VERTIGO 42

This Large Print Book carries the
Seal of Approval of N.A.V.H.

A RICHARD JURY MYSTERY

VERTIGO 42

MARTHA GRIMES

THORNDIKE PRESS

A part of Gale, Cengage Learning

GALE
CENGAGE Learning·

Farmington Hills, Mich • San Francisco • New York • Waterville, Maine
Meriden, Conn • Mason, Ohio • Chicago

GALE
CENGAGE Learning®

LIBRARY OF CONGRESS CATALOGING-IN-PUBLICATION DATA

Grimes, Martha.
    Vertigo 42 : a Richard Jury mystery / by Martha Grimes. — Large print edition.
        pages ; cm. — (Thorndike Press large print basic)
    ISBN-13: 978-1-4104-7275-5 (hardcover)
    ISBN-10: 1-4104-7275-2 (hardcover)
    1. Jury, Richard (Fictitious character)—Fiction. 2. Police—England—Fiction. 3. Large type books. I. Title. II. Title: Vertigo fourty two.
PS3557.R48998V48 2014b
813'.54—dc23   2014022077

Published in 2014 by arrangement with Scribner, a division of Simon & Schuster, Inc.

Printed in Mexico
1 2 3 4 5 6 7 18 17 16 15 14

To that incomparable
couple of attorneys,
Alice and Andrew Vachss
"women and children first!"

■ ■ ■ ■

HARBOR LIGHTS

■ ■ ■ ■

"They only told me we were parting . . ."
Jimmy Kennedy and Hugh Williams

1

Vertigo 42, the City
Monday, 6:00 P.M.

It was far too high to see Old Broad Street down below, but the windows that traveled all the way around the lozenge-shaped room gave as great a view of London as he'd ever seen. The Thames, Westminster, St. Paul's, Southwark, everything miniaturized. He was so high up he fancied he'd almost had an attack of vertigo on the fast elevator that made only one stop, and that one at the top of Tower 42: Vertigo.

Jury was looking down at the Thames, moving off in one direction toward Gravesend and Gallions Reach, which he couldn't of course see; in the other direction, the Isle of Dogs, Richmond, and Hampton Court. He tried to picture all of those ships that had once steamed toward London's docks, toward Rotherhithe and the Blackwall Basin in the not-so-distant past, and in just such

9

light as Jury was seeing now, the sun setting on St Paul's. In the deep sunset hovering over buildings, the outlines blurred. They might have been dark hills.

He was looking toward Docklands, an area that used to comprise the West India Docks and beyond to the Blackwell Basin, one thing that remained after the docks closed. Eighty-some acres of what was now the Canary Wharf estate. Hundreds of dockers had once lived and worked there; now it was office workers, glass buildings, and converted warehouses.

Vertigo 42, this bar at the top of one of the financial towers in the "square mile" that made up the City of London — London's financial district — might have been designed to create the illusion of a city down there. Or perhaps that thought was merely brought on by the champagne Jury was drinking. Champagne was something he never drank and wasn't used to; but that's what you got up here, that's why people came here — to drink champagne.

The champagne had been brought by a waiter "at the request of Mr. Williamson, sir." The waiter set down two glasses and poured into one of them. Jury drank. He had forgotten champagne; he had certainly forgotten great champagne, if he'd ever known it at all. This lot (he had checked the wine list) was costing Mr. Williamson in the vicinity of 385 quid. One bottle. That much. It was Krug. Was wine this expensive meant to be swallowed? Or just held in the mouth as the eye held on to the barges streaked with orange light there on the river.

The waiter returned with a dish of incandescent green olives, big ones; he placed them on the counter that ran beneath the window and between the rather trendy-looking but very comfortable chairs.

Jury was there to meet not an old friend, but a friend of an old friend, Sir Oswald Maples. The friend of the friend was Williamson, who had ordered the champagne. Oswald Maples had asked Jury if he could spare some time to talk to Tom Williamson, and Jury said, "Of course. Why?" To which Oswald had said, "You'll see." Jury filled his glass again before he moved to another window and another view of the Thames.

"My favorite view," said a voice behind him. Jury turned.

"Superintendent Jury? I'm Tom Williamson. I'm very sorry I'm late."

"I'm not," said Jury, lifting the Krug from its ice bed. "You will notice this is considerably below the waterline."

Tom Williamson laughed and poured a

measure into his own glass. He was a tall man, taller by an inch than Jury himself. "Fortunately, there's a lot more sea." He raised his glass, tipped it toward Jury's. "You like ships, Superintendent?"

"I don't know anything about them, except there's a waterline on the hull."

Tom smiled. "I love them. My grandfather was in the shipping business. Down there used to be steamships of the East India Company loaded with stuff — tea, spices, as many as a thousand ships going toward the docks. And barges. Now we've got tourist cruisers and speedboats. Still a lot of river traffic, just not the same traffic. Thanks for meeting me."

The thanks came without a pause between it and the river traffic. The way he talked, the directness, as if he didn't want to waste any time, made Jury smile. Williamson had yet to remove his coat, which he now did, and tossed it over one of the coolly blue amoeba-shaped chairs.

"An interesting bar to choose," said Jury. "Light-years above the ones I frequent down there." He nodded toward the window and approaching dark. "Do you work in the City?"

"No. I know nothing about finance. You wonder why I chose it?"

12

Jury laughed. "I'm not complaining, believe me. It must have the best views of anyplace in London."

"Yes. I don't come here often." He sat back. "Perhaps I chose it because up here is quite literally above it all." He sipped some champagne.

Jury smiled. "What's the 'all'?"

Williamson looked perplexed.

"That you want to be above?"

Williamson picked up an olive but didn't eat it. He put it on one of the small paper napkins the waiter had supplied. "You know a man with the Devon-Cornwall police. A Commander Macalvie?"

Jury was so surprised by this sudden segue he spilled his champagne, fortunately only on himself. "Sorry." He brushed at the spill with a napkin. "Brian Macalvie? I certainly do. But it was Sir Oswald Maples who spoke to me about you —"

"Of course. I'm sorry. I'm tossing too many balls in the air." He plucked the bottle from its stand and poured more for each of them. "I don't know how much Oswald told you . . ."

"Nothing, other than that you worked for the Government Code and Cipher School, GC and CS. Not when he was there, but after it changed to GC Headquarters and got moved to Cheltenham."

Tom Williamson nodded.

Jury went on: "Sir Oswald knows I'm a sucker for that stuff. I stopped at Bletchley Park to see the Enigma machine. It was incredible work they did, Alan Turing and the others."

Williamson said, "Oswald was at Bletchley Park during the war. He was really into it, very high up. I wasn't so much; my work was small potatoes by comparison. Your name came up — that is, he thought of you when I was visiting him one evening in Chelsea. It's about my wife, Tess."

"Your wife?" Jury looked over his shoulder, quite stupidly, as if he expected to find Tess there, behind their chairs.

"She's dead."

Somehow, Jury had known that, even as he turned to look for her.

"Seventeen years ago." He paused long enough to have counted every one. "We had — I still have — a house in Devon, very large, too large for us, certainly. Woods, extensive gardens, tiered and rather Italianate, I suppose, and too much to maintain, even with the gardener, who's been there for years. But Tess wasn't really interested in bringing it back, as they say, to its former glory. She liked the unruliness of it, the

14

wildness. She was a bit of a romantic, Tess."

It had grown dark now and the lights had come on along the Embankment and across the river in Southwark. "I met Tess in Norfolk, along the coast. We liked to watch the lights in the harbor. That's the other reason I like this bar. Down there. The lights coming on." He stopped.

Jury waited.

Tom cleared his throat and went on. "I was talking about our house in Devon. As for me, I saw a lot of unkempt lawn, tangled vines, rioting weeds, and tree rot." The laugh was perfunctory, not happy. "At the rear of the house in the gardens there were — are — two concrete pools, ornamental once, I expect. Empty now. There's a wide patio and a flight of wide stone steps. Urns placed strategically round the patio and at the top and bottom of the stairs." He looked away from the dark Thames below, curving in the distance. "Excuse all of the detail, but this is where she died, you see. At the bottom of these stairs. Tess was given to attacks of vertigo."

Jury felt disturbed by this accounting because he knew behind it lay another accounting.

"She apparently —"

Jury could see the man's mouth working

15

to get beyond "apparently" and said it for him. "Fell."

Williamson nodded. "Her head hit a stone plinth at the bottom. Pedestal of an urn. Grecian."

As if Keats might help out here.

Then to keep going, Tom took a pack of Silk Cuts from his pocket, stuck one in his mouth before he remembered to offer the pack to Jury, who, after gazing at the cigarette for half his life, declined. Tom lit one with a cheap, no-nonsense lighter, which he placed on the table beside the cigarettes. The man was obviously wealthy but didn't express it in silver cigarette cases and lighters.

Out of another pocket he took a folded paper. It was worn with creases from countless refoldings. "This is a poem she liked by Eliot; the book was given her by a photographer friend. It sounds almost like directions for a pose, doesn't it?" Tom smiled a little and read:

"Stand on the highest pavement of the
   stair —
Lean on a garden urn —
Weave, weave the sunlight in your hair . . ."

Setting aside the poem for the moment,

he reached into the breast pocket of his jacket and took out a small picture, hardly more than a snapshot, but paper of studio quality. A portrait in little. "This is Tess."

Jury took it. "The pose is like the poem, yes."

"It is. I've the original photograph at home. Tess was pretty."

"That's an understatement, Mr. Williamson." Jury felt, for some reason, oddly forlorn.

" 'Tom,' please."

"Where is home? Devon?"

"Devon? Oh, no. Not that house. I live in Knightsbridge. That's our London house."

Jury went back to the problem, or what he took it to be: "There would have been a police inquiry. What was the result?"

Williamson shrugged, as if the result were irrelevant. "Open verdict. There wasn't enough evidence to determine one way or another."

"You didn't agree."

Enter, Brian Macalvie. He would probably have been a detective inspector seventeen years back. "Was Commander Macalvie — he wouldn't have been commander then — was he the primary on this?"

Tom shook his head. "The man in charge

was a Chief Inspector Bishop, no, Bishoff. He was convinced it was accidental. There was, of course, reason to believe it was an accident because of the vertigo. The steps there are high."

"But they were her steps."

"Precisely. She was all too familiar with them. Chief Inspector Bishoff made the point that it was probably a misstep, or something fallen on one of the steps, in her path. But it wasn't. No, I'm sure someone arranged to have it look like an accident."

"But why did you think that? Purely on the basis that it wasn't vertigo that caused it?"

"No." His fingers were on the stem of his champagne flute. He turned and turned the glass. "No. It was the way Tess was lying." He looked toward the window.

Jury was sure he wasn't seeing London beyond it.

"She was lying with her arms outflung, the flowers she'd been carrying scattered."

"Do you think it was some sort of enactment of the figure in the poem?"

Tom read more lines from the poem still lying on the table:

"Clasp your flowers to you with a pained surprise —

18

Fling them to the ground and turn
With a fugitive resentment in your eyes."

"It did look a little like it. Arranged."

"What about this photographer, then?"

"Andrew Cleary. She called him Angel Clare, after the character in *Tess of the D'Urbervilles;* she was very fond of Thomas Hardy. He had nothing to do with her death; he was in Paris."

Jury was silent for a moment. Then he said, "Was there someone you think had a reason to kill your wife?"

He did not answer but rose and took a couple of steps toward the window.

Jury had the strange feeling Tom was in some way reentering his wife's death, standing there as if there were a stone stairway down to Old Broad Street. Then he turned back, sat down. "There was an incident, something pretty dreadful that involved Tess five years before she died. I said 'incident.' Ridiculous. It was more than that; it was another accident at the same house, the same rear gardens . . ." He rubbed the heel of his palm against the side of his head, as if trying to call something up.

"Tess had a party for some children at Laburnum. That's the name of our Devon house. Six of them, the children. Tess was very fond of children and we had none, unfortunately. She would get up parties for kids, their birthdays, or holidays, even arcane Welsh or Scottish holidays most of us have never heard of . . ." He moved his shoulders a little, as if resettling a coat around his neck. As if he were cold.

"Anyway" — he continued with the story — "at one of these parties at Laburnum, a child named Hilda Palmer fell into one of the drained pools. They were concrete pools, fairly deep. They should have been filled or fenced and Tess was in the process of organizing that; she was lining up an Exeter firm; unfortunately it hadn't been done yet. Of course, the kids had been told not to play at the rear of the house in the gardens around those pools. But Hilda went round, apparently, when they were playing, got near the pool, missed her footing, and fell in.

"Tess was in the house, getting the cake and other party food ready. It was some-body's birthday. She heard a shout, some noise. The kids were supposed to keep to the front of the house — this is a large house, as I told you, with extensive gardens and woods.

"What she told us was that she went out to investigate, but didn't see anything. She went down the steps and looked around, saw nothing, heard nothing, and then she got closer to the drained pools. There was Hilda lying crumpled at the bottom. She wasn't moving. Tess said she thought she was unconscious and jumped down into the pool. But Hilda wasn't breathing. She was dead. Just like that."

"How terrible."

Tom closed his eyes briefly, shaking his head. "The children told her they were playing hide-and-seek. So they didn't see which way the others had gone. Behind a tree, into the maze, into the shrubbery . . . They were all in different places." Nervously, Tom picked up his packet of cigarettes and lit one.

This had happened over twenty years before, yet it still made the man's hands shake. "That this Hilda Palmer missed her footing and fell in, this was the inference drawn by police?"

Tom shook his head. "This was the inference Tess drew. No one saw anything. When she discovered the girl was dead she yelled for help. Elaine Davies, a friend of Tess, and the kids all came running. Tess called the police; the ambulance came; detectives and all of their people came.

"So to answer your question: the inference drawn by police was that Hilda Palmer was killed by someone; that she was struck, and that's what caused her fall. There was a good deal of blood. Tess had it on her hands, her dress. The coroner argued that there appeared to be no reason for the fall; that is, unless the child was given to bouts of dizziness. Police said there was nothing around the pools that anyone could trip over —"

Jury snorted. "She could have tripped over her own feet, tripped over air."

"I know. But that was the argument."

"Why would someone have tried to kill her?"

Tom shook his head. "Hilda was only a child, nine years old, but she was an unpopular child. She was a bit of a bully. But worse, she had even gotten some adult backs up because she seemed to be able to ferret out information, God knows how, and would hold it over people's heads."

"Blackmail, then."

Tom shrugged. "Something like that." He pulled their champagne bottle out of the cooler, saw it was empty, shoved it back in. "I wouldn't mind a whiskey, myself. You? Or more champagne?"

"A whiskey would be fine."

"Brand?"

"You choose."

Tom motioned a waiter over and ordered Laphroaig 18.

Not what Jury would have chosen, only because he couldn't afford it.

Once the waiter left, Tom went on. "At the inquest there was a great deal of disagreement as to what had happened. Not everyone believed Hilda was struck and shoved into the pool. Some thought it, as Tess had reported it, an accident and that the blow to the head had come when she hit the bottom. There are big pieces of broken cement down there, chunks of it, and rocks as well."

"Those would have been quite different events, though."

"Not according to police forensics. The forensic testimony was rather amazing. Both of them had very good evidence for reaching these conclusions. Finally, it was an open verdict. The evidence wasn't conclusive.

"It was Tess who was under siege," he said, turning to Jury. "It was Tess who would have been indicted — and she was, by the mother and others. People held Tess responsible. It was her property the children were on; they were in her care; Tess should never have allowed them to be around those unfenced pools. God knows Hilda's mother blamed her. She was in a rage; she had to be physically restrained. Grief, of course, explained much of it. But the hatred of Tess never stopped."

The waiter appeared and set down the two drinks, offered snacks, which they both declined.

Jury took a drink of the pricy whiskey. "Do you think there's a good possibility that the mother murdered your wife?"

"It was five years later, I know. A bit long for revenge."

"Hamlet managed. Had this woman tried to contact Tess during those five years?"

"Oh, yes. A number of times."

"Then did the Devon police see this Palmer woman as a viable suspect?"

Tom shook his head. "The chief inspector was convinced Tess's was an accidental death. Vertigo. Tess was always taking tumbles, catching her high heel on a curb or uneven pavement, miscalculating a step down — that sort of thing. The way she fell down those steps, the way her head hit the base of the urn — all of it appeared evidence of an accident."

They were silent for a moment. Then Jury said, "Was there something you wanted me to do, Tom?"

"Yes. When I was talking to Oswald, he said he had a good friend who was a superintendent at New Scotland Yard. That got me thinking . . . Well, I'll certainly understand if you don't —" Tom Williamson rubbed again at his wrist at the place where the watch wasn't.

Jury wondered what had happened to it. "If I don't — ?"

"Want to have a word with Commander Macalvie."

"You mean try to reopen the case? That would be somewhat — unorthodox, wouldn't it? Someone in my position interfering with someone in his position?" To say nothing of being highly improper, against every tenet of police procedure, against propriety, and, probably, against the queen. Jury could hardly wait to ring him.

"Right. Sorry. I know it's a harebrained idea." Tom Williamson tossed back the rest of his whiskey.

"Not at all. I can understand how hard it must be, not knowing." How many other platitudes had Jury got waiting in the wings? "But, yes, I don't mind putting a question to Mr. Macalvie. He's a friend of mine."

Tom looked as if he'd just been given the City below them. "That would be extremely kind."

25

"But, listen: if by some miracle police did reinvestigate your wife's death and found it was murder, what then? What would you do? What could you do?"

Tom thought for a moment. "Well, I expect I'd better get a solicitor."

Jury looked puzzled.

Tom smiled wryly. "Because I'd be the prime suspect. My wife was a very wealthy woman." He pulled the empty bottle of Krug out of the bed of ice. "This kind of wealthy."

Smiling slightly, Jury said, "If you're to be the prime suspect, I take it you have an alibi?"

"I was in London. As a matter of fact I was visiting Oswald."

"That should do it." Jury set down his glass.

Tom said, suddenly, "Where are you going after this, Superintendent?"

"Going? Nowhere. Back to my digs. I live in Islington."

Tom had his mobile out and said, "Would you pardon me for a moment while I make this call?"

"Of course." Jury was happy to be alone here at the top of Tower 42, looking out on a London that at this point was inaccessible to him and he to it. He rose to move closer to the window. Tess Williamson would not have been able to look down on London without being terrified, he supposed.

Tom Williamson was back, sitting down, picking up his drink. Jury joined him.

"I canceled a dinner engagement. I wonder if you'd like to have dinner with me? I was thinking of the Zetter in Clerkenwell. It's close to Islington, so you wouldn't be too inconvenienced getting home. Do you know it?"

The Zetter was where he had met Lu Aguilar; she had then been a detective inspector with Islington police. And she was now, after a terrible car wreck and its aftermath of weeks in a coma, back home in Brazil. She had regained consciousness, but the consciousness wasn't telling her much. Jury was a stranger.

"Oh, yes. I know it."

2

"Devon?" said Carole-anne Palutski, Jury's upstairs neighbor who was at the moment downstairs, sitting on his sofa, flipping through the glossy pages of a magazine called *Hair Today*. She tossed it aside, apparently liking nothing in there better than what she already had.

"The plan was, you was to go to Northants and visit your chum." As if she had made the plan.

Jury was stuffing assorted clothes into a duffel bag and, at the moment, studying a tie, or a selection of ties he had arranged over the top of his easy chair. They all looked alike, in the way all of those hairdos must have looked to Carole-anne. He was only studying the tie because she had insisted he wouldn't need a tie, not "up in the country, like."

28

"Northampton is not really the country, like."

That had preceded the question, "Devon?"

"I am going to Northants, only for a day or two, and then to Devon. Exeter."

Carole-anne was studying Jury far more closely than she was studying *Hair Today*. "You know Devon's the other side of England, don't you? It's miles."

That "miles" rather stunted her grasp of distance; still he was pleased by her rudimentary knowledge of geography. Until now, he thought she couldn't follow a line anywhere past Clapham Common. Jury said, "From London to Exeter is a hundred and seventy miles."

"Like I said." The magazine had resurfaced in her lap and her head was bent over it, the lamplight showing her hair in all of its flame-throwing glory.

"Perhaps I'll take my chum with me."

"Him? Lord Ardry as once was?"

Dear God, where had she picked up this arcane upstairs-downstairs idiom?

"You don't think he rides in cars, Lord Ardry, as once was?" Jury spent a moment imagining the 170 miles with Melrose Plant. They'd be stopping at every Little Chef along the way. Plant was as bad as Wiggin

— no, worse. "Mr. Plant is a chum of Commander Macalvie, my chum in Exeter."

"So you're all chums together. You and him and the Devon police."

"Correct. The Devonshire and Cornwall Constabulary."

"Sounds like lead feet."

Jury liked that. He'd be sure to tell Macalvie. "Does, doesn't it?"

"My guess is he's trying to get you to join it."

Jury stopped pushing a sweater into the bag, startled by her prescience. That had been just what Macalvie had been doing, off and on for some years now.

Carole-anne decided to lie down on the sofa, shedding her strappy sandals. "Well, you won't want to leave London." And me.

"True. I might not want to leave London." And you.

On the little table, the phone rang.

She said, "It's probably that Dr. Nancy."

He had started for it and stopped. "Why do you say that?"

"Because she rang just before you came in. Didn't you read your messages?"

The phone still brr-brr'd.

Jury leaned over her. "Carole-anne, I've been here for an hour. Why didn't you tell me?"

"Because I'm supposed to be careful and write down messages exactly —"

Brr-brr.

"What were you doing in my flat anyway?"

She tossed the magazine on the floor. "I like that! I told you this morning I'd come in and do you a nice fry-up —"

"Has anything been fried up?" Dramatically, Jury sniffed.

Brr.

He grabbed up the receiver.

Dead. Damn! Why did he have these inane arguments with Carole-anne?

"There, now you went and missed your call." Pleased with the dead phone, she picked up *Hair Today.*

Jury fell into the easy chair. *And gone tomorrow.*

Lead feet.

3

Ardry End
Tuesday, Noon

The first person Richard Jury saw as he got out of his car the following morning was Mr. Blodgett, Melrose Plant's hermit-in-residence. On the far side of the grand grounds of Ardry End sat what Melrose Plant insisted upon was a hermitage. Melrose had seen a similar structure, stone and wattle, in the pages of *Country Life.* In an ad for an ostentatious and overpriced property, a large, eighteenth-century-style house, was this little stone structure on the grounds.

In the real stone-and-wattle eighteenth century, all the best people had hermits, Melrose had read somewhere, although he was vague on details. But he wanted one expressly for the purpose of the hermit's moving about, looking wild-eyed and a little dangerous, popping up at windows when his aunt Agatha was inside wolfing down cream teas and sherry. He meant to scare her off.

The position paid well. Melrose Plant always paid well.

If there's one thing you aren't, Jury had said to him once, it's a skinflint. Melrose had not taken well to the compliment; he wanted to know the left-out things Jury thought he was.

In the distance, Mr. Blodgett was waving him over.

Jury returned the wave and made the longish trek to where Mr. Blodgett stood beside his hermitage.

Originally Mr. Blodgett had worn a beard and long hair and an unkempt look befitting a hermit. Of late, he had cut both hair and beard and generally smartened himself up. And Jury saw that the hermitage itself had been smartened up, for it appeared to have a new extension. Closer, he could see it was a screen-enclosed room, a sort of sunporch.

"My Florida room, Mr. Jury," announced Mr. Blodgett. "Built 'er on me own, I did. Come in, come in, look around." Mr. Blodgett held wide a screen door.

The ceiling was a bit low for Jury but would accommodate Mr. Blodgett's short stature nicely. Jury wondered where in heaven's name he would have come by the patio furniture, two chairs and a lounge grouped about a glass-topped table. The cushions bore a pattern of coconut palms.

"Well, Mr. Blodgett, this is very, very pleasant. And you did it all yourself?"

"Ev'ry bit. Now it'd be nice t'ave a telly, but o' course, no electric's laid on out 'ere."

"You make do with your oil lamps, then?" There was one centered on the table. "And candles." A fat one sat on a little metal table, not part of the patio suite, probably. "And you've a wood-burning stove inside, right?" Jury nodded toward the hermitage proper.

Mr. Blodgett nodded as he removed his cap, scratched his head meditatively, and repositioned the cap. Jury was not sure, but he thought the very faded intertwined letters were MU.

"If you're a Manchester United fan," Jury said, smiling, "you really do need a telly."

Mr. Blodgett removed his cap then and turned it in his hands, as if addressing the lord of the manor. "Oh, I don't think Lord Ardry'd look too kindly on electric in the 'ermitage. Well, you can see his point —"

Jury merely smiled and thought, No, I don't see his point. Anyone who would engage a hermit in the first place would be able to entertain any wacky idea. Jury was about to speak to this point when he heard a short bark and turned to see the dog Joey barreling toward him, with Melrose Plant (aka Lord Ardry) advancing at a much more leisurely pace.

"Joey!" he called.

The dog jumped on him, then got down and circled around him a few times, after which he ran off, not toward Melrose, whom he didn't seem to give a fig about, but toward the barn where lived Melrose's horse and goat, Aggrieved and Aghast.

Jury had found Joey in a Clerkenwell doorway, nearly starved to death. He'd taken him to a vet, then, later to an animal refuge, where he had, still later, claimed him back and taken him to Northamptonshire. The girl in True Friends, named Joelly, had found an old collar with the name JOE engraved on a little metal nameplate. She had so impressed Jury that he thought the dog should be named after her, so they settled on a *y* being inscribed after the *Joe* to make "Joey."

The dog, she had said, being an Appenzell mountain dog, needed space and air. It was a working dog, one that worked with herds — sheep, goats.

Jury's one-bedroom flat was hardly a place of space and air, and he had nothing to herd unless he counted Carole-anne, so he had hit on the idea of taking Joey along to Ardry End and pretending that the dog had just turned up there on his own. "Lost," a stray, whatever. Joey had immediately made for the barn and the goat. One goat (Jury guessed) was better than none.

Thus the "lost" dog had to be named. No one at the Jack and Hammer paid any attention to Jury's protests that "the name's right on the collar. Joey."

"Aggro!" called Melrose. The dog went on about his business.

"His name's Joey," said Jury for the millionth time as they made a swing round the Florida room before returning to the main house.

Melrose ignored that, as usual. "Glad you got here in time for lunch. It's Soufflé Day. Come along." He turned to Blodgett. "Ruthven'll be bringing yours along in a bit, Mr. Blodgett."

"Blodgett gets soufflés?"

"Of course. I told you. It's Soufflé Day. I had scrambled egg soufflé for breakfast. Delicious."

"What's for lunch?"

"Tomato soup soufflé, cheese soufflé, and chocolate soufflé for the pud. Don't you like soufflés?"

36

They had by now reached the drive where Jury's car was parked.

"Of course, but how in hell do you make a soup with it?"

"Can't imagine. Help with your luggage?"

"No." Jury gave him a look and dragged his duffel bag out of the trunk.

"Are we going camping? Should I get my bedroll?"

"The Beamo one? Why not?"

They walked up the wide steps and into Soufflé Day.

The tomato soup soufflé had turned out to be a creamy tomato basil with a puff of pinkish baked egg white floating atop it. Then there was the cheese, then the chocolate. Coffee, brandy.

As they were now walking down the drive, Jury said, "I could do that all over again. What's for dinner?"

"Well, at this point in things, Martha runs out of steam, so dinner will be ordinary roast beef or something, but dessert will be a Grand Marnier soufflé."

"I'm for it." Jury stopped, and so did Melrose, toward the end of the drive to look back and see in the distance, Ruthven swanning across the grass, carrying Mr. Blodgett's soufflé.

"How does Ruthven feel about waiting on a hermit?"

"Oh, you know Ruthven, he's so self-contained he'd happily take on the Mad Hatter's Tea Party if asked."

They continued walking, stopping when they got to the Northampton Road, which, although not famous for speeding cars, still remained a proving ground for the odd motorcycle gang who seemed bent on turning it into that twenty-four-hour race at Le Mans.

"You should get electricity laid on back there." Jury tilted his head toward the long lawn and the hermitage.

"What? Blodgett's supposed to be a hermit. They write religious tracts by candlelight. Next, you'll say he needs a telly."

"He needs a telly."

Melrose ignored that and walked on. "So you're off to Exeter tomorrow? Say hello to Brian Macalvie for me."

"I will." Over lunch, Jury had told Melrose about the death of Tess Williamson. "Her husband wants me to see this house, Laburnum."

"A name suggesting poison. Were it mine, I'd change it."

"I'm sure you would. You're always changing names."

"Very funny."

4

Jack and Hammer
Tuesday, 2:00 P.M.

"I've got it," said Trueblood. *"Agape."*

"You mean," said Joanna Lewes, "*a-ga-pe,* three syllables, meaning 'peace and love'? That sort of thing?" She frowned.

"No, I mean *'a-gape.'* " When they all turned judgmental eyes on Trueblood, he said, "For God's sake, just *look* at him. He's been sitting there the whole time with his mouth open."

The eyes now turned to the lightly panting dog Diane Demorney had found, inexplicably, on her doorstep. It had indeed been sitting with its mouth open, tongue hanging a bit to the left.

Vivian Rivington said, "But the dog is not part of Melrose's household. We don't have to follow the *Ag* rule, every name beginning with *Ag.*"

"I have an even better idea," said Richard

40

Jury, settling his pint of Adnams on the table. "We could call him Stanley. Stanley's the name on his collar." Indeed it was, right there engraved on a brass nameplate on his brown leather collar. There was also a leather lead now unattached to the collar and draped over Diane's chair.

"Stanley! That's an absurd name for this dog," said Trueblood. "He's a Staffordshire terrier."

"Marshall's right," said Diane. "It doesn't suit him at all. He's more of a . . . Tony. What about Tony?"

"What about the name on his collar?" said Jury.

"Hm. An-ton-i-o!" said Trueblood in a fake Italian accent. "Not bad."

Stanley didn't bother looking at him. He went on lightly panting.

Jury said, "Would you like me to tell you what I find most interesting about this insane desire to name lost dogs? You do agree the dog is lost?"

Melrose sighed. "Is this going to be one of your Socratic arguments where you ask a series of questions that can, by their nature, have only one answer?"

Jury ignored him and continued. "What is interesting is that no one, not one of you, has made any attempt to find its owner."

Diane Demorney, who was drinking her postlunch martini, straight up with a twist, stopped it on its way to her mouth. "I beg your pardon! I most certainly did look for the owner, all round my front steps and down the walk. I went from my door straight down to the road, looked and saw absolutely no one. And, whilst Tony and I were walking, I looked all along the road, both sides —"

"His name's Stanley."

"— while making our way to here." Diane pointed down at the floor of the Jack and Hammer.

Mrs. Withersby, the pub's char, had come slapping up in her carpet slippers with her mop to stand and listen. She had a cigarette she'd bummed off Marshall Trueblood behind her ear.

"Tony," said Trueblood. "You know that's not bad. Yes, I'd say that rather fits him, but if we're to have carte blanche with names, then, my God, it'll take forever. If there are no limits. No, I think we should stick with the rules. It should begin with *Ag.*

Said Mrs. Withersby, "Agony. How 'bout Agony. It's what I feel whenever I run into you lot."

Jury laughed and called into the public bar to Dick Scroggs: "Dick, set Mrs. Withersby up with whatever she wants."

"Withers, you can spell!" said Trueblood.

Dick called back she was "on duty," to which no one paid any attention, mostly Mrs. Withersby herself. Dragging mop and pail behind her, she said "Ta" to Jury and set off for the public bar, the one on the other side of the arched doorway.

Melrose recited:

" 'The witch that came (the withered hag)
To wash the steps with pail and rag
Was once the beauty, Abishag.' "

Diane looked at him admiringly. "That's quite good, Melrose. You made that up just sitting here?"

"No, Robert Frost made it up just sitting in New Hampshire." He said to Jury, who was rising from his chair, "You're not leaving, for God's sake?"

"To see if I can round up some information."

"Information? About what?"

"Stanley, of course." He looked down at the dog. It looked back at him with a *Who are these people?* expression, followed by *And why are you not getting me out of this?* Which begot not a change in expression but an intensifying of it.

43

"Where are your animal control people?" asked Jury.

"Not here," said Joanna. "I expect there's something in Northampton. A pound. Or a shelter."

None of which they'd put themselves to the trouble of contacting. Jury walked through the doorway to the public bar, where Mrs. Withersby raised her double whiskey, her expression (like the dog's) difficult to interpret: Was she thanking him for the drink or asking for a refill?

He held up his mobile, saw it was spent. "Battery down, Dick, may I use yours?"

Dick Scroggs shoved the house phone toward him. "I hate them mobiles. Always got a glitch in it, mine does."

Jury pointed toward the directory by the row of bottles and Dick handed him that. Then Jury nodded toward Mrs. Withersby's glass. "Another, Dick."

Dick went down the bar and collected her glass. Jury thought it great that he could treat his char as one of the customers.

He had dialed and got the Crawley Animal Refuge somewhere in Northampton. He gave the woman who answered the information about the Staffordshire, where it had turned up, the name on the collar, the ap-

44

proximate time his friend had found the dog.

"Does the dog have a chip?"

What an idiotic question. If the dog had an ID, would he be asking about it? They weren't the owners, for God's sakes. "You mean something implanted under its skin for ID?"

"Yes."

"I don't know, do I? I haven't had the time to perform minor surgery to tell if he does or doesn't."

Dick Scroggs snickered and proceeded to wipe glasses.

"You needn't take that tone."

"Apparently, I do, madam. Your first act was not to go and check on recent calls about a missing Staffordshire terrier, not to refer a question to your computer or somebody else, but instead to ask me for information I couldn't possibly have, not being the dog's owner. The dog has strayed into our presence. I've clearly given you all of the information I have: the dog's apparent breed, its color and size, a description of the collar and the name on it. I'm a Scotland Yard detective superintendent. I don't ordinarily have time magically up my sleeve, and what little time I do have, you're wasting. Now, if you're unable to give me an

45

answer, one that strikes me as spectacularly simple, then I'll come to the facility with my warrant card and two detectives and see how things are run there."

Not enough attention has been paid to the silence we call "dead." A black hole opened down the line and apparently sucked her in.

Mrs. Withersby cackled and slapped the bar.

In a little while, a new voice came on. "Superintendent. I'm Bill Nevis. I'm the director here."

"Yes, Mr. Nevis."

"No one has reported a dog of that description missing. There are no rabies tags I take it."

"None. Only the name on the collar. It's one of those little metal plates that's screwed into the collar."

"Right. Here's the thing. There's a shelter in Sidbury that might have a scanner — just a minute —" He gave Jury the number. "Or if someone has the time to bring the dog here, we could scan for the chip. We're actually on the outskirts of Northampton, toward Sidbury, so you wouldn't have to fight traffic and could avoid the carriageway." He gave Jury the directions. "In case you decide to come."

It made Jury smile. He pictured Bill Nevis as rather eager to take on the project of Stanley.

Bill Nevis went on: "There are a number of other things that provide clues as to ownership — that is, that can narrow it down. I once found the owner of a superior-looking hound by canvassing the various hunts within a several-mile radius. Turned out to be much the easiest thing to do. Once I tracked a terrier by means of a collar that was made only by a small leather goods shop in Jermyn Street. Oh, yes, pets can be snobs too . . ."

Jury laughed. "That's ingenious."

"Always check the collar for clues. And if there's a lead attached to the collar, that too . . . well, pardon me for giving you instruction; you're with Scotland Yard, after all. But, see, I've started a database. By now it's quite extensive and shows some surprising results. Do you know that I can tell what area of the country will produce the highest rate of lost animals, dogs and cats? Not Greater London, which I'd have guessed. No, it's Slough."

"Slough? Good God. Slough's always getting bad press, isn't it?"

Bill laughed. "I can't say, at the moment, exactly why this is. Industrial parks? A lot of transients?"

"Mr. Nevis, this is the most heartening conversation I've had with anyone all year. Do you realize you could revolutionize the entire pet-finding operation in this country?"

"Well . . . I don't know about that, but I'm certainly going to give it a go. I'm wondering, for instance, if identification could be helped by taking paw prints. Obviously, not conclusive, like fingerprints. But could it narrow things down a bit?"

"Ever think of working for the police? Or with the police?"

"With the police? I like that idea."

"We'll be in touch. Thanks for your help. Stanley thanks you too."

Jury hung up and then rang the number Nevis had given him for the Sidbury place. He asked the woman who answered the phone if their office had a scanner that could read an implanted chip.

"Has the dog got a chip, then?" she asked.

Jury bit his tongue. Had all places given the job of telephone reception to those who could ask the stupidest questions? "That's the point. I don't know, do I, unless a scanner shows one."

"Oh. Just a tic."

Jury waited while the tic went into overdrive. Finally, she was back.

"No, we don't have one."

Silently Jury cursed and hung up. He started ordering a round of drinks for his table when he saw Theo Wrenn Brown crossing the road from his bookshop. "Sweeping" across would not be an exaggeration, his coat flapping back from his black sweater. It was another instance of Theo reinventing himself, as the last one didn't smoke cigars or wear black turtlenecks.

The outside doors of saloon and public bars faced each other across a small entryway. Jury walked through the inside connecting door of the two bars as Theo kicked a chair up to the round table in the window. He must have gotten word of the universe shutting down, so confident did he appear of his reception. Nothing short of that would get their attention, as none of them liked Theo.

He had chucked his cigar in favor of a cigarette, which he lit with a match cupped between his hands for the sake of the shadow he thought it would cast across his face.

Jury set down the three drinks he was carrying, Dick Scroggs to come with the rest. "Dick, a drink for Theo too." Jury's irritation at telephone answerers dissipated when he thought of his conversation with Bill Nevis. He flattened out the bit of paper on which he'd written the sparse directions, then put it in his pocket. He unwound the lead wrapped round the table leg and said, "Come along, Stanley."

Stanley seemed to like the idea. Got him out from under the feet of this lot, at least.

Surprised, Diane gave Jury a hard look. "Where're you going with him?"

"To a shelter that can scan for a chip. See if there's any ID." Jury returned Diane's flinty look with one of his own. "So while we're away, you can carry on with your name competition."

Diane was about to protest.

"Save it, Diane. Dick," Jury called into the public bar. "Can I borrow your car?"

"You could have mine," said Theo, "only I've business in Sidbury." He checked his watch. "Got to go. Cheers." He polished off his drink and departed.

Dick Scroggs came round from the bar into the saloon bar, fiddling some keys off a giant ring. "It's not much more'n a heap of rusty parts, but you're welcome to it."

"Thanks, Dick." Jury picked up the keys and left.

The Crawley Animal Refuge was just off the Northampton Road a mile or so south of the market town of Northampton. It was a long, low cinder block building, white-washed. Its institutional look was softened by the clipped grass and hedgerow and nearby woods.

Bill Nevis was waiting for him or, rather, waiting for Stanley. Upon seeing Bill, the dog woke up and looked expectant.

They were in Bill's small office furnished with a plain wood desk and chairs and three computers. "Let's have a look first for a chip." He picked up a small object about the size of a remote control and ran it over Stanley's body. "Nope. Nothing here, unfortunately. Strange for a dog that seems to have had such good care." He sighed, as if at the strange behavior of dog owners. "I want to find out what kind of training he's had." He turned to the dog, said, "Stanley, sit."

Stanley sat, so suddenly he might have been waiting half his life for this command.

That was the only voice command. From then on, it was hand movements, some so slight and nuanced that Jury barely detected

51

them. Movements or perhaps mind reading. The dog looked entranced.

That stopped and Bill had Stanley lie down. "This dog is extremely well trained. Far beyond the average. It's not something you pick up at Bark-Along." He smiled at Jury. "That's a pet shop that holds obedience classes. Look, I'll do a bit of searching around. If I come up with any ideas, I'll ring you, okay?"

"It's not necessary to leave Stanley here, is it?"

Bill Nevis shook his head. "Well, you can do, if you want —"

Stanley looked as if he'd much prefer to be left.

As Jury was driving the Northampton Road, he was overtaken by a mob of Northampton police cars, headed in the direction of Sidbury, the larger town a few miles southwest of Long Piddleton.

Back at the Jack and Hammer with Stanley in tow, Jury saw that the window table was still occupied, and he wondered if they ever left. Or did they leave and then leave cardboard cutouts of themselves in the window?

"What was that all about?" he said, dropping into a chair.

Stanley went under the table and sulked.

"What was what?" asked Trueblood, lighting up one of his colorful Sobranie cigarettes.

"Police. Half a dozen cars. Northants police nearly drove me off the road. You didn't see them?"

"Well, they didn't drive through here, old bean."

Then Theo Wrenn Brown was back, bursting through the door of the saloon bar like a stripper coming out of a cake, thinking himself the surprise of the day.

"What's up, Theo?" said Jury.

"You don't know?"

"Know what?"

"Police are all over the Old Post Road. You know, just outside Sidbury. A body. They've found a body."

Theo had never looked happier.

5

Old Post Road
Tuesday, 4:00 P.M.

The Old Post Road lay between the market town of Sidbury and Long Piddleton and fed into the Northampton Road. It was now little used. Jury pulled up across the road from the scene squared off now by yellow crime scene tape. There were several police cars, all Northamptonshire police. The cars were pulled up in front of Tower Cottage, or parked on what must have been an old dirt road that ran by the tower that sat some distance from the cottage. The road might have run into the Northampton Road, but more likely, dead-ended in the field. There was no ambulance as yet.

As he got out of the car, he looked up at the tower, probably about fifty or sixty feet high. It looked to be structurally sound from this distance. He asked a constable to point out the person in charge and was directed to a tall, thin man who could have been forty or fifty.

"Her license says she's Belle Syms, lives — lived — in Clerkenwell." Chief Inspector Ian Brierly was holding a small bag of the sort women referred to as a "clutch." This one looked very expensive — gold, silver, and ebony. Its clasp was topped by a tiny gold skull. It was this bag he'd taken the license from. Brierly was a chief inspector with the Northamptonshire police; that Jury was part of the Metropolitan Police did not seem to dismay Brierly at all.

The body of the young woman lay on a black body bag that had not yet been closed. The scene-of-crime officers were scattered about between body and tower doing their work. The victim was wearing a red silk dress, the entire top covered with red sequins and bits of marquisette outlining a deep-V of a neckline. Jury thought it was a stunning dress. He asked Brierly if he could check the label.

"Sure. It's Givenchy. Pretty haute couture for a shopgirl, wouldn't you say?"

"Why a shopgirl?"

Brierly shrugged. "The nail artwork. Phony fingernails over the real, bitten ones." Brierly kneeled and raised her hand. The hot-pink polished nails were dotted with crystals; one nail on each hand was covered with a metallic-looking silver. It was elaborate and quite beautiful. One of these enhanced nails had come off to show a down-to-the-quick nail. "Just doesn't strike me as a Hooray Henrietta type."

Jury smiled. He'd always liked that "Hooray Henry" designation for the young upper class.

Her shoes were strappy sandals in red patent leather with the designer's name on the insole. One shoe was half off one foot and the other a short distance from the foot. Jimmy Choo. Jury was feeling almost at home, back in the world of Upper Sloane Street fashion. Givenchy and Jimmy Choo.

The tower sat in the middle of a couple of acres, the old thatched cottage some hundred feet or so off to one side. There were no battlements, and as the door was set level with the ground, rather than high enough to need a ladder, Jury assumed it was never meant for defense. A bell tower, perhaps. There were actual windows, rather than mere slits for openings. The property was listed with an agent in Sidbury. Jury wondered what price it would bring.

"What was this built for?" asked Jury.

"No idea. It seems to be a folly. Possibly someone thought they'd live in it; there are several floors. Question is, of course, why would this Syms woman visit it? It's never been considered of much tourist interest, and the road's hardly used." They were walking closer to the tower as they talked, and now DCI Brierly pointed upward. "Fell right from the top, or rather, the level right under the top. Bell tower, I suppose. That was some dreadful fall."

"Yes. How can you be sure it wasn't from farther down?"

"Windows, for one thing. None of them open, except at the top. They're not barred, but they're shuttered, as you can see."

"So are you thinking accident? Suicide?"

DCI Brierly shook his head. "Hard to say. She paid a visit to her aunt, Blanche Vesta, but was staying somewhere else. We haven't got where yet. Right now the aunt's with a WPC over there in the cottage and she's pretty upset." Brierly paused to look over at the body on the ground. "With what we know at this point, I find it hard to think 'accident' because why would she be up there in the first place? For the view? The way she was dressed? Not kitted out for a climb, that's for sure. Red silk and designer shoes with four-inch heels."

"Wouldn't she have taken them off if she'd jumped? They'd make the jump that much more difficult. And there was no sign of anyone else?"

"We're waiting to talk to the owner, who might be able to tell us if anything was disturbed. He's an American antiques dealer. There're antiques on several levels, old rugs, stuff. He's in London, according to the estate agent."

"Antiques dealer in the U.S. Could be a friend of the dead woman, maybe? Maybe she stopped by —" He ran a thumb across his forehead, perplexed. "But that doesn't explain going up there . . ." said Jury. "Have you got the time of death?"

"Not yet. Late last night, early this morning."

"And the body lay here all that time before — ?"

"A delivery lad found her just an hour ago. This road isn't much used, and that tower sits far back from it."

"I would have thought the red dress —"

"The red might have meant flowers to someone — roses, poppies. It's quite a distance from the road. You'd have to be closer than that to make out a body, I think."

"It could have been murder; she could have been forced out of that window." Jury looked up.

"There's always that," said Brierly, dryly.

58

Jury looked toward the cottage. "The aunt, how —"

"Did we find the aunt so quickly? Bit of paper with a phone number written on it." Brierly held up a scrap of paper. "The aunt was a bit surprised when her niece stopped to visit. Hadn't seen her in some time. So they had a drink and a wee chat and Belle seemed to be in good spirits, you know."

Jury didn't know.

"The aunt said Belle didn't like to drive as it makes — made — her nervous."

Jury was reminded of Stanley's redundant renaming. "So this Blanche Vesta has no idea why her niece would have driven here?"

"She called it a 'very queer thing indeed.' Kept repeating that."

Jury looked over toward the little cottage. "She's there?"

Brierly nodded. "Our WPC organized some tea I shouldn't wonder."

Jury thanked Brierly and walked across the grass toward the cottage, where smoke was curling out of the chimney.

The woman police constable, WPC Mary Wells, said, "I expect I shouldn't have taken the liberty, sir," speaking of the fire, "but it was so chilly and the fire was already laid,

59

as if someone was meant to put a match to it."

WPC Wells had a fey quality about her, as if she might expect to see fairies dancing on the hearth. "I hope it's all right, sir, that I made tea."

"I'm sure your DCI can square it with the owner."

Blanche Vesta, who lived, she said, in Meecham Lane just off the Old Post Road, had not known Belle all that intimately, her living in London as she did. Wembley, near the park.

"Wembley Park?"

Blanche nodded. "At least when she was married. I went there once or twice to visit. I don't care for London; it's too big."

The cottage was probably being used by its owner only intermittently, and had no heat laid on when he wasn't there; fortunately, the electric was, and the resourceful WPC had put the kettle on and managed to scare up a packet of PGs. Despite its chilliness, Tower Cottage was quite cozy, the armchairs deep and comfortable. With the round deal table between them, Blanche and Jury were both having a cup.

"The thing is this, sir," said Blanche, pulling her dark wool skirt tighter over her knees, not from modesty, but against the chill.

Jury noticed the skirt adjusting and reached behind him for a wool throw he'd seen on a nearby stool. He handed this to her.

"Why, thank you." She took a moment to be flustered and to arrange the blanket over herself. "The thing is this," she said again. "Belle completely surprised me, her turning up in Sidbury. Last time she did that — it was practically a year ago. When she was living with her husband, Zachariah, I'd visit them occasionally in Wembley, as I said. They're separated, but they're still friendly. I know he'd like to get back together, but . . ." She stopped, then said, "Well, her going up that tower's not that surprising. She always liked heights. Ferris wheels, roller coasters, slides, when she was little . . ."

"Could she have been going to meet someone? A man?"

"Dressed like that, she must've been. She was married, but they separated. A pity, that was, as I always liked Zachariah. He was such a sweet boy. But I guess Belle wanted more."

"And she didn't tell you where she was staying?"

Blanche Vesta shook her head.

"Blanche. Forgive me for asking this, but I must, in the circumstances. Is it possible Belle might have thought of suicide?"

A curt shake of the head, and then a little laugh. "Belle? Kill herself? Too flighty was Belle for that."

Jury had heard reasons for not committing suicide, but flightiness was never one of them.

"No. Besides she was Church of England. You know what the church has to say on that score."

Jury wasn't sure what the church had to say on any score. He sat back and looked at the weak fire. "Did she know anyone else in Sidbury besides you, Blanche?"

She shook her head slowly. "No one I ever knew of. But it's not impossible she did. There's other places she might've been going. Northampton, maybe? Not that I ever heard her mention anyone there. She did get a call . . . or did she make one? I'm too flustered to remember right."

"That's all right. You'll remember later. You can't think of any reason why she suddenly turned up to visit you."

Blanche Vesta looked about the room as if just now assessing her presence in it. "Maybe she didn't."

62

Jury frowned. "Meaning — ?"

"It wouldn't be me she got herself turned out as she did. That dress, those shoes! That's never the way Belle dressed. Skirts and cardies, fawn and brown: that was Belle's style. Such a dress that was. Beautiful, but it must have cost the earth, and wherever was Belle getting that kind of money? Well, it's like you said: maybe her purpose was to see somebody else, and her visit to me was just, you could say, because I was here?"

And they were all there, lined up on the other side of the police tape — Melrose Plant, Vivian Rivington, Diane Demorney, with Stanley in tow, and Joanna Lewes. Marshall Trueblood was pouring words into the ear of one of the police constables, as if the PC were a jug, but who, to give Trueblood credit, appeared to be listening. It was not getting Trueblood under the tape, however.

Theo Wrenn Brown was moving among some other people who either had heard of the death or had been driving by, though hardly anyone ever used the road. Cars were pulled up in the lay-by, or off on the grassy verge. Theo Wrenn Brown was exhibiting what he considered his special status as the one who had passed the scene first. He was pointing at the tower and sweeping his arm about, taking in the scene.

When they saw Jury coming, Diane and the others waved and grinned as if they were a party of six announcing their presence to a maître d' who could be absolutely counted on for a table by a window.

Jury thought Trueblood was about to raise the police tape as if it were a velvet rope.

Diane Demorney was pulling back on Stanley's lead. The dog seemed very interested in the police business at the tower. Diane had a thermos that Jury assumed held vodka, but he was surprised to see her produce a little bowl from her suitcase-size purse, which she filled with water from the thermos and put on the ground for Stanley. The dog slurped it up. Jury thought Diane would have been the last person to ever bring water for an animal. So much for his profiling ability.

Jury said, "You don't suppose the lady in red is Stanley's owner, do you?"

"No, of course not," said Diane.

Jury let that subject drop. Brierly would find that out.

Joanna Lewes asked, breathlessly, "But what happened?"

"Did she really jump?" asked Vivian. Her

dark red hair was tucked in the collar of a hyacinth-colored coat. Jury kept forgetting how beautiful Vivian was.

"We don't know yet."

"Don't know?" said Trueblood. "All of this police presence and you can't tell if someone jumped or fell accidentally?"

"The way your minds work — like bullet trains — well, we police have to slog along muddy trails of thought and evidence until we finally, perhaps luckily, come to a conclusion."

Jury walked across the grass to where DCI Brierly was standing, writing in a notebook. Jury said to him, "Blanche Vesta is a clear-headed woman. According to her, Belle Syms rather enjoyed heights and her aunt thought she might have gone up the tower, but it's hard to believe she'd gone on her own. And where's her car?"

"Right." Brierly looked up toward the top of the tower. "Larking about with her date, you think?"

"With her date, possibly. But I wouldn't call it larking." Jury looked down at the body, turned away. "You see that Staffordshire terrier over there —" Jury nodded toward the group. "The dog's straining at his lead. We found him."

"You think it might have been the victim's?"

"But if her niece had a dog in tow, Blanche Vesta would surely have mentioned it."

Brierly nodded. "Good-looking dog."

Jury looked down. "Good-looking girl."

6

"They're going to be all over it, you know," said Melrose Plant to Richard Jury that evening as Ruthven placed two whiskies in cut glass tumblers at their elbows.

The dog Joey lay snoozing by the fire on an old scrap of ratty-looking rug that he had developed a special attachment toward. Ruthven couldn't get it away from the dog, much to the butler's distress. Right now, Joey patrolled Ruthven's every move through half-closed eyes.

" 'They'?" said Jury, raising glass and eyebrows simultaneously. "Why 'they'? You're the ringleader."

"Don't be daft." Melrose was fingering a cigarette out of a silver box. "Trueblood is."

"Ah. So you admit there *is* a *gang*."

"There's no gang. We all go our separate ways."

67

"No, you all go the same way. The interfering way."

"The Interfering Way. Sounds like a sequel to *The Guermantes Way* or perhaps a highway on the Isle of Skye. Could we just stick to the subject?"

"Was there one?" Jury had bolted his whiskey and was about to summon Ruthven, only he didn't see a summoning device.

"The lady in red, of course."

Jury held up his empty glass. "Another?"

Melrose left the comfort of his wing chair and tugged at a damask bell pull to the right of the mantel.

"I haven't seen anyone do that since *Upstairs, Downstairs.* Does it really ring a bell someplace?"

"In the stable. You'll see Aggrieved pass the window with your whiskey. Now, all I was saying is that Trueblood will have all of us investigating. It will be really silly."

"It usually is. You better steer clear of the crime scene or Brierly will charge you with interfering with an ongoing investigation."

"Well, *you* certainly lost no time getting to the Old Post Road to interfere."

"I'm a detective. I get to interfere."

Joey looked up smartly when Ruthven appeared.

Jury held out his glass. Smartly. "What's

for dinner, Ruthven?"

Melrose interfered. "Black pudding and Spotted Dick."

Ruthven offered a crimped little smile and was about to answer when there was a knock like doom on the front door. The knocker was raised and lowered several times before Ruthven could get there. They heard him politely murmuring, the murmur overridden by the voice of Melrose's aunt, and a third voice, belonging to her bosom friend, Lambert Strether. Both voices had Melrose sliding down in his chair.

And Jury rising from his with undisguised glee, sensing the door opening on a bit of theater.

Ruthven announced both of the visitors: "Lady Ardry and Mr. Strether, sir." They were in the room before it was out of his mouth.

She stumped in, short and stout, Lambert Strether in her wake. "Superintendent! How good of you to come!"

As if it were her house rather than her nephew's. Melrose now got up slowly from his watered silk chair like a sponge from the bottom of the sea. "Ah, Agatha. I've not seen you all day." To Strether, he nodded and mumbled an hello.

"I've been to London!" she said.

As if no one else ever had.

Not having waited for Ruthven to take her cape, she was divesting herself of it now, unhooking the cord that joined the two big buttons. It might simply have landed on the floor had Ruthven not stepped up to collect it. It was a swirl of tartan, and Melrose was trying to decide whether she put him in mind of Batman on the Isle of Mull or Dame May Whitty in *The Lady Vanishes*.

And would she? No, she would not vanish; she would sit and ask for a Shooting Sherry. Strether settled for "whatever you two are imbibing, ho ho."

His name was Lambert Strether, born to a mother who was so fond of *The Ambassadors* that she named him after its protagonist. This Lambert Strether was not what Henry James had in mind. He was a con man who had tried to pass off phony papers claiming he was the inheritor of their old pub, the Man with a Load of Mischief. Had tried until the little group sitting in the Jack and Hammer's window had killed this plan quickly, and Richard Jury had come along and driven nails into its coffin.

Agatha thought the world of Lambert, but then Agatha's world was a restricted field of Agatha-stuff, like dusty owls on the mantel and ratty fur pieces and custard over nursery puddings, which she thought the very essence of British-ness. Agatha had come from America decades before to claim whatever she could as Melrose's aunt-by-marriage to his uncle, the Honorable Robert. She called herself "Lady Ardry," whereas she was merely a widow, a wiped-out Mrs. It both irritated her and pleased her that Melrose, as his father had been the seventh, was the eighth Earl of Ardry, a title that he had jettisoned years before. So now he was merely an irritant.

Having greeted his uninvited guests, the irritant resat himself while Ruthven served the Shooting Sherry and whiskey.

"What brings you here, Agatha?"

"You haven't heard?"

"I don't know if I've heard, since I don't know what it is."

Lambert Strether drank his whiskey and waded in. "Been a peculiar bit of bother at the Blue Parrot. You know the place?"

"What bother?"

Lambert had lost interest in his own announcement and was already looking around for the decanter, ready for a top-up.

Melrose repeated, "What bother? Has Trevor Sly finally realized that Rick and what's-her-name — Ida? Irma? — are not going to show up in the Blue Parrot?"

What's-her-name being Ingrid Bergman, thought Jury.

"Or," Melrose went on, "has that cardboard camel Trevor keeps parked by the door got bored with the whole thing and just wandered into the sandbox he calls his car park?"

Jury quite liked the Blue Parrot. The film posters all depicting outposts in exotic places; the swinging beaded curtains, the questionable life of the colorful parrot itself. Jury thought it might have been a little dead the last time.

At just that moment Ruthven appeared with stunning prescience, announcing dinner. Coughing lightly behind his hand, he asked, "Shall I set another —"

Melrose cut that off with a swift rise to his feet. "No, Ruthven, you shan't." He turned to the visitors. "So sorry, Agatha, Mr. Strether, but the superintendent and I can't delay dinner. It's Soufflé Day, and you know how Martha is about that!" He turned to Jury. "Richard."

Thus commanded, Jury rose. This managed to get Agatha up, but with a struggle. Strether said, "Haven't finished my drink, dear boy."

Melrose wouldn't have cared if he hadn't finished his blood transfusion; he took Strether's elbow, difficult as it was, since it was planted on the chair arm, and helped him and his whiskey to their feet. "Nice you could drop by."

Of course, it infuriated Lady Ardry (as wasn't) that her nephew and his friend weren't chaining her to her chair to force her to talk about the "bit of bother." "Very well, you'll have to go to the Blue Parrot to find out."

Melrose ushered them, one on each side, to the front door. Out of sight, his frosty Good night spun into the dark.

"Come on." Melrose motioned from the big marble-floored foyer for Jury to come. The dining room was on the other side of the house.

As they walked toward it, Jury said, "What do you suppose she was talking about?"

"Look, if anything had happened at Trevor Sly's we'd've heard the parrot squawking all the way here." He frowned. "Ilda? Inga?"

"What are you talking about?"

"Ingrid in *Casablanca*. What the devil is her name?"

Jury shrugged. "Can't remember."

They had arrived in the gleaming rosewood dining room, white napkins, polished silver, candles.

"Elsie?"

Jury sighed. "Look, she walked into Bogart's gin joint and changed the world. Who cares what her name was?"

They sat down. "Certainly, that's one way of looking at it." Melrose snapped open his snowy napkin and stared at the ceiling. "Ilka?"

The Grand Marnier soufflé having been floated in double helpings onto their plates, the brandy sipped, the cigarette — just Melrose's — been lit, they decided there was nothing for it but to go to the Blue Parrot and check out the "bother."

"Ruthven," called Melrose toward the kitchen. He hated using the little bell.

Ruthven appeared. "We're going out. I think I'll wear my camel coat."

Jury winced. "That's beneath you."

Melrose was still snickering as Ruthven assisted him with his bespoke, camel-haired coat. And Jury with his unbespoke mack.

7

The Blue Parrot
Tuesday, 10:00 P.M.

Trevor Sly, owner of the Blue Parrot, appeared to be a more broken man than usual, not spiritually, but actually, physically broken. This seeming dislocation of joint and vertebrae was owing to Trevor's tall spindliness and his ability to bend himself in just about any direction, as if he were a collection of pipe cleaners.

To say he was tall and thin, with sticks for arms and legs, didn't quite catch it. This physical bending into any position went right along with his obsequiousness, this bending of his own wishes to meet those of whoever was in front of him, who at the moment happened to be Melrose Plant, and Melrose didn't trust Trevor any further than he could throw him. Fortunately, he'd no need to throw him anywhere.

Trevor loved to think of himself as every

man's confidant. He was not a man to confide in; he'd probably use a confidence as a cudgel. On the one hand he was servility itself; on the other, a man with strong tendencies toward blackmail.

This Uriah Heep of Northamptonshire ran his public house all on his own, employing neither cook nor barmaid nor bottle washer.

Jury had always liked the place, not in spite of its rather kitschlit ambience, but because of it. To Jury it was almost bad taste turning a corner and running into something else — prepackaged nostalgia, maybe. The walls were adorned with old film posters, *Casablanca* prominent among them.

He tried to recall her film name and still couldn't. He looked at Ingrid and Humphrey looking at each other. It was on the tip of his tongue.

On one wall a big poster advertising *The Road to Morocco* showed Bing Crosby and Bob Hope riding a camel. There was Peter O'Toole as Lawrence of Arabia. There was *A Passage to India.* Peter O'Toole he supposed was still alive, but what a loss to theater had come with the death of Peggy Ashcroft. The film posters hung side by side, Lawrence on top of that train and Peggy in a howdah atop a camel. They seemed to be moving toward one another as if about to meet, but it was a meeting that would never take place.

Beneath the kitsch, Jury saw a crushing sadness. Bogart and Bergman, Peggy, Bing and Bob — how could all of these people be dead? They seemed to lie at his feet in terrible heaps, as if he'd shot them.

It was the desert Trevor Sly seemed to like, exoticism that he featured. The tables were covered with red-and-white-checkered cloths, and on each was a little desert scene: palm trees, camels with howdahs or grouped as a family, little tents, figures of nomads. Palm frond fans creaked above the eight tables and their little enactments of desert life.

He left off looking at the camel train, much like the cars of the actual train atop which Lawrence moved, and joined Melrose at the bar.

"What can I get you, Mr. Jury?"

Jury studied the optics, saw Glenfiddich, looked at the beer pulls, saw Guinness, decided on that, partly for the aesthetic experience.

"All right, Trevor, go on with what happened. Incidentally, was my aunt here with that Strether-fellow when this 'An Occurrence at Owl Creek Bridge' incident took place?"

Jury was watching the foam gather atop his glass, Guinness foam being like no other in the way it perfected itself. Jury turned from the foam to Melrose. "Owl Creek? What are you talking about?"

"You recall that story by Ambrose Bierce. The Confederate sympathizer captured and being hanged on Owl Creek Bridge. The rope's round his neck and he goes down. Then you see the rope snap and he drops, free, into the water below. He swims like hell, all the while they're shooting at him. Farther upriver he drags himself onto the bank and then starts running for home. Home we see is an antebellum mansion, a lovely wife and sweet children. He runs through woods toward it and her, his arms outstretched, yet oddly, they don't meet."

Jury thought of Peggy Ashcroft on that camel and Peter O'Toole running across the cars of the train, fated never to meet.

"In the film version of this story, he keeps on doing it," Melrose continued. "I mean, runs toward her again and again, the film repeating the incident over and over. Now, suddenly, we're back at Owl Creek Bridge, where the rope's round his neck and he drops and is dead."

"You mean the escape never happened? All of that running and finding his wife, all of that was what he thought of in the few seconds between dropping and dying." When Melrose nodded, Jury said, "That's one of the saddest things I ever heard." He turned to Trevor. "So what happened here?"

Trevor, having sliced the foam from the pint with a knife and served it to Jury, pulled up a stool behind the bar and leaned over to get a bit more cheek-by-jowl experience. "Well, a gent comes in here, four-ish it was, looking distraught, clothes a bit all anyhow — you know, tie askew, mud on the shoes. He's wanting to know where the Old Post Road is —"

Melrose opened his mouth to say something, but Jury put a hand on his arm.

"— and he'd really like a drink, double whiskey. I pour it, he downs it in ten seconds. I give him directions to the Old Post Road as best I can, he pays and runs out. I walked to the door to see his car speeding away. In a right hurry, he was."

"Didn't he give any clue —" Jury said before Trevor interrupted.

"Oh, but that's not the end of it. Just wait now." Trevor drew even closer. "Then he's back again, asking for a drink. This about five, only an hour later."

"How strange," said Jury.

"Stranger still. He asks me again where the Old Post Road is. I told him he'd been in before, asking the same question and that I'd told him. Well, he gives me this odd look but doesn't say anything for a bit. Then he asks —"

"You'll love this." Melrose gave Jury's side an elbow.

"You see a strange dog around here?"

Jury choked on his beer.

"Well, I says, 'No, there's no dog been round the Blue Parrot today.' " Trevor went on, "And I ask him, 'Is it your dog, then?' And he nods. Then I ask him where he'd last seen the dog. He says, 'The Old Post Road.' " Trevor shrugged. "And just like that, he turns and walks out. Then, a minute or two later I hear a shot ring out. Came from the direction of the car park out there." He pointed toward the front of the pub.

"A shot? Just a single shot?" said Jury.

"That's what I heard."

"Did you do anything?"

"Such as what, I'd like to know? Go dashing out and get shot meself?"

Wryly, Jury answered, "I was thinking more along the lines of calling police."

Trevor said, no, he hadn't. Would police

have come? Probably thought he was barmy.

They conferred for a while longer about the man and his dog before Jury and Plant left.

Melrose pushed into the driver's seat and started up the hummingbird engine of his Silver Shadow. Jury thunked closed the passenger seat door and clicked on his seat belt.

Said Melrose, as they slid along the rough dirt road the Rolls mistook for silk, "Well, there'll be no living with them now." He spoke, of course, of his friends at the Jack and Hammer. "What do you think?"

"That I'm glad I'm going to Exeter."

If the dirt road to the Blue Parrot was silk, the Northampton Road was air, and they fairly flew all the way back to Ardry End.

8

Exeter, Devon
Wednesday, 1:00 P.M.

Exeter Cathedral was one of the fifty-six cathedrals in England, and Jury had been in very few of them. He tried ticking off on his fingers the ones he had visited — Salisbury (not far away), Lincoln, Wells, Canterbury — and found he had many more fingers than cathedrals.

He wondered how he could be so ignorant of cathedral architecture. Did all of them have vaulted ceilings such as this, such intricately designed ceiling bosses? Probably.

But none of the other fifty-five had Brian Macalvie walking down the nave in his signature macintosh and carrying a book into which several file folders were stuffed. The Devon-Cornwall Constabulary was headquartered in Middlemoor, outside of Exeter. Macalvie was a divisional commander.

Jury had last seen him two months before. It seemed like yesterday and it seemed like years. Time had a way of dissolving.

"When you weren't across the street, I figured you'd be here."

"Why?"

"You are, aren't you?"

Jury smiled slightly and shook his head. They were both looking at the rondels, brilliantly colored tapestry cushions, lined up all along the ledge of the nave.

"Remember," said Macalvie, "Fanny Hamilton?"

"I remember her."

Fanny Hamilton had been their case.

They left the cathedral and crossed over the square to a small café that looked out on the green.

"And Tess Williamson," said Brian Macalvie. "I remember her. She'd be hard to forget."

They were sitting in the same café in which Jury had met him years before when Macalvie had been working on a case involving the deaths of three women, Fanny Hamilton having been one.

They were drinking coffee and eating from a double-tiered tray of miniature pastries — small brioche and croissant, others dappled with apricot or peaches in a custard. Jury had eaten three of them while drinking his first cup of coffee.

Macalvie had eaten none; rather, he looked at them as if they presented a fresh puzzle. To Macalvie, everything was a puzzle, a murder case being the Great Puzzle.

"Tess Williamson." He said again and smiled briefly. "Unforgettable."

Jury picked up a miniature croissant. "You make it sound as if you knew her well." He stuffed the croissant into his mouth. One bite.

"I did."

Jury nearly choked. "What?"

"I knew her. I met her in here one day. All the tables were taken. She waved me over to hers. She was sitting alone. This table, actually. She said she liked the view of the cathedral." He now picked up one of the fruit-filled pastries. "She loved this stuff."

Jury was astonished. "It sounds as if you met like old friends. Tom Williamson didn't mention that."

Macalvie shrugged. "She probably never mentioned it to him. As to old friends, we weren't. Friendship has a history. We didn't."

"Then how?"

Macalvie sighed. "Let me give you the facts, since you have clearly stereotyped the whole thing."

Jury smiled. "That's me. More coffee?" He looked around for the waitress.

"I had coffee in here with Tess Williamson maybe five times. She used to come to Exeter to do charity work for the cathedral. One of the holy dusters."

"What's that?"

"They dust, don't they? Polish, clean. She thought it her proper station in life." Macalvie smiled.

Jury thought for a moment. "It sounds like penance."

"You're getting clever. Yes, I'd say she had the makings of a penitent. She was here like clockwork. I, of course, don't exactly have a clockwork schedule. But I did meet up with her those several times. Originally, when she introduced herself, I remembered the Hilda Palmer case, nearly five years earlier. I'll tell you, I wished I'd been working it." The book holding the files was on the table. He took out one of the files, held it up. "Ludicrously inconclusive. You know what happened?"

"I know what her husband told me." Jury repeated what he knew about Hilda Palmer's death.

"So these kids were all over the grounds, the other woman" — he turned over a page — "Elaine Davies was in the front and supposed to be watching the kids, but not very hard, as she knew sod-all about what was going on, or so she said. Then the discovery of Hilda Palmer at the bottom of that dry pool and Tess Williamson with her."

Jury said, "What about Tess Williamson's own death? Tom Williamson thinks she was murdered. Shoved down that flight of stone stairs."

Macalvie nodded. "There was that possibility. Forensic did a computer simulation of the fall, posited on the direction in which she'd been standing, the blood spatter along the way, the bruising, et cetera, et cetera. They decided that it was an accident. They were wrong."

The waitress was at their table looking annoyed. Macalvie ordered two more coffees, and she turned and left.

Jury always liked the way Macalvie discounted evidence so calmly and unambiguously.

"So you think it was murder too?"

"Of course it was. Or suicide."

"Why?"

"The fall. You'll see what I mean when you see the house."

"I expect it struck you, the points of similarity between the death of the girl Hilda Palmer and Tess Williamson," said Jury.

"It struck me. What you're getting at is some motive for murder, right? The girl's mother might have wanted to duplicate the circumstances in Tess's death. Yes, it occurred to me, but I didn't think about it for long before I decided it was coincidence. Whatever similarity there was in their both dying at Laburnum isn't strange, since Tess Williamson spent so much time there. But the fall down that flight of stairs? I'd never put that down to vertigo. Perhaps suicide made to look like an accident. Also, five years seems a long time to wait to seek revenge, especially if it was a parent. A parent's emotions would be boiling hot right afterward, but she'd simmer down over the years."

Jury nodded, though he didn't necessarily agree. "Those times you met her, did she bring the case up? Did you?"

"Did I? Of course not. Had she wanted to talk about it, I guess she would've. She didn't."

"What was she like?"

Macalvie stirred coffee already stirred to death. "Generous. Compassionate. But what I noticed most was the way she paid attention. You've known people like that? They're rare, the ones who really listen. But the generosity . . . the kind of person who'd see a stray cat and go get it some milk. Nothing escaped her notice. We talked about nothing in particular: my work, her house, which she loved, her husband, Tom, whom she also loved. And Thomas Hardy's books. We talked about having lunch one day —"

"Brief Encounter," said Jury, drinking his coffee.

"What? Bloody hell. You're revoltingly sentimental. It was nothing at all like that." Macalvie drew a match across the upright box on the table held straight by prongs. He inhaled, said, "You still stopped?" He wiggled the cigarette.

Glumly, Jury nodded. "When are you going to stop?"

"Never, seeing the effect it's had on you."

Jury laughed.

"You want to see it?"

Jury's hand was hovering over the last of the little pastries. "See what?"

Macalvie stared at the ceiling, shook his head. "What we've been talking about, for God's sakes. Laburnum. The Williamsons' house. It's not far from here."

"You bet. Now?"

"If you're not going to order another pastry selection."

VERTIGO GIRL

9

Old Post Road
Wednesday, 1:00 P.M.

Melrose Plant pulled his early-model Jag
into the leaf-matted drive of Tower Cottage
and its FOR SALE sign, FREEHOLD (believable); LOVELY VIEWS OVER THE COUNTRY-
SIDE (Aren't there always?), ALL MOD CONS
(unlikely).

He crunched across the gravel and leaves
to the front door, passing by some pots of
geraniums that looked the worse for wear.
Owen Archer was not one to be out here in
all weathers in his gardening togs, deadhead-
ing roses and pushing a wheelbarrow of
manure around.

Melrose stood on the stoop and gave the
dolphin doorknocker a couple of goes,
admiring Archer for his scruffy front garden.
One did get tired of perfect pruning and
grass cut to glassy smoothness. Had Melrose himself not had people who came at

mysterious times (for he never seemed to see them) to shear and trim, Ardry End would have looked like Kurtz's place in the Congo.

As he stood leaning against the doorjamb, he observed some very tall dark green plants crowded at the corner of the cottage that looked to be swaying in the breezeless air. Melrose wondered if there were any more triffids around, or if John Wyndham had used them all up. Triffids marching, one, two . . .

The door opened suddenly, and since Melrose's shoulder had been against it, he nearly fell into the little hallway.

"I do beg your pardon," he said as he righted himself and reset his jacket on his shoulders.

Owen Archer laughed. "Quite all right. I do it myself. Come on in."

"I do it myself?" That rather overflowed the banks of hospitality, didn't it? "Thank you. You're Mr. Archer?"

"I am. You're Lord Ardry?"

Melrose nodded. He trotted out his title once in a while when it suited him. He had been resourceful enough to get Owen Archer's name and number from the listing agent, and had called.

"Sit down, won't you?" Archer waved

vaguely in the sofa's direction. "Tea?" A teapot sat on the round table between sofa and armchair.

Melrose took a seat on the sprigged muslin sofa, finding it quite comfortable. Archer had been seated in the opposite armchair, to judge from the cup, the book, and the lamp. Right now he opened a corner cabinet, which housed some very old china, and took out a cup and saucer. He set it before Melrose and poured tea into it. He moved the small milk jug and sugar bowl from the middle of the table to keep company with the cup.

"I hope you don't mind the intrusion, but as I said over the phone, the Scotland Yard detective superintendent who's been staying with me had to go to Devon and asked me to visit in his stead . . ." How banal, how unconvincing, how, indeed, absurd.

But Owen Archer apparently didn't need convincing and took Melrose's visit at face value. "Yes. Imagine returning from London to find your place overrun by police, dead bodies, ambulances, patrol cars —"

Melrose wondered how long the list would be. Especially since nearly all of those things had vanished by the time Archer returned. "Then you saw her?"

"The victim? No. Sorry. I was dramatizing

everything. One of the detectives had me look at police photos. Poor woman. It's a helluva way to commit suicide or murder, though, don't you think?"

Melrose started in his chair. "I don't understand. Police think it wasn't an accident?"

"Apparently not. Not according to that inspector — Briars? Is that his name? I was somewhat concerned there for a while, that I was a 'person of interest,' as they say. But I got the distinct impression they'd someone else on the books, though he didn't say that, not directly. They had me go up in the tower to see if I could tell them if anything looked strange or out of place . . . you know."

No, Melrose didn't know. Owen Archer was a mine of fresh information.

"And was there anything?"

"Just a chair and a small table pulled round in front of the window, ostensibly to help her get up to the window. I can't imagine choosing that as a site for a suicide, the window's too difficult to reach."

He went on. "People do sometimes pull up here to look at the tower. Well, it's a folly, isn't it? The Old Post Road isn't much used, which is one of the reasons I bought this place. I expect it's going to be heavily trafficked now. At least a dozen cars have stopped, but no one has attempted to cross over and investigate. I don't think the whole experience is going to do much for property value."

"On the contrary. As it didn't happen in the house itself, there might be a certain ghoulish attraction to owning the tower. You're just back from London, then?"

Archer nodded. "Christie's auction. Not much there, and what there was I thought too pricey. People lose their heads at auctions, don't they?"

"I see you have one or two very handsome pieces: that chest by the fireplace."

"That? Oh, yes. Restoration, that is. I've got a number of things I'll have to sell."

Why in hell wasn't Trueblood handling this assignment? He had the perfect excuse to come here. "I've a good friend in the village — well, you might have been to his shop. Trueblood's Antiques. It's next door to the Jack and Hammer."

"Yes, I have. He's got very fine stock for being out there in the sticks."

The sticks? "Yes, I expect we probably are too far from London for our own good." Hardly little more than an hour. "Agrarians, you might say."

"Really? Farm country? I wouldn't have thought —"

Melrose wondered, then, what are "the sticks"?

"— since I haven't seen any farming around."

"Well, I do keep animals. Horses, goats —" Melrose recalled some article in *Country Life* which always featured an aspiring debutante, this one a young woman who "kept a pig." Meaning kept it for photo ops. Melrose was now thinking of getting a pig of his own.

Archer smiled broadly. "Gentleman farmer, are you?"

"Oh, no, just a gentleman."

Frowning the tiniest bit, Archer said, "It's Lord Ardry, right? Then that means you sit in the House of Lords?"

Melrose was as far from sitting in the House of Lords as he was from sitting in Agatha's lap. But having presented himself at the door as "Lord" he could hardly drop the title on the other side of the sill, and he had no intention of giving Owen Archer his reasons for abandoning his title.

He got back to the business at hand: "The victim, Mr. Archer, you only saw photos? You didn't see the body at all? I mean, police didn't ask you to identify it?"

"Me? Why would they?" He was peering into the teapot and apparently finding it

98

wanting. He rose. "I'm going to put the kettle on again. Won't be a minute."

Archer had seemed unoffended by the questions. But why take that particular moment to escape to the kitchen?

He said he had gone up to London. How hard would it be to get someone, a woman friend, to lure one's lover, say, by telling her over the phone, "Listen, darling, take off those four-inch heels and meet me at the top of the tower where I've got a surprise for you."

Melrose flinched when the kettle screeched.

Archer was back and pouring fresh water over old tea leaves. Melrose wondered if Ruthven or Ruthven's wife, Martha, ever did that. He hoped not. Yet it was an oddly British practice, wasn't it? Most Americans didn't do it, he guessed.

"You were saying . . . ?" Melrose said as Archer handed him his refilled cup. Melrose sipped it and set it aside. "About its being your tower."

"Yes. Well, I can see that a death in my backyard might make me look suspicious. Only, it's not literally in my backyard, is it? It's a tower, a folly that tourists just take it upon themselves to go into. If they see signs of my presence, they go ahead and investigate anyway. I suppose they don't necessarily attach the folly to the house. I mean, it's a bit of distance from it." Archer's frown deepened. "Why would anyone choose that tower?"

"That, of course, is a good question. You keep some of your antiques there?"

"Yes, until I have enough to fill a container and get them back to the States." He thought for a moment. "If it wasn't premeditated — the murder, I mean — if it wasn't premeditated, if he just suddenly went into a rage or something . . ."

"That's possible."

"It still doesn't explain," Archer went on, "why they'd gone up in the first place. Unless, again, it caught their eye in passing, you know, like any tourist might." He shook his head, slid down in his chair a little. "But dressed as she was, seems unlikely."

10

A brass plate set in the ivy-covered brick of the stone wall said *LABURNUM.* Jury got out to push open an iron gate nearly hidden by vines and overhanging branches which Macalvie then maneuvered the car through. The quarter-mile drive was so thick with vegetation that Jury had again to get out to remove a fallen branch from their path.

"Thought there was a gardener who still saw to things," he said, slamming the car door. "Tom Williamson mentioned one."

"He still comes; it clears out once we get to the house."

Jury looked at him. "You've been here before."

"Of course I've been here. Remember? I was on the case."

No, thought Jury, more recently. It wouldn't have looked like this back then, wouldn't have needed clearing at the time Tess Williamson died.

What he said instead was, "I'd have thought she'd find this house awfully painful. But she kept returning."

"Some things you can't stay away from. Obsession."

Jury glanced at him, thinking that comment strangely out-of-character for Macalvie, until he remembered that Melrose Plant had mentioned some terrible experience Macalvie had been through in Scotland, but not told him the details. It was clear it had involved death and a woman.

"You think this place was an obsession with Tess Williamson?"

"I'd say so."

They left the car, but instead of walking through the house, they walked round it to the rear, to the patio, the gardens, the pools. There were large stones lying near the side of the house, partially sunk into the ground.

"Sarsen stones," said Macalvie. "Like the ones in Avebury, only smaller."

They were on a path that ran between the pools where a marble statue of a Grecian or Roman maiden stood, its granite surface pitted. On her slightly down-turned face Jury could see tiny marks, discolorations near her eye, a little line of them down her face, like tears. One was tempted to be a fool and try to wipe them away.

Standing between the empty pools, they looked back toward the house, at the wide patio with its bank of French doors behind and the high stone steps below it.

"Those are the stairs she fell down?" said Jury. *Stand on the highest pavement of the stair.* Iconic, the stairs seemed, almost a staircase wedded to myth.

"Right," said Macalvie, to some thought process of his own as he folded a stick of gum into his mouth. "Husband said she suffered from vertigo, which went a long way toward convincing the coroner it was an accident. Forensic reconstructed the fall." Macalvie once again removed the computer-generated picture from the file in his hand and handed it to Jury.

"This shows she fell forward —"

"Pretty much took a dive, sustaining multiple injuries, none serious, mostly bruising on the left side of the torso, arm, thigh. Minor wounds, abrasions from the stone, chipped edges, loose rocks, so there was blood spatter."

"Hell of a memory, Macalvie."

"For this."

Jury looked at him. "You really liked her."

103

Macalvie nodded briefly. "I did."

Jury looked again at the stairs, the urn at the top. *Lean on a garden urn.* The marble statue on the base of which she had struck her head. From this distance he couldn't tell much. He would have to look more closely. Although he wondered why he thought he might have something useful to add to the forensic analysis.

Wondering about the scene, Jury said, "She couldn't have fallen backward?"

Macalvie frowned slightly. "No. That would have set up a different pattern of wounds."

"Possibly. But what if she tumbled —" Jury's hand twisted, trying to simulate a circular motion. "She could have hit the steps on her back, been 'bounced' by the force, gone over on her left side, scraped along enough to bruise and cut herself."

"Why? I mean, why do you like that scenario better?"

Jury was silent for a few moments, then said, "There were flowers everywhere."

"Yeah. She must have been collecting them, roses mostly, then peonies, some feathery fern, picking them for the house. She liked flowers."

"They were all over the steps —"

"What's the problem?"

"The roses, the flowers."

Macalvie waited.

"Wouldn't she have been taking them into the house? Wouldn't she have been going up the stairs? Made a misstep, gone backward . . ."

"She could have simply turned to go back down, or just to look at something."

"I saw the photograph of her taken on those stairs. Photographer . . . what was his name?"

"Andrew Cleary. We talked to him. He was, he said, just a friend. My own guess was he was just something else."

"You're probably half-right. According to Williamson, Cleary was probably in love with her. A feeling she didn't return."

"Cleary had an alibi. He was with her in Paris. The alibi, that is. His lady friend. Not only was he with her, he was in hospital with pneumonia. So it's not just his girlfriend vouching for him. They're living there now, I think. In Paris, I mean. You're bothered by the way she was posed?"

"I'm just standing here now, seventeen years later. I don't know anything about the Williamsons other than what he told me. I wonder how they fell. I wonder if they fell, or were thrown."

"Are you still talking about the flowers?"

"You don't think it would make any difference?"

"Whether the flowers simply fell from her arms or she tossed them down? Yes, it would make a bloody difference; she'd have been angry."

Jury drew the Eliot poem from his raincoat pocket. "It's a poem that she and Cleary were fond of."

Macalvie read silently in the dusty light.

"You never wear glasses, Macalvie."

"Never needed them." He read aloud, 'So I would have had her stand and grieve —' What happens here? It seems staged. I don't get it."

"I don't either. Especially given the irony, or the lack of sentiment. She's not really grieving; he's not necessarily leaving. The effect the speaker wants is all in his mind. It's all posturing."

Macalvie shook his head. "I don't know. He seems disturbed that it didn't happen the way he saw it: the grief, the leaving. I think the point is — it didn't happen. None of it."

"Andrew Cleary," said Jury, meditatively. "She called him Angel Clare."

"Who?"

"A character in *Tess of the D'Urbervilles*."

"The Hardy book. Yeah, she really liked Hardy."

"Hardy's Tess was in love with the solemn sod named Angel Clare."

"Where we are now is practically in Dorchester. This is Hardy country."

Jury looked around at the thick trees filtering the pale light. "Fate."

"Fate?"

"Thomas Hardy. Hardy seemed to think destiny was irrevocable." He looked at the folders Macalvie didn't seem to want to let go of. "You've got the file there about Hilda Palmer's death?"

"Got it all. It was the pool to your right where she was found. Or I should say, they were. Hilda Palmer and Tess Williamson. At the end closest to the house."

They walked toward the house, stopped at the bottom of the drained pool. It would have been fairly deep for a child, five or five and a half feet. What he saw was broken rock and concrete and fallen branches. "Was it like this then?"

"Pretty much, from what I read. No branches in it twenty years ago, but as much broken stone and concrete, I'd say, given the injuries."

"Who were these kids?"

Macalvie turned a page in the file. "Children present: two boys, four girls. Boys were Kenneth Strachey, twelve; John McAllister, ten. Girls were Madeline Brewster, aged twelve; Veronica D'Sousa, nine; Arabella Hastings, eight; and the victim Hilda Palmer, ten years old. The adults present were Tess Williamson and a friend of hers, Elaine Davies."

Macalvie went on. "Except for Tess Williamson, who was in the kitchen getting food ready. Here —" He produced a colored snapshot of Tess and a woman Jury took to be Elaine Davies, both standing by a white enameled kitchen table on which rested an elaborately decorated chocolate cake. Frills of chocolate and honey-colored icing were looped around it.

"It was one of their birthdays. McAllister's I think."

Jury kept gazing at the picture. "God, but she was beautiful, wasn't she?" Her hair was as honey-colored as the icing where the light hit it through the kitchen window.

"She was," said Macalvie.

"Mind if I keep this for a bit?"

Macalvie shrugged. "Okay by me, I made copies of everything. Anyway, to go on with logistics: Everyone else was in the front or near the front. All outside —"

"But isn't this the Davies woman? She's inside."

"That picture was taken much earlier. Elaine Davies wasn't one of the parents. She testified she came along just so there'd be another adult present to watch the kids. Except she didn't do much watching, just sat on a bench reading *Country Life*. She claimed she could see the kids from there, but how closely was she looking?"

"The children could have been anywhere when they were hiding."

"Well, not if they were following the rule Tess had laid down: they weren't to play around the ponds. And the kids themselves had made the rule that they couldn't go back in the gardens; otherwise the place was just too big and the one playing 'It' would never have found them all."

"Hide-and-seek's a short game. Counting to ten —"

"Veronica D'Sousa, who was 'It' —" Macalvie held up the file. "This is her statement if you want to read it."

Jury shook his head. "Not now. Go ahead."

"Veronica said they always counted up to a hundred, for nearly two minutes to give the kids plenty of time to hide. First one she found was Kenneth Strachey, who had stuffed himself between two of the sarsen stones you saw back there. Arabella Hastings was simply hiding behind a tree. It took Veronica a long time before she found Madeline Brewster, who'd climbed up on the front iron fence, hiding in plain sight, she said.

"The other boy, John McAllister, was found after they'd discovered Hilda Palmer. He'd been hiding in the laburnum grove, up a tree, a place strictly off-limits. He was sick from eating the seeds of the tree. After they pumped out his stomach, he said he'd gone there because 'Hilda dared me —' " Macalvie thumbed the page over. "When they started in playing the game, she'd said John wouldn't dare go into the grove. They took him to hospital, pumped out his stomach. DCI Bishoff asked him why he ate the seeds. 'Didn't you know they were poisonous?' "

" 'I just wanted to see how much. Veronica was taking too long to find me. I guess it was because of Hilda.' Starts to cry. 'Did you like Hilda especially?' Shakes his head hard. 'No. She was mean.' "

Macalvie stopped reading. "That was pretty much a standard response. All of the kids thought she was mean. Mean or hateful or awful. None of them had anything good to say about Hilda Palmer."

They had begun to climb the stone steps. "Then what was she doing at this party?"

"Good question. Tess Williamson said that she felt sorry for the girl and thought maybe she'd settle in and not be quite so 'ireful.' Her word." Macalvie smiled, mouthed it again.

Jury looked at him, smiling himself. "You got a kick out of her, didn't you?"

"Big kick. Who else would say 'ireful'?" They were standing on the stone patio, its front circled by pollarded shrubs. "Maybe you should talk to the kids. Not kids now, of course, but they must be around, here and there, in some guise, doing something."

They sounded like ghosts. "I will. Were they all London children?"

Macalvie nodded. "South Ken, Chelsea, Clapham, I think. North London, the little Hastings girl. The parents were friendly with the Williamsons to one degree or another. You want to talk to them, I mean the children who were there? There are no current addresses, but you can have the ones here. As I said, I made a copy." He handed Jury the file from which he'd been reading.

"Thanks, Macalvie." He looked at one of the photos, one showing the six children in the front garden of Laburnum. They smiled dutifully as the picture was snapped. He pointed to one image.

"Madeline Brewster," said Macalvie. "I think they called her Mundy. Funny nickname. She's the pretty one."

"Is this one Kenneth Strachey?" He pointed to the tall boy with brown hair and a confident look.

"Right. The other one's McAllister."

John McAllister was small and wiry-thin, wearing black-framed glasses, which he was adjusting as the picture was taken, as if they were about to slide down his nose. The glasses were awfully old-looking and heavy for a small boy. The sunlight caught at his hair and made runnels through it; it was a beautiful chestnut color with golden highlights. Jury could understand his appeal to someone like Tess Williamson; he appealed to Jury too.

The other girls, Veronica D'Sousa, Hilda Palmer, and Arabella Hastings were nothing like Madeline Brewster. Hilda Palmer had black hair, cut sharply around her neck, and a fringe that looked razor sharp like the rest of the hair. Her chin was up, her arms straight at her sides, and she looked as if she owned the world. Veronica D'Sousa and Arabella Hastings were the same size, despite their difference in age, with the same pale faces and brown hair. Even their pouts were similar. Madeline Brewster was a beautiful child with a heart-shaped face and long tawny hair.

"You want to see the house, don't you?"

Jury nodded.

Macalvie went upstairs and Jury into the living room, where he was reminded at once of Watermeadows, the old and now unoccupied mansion not far from Ardry End. Watermeadows had presented more elaborate trappings, greater vistas, more Italianate tiered gardens.

But there were the echoes, that sense of footsteps only just retreating when he walked into this living room, uncannily like the one in Watermeadows in its spartan display of furniture, or, rather, lack of it. A little bonheur du jour sat against one wall; on the right side of the door Jury had entered was an inlaid bureau. Then nothing else except for a large, comfortable-looking sofa square in the middle of the room, as if it had been stranded there. Yet there was a tall lamp at its back, a small belle epoque table beside it, a book on the table, and a scattering of silk cushions on the floor.

That taken together with the imaginary footsteps, it truly looked as if someone had just now been sitting there and had hastily departed.

The architecture of the room was quite formal: it was octagonal with three doors leading into what Jury discovered were a sitting room or study, a dining room, and the hall down which he had come. The walls were paneled and papered in pale yellow, wallpaper decorated in the manner of very delicately drawn Japanese prints.

He could hear footsteps overhead, Macalvie's, of course, but they still sent a momentary chill down his spine. He walked back to the wide hall that went from the front door to the bank of French doors at the rear of the house. Beyond those doors was the patio, wide and semicircular and beyond that the steps down to the ponds, the walks, and the gardens. He walked across the patio to stone stairs, and then down them. He turned to look back up and shook his head and went back into the house.

The front staircase which Macalvie had climbed was actually a double staircase, one running upward against each wall to a landing where a tall window gave out over the gardens. The stairs turned and went up another half-dozen steps to the first floor.

Jury called out to Macalvie, whose voice came muffled from one of the rooms. He

114

counted six bedrooms, three on each side. He turned from the stairs, going to the room at the right, which overlooked the same scene as did the landing below. He assumed this was the master bedroom, given its size and position and very large, four-poster bed with a canopy. Unused, except for the infrequent visits of Tom Williamson, fewer and fewer over the years until, he supposed, none at all over the last ten. It was strange to think that no one had slept here for a decade. There was a very large Aubusson rug stretching nearly wall to wall, a dressing table, a bureau, a few scattered chairs covered in watered-green silk.

Again, the wallpaper caught his attention. It could have been very old or looking as if it had the patina of age, an antique paper. The pattern was so eerily like the scene outlined in the window, one would suppose that the outside had come inside.

He saw by his watch that it was after three on this October afternoon. October can sit well or ill on an unoccupied and neglected country house. On this one, it sat well. The house belonged here.

Jury left this room and went to the one down the hall, the one he thought Macalvie's voice had issued from.

"He usually kept this locked," said

Macalvie, without preamble. "I had to get a key from the housekeeper."

"Why did he want it locked?" It was a comfortable, very lived-in study or library. There were shelves holding ships-in-bottles.

"Because of those." Macalvie nodded toward the ships. "It was the kids, he said. He didn't care who else came in here, but he was afraid the kids might get too interested in ships, mess with them, break something."

"He was a collector?"

Macalvie shrugged. "Looks like it. Understandably, he wasn't talking much about ships-in-bottles at the time."

Jury moved to the back of the room where a glass-fronted armoire held three models, one on each shelf. In the bottle on the top shelf was a three-mast wooden schooner; on the second shelf, a freighter with tiny strips of paper — twenty or so — replicating hatches and with dark smoke coming out of its stack. The blue water on which it sailed was probably some sort of putty. A third bottle looked like a whisky decanter. In it was a schooner and a lighthouse, colorfully detailed. "I used to wonder as a kid how anyone ever could get a boat into a bottle."

" 'Impossible bottles,' " said Macalvie.

"What?" Jury moved over to the desk

where he was standing, inspecting a wooden carving.

"Things like that, I mean getting objects, not only ships but stuff like playing cards, stuff that really couldn't go through the neck of a bottle — they were puzzles; they were called 'impossible bottles.' "

In several bottles, including the one on the fireplace mantel, were tightly rolled pieces of paper. Probably identifying the ship or telling its history or stating the provenance. The bottle on the mantel was larger, containing not one ship but several, a harbor scene. There were tiny buildings, tiny copper lights. Jury was once again at the top of Tower 42 listening to Tom Williamson talk about the lights along the Embankment. *"I like to imagine they're harbor lights."*

"You remember a song called 'Harbor Lights'?"

Macalvie came up to look at the ship on the mantel. "Hm. 'They only told me we were parting.' I remember that line."

Jury stared at him. "You're getting sentimental, Macalvie."

"Always have been. Well, if you mean to get back to Northants this afternoon, I guess we'd better leave."

"Yes," said Jury, with a curious reluctance

to do so.

He made one stop at a Welcome Break along the M5 to have coffee and another look at the file Macalvie had given him. He liked the picture of the children, standing in an awkward row, trying to blend for the photograph, and of course not blending at all. Children somehow refused to.

Madeline Brewster, Mundy. *"She's the pretty one."* She was indeed pretty, beautiful even, even with her hair pulled to the sides in bunches, and the sun causing that squint to her eyes. Girls wore dresses then, and hers had a pleated skirt, a top with slightly ruched sleeves, all quite smart for a little girl. Kenneth Strachey in his sleeveless sweater and checked shirt, held his chin up and his eyes at a slant, as if he were finding the picture-taking pretty silly. Kenneth felt superior to the little operation. Veronica didn't, though. She wasn't quite in the line, but a half-step backward. Hilda Palmer was quite the opposite. She'd stepped forward. With her square face and bobbed hair, Hilda was not pretty at all. Yet she posed like the belle of the ball, as if she knew all of the steps.

Tess Williamson. A photograph the police had collected, not the one Jury had seen, but one done in a studio, probably, a head-and-shoulders pose. Hair long and light, eyes possibly light blue. It was a black-and-white photo. Much of her beauty lay in her expression — good-natured and empathetic.

Jury put the papers back together, and drove on.

11

Thinking Melrose Plant would be there, as he often was before dinner, Jury stopped in at the Jack and Hammer on his way back from Exeter.

They all sat in the pub, heads together, scratching on bits of paper or napkins, drinks forgotten momentarily.

When Jury saw Melrose was not there, he turned to go, but then thought better of it.

"Superintendent!" said Trueblood. "You'll never guess!"

"No, I won't. We could play charades."

Vivian laughed. Trueblood wrinkled his brow, as if considering it, then said, "Murdered. Our lady in red."

He noticed the lady in red was theirs. "You got this report straight from Northants police did you?"

"No. Basically rumor," said Joanna Lewes.

"And the rumormonger was?"

"Melrose." Vivian said this. "He was just here. He's gone home."

"Thanks. See you later." Jury left.

He slammed the door shut, turned the key, and woke up the engine. He slowed the car when he found himself near Lavinia Vine's cottage. In her front garden was what looked like a laburnum tree, no longer golden, most of the foliage shed. He stopped the car and got out.

Lavinia was talking across her fence to Alice Broadstairs. Miss Vine and Miss Broadstairs, archrivals in the field of botany and champion blooms, were otherwise the best of friends.

"Miss Vine, Miss Broadstairs," said Jury, approaching the cottage. "How are you keeping? Or I should ask, how are the peonies, the pansies, the roses keeping?"

"Why, Mr. Jury," said Lavinia, as Alice Broadstairs thumped up an "Hello!" They were both in their eighties and gave the impression of two sweet, elderly women whose common interest was gardening. They were annual fixtures at the Chelsea Garden Show. But Jury knew gardening was a vocation, not an avocation for them. Their minds were rigorous, their dispositions determined.

Jury nodded toward the tree. "That's a laburnum, isn't it?"

"Yes, it is. We English do love our laburnum trees, don't we? The golden chain tree it's often called. Absolutely gorgeous in spring. Not so interesting now."

"Is it true everything about the tree is poisonous?"

"Leaf, seed, root, bark," Alice Broadstairs said. "Lavinia has to watch out that cats don't use it as a scratching post. When they wash their faces they ingest it. That cat of yours, Lavinia; I've caught him at it!"

"Desperado? He's proof against anything. But children, you know, sometimes take the pods for pea pods and open them and eat the seeds, or try to. They're very bitter, so most children stay away from them. But there have been accidents."

"How toxic is it? How much would it take to kill a person?"

"Um." Lavinia Vine thought a moment.

Alice Broadstairs jumped into the breech. "Fifteen to twenty seeds might do it. On the other hand, I heard of one death occurring when a gentleman used the leaves for tea."

"If the taste is so unpleasant, why would one keep on eating the seeds?"

Alice shrugged. "Depends on the child, I expect. Some children are just slow-witted —"

Lavinia stepped in. "The laburnum's dangers are overstated. It's quite true that all of its parts are toxic and a little child's eating the seeds, I've heard of one's becoming ill. Yet, I haven't heard of any deaths resulting from it. Are you sure about the tea, Alice? It sounds unlikely."

"Quite sure, Lavinia."

Jury nodded. "Thanks for the information." He said good-bye, gave them a brief salute, returned to the car.

As he drove on and across the Northampton Road to Ardry End, it occurred to him that the little McAllister boy hadn't looked at all slow-witted. Far from it.

12

Melrose Plant was standing at the top of the drive with his hands in his pockets when Jury's car pulled up.

"Sorry I'm late," said Jury, getting out of the car. "I stopped in at the Jack and Hammer. I thought you might be there. They told me you were passing around a rumor that the woman who fell from the tower didn't fall. She was pushed."

"It's not my rumor, it's Inspector Brierly's."

"Detective chief inspectors are not rumormongers. You were talking to DCI Brierly?"

"Of course not. I was talking to Owen Archer. The owner of the place. Brierly spent some time questioning him, apparently. But then he would do, wouldn't he, seeing that Archer is the owner of the property."

"Where was he?"

"London. Auction at Christie's. Archer's into antiques; has a shop in the U.S."

"I take it he also has an alibi?"

"A dozen people can vouch for his where-abouts."

"And he has no idea what she was doing there?" When Melrose shook his head, Jury went on, "Did he tell you anything else of interest?"

"Meaning, did the police tell him? Why don't you just ring DCI Brierly? He'd tell you."

"I hate being seen as an interfering CID guy."

"Hell, you *are* an interfering CID guy. You've already stuck your nose in, and Brierly didn't bite it off. Probably glad of the help."

Jury smiled. "No he isn't. It's his case."

Melrose shrugged. "He seemed perfectly happy to have you at the crime scene. He didn't mind your interviewing the victim's aunt."

"If she wasn't staying with her aunt, where was she staying? Did Brierly give up that information?"

They were by now sitting in the living room. Melrose looked up at the beautifully detailed cupids and garlands around the ceiling molding. "Brierly asked Owen Archer if he'd ever been to the Sun and Moon Hotel; Archer said yes, a long time ago. I inferred from this discussion the Sun and Moon must have been the place where the victim was staying. It's about two miles farther along the Northampton Road from here. Calls itself an hotel, but it looks rather scruffy. It's really just a pub with rooms and bar food."

"Belle Syms was there with somebody?"

"She was?" said Melrose.

"That was merely an assumption. She comes here from London, stays overnight, yet doesn't do the obvious thing, which is to doss down with Aunt Blanche. From this, I assume she was sharing her room at the hotel with somebody."

"Ask Brierly, for God's sake. You've got your mobile? Ring him."

"Battery's down."

Melrose got up, went to the fireplace, and pulled the tapestry bell pull that hung beside it.

Ruthven appeared a few seconds later.

"Could you bring Mr. Jury a phone, Ruthven? Thanks."

The battery was for once charged in Jury's mobile. He just loved the ritual of a landline being brought to him where he sat, and

126

in less than a minute, he had it. While he waited he went through several bits of paper in his pockets until he found DCI Brierly's number. "Thank you, Ruthven," he said when the butler placed a black telephone on the table before him and then plugged in the cord.

"Sir." Ruthven bowed himself out of the living room.

After informing Jury that DCI Brierly was right there, a PC at the Northampton station handed the phone over, and Brierly asked Jury what he could do for him.

Given that Jury had been permitted to question Blanche Vesta, he didn't think it would be taken as interference if he asked Brierly about Belle Syms's stay at the Sun and Moon. "Was she with someone?"

"Most definitely. They arrived separately, though. Mr. and Mrs. Guy Soames went down on the register. He later returned to London for something involving business. He of course would have been the reason she didn't stay with her aunt."

"But she stayed after the boyfriend left?"

"Oh, yes. He'd told her he'd be back in several hours, but that was apparently the last she saw of him."

"Who told you this?"

"The owner, who's also bartender. She

told him."

Jury paused, then said, "Listen, would you mind if I stopped by the Sun and Moon and had a chin-wag with this owner?"

"Help yourself. His name is Whorley. He chatted her up, so you might get some more out of him. He's pleasant enough, albeit a little nervous about police popping in and ransacking a room."

Jury smiled. "Funny how people usually are. Thanks very much."

"Wait a tic: forensic found prints — I mean shoe prints — leading up to the door of the tower made by a shoe that was definitely not that high-heeled sandal. The only other fresh ones."

"What sort of shoe?"

"Low-heeled, squarish, but a woman's shoe. The shoe would have fit the victim. The ground was hard, so we had to bring it up with ultraviolet."

"No man's shoe?"

"Old ones. Made by the owner and a few others. Possibly curious passers-by, tourists?"

Jury thanked him, and after assurances he would let Brierly know if he found out anything, Jury said good-bye and again was about to hang up when Brierly said, "Oh, yes. About the Staffie. No, Belle didn't have a dog with her. She didn't care much for animals, though her husband did."

"Right. Thanks." To Melrose Jury said, "I'm stopping in there on my way back to London."

"At the Sun and Moon? But you haven't said anything about your trip to Devon. How's Macalvie?"

"As always. It turns out that Macalvie knew Tess Williamson."

"Outside of the investigation, you mean? What are you going to tell me next?"

"I'm not going to tell you anything next. Get that look off your face. Macalvie met Tess Williamson purely by chance in a coffee house near the cathedral. They met there several times afterward —"

"Not by accident."

Jury ignored the implication, especially since he'd implied much the same thing. "He found her intelligent, nice, empathetic."

"So what does he think happened?"

"As in the death of Tess Williamson? Or the Palmer girl, Hilda?"

"Either. Both."

"I think he's uncertain about Hilda Palmer's death. The coroner's ruling at the inquest was an open verdict. Macalvie certainly didn't think there was enough evidence to indict Tess Williamson. Then the case was dismissed.

"As to her own death, Macalvie didn't go along with the 'accident' theory. Tess Williamson did have vertigo, which might argue the 'accidental' nature of it, but such a fall wouldn't take the person all the way to the bottom of the steps. Supposedly, her head hit a hunk of stone at the base of the statue at the bottom of the marble stair. To all appearances. Yet, I'm still wondering, and I know her husband is, if someone might have caused that head injury."

"But if it was a person who'd given her a brutal head injury, there'd have been a lot of blood thrown about on the way down the stair, surely."

"You'd think so."

"I'd think so? For God's sakes, is that the way your forensic experts put things?" Melrose changed his voice: " ' 'ey Alf, 'ave a look at this tennis racket. See 'ere where the cat gut's been ripped out. The victim was lying on the court garroted with a stringlike substance, right? . . . Could this be it, then?' Alf shrugs. 'Well, you'd think so.' "

Jury laughed. "The forensic team was a little hostile toward this newcomer proposing a theory that didn't match their findings."

"Macalvie a newcomer? Hard for me to believe he was ever that. I doubt he was a newcomer the day he was born."

Just then the dog Joey raced in.

"Joey!" Jury exclaimed and gave the dog a good rubbing.

"I wish you'd stop calling Aggro 'Joey.' It's grown into an obsession with you."

Jury tugged at Joey's collar. "The original owner apparently shared the obsession." He pointed to the small nameplate. Jury had suggested Joey because he liked Joelly's name. She was the person he'd dealt with at True Friends Animal Shelter. "You want to talk about obsession? The way you lot sit around in the Jack and Hammer naming animals, insisting every name begin with *Ag*— Aggrieved, Aghast, Aggro — that, old chap, is obsession!"

13

Sun and Moon Hotel
Wednesday, 9:00 P.M.

It was a mock-Tudor wayside inn, white-washed and black-beamed, the beams rough hewn. The Sun and Moon Hotel probably didn't live up to either part of its name.

Jury pulled in under a sign that depicted a sun shining on one side, and a moon floating on the other, neither realistically presented, just as he imagined the word *Hotel* was more fantasy than reality. Beneath the gold and the silver was carved A. WHORLEY, PROP.

He got out of the car and crossed the gravel to the front door, which sported a small carved sign SUN AND MOON HOTEL. Jury went through to find the area around RECEPTION empty. A door on his left was signed SALOON BAR. He heard voices and the clinking noises of glasses and bottles. He pushed in through the door and found two tables occupied, one by a single man, the other by three women.

Jury went up to the barman, said, "Mr. Whorley?"

"That's me, right. What can I do for you?"

Whorley was a small, wiry man with intelligent brown eyes.

"I'm Superintendent Richard Jury, New Scotland Yard." Jury produced his warrant card, noting that Whorley was neither suspicious nor alarmed.

"Bloody hell," said Whorley, but without emphasis. "This bad business is bringing in the top guns, ain't it?"

Jury smiled. "Me, I'm just helping out Northants police. What can you tell me about this Mr. and Mrs. Soames?"

"No more'n I told them." Whorley paused to extract a pint glass from a rack and place it beneath the Guinness tap. "Care for one?"

"No, thanks, driving to London."

Whorley filled his own pint.

"The Soameses. They checked in on the Monday, correct?"

Nodding, Whorley placed his pint before him. "She comes in by herself, four-ish. Goes out again, comes back in an hour, maybe hour and a half, and him, he gets here a bit later. Round about half-six, it was. I wondered what they had in mind to do 'round here, dressed to the nines, they were. 'Specially her. Well, you saw what she was wearing: that red silk and sequins dress with glitter all round the neck." Whorley whistled. "Dishy. He had on a blazer, brass buttons. Goin' out on the town, he says; I says, 'What town' and he laughs fit to kill."

"Where had they come from?"

"London. 'Guy' was the first name. Guy Soames. Mr. and Mrs. Anyway, they go back up to their room; an hour later he comes down, coat on, says he's been called back to London and would I see to helping his wife find a nice restaurant for a meal, as he doesn't know when he can get back." Then off he goes in his little car, one of them Italian things."

"Leaving her stranded?"

Whorley merely shrugged. "She come in her own car. Old Morris, I think. Still there till the coppers shanghai'd it."

Jury nodded. "Go on."

"Awhile after he leaves, she comes down and asks for a gin and sits here at the bar and drinks it. In a right temper, she was."

"And did she tell you what took him back to London?"

"Business, she says. Furious, you could tell. No wonder. So I tells her about a restaurant in Sidbury supposed to be decent. She said she'd go there and left."

"Did you see her again, after she left for dinner?"

"When she came back and had to drag me to the door because she'd forgot her key, yeah. That was around ten, ten-thirty, I think."

"Thanks, Mr. Whorley. Do you think I could see her room?"

"Yeah, sure. So'd the others." He called out to Jimmy. "Jimmy can take you up."

Jimmy came from somewhere in the back, a tall lad, perhaps fourteen or fifteen, with the usual fifteen-year-old surliness. Whorley told him to show Jury to the room.

The Sun and Moon was one of those places Americans had such a liking for, trading threadbare and dry rot for a shot of antiquity they couldn't get at home. Which, Jury thought, was sweet of them. He liked Americans. They were less ironic, less cynical than a lot of Brits.

Jimmy led Jury up a staircase that was in need of propping up. Through the thin runner he could almost feel the wood wanting to give up. He followed Jimmy along a hall only marginally wider than the staircase, up three more crooked steps to a room on the right, whose ceiling sloped on the far side, above the little gabled windows. The ceiling was whitewashed and beamed, the walls papered with a rosebud and vine design on a malt-covered background. The wallpaper looked as old as the beams. On the left a door led to a tiny bathroom where a few toiletries had been arranged on a shelf above the sink. A hand towel had been used and replaced on the rack. He looked at the bathtub, which had one of those handheld shower attachments that he personally couldn't stand. He got down on one knee and ran his hand along the inside, looked at the drain.

The bed was still made up and was rumpled a bit, though unslept in. "The maid hasn't been in here?"

"No. Coppers said not to mess nuffin' about."

Jury opened the door of an old wardrobe that was serving as a clothes cupboard and looked at the contents. Nothing but an extra blanket, ironing board.

He moved to the dresser, opened a drawer. Empty. Another and another, both empty. Finally, there was one with a garment. Panties, forgotten. A tiny Marks & Spencer tag dangled from a bit of thread.

"Into the lady's intimates. Wait'll I tell the commiss'ner." Jimmy stuck thumb and little finger over his ear to mimic a phone.

Jury handed the silky underwear to him. "Go ahead, have a look."

Jimmy did. He saw the sales tag. "Yeah, new." He squirreled his brows together.

"What does that suggest, Jimmy, detective manqué?"

"You callin' me a monkey?"

"Don't be daft."

"Well, it tells me nuffin'."

"It ought to tell you sumffin' if you think about it." He put the underwear back in the drawer, closed it, and handed Jimmy one of his cards. "Call me if you remember anything."

Jimmy was gazing at the card. "Scotland Yard."

"Tell me, did you talk to her at all?"

"Only when she asks for some crisps. Sits there on her own until Sonny — that's Mr. Whorley — comes back. I don't think she's used to sitting around in pubs on her own, I mean, the way she looked. Some rags she was wearin'!"

"Hm. Well, sorry old chap, but I've got to get back to London." Jury was about to leave when he remembered Stanley. "What about a dog? Did they have one?"

"What dog?"

14

Knightsbridge
Thursday, 11:00 A.M.

He knew the kind of place Tom Williamson would live in: not ostentatious, but rich in detail. Velvet, silk, down, somewhere a sofa soft enough for one's whole self to sink into. Gauzy curtains for added light, or Roman shades for the same purpose. Depending on which way the sun slanted, and when.

Tom Williamson answered the door with a mug in his hand on which were worn-down letters spelling, or only half-spelling: BURN-HAM, the other word which might have been OVERY was hard to see. He had spoken of meeting Tess on the Norfolk coast, Jury recalled. Burnham. The mug was a seaside souvenir that amused him, as it seemed out of place in these refined surroundings. Maybe everybody had a cupboardful of seaside stuff.

Tom was wearing slacks and a gray cardigan and an expression that was a little less bereft than when Jury had last seen him.

"Superintendent! Come on in." He flung the door wider and Jury stepped into a long, narrow living room that looked rather remarkably as he'd imagined it, as if he'd been here before. Not déjà vu, but something similar.

"Come on through to the kitchen. I'm drinking tea. I'm out of whiskey, though I expect it's a little early for that." He turned, held up his mug, an invitation.

"Tea's fine." Jury was getting out of his coat.

"Just toss the coat anywhere."

Jury put his coat over the back of a counter stool. The counter was white granite; the rest of the kitchen also white — tiles, paint, cupboards. Glossy but chilly. Tom Williamson was neither, and nor, Jury imagined, had his wife, Tess, been.

Tom got down a thick white mug with another seaside inscription, this one in sunset orange: A PRESENT FROM EASTBOURNE. "I like the mugs," said Jury. "They don't match."

"Neither do the places," said Tom, over his shoulder, as he added milk to Jury's tea. "I forgot to ask. You do take milk in it? Sugar?"

"Both."

Tom added a rounded teaspoonful of sugar, stirred, and set the mug on the counter. "You know what I've always got a kick out of? The public places, train stations, caffs, museums — that already have the tea made up with milk and sugar. Yet, it always seems to be the right amount. Are we all that much alike?"

"Probably."

Tom laughed. "Let's go back to the living room."

As they walked back, they passed a long polished table toward the rear of the room. It seemed to be a catchall, as it was layered with gloves, scarves, a hat, the morning's post, magazines. At its center, Jury saw one of the ships-in-bottles he'd seen at Laburnum. Jury stopped. "Is this one of yours? I saw these ships at Laburnum." Jury picked up the bottle from the table, looked at it carefully. "Isn't this the *Victory*?"

Tom smiled. "Nelson's ship, yes."

"The detail is marvelous."

The sofa that Jury sank into was down, as were the companion armchairs opposite it, one of which Tom Williamson took. The walls were covered in a dark green fabric, damask, perhaps; the graceful banister of the staircase against the right-hand wall was mahogany. The fireplace mantel was a gray granite that reminded Jury of the stone steps of that house. The photograph of Tess Williamson that sat upon it reminded him even more.

Tom saw the direction of Jury's look and said, "That's the original of the photo I showed you." He sipped his tea and settled the mug, careless of its leaving a mark on the fabric, on the arm of his chair. "You went to the house?"

"I did. Tell me about Tess and that house, if you don't mind."

Tom smiled. "No, I don't mind at all. What would you like to know?"

"Anything."

Tom slid down in his chair a bit, leaned back, as if he were settling into a more comfortable time and place. "She really loved Laburnum. I think part of it was because it was near Dorchester, where she was born. Tess liked that Hardy country, even though she lived in London most of her life. Unfortunately, Laburnum is a little too far from London to make it viable for a weekend place, which was the only time I could get away."

"She didn't like being there on her own?"

"It wasn't that; she never minded being on her own. But she seemed to feel that it wasn't fair to leave me on my own. Even though I told her again and again it was all right." He looked at Jury. "She was a very considerate woman, Superintendent."

Jury nodded. "Commander Macalvie certainly thought so."

Tom looked surprised. "Commander Macalvie?"

"He'd met her in Exeter, purely by chance."

Tom was thoughtful for a moment. Then he snapped his fingers and said, "Of course. She told me she'd met up with a Devon policeman. That's so strange that it turned out to be him."

"She really impressed him. And believe me, he's not easily impressed."

"Tess was impressive." Tom looked at the photograph. "At the house, how did the whole thing strike you?"

"I must say, pretty much as it struck you — ambiguously. The point you made about her position, Macalvie thinks it wouldn't have happened that way. The coroner's report, the reconstruction of the fall —"

Tom nodded. "It wasn't much of an idea, I expect. It only occurred to me just recently, looking at that photograph."

"On the contrary, it's quite a good idea." Jury thought for a moment. "What did she do when she was there on her own? Was she a gardener?"

Tom laughed. "God, no. Tess always said she was too damned lazy for that. No. The old fellow, Sturgiss, who more or less came with the place, he did what was absolutely necessary, though I'm not sure what that was. His wife came in to do a bit of cleaning now and again, still does. I don't want the place to go completely to seed, you know. But Tess seemed to like everything about the house just the way it was." Tom picked up his mug, set it down again. "She used to wander about that desolate garden, waiting — she said" — here Tom smiled — "for something frightful to happen." Tom's smile was abrupt, as if he'd suddenly remembered that something had.

"What did she mean?"

"Tess was a kind of fatalist." He smiled slightly.

"A fatalist?"

"With a capital *F.*" Tom drew a stroke in air and crossed it twice. "Always had been. I told you she loved Hardy. *Tess of the D'Urbervilles, Jude the Obscure.* Dorchester was Hardy's home. She loved all of that fatalistic stuff."

He sounded, Jury thought, almost resentful of Tess's fatalism, as if it had steered her toward that unlucky house. "And you don't?"

"No. Chance, that's what I believe in, if one can call it a belief."

Jury frowned. "But isn't that what Thomas Hardy believed? Wasn't it chance that ruined his characters' lives?"

Tom frowned, looked into his mug. "Was it? Do you suppose they're two sides of the same coin?"

"Shouldn't they be opposites?"

"Perhaps. But I think that whole fatalistic belief might have helped Tess through that damnable inquisition. She would have said it was meant to happen. No escape, no accident — in the larger sense, I mean."

"And in the smaller, you believe it was."

"Hilda Palmer's death? An accident? All I know is, Tess didn't hurt the girl."

Jury nodded.

Tom went on. "Tess was fanciful. That was one of the reasons she got on so well with children. She could make things up; she could invent games; she could concoct scenarios. They loved it."

"Tell me about the children. What you remember."

Tom ran his thumb over the faded gilt lettering of his mug. "Not much, really. It's a bit of a blur."

144

Jury shook his head. "Don't do that. Don't dismiss it." When Tom Williamson remained silent, Jury said, "These were kids your wife entertained often. Even if your contact was limited to sightings in the garden or voices in another room, still, Tess talked about them. Six children, Hilda Palmer being one. You described her quite well. What about the boy who got sick?"

"Yes, yes, of course. John McAllister, the littlest boy. Nearly poisoned himself eating seeds from the laburnum tree he'd climbed. He was Tess's favorite. Possibly because he'd lost his parents in some kind of accident. Car accident, a collision on the M1 or M2."

"What about Madeline Brewster?"

Tom leaned his head against the back of his chair, frowned up at the ceiling. "I think she was the pretty little girl with the odd nickname. Mandy . . . ?"

"Mundy."

"You seem to know more than I do." He said this ruefully.

"Only what was in the police report." He thought of the photo of the children and Madeline Brewster: hair in bunches, heart-shaped faced, a rather smart little pleated dress. "Commander Macalvie let me see them. But these are facts. What I'm interested in is impressions."

Tom nodded. "Madeline Brewster, as I said, was very pretty. The other girls were jealous of her, at least that's what Tess said." He was silent for a moment. "Especially the girl with the intimidating family name . . . Victoria? No, Veronica, her name was . . ."

"D'Sousa."

Again, Tom nodded. "Funny how this comes back in bits and pieces. The D'Sousas were severely 'arty.' I wonder if the name was real."

"The other boy, Kenneth Strachey, what about him?"

Tom seemed to be trying to drain tea from his empty mug, then said, "Strachey." He sat thinking, then shook his head. "Oh, yes. Kenneth's father claimed he was descended from Lytton Strachey. There was a drinks party and I remember being cornered by this neo-Bloomsbury set. There was much talk — but I imagine little reading — of Virginia Woolf and Clive Bell and Forster. He was fascinated by Dora Carrington — you know, the artist? She was mad about Lytton Strachey. She was living with him and a friend of his and she married the friend just to stay together with Strachey. That's the most spectacular ménage à trois I've ever heard of." He laughed.

146

"These kids, were they close? I mean were they what you'd call a gang?"

"I don't think so. They seemed to be too different —" Tom frowned, thinking back. "But perhaps that was just Hilda Palmer who was different. The others —"

"Why was she included in this trip, do you think?"

Tom shrugged. "Tess's kindness, I expect."

"I interrupted you. You were saying 'the others' — ?"

Tom smiled. "I do seem to recall Tess remarking 'thick as thieves.' "

"That's pretty much a gang, then, isn't it? Now, this friend of your wife's, Elaine Davies. She went along to help Tess keep an eye on the children. But according to the police report, she seemed to have spent most of the time reading *Country Life*."

Tom laughed briefly. "Elaine Davies is so unlike Tess, I can't think what Tess saw in her. Probably Elaine invited herself along. She's a bit of a social climber, a woman who spends a lot of time at Toni and Guy's getting her hair done."

"Then she lives in London? I'd like to talk to her."

"I haven't seen her in some time, but if she's in the same house, she's not far. Belgravia." Tom rose and went to a small teak

147

table, picked up an address book, wrote down the address, and handed it to Jury.

"Thanks. Now I'm afraid I must go."

"This has been extremely kind of you, to go all the way to Devon and have a look round."

Jury got up. "I've an idea I'll probably be going back."

At that, Tom smiled brilliantly. He rose too. "I can't tell you how much I appreciate it. You see, not being sure —"

"I know exactly what you mean." Tom Williamson retrieved Jury's coat from the chair in the kitchen. As he was shrugging into it, Jury said, "I'll let you know how this goes on."

Tom still held to the seaside mug he'd had when he'd come to the door. Now they were at the door again.

Jury nodded toward the mug. "Do you like Burnham, then? It looks as if that mug has got some use."

"Oh. I told you I met Tess on the Norfolk coast. That's where I met her."

"You were both on holiday?"

Tom laughed. "Tess was. But me, far from it. I lived there for years. I worked there; I mean, I had a shop. Model ships."

Jury was surprised. He wouldn't have thought of Tom Williamson as a seaside

148

merchant. "You sold them?"

"I made them."

Jury's surprise was so great that his mouth fell open. He looked over Tom's shoulder toward the table and the ship-in-a-bottle. "You mean you made all of those ships that I saw at Laburnum? Macalvie and I just assumed you'd collected them. And that's one of yours? You made that?" Jury walked past him, back into the room to the long table. He bent and looked again at the *Victory.*

"You like ships, do you?"

"I'm completely ignorant of them. Except for this one. I thought Nelson was something."

"He was indeed. There's a lot of Nelson history in Burnham. Or 'the Burnhams' as they say. There are several villages. Anyway, I made hundreds of ships. This was in the years before GC and CS. Tess just came into the shop one day and looked all around and took a long time doing it. That one she looked at for so long I wondered if she had some family connection to Nelson. It was rather expensive, but she bought it. And she seemed absolutely dazzled by the fact I'd made it. She asked me a lot of questions about the craft and I finally invited her to dinner, where she asked me a lot more.

"I think I would give anything to go back

to the old days. To be sitting with Tess over fish and chips talking about these ships." He had picked up and now replaced the bottle. "Or any ships. Or anything at all."

It sounded as sad as anything Jury had ever heard.

"Why didn't you go back to Norfolk?"

"Because she wasn't there."

They were at the door again. "But this house . . . she isn't here, either."

"No. But this is London. London tends to drown out things." He stood there for a moment, hands in pockets, reflecting. "Do you know what she told me? She told me I was the one who made her dreams come true. It's a line from another song, 'I Remember You.' Tess loved old songs." He looked away. "I can't imagine I made her dreams come true." Tom held to the mug and looked at the carpet.

"I can. Good-bye, Tom."

15

"I located two of them," said Detective Sergeant Alfred Wiggins, who shared Jury's office at New Scotland Yard. "Kenneth Strachey and Madeline Brewster. I'm working on the other three. Where are you now?"

"Knightsbridge." Standing in front of a patisserie.

"You're in luck. Madeline Brewster lives in Clapham, but works in Knightsbridge. Harrods."

"I'm looking at it." Jury was. He'd walked up to the Brompton Road to hail a cab. Harrods, with its usual swarm of people moving in and out, back and forth, crossing and recrossing before the building that stood like a mountainous honeycomb among bees, was directly across from him. "What department does she work in? Harrods is a city unto itself."

"In the Armani Col-ez-i-on." Wiggins gave Armani his best. Jury thought he heard an air kiss in there somewhere. "Speaking of fashion, what about the Givenchy? Should I visit the salon on Upper Sloane Street?"

"I imagine Brierly is trying to track that down. But go ahead, it wouldn't hurt. What about Kenneth Strachey?"

"Lives in Bloomsbury —"

With a name like that, wouldn't he just? Jury smiled.

"— appears to dabble about in writing. Mostly for small, terribly intelligent periodicals. Lives with another dabbler, who wasn't there. That one's in the theater, maybe an — uh — actor, not currently working."

"You say 'resting between roles,' Wiggins." Anyone not gainfully employed and following an artistic bent was, in Wiggins's eyes, a dabbler. "Is the uh-actor male or female?"

"Male. They're probably, you know, matey."

Add to dabbling, men living together, and you get gay.

"Strachey's good-looking, but in a kind of arty, pretty, girl-y way. There was an author photo with one of the pieces he wrote; I looked up a couple of the periodicals."

"Not necessarily gay, Wiggins. See if he's at home."

"Right. Shall I tell him you're coming?"

"No. Tell him *you're* coming."

"Me? What is this case? Not one of yours. And I was about to have my elevenses."

Jury was regarding a tray full of doughnuts, some powdered, some glazed, some leaking a custardy sauce. He looked at his watch: 11:56. "It's noon. Too late for elevenses and, anyway, I'll take you to lunch at Ruiya's."

This Soho eatery always had a half-block queue and Wiggins loved it for the crispy fish and because he got to bypass the queue.

Wiggins perked up immediately. "Right, boss."

Boss. "Say one-thirty at Ruiya's. That gives us both an hour and a half. If Kenneth Strachey takes up more time than that, ring me on my mobile. Same for me. Otherwise, one-thirty. Oh, and get hold of Armani and see if Madeline's there today and ring me back."

"Will do. 'Bye."

"And what about Andrew Cleary? Did you find him?"

"You mean the photographer chap?"

"The very same, Wiggins. He lives in Paris now."

After Wiggins assured him he'd ring Cleary, Jury pocketed his mobile and stood looking at the doughnut tray, deciding. He glanced over his shoulder at Harrods and its endless flow of people. Having tanked Wiggins's elevenses, he really shouldn't go into the patisserie.

He went in.

Jury was drinking excellent coffee and eating a custard doughnut, remembering that Oswald Maples lived not ten minutes away in Chelsea. Sir Oswald had known Tom Williamson, but he had not been at Laburnum, and Jury wanted to talk to those who had first.

When Wiggins called, Jury was just polishing off a sugar-glazed doughnut, drinking a second cup of coffee.

"Sorry for the delay, but getting round Harrods on the phone is almost worse than doing it in person. Takes effing forever. She's there now. And I got Andrew Cleary too. He's going to be in London this weekend and can see you whenever you like."

"Okay, good. Tell him Sunday. Well, getting that information ate up" — he ran his finger over a dribble of sugar — "enough of your time that we better change Ruiya to two o'clock."

"Right. Two o'clock at Ruiya. And Madeline Brewster, she's modeling Armani. That might be worth a look."

16

It definitely was worth a look.

After the initial squash and holler of Harrods, Jury found the designer collections: Armani, Saint Laurent, Givenchy, Sonia Rykiel, and others together and yet apart. Jury went to Armani.

He saw her almost immediately. She still looked, in some odd and lovely way, like the little girl at that fatal party. Her hair was no longer in bunches, but thick and long, and looking unmanageably curly, a look he supposed was very well managed. She wore a silk cinnamon-colored dress with long sleeves, slightly ruffled at the wrists. She turned, walked, turned, hand-on-hip turned again. Behind her were a half-dozen glass doors, reflecting a half-dozen girls in cinnamon dresses.

A tall woman in black, no doubt Armani

black, who appeared to be overseeing all of this, Jury took to be the manager. He alarmed her by pulling out his ID. Her heavily brown-shadowed eyelids flew up.

"Police?" She was not so far gone she forgot to whisper.

Jury smiled and whispered back. "Nothing to do with Armani. And you are — ?"

That her own name would get into this possibly sordid affair gave her pause. But she answered, "Artimis. Joyce Artimis. I'm in charge of the collection."

"Fine, Miss Artimis. That dress is gorgeous. I'd simply like to speak to the young lady modeling it. I believe her name is Madeline Brewster?"

"Mundy? What's she done?"

Clearly, police wouldn't be standing here if something hadn't been "done." And if Armani hadn't done it, Mundy must have.

"Nothing at all. I need to ask her a few questions, that's all."

Mundy Brewster had finished her turn in the cocktail dress and gone through one of the mirrored doors. Miss Artimis followed and went through it too.

Jury entertained himself while he waited by walking from the Artimis-Armani gang to a less-heady selection a few steps away. Clothes here were cheaper, but showier. He

156

inspected a mannequin dressed in a hot pink knitted skirt topped by a fiery orange cap-sleeved T-shirt down the front of which spilled a thin strip of glittering zircon. This ensemble, by an outfit called Juicy Couture (what a wonderful name!), was just biding its time until it found its way to Carole-anne Palutski. He was searching around for a price tag when a voice at his elbow said, "That's all the rage, you know."

He looked around at Mundy Brewster. "Do the rich actually have rages when it comes to this? I thought it was only middle-class-me."

Mundy laughed. The sound sparked the air far more than the faux-diamonds on the shirt. "Why do I have a hard time seeing you front and center at a Juicy Couture show?"

"Can't imagine. You should hear me on the subject of shoes. Such as your Christian Louboutin." He looked down.

She was genuinely surprised. "Wow!"

"Red soles."

She wowed again.

"Miss Brewster, I just wanted to talk to you about the past. Could we go somewhere and sit down?"

"Certainly. But could we do the sit-down outside of Harrods?"

"I can think of nothing I'd rather do."

"Good. There's a Pret just down the Brompton Road I go to a lot. Just let me take off this thousand-quid rag and I'll be with you in five."

He watched her walk away. The cinnamon silk looked like a thousand quid, not a rag.

They sat in the Pret A Manger's slick and silvery environs, she having a heavily garnished cheese sandwich and a glass of wine; he having coffee.

He spoke about Laburnum and the party.

"Of course, I remember." She set down a piece of the sandwich, which she'd cut into neat quarters, and picked up her wine. "How could a person forget something like that?"

"Fairly easily. Because you were little children then, or because it was a traumatic event you might have suppressed."

Mundy picked up the quarter of sandwich and bit into it. In a moment she asked, "Did anyone tell you about Hilda Palmer?"

Jury nodded. "That she was good at finding out things and using the information. Blackmail."

Mundy nodded and drank some more wine. "Remember that old movie called *The Children's Hour*? Shirley MacLaine. One of the students in the school, boarding school, I think starts a rumor about the two women who run it, that they're lovers. It destroys the school; one of the teachers, the Shirley MacLaine character, commits suicide."

"Was that the sort of rumor Hilda started?"

Mundy half-shrugged. "I don't know. But that's the sort of girl Hilda was. I think she was the most vicious person I've ever known. On the surface, she was sweet. But underneath, she was really cruel. She'd pretend to save things — you know, chipmunks or birds. It would be some creature she'd hurt in the first place and then set about fixing it. Imagine the ruination that lay in her wake if she'd ever gotten to our age now."

"And do you think she knew something, or was some kind of a threat to Tess Williamson?"

Mundy regarded Jury with her deep brown eyes. "Hilda was a threat to everyone."

He hadn't expected that. "Including you?"

She nodded. "Hilda saw me take something once. It was a school outing to Hampton Court. All of these stately homes have souvenir shops. I picked up a ring, just junk, I expect. I put it in my shirt pocket." Here she touched her heart, where the pocket

159

must have been then and blushed and looked down at her plate.

The child never dies in us, he thought. "We all did stuff like that, Mundy. I know I did."

She looked up in surprise at him, a copper. "You did?"

"In Brighton, when we visited the Prince Regent's palace. I slipped a pen into my pocket." He patted his jacket, where there was no pocket, and nor had there been one then.

She smiled. "A bent copper."

He smiled too. "Right."

"What Hilda did was wait until we were on our bus again, when there'd be no chance of my putting the thing back. 'What are you going to do?' I asked. I was really scared.

" 'Nothing, at least not now.' That was even worse."

"To think the axe might fall at any time."

Mundy said, "I wasn't sorry she was dead. I could have shoved her myself into that pool. Only I didn't." Her smile was swift and bright.

He noticed a dimple in only one cheek. "And do you think Tess Williamson did?"

Mundy shook her head. "No, she couldn't have done. She loved kids. She didn't have any of her own, which I bet was hard on her. I can't imagine her shoving one into a concrete pool."

"Yet she was found alone with the dead girl."

"She was in that drained pool trying to help."

"Very possibly. What about the other kids who were there?" Jury looked at his notes. "Kenneth Strachey, John McAllister . . ."

"Ken Strachey. He was good at sorting things: he could work out anything, an argument or the right answers on a maths quiz — Ken was a fixer."

Beneath the cinnamon sleeves she'd modeled, the girl was smart.

"Do you keep in touch with any of them after all this time has passed?"

She shook her head. "Only with Johnny McAllister."

The way she said his name told a lot. "According to Tom Williamson, his wife was very fond of John McAllister."

"She was. Johnny was . . . a little sad, really. He was small and fragile and picked on by other kids. But he was so sweet. And also very smart; he read so much, carried books around in a backpack all the time. That old backpack; it had been patched up so often I wonder how it didn't fall apart.

161

Johnny was smarter than Kenny, although it wasn't obvious. Did you know he was an orphan? Or, rather, his parents were both dead and he was living with guardians." Mundy frowned. "I visited them once or twice and thought they were cold and distant. I always got the feeling Johnny got chilly when they were around, as if someone had blown snow into the room. It was a good thing he had Mrs. Williamson. She gave him confidence. Even hope."

Jury frowned. "You say Johnny was smart. Did you wonder why he chanced eating those poisonous laburnum seeds?"

She smiled. "To see what would happen, maybe? He was like that, taking chances. He loved formulas — or I guess it's 'formulae,' right? Can you imagine a ten-year-old fascinated by molecules and maps of numbers?" Mundy went on. "It didn't surprise me when he turned out to be a brilliant doctor. He knew so much; he was a wizard in science and biology. He's usually off in Kenya and Botswana, taking care of the natives, trying to cure diseases. He's brilliant. He's in scientific research. He's an M.D. He was with something like Médecins sans Frontières for several years. Which is just like him."

She looked sad as she went on: "When

Mrs. Williamson had that accident, I think Johnny cried for days. I went to see him every day because I knew he had no one to lean on. When Hilda Palmer died, because of the death and the awful publicity, his guardians wouldn't let him see Tess, and it was crushing." She looked up at Jury. "Then she died. But we went to the funeral, despite parents. Well, Mum was okay with that. But the others snuck off and went to it and we kept well back so no one would see us. I nearly had to hold Johnny up all the way through."

"That must have been painful. I'm sorry. But he recovered, didn't he? From what you've said, his life seems to have taken a very good turn." He watched her.

She shook her head. "He never recovered. But, yes, his life took a good turn." She rested her chin on her folded fingers. "Johnny has a way of — I don't know — disappearing? He's there, then he isn't. I just don't understand why he lives in East London, for God's sake. He has money. Mrs. Williamson left him quite a lot."

He heard something in her voice that was more than casual. "Did she? What about the rest of you? Did she leave anything to you?"

"Oh, no. She probably figured the rest of

us were well taken care of. But John was her pet. She couldn't stand thinking he'd be at the mercy of others. She was right."

"What about the other girls, Veronica and Arabella?"

"Veronica D'Sousa. Arabella Hastings. Veronica's mum had her taking every kind of lesson: ballet, acting, singing, dancing —"

"I'm surprised she had time for hide-and-seek."

"It was kind of pathetic, really, Veronica being not very talented. Probably she grew up to be gorgeous and has just nabbed the lead in the latest revival of *Anything Goes*."

Jury laughed. "And Arabella? From what I've seen in the file, she wasn't exactly a knockout."

"No, she wasn't. She was absolutely crazy about Kenneth. But why shouldn't she be? Kenny was the very essence of charm. Really, it was like perfume, an expensive and exquisite scent. If he could bottle it, Harrods would be happy to sell it, I'm sure. And he was incredibly manipulative. Still is, I expect."

This summation of Kenneth Strachey made Jury smile as he looked at Mundy's glass. Her fingers were circling it as if it were the glass that kept her afloat. "Would you

164

like more wine?"

She looked down. "I'd like a cappuccino, actually."

Jury rose and went to the coffee urns and asked for a black coffee and a cappuccino. He looked at her, at her back, her head turned slightly so that he saw her perfect profile reflected in the window glass. He thought of what she'd said about John McAllister and shivered, as if a door had suddenly opened on rain.

That was because Jury had been there, himself, an orphan, out of luck with relations for a few years, and spent those years in a home. It had been three years of nothing to look forward to, every day like every other: powdered eggs for breakfast, fish paste in a sandwich for lunch (no Pret A Manger on every corner in those old days). He was not sure, actually, how he'd landed there. There was a gap in his memory between his mother's death and the orphanage. He recalled vaguely a woman from the Social —

"Sir?"

He looked away from the window to the lad who worked the coffee machine. "Yes? Oh, thanks." He paid and took the creamy cup back to Mundy Brewster and the black coffee for himself.

165

Sitting down, Jury said, "Tell me, what did you think of Tess Williamson? Other than that she was very fond of children?"

Mundy spooned up foam from her cup. "I know that she'd been born into money, always had it. Her family. They were wealthy in the way very old money can be distinguished from new." Mundy smiled. "Not that I've ever had either. I expect she was envied. I mean, never having to scrimp or go out and get a job. Somehow I think it told against her, I mean, it wasn't a point in her favor with some people."

"And envious people enjoy seeing the Williamsons of this world brought to heel?"

She nodded. "Exactly. I heard this from my own mum, who said, 'She'll come to no good, that girl, you wait and see. Too beautiful, too rich.' "

"It sounds like a Victorian novel. And it sounds more like a curse than a comment."

"Well, Mum didn't really dislike her, although I'm sure she envied her. Mum just thought such a charmed life as Mrs. Williamson's would find something beastly plunked down in the middle of it. That came from Mum having a pretty hard life herself. I'm adopted too, you know, but Mum was nothing like Johnny's guardian. She had to work two jobs to keep me in that school where the well-off kids went. It was because she wanted me to get a good education right from the start. Anyway, as I said, Tess Williamson could never have pushed Hilda, absolutely not."

"Did many of the parents agree with you?"

"I'm sure they did, at first. Then, you know, it dragged on and on, with her being taken in and solicitors fighting and the newspapers. The longer it went on, the more guilty she must have appeared. So much talk, so much printed, accusations flying back and forth. Even after the whole case was dismissed for lack of evidence, some people wouldn't let it go." Mundy turned her coffee cup round. "And then she died in the very same place. I could not believe it; I just couldn't. I was seventeen by then and thought the entire world was going to hell anyway . . . It made me so sad."

For a moment, she was silent, then she said, "We were so happy back then. You should have seen Laburnum that summer, the woods full of maples and oaks, the laburnum grove burning like fire, waves of bluebells and crocuses, stone walls where bloodred roses grew, the vastness of it, those precipitous stairs. The house looked to me like one of those cool Venetian castles, pillars around, footsteps that echoed, endless marble stairs, silence —"

"Mundy."

"Yes?" She looked as if she were coming out of a daze or a trance.

"You missed nothing; you remember all of those details as if you were looking at a photograph. Yet you can't recall much of what happened around the time of Hilda's death. Why is that?"

She puffed out her cheeks, then seeming to realize that looked childish, stopped. She turned her head. Propped her chin on a fist and looked out of the window, presenting a profile that was one of the most perfect Jury had ever seen: the graceful slope of the forehead and eyebrow, the perfect nose, straight to its tip, where it turned up slightly, the curve of the lips, the long neck, swan-like. No wonder people remembered her as "the pretty one." Then that view dissolved like a watery reflection when she lowered her head, turning back.

"Well. I expect I didn't want to talk about it. Where we were, where we went. We were supposed to stay in the front garden, not go all over, because it would make finding everyone nearly impossible. Kenneth and Arabella and I followed the rules. He hid behind the sarsen stone; I was on top of the wall. I don't know where Arabella was, maybe behind Kenneth's stone. Of course, everyone knows about Johnny being in the laburnum grove because he got sick. And, of course, Hilda. Obviously Hilda broke the front garden rule. Nicki, of course, was "It." Doing the counting.

"Nicki?"

"Veronica's nickname. We all seem to hate our given names, especially girls. 'Mundy' I got from my little brother, who had a hard time saying 'Madeline.' "

"But you wouldn't know if Kenneth left his place behind the stone and went back there."

She shook her head. "No." She paused. "I hate pointing a finger at anyone."

"You all disliked Hilda, though, didn't you?"

Leaning back, she gave Jury a sardonic look. She seemed much older than her thirty-four years. "You think this was our version of *Murder on the Orient Express*? That we all picked up a stone instead of a knife and bopped Hilda on the head? Do you have a cigarette?"

He blinked, jarred by the question. There was something dreamlike in its irrelevance; indeed he felt there was something dreamlike about Mundy Brewster. She felt like a thing in a dream.

"No. I quit." He made to rise. "I can get you some —"

She pulled at his arm. "Oh, don't. I'm sorry. There are times I feel the need of a cigarette like some people do a drink. I'm trying to quit. Is it hard?"

"It's endless. The only thing you can do is turn your mind away from it. Go on talking."

"Yes. Well, when Veronica was counting, I never realized how long one minute could be. And two of them? It's plenty of time to kill someone if that's what you mean to do."

With this rather surprising appraisal, Mundy scraped her thick tawny hair back from her face, as if she could finally reveal herself and looked at her watch. "Oh, my God, look at the time."

Jury got up to help her with her coat.

"Thank you for lunch. I needed a wine and caffeine jolt."

"Why's that?"

"My boyfriend left me."

"Christ, I'd say he's the one who needs a jolt."

"Thank you."

As they passed through the door, he said, "Someone in London?"

"In and out. I told you how he has a way of disappearing."

Jury let the door suck shut behind them. "McAllister? He's the boyfriend?"

She smiled up at him. "He doesn't know it. It wouldn't make any difference if he did." She sighed. "I guess I've always been in love with him, even when we were kids, even though I was bigger than he was." She sighed again. "Talk about Victorian novels. Talk about unrequited love." Then she laughed, briefly. And then she sighed a third time.

"Why it isn't requited is a mystery beyond even Scotland Yard's power to solve."

"That's nice of you to say that." She put out her hand. "Thank you for lunch and for listening to me." He took her hand; her grasp was not the usual soft touch, of fingers slipping over palms. It was quite strong.

"Anytime. And if you think of anything at all about this whole sad business of Laburnum, give me a call, will you?" He handed her a card.

He watched her walk away. A while on, she turned and waved.

What a girl.

17

Bloomsbury
Thursday, 12:30 P.M.

Wiggins himself got no less lucky.

Kenneth Strachey's Bloomsbury digs were open and airy, as was, indeed, Kenneth Strachey himself. He was absolutely delighted to have a visit from New Scotland Yard, especially a detective who knew the merits of afternoon tea.

"And scones," he added, hooking his hand over his shoulder to indicate Wiggins should follow him.

They made their way across the large, white, and well-lighted living room into a kitchen equally as large, where Kenneth Strachey opened one of the several doors of a black cooker and slid out a thin tray. "Just done." He put the pan on the giant butcher-block table in the center of the room. Around it, bamboo stools sat, neatly aligned. Above it hung a cast iron pot-rack from which were suspended a dozen sun-bright copper pots and pans.

"My word. This kitchen means business," said Wiggins, taking one of the stools and eyeing, with pleasure, the fresh scones. Smelling them too. "You like to cook, sir, I take it."

Strachey grinned. "If I weren't a writer, I'd seriously think of becoming a chef. I love to cook. I get up in the middle of the night and cook. Tea!" From a marble countertop he took a kettle that looked to Wiggins of such substance and streamlined modernity that it might have come off a Boeing assembly line. The chrome handle seemed to roar back over the kettle, and the whole thing might have taken wing. Strachey touched something in the cooker's control panel and came back to the scones. "Butter," he said, pulling over a white crock. "Marmalade? Or some blackberry jam?" He looked at Wiggins, apparently expecting him to chip in with decisions.

Wiggins was only too happy to say, "Marmalade, definitely."

Strachey went to a shelf, pulled down another crock. "Now, what kind of tea?"

"Anything, long as it's black. I can't stand those sniffy little cups that look like water with bits of wheat and stems floating about."

173

Strachey snickered and turned back to pick up the kettle, water already on the boil.

"That's some cooker you got there, Mr. Strachey. That boiled faster than my electric kettle."

"It's an Aga." He was spooning a Fortnum & Mason Afternoon Tea into a bluish glazed pot. "If they gave me a choice between this cooker, a Jag, or a private jet, I'd take the cooker." He turned over a little hourglass timer sitting on the table, then went to a cupboard and retrieved small plates and opened a drawer for a couple of butter knives. Then he sat down.

"Don't let Jamie Oliver get wind of this kitchen. He'd be in it in an eye-blink."

Strachey thought this hilarious. "God, does everyone at the Met have your sense of humor?"

It was the first time Wiggins could recall ever being cited for his sense of humor. He scratched his neck with a finger, frowning slightly. "Not much to laugh at in our job, you know."

Sense of humor. Tea preference. Homemade scones. Wiggins could move in here and live out his days.

Strachey had taken a pint of milk out of the industrial-size fridge, closed the door with his foot, and brought down a blue-and-white jug. Into this he poured the milk. "Tea's up!" he said, seeing the sand had run to the bottom of the timer. White porcelain cups had appeared from somewhere, and Strachey poured. He shoved the jug and plate of sugar cubes toward Wiggins.

Smiling broadly, Wiggins poured in a measure of milk, added three cubes.

Strachey added only milk, raised his cup. "To your health, Sergeant!"

"And yours, sir."

They sipped. Strachey said, "Cut out the sir stuff. My name's Kenneth. What's yours?"

"Alfred." He spread some butter on a scone. "But everyone calls me just Wiggins."

"Ah. Like Morse. Very high level of policing, Morse did."

"Thanks, but I doubt mine's that good."

"I suppose neither was Morse's, given he's complete fiction."

"True. Good man with a crossword, though. Thanks." That was for Kenneth, who was holding out the teapot. "Never be too much tea for me."

Finished pouring, Strachey said, eyes narrowed, as if in fierce combat with a thought: "You know what I'd like right now, right this minute? Cheesecake!" He slammed his hand on the table, making his cup jump, and was off his stool and looking into the vast Arctic reaches of his refrigerator.

"Right!" said Strachey, as if he'd found he was on the right track to the Pole. He reached both hands in.

Drinking his tea, Wiggins expected to see a cheesecake emerge. But what emerged was a pint of sour cream, some cream cheese, more butter, a lemon, and a half-dozen eggs. All in one go, he'd grabbed these items and, with them, did his signature kicking shut of the door. He put all of this on the table, went to a cupboard, pulled out a slim box of digestive biscuits, and slapped those in front of Wiggins.

"Just open this and dump the biscuits into a bag . . . Here." Kenneth tossed a box of plastic Ziplocs toward Wiggins.

Who still sat with his mouth open. "You don't mean to tell me you're going to *make* a cheesecake."

"Of course." He tapped two different controls on the Aga, plunked a stainless steel pan on the large warmer, tossed in butter. "You're supposed to crush those digestives up, man."

"Stomp on this lot, is that it?" Wiggins had the package open and the biscuits transferred.

"Right." Kenneth pulled a long circle of

marble out of a drawer, plunked that in front of Wiggins.

Wiggins couldn't have said whether it was a small Corinthian column or a rolling pin. He looked around, still trying to take Kenneth Strachey's intention in.

"Get your skates on, Wiggins," Kenneth said, over his shoulder. "This the way you stand around a crime scene, is it? Mouth open, wondering what to do with the knife?"

Wiggins started crushing. They were chocolate digestives, and he began enjoying his role as sous chef. "The knife's the job of forensic. Nothing to do with me."

Kenneth snickered, butter melted, pan on table. He started a whirlwind of activity over the mixing bowl, cracking, whipping. "Okay, that looks okay. Take a dab of butter and rub it round this." A spring-form pan emerged magically. "Then pour the crumbs in and then the melted butter. Good man. Finished in a breeze. Mix it up good, there, then pat it all down and around."

"I think I get the picture. This is the crust."

"So you do know your way round a crime scene after all!" Whipping up a storm. "God, I could do with a lemon-drop martini."

"No way. We've got enough on our platter." Wiggins was pressing the crumb mixture round the sides of the pan. "Tell me this, when do you do your writing?"

"When I'm drinking my martini and eating my cheesecake. For God's sake, haven't you finished there?"

"Just about. Now I know how those idiots feel on the telly when Gordon Ramsay's around. Done!"

Kenneth grabbed the pan, poured in the makings of the cake, spun it around while he kept a spoon on the go, smoothing a perfect circle. He grabbed it up, went to the Aga, opened a door, and slid it in. "Excellent. Forty minutes that'll take." Back to the fridge, and opening the door, he glanced in, pulled out a dish of raspberries. More tea?"

"I wouldn't say no. Thanks." It was his third cup. Same fill-up on sugar. "Have you always lived in Bloomsbury, then?"

"Half of my life. I wouldn't live anywhere else. It's got everything, part of museum mile, the Renoir Cinema, King's Cross St. Pancras, so if you get the urge to toot off to Paris, the Eurostar's only a stone's throw. And of course, Bloomsbury's where all of them lived, the literary greats — Virginia Woolf, the Bells, and my great-great-great cousin —"

"That'd be Lytton Strachey, wouldn't it?"

"It would. At least that's what Pa claims. Of course he wants me to pick up the cudgel. As if I could. You know his work? *Eminent Victorians,* that's the main one."

"Can't say as I do."

"But me, I want to be a chef. Pa is appalled to think that's my ambition."

Wiggins smiled. "Well, it's not exactly up to Pa, is it?"

"Isn't it? You see this kitchen? You don't think this came from a journalistic spree, do you? My parents are wealthy. My grandmother was even wealthier. I have a trust fund. My father's the executor."

"Uh. That throws a spanner in the works, I expect."

"It does, indeed. Did you always want to be a policeman?"

"God, no. I happened on to policing by accident, almost. In school, I went on a tour of a police academy and thought it looked like interesting work, then forgot about it for years, then a friend of mine joined the force in Manchester — where I'm from — and one thing led to another, and here I am. It's not like police work is in my blood, or anything. My father worked in an office all his life. He thought I was being frivolous. That was his word: *frivolous.*"

Strachey laughed. "Does he still think so?"

"Probably. So, would you say writing is in your blood?"

"You mean because my pa claims to be in the Strachey line? No. Actually, that's not my blood. I think Pa's just forgotten that."

Wiggins tried to make sense of that.

"Anyway, I'm writing a long piece for a small journal right now on the Foundling Hospital. It's in Bloomsbury. You ever been there? Of course, it's a museum now. The history is fascinating though."

"What was it a hospital for?"

"Deserted children."

They talked about the hospital for a few minutes, and about foundlings — Strachey seemed to have a whole raft of them in his head, beginning with seventeenth-century revenge tragedies like *The Duchess of Malfi* and *The Changeling*. Until some twenty-five minutes later, Wiggins looked at the kitchen clock. He had completely forgotten. Lunch with Jury. Soho. The big clock stood at one-forty-five. "God, I'm late, sir. I'll have to leave."

"What? Now? Before the cheesecake. Another ten minutes — ?"

"Another ten minutes and my boss will have my head."

They both got up, Wiggins apologizing,

thanking him as they walked to the front door.

There they shook hands. Then Kenneth Strachey said, smiling as he leaned against the doorjamb, "I'm truly sorry you have to leave, Sergeant. There's just one thing I'm curious about."

"What's that?"

"Why did you come?"

18

Jury waited for Wiggins to embellish.

When he realized his wait would be in vain, he said, "That's it? The sum total of your talk with Kenneth Strachey? You tell me Strachey remembered they were playing hide-and-seek. Then there was 'the most awful row' and they all ran around to the back and there was Hilda dead at the bottom of the pool. That's it?" Jury went mercilessly on. "Wiggins, my dog Joey knows that much."

The menu lowered. "I didn't know you had a dog, sir. That's really —"

Jury shut his eyes. "The dog's not the point."

Wiggins, who had arrived at Ruiya forty minutes late, raised the tall menu so as not to be stared at by his superior. He replied, "That's pretty much it, yes, sir; that's about

182

all Kenneth Strachey had to say." It wouldn't even have been *that* if Kenneth Strachey hadn't reminded Wiggins that he must have had a reason for visiting in the first place.

So by the time Wiggins had asked him one or two hurried questions, which Kenneth had answered, the cheesecake was, of course, done. Wiggins couldn't be allowed to leave at *that* point — "For God's sakes, Detective, you helped make it!" Kenneth's hand hooked over his shoulder again, as it had done when Wiggins had first come, and they retraced their steps back to the kitchen. And that had accounted for twenty of the late minutes. They each had had two helpings.

Relentlessly, Jury kept on: "You were at Strachey's for at least an hour. No, at the very least, an hour and fifteen minutes. At *least.* Unless you were lollygagging all over Bloomsbury with the ghost of Leonard Woolf."

Wiggins's snort showed how much he valued that bit of commentary. "Really, sir." He paused. "I'll have the crispy fish."

"I know. You always have the crispy fish. What were you doing all that time?"

Having made his luncheon selection, Wiggins could no longer — logically —

pretend to study the menu. He moved his cutlery around, which didn't take up much of the reporting-on-Strachey slack, given there was only a set of chopsticks to reposition. He said, "Well, I'm sorry to say it, as I don't imagine you'll think it was time well spent, but" — here he glanced at Jury — "but I did pop into the Foundling Museum." He coughed behind his fist.

Ordinarily, Jury's eyes were a calm, even a warm, gray, but when he got massively irritated, the eyes could go as cold as chrome. "The Foundling Museum. What in bloody hell is that?"

Seeing his chance, Wiggins took his superior's question as literal interest and answered it. He spoke steadily for three minutes, which is forever in liar's language. But, of course, his commentary on the museum itself wasn't a lie at all; he was merely embroidering upon what Kenneth Strachey had told him. And the three minutes of embroidery gave him time to work out a reason for the museum visit.

"Since Kenneth Strachey is writing a series of pieces about it, I thought it might tell me something —" Wiggins went wandering around the liar's maze. A way out . . . Ah! "Like, why is he so interested in that place? I mean interested enough to write a *series* of articles on it?" He'd almost forgotten that detail. He wandered on and finally saw a gap in the maze. It was almost eagerly that he went on: "See, I thought you'd want my impressions, sir, I mean, since you already had the basic facts and Strachey added nothing in that department."

Jury had been watching him closely all through this disquisition, and when Wiggins finally screeched to a halt, his boss was still staring at him. Then he slowly smiled and the smile widened and widened again.

Wiggins wanted to think he had safely left the maze, but then he recalled that line from Shakespeare Jury loved: *"One may smile, and smile, and be a villain."* In his mind, he could hear Jury repeating it. Again and again. Then Wiggins remembered he had found out something: "I did find out Kenneth Strachey was in London the night Belle Syms was murdered. His housemate Austin was there." He had found out Kenneth's whereabouts during the first helping of cheesecake; he had found out about Austin during the second.

"When in London? The entire night?"

Wiggins cleared his throat. "Well, I didn't get all the details, but . . ." He looked away. Then he looked up at the approach of Ruiya's owner. "Here comes Danny Wu!"

He was so delighted to see Danny that he was half-out of his chair.

"Sergeant Wiggins; Superintendent Jury. What a pleasure. It's been awhile."

"At least a week, Danny. The menu hasn't changed."

"The menu never changes," said the impeccably tailored owner. He was wearing dead-black — a finely spun wool silk with a stripe so razor thin it could have been an optical illusion. His tie and pocket handkerchief were the pale yellow of jonquils. All Jury could think of, looking at that black suit and yellow tie was Black Narcissus. The yellow presented an astonishing contrast that Melrose Plant would have passed up and Marshall Trueblood would have taken a step further. These were the three best-dressed men that Jury had ever seen.

If he himself could have afforded such suits, he wondered how he'd look. He imagined viewing himself in the long mirror of Plant's bespoke tailor, engaged in the elegant process of a final fitting. How did he look?

Like a cop.

Danny, had he not been a superb restaurateur, would have made a superb photographer's model as a second career; or, as a third career, a superb criminal, which Jury was inclined to believe was Danny's first career, though Jury had never been able to work out what criminal activity he might be engaged in. He did not have form, but he *had* had a dead man on his doorstep, which, quite naturally, had raised suspicion.

Not (for Jury) the suspicion entertained by Chief Superintendent Racer (Jury's superior), which was that Danny Wu was the drug lord of Docklands, an allegation Jury had thought absurd at the time and still did. But Danny was so — what Jury's uncle had called — "plausible." Meaning completely, disarmingly believable. It was not a compliment. "A man you'd not for a moment doubt." His uncle would smile broadly and wink. "Sucker."

"Where do you get your clothes, Danny?" Jury was back to that.

"Off a hanger in my cupboard."

Jury smiled. "Wish I had your tailor. Or anyone's."

"You don't need a tailor, Superintendent. You're a man clothes could never compete with; they'd always lose."

Jury was stunned. So he picked on Wiggins's astonishment. "So? By your look, I'd say you utterly disagree?"

"What? No, no . . . Well, it's an inscrutable thing to say, is all," said Wiggins.

"I'm an Oriental, Sergeant. That's what we do."

Jury laughed.

In his mind's eye, his uncle winked.

"Crispy fish," said Wiggins, after blowing in and out his cheeks.

"Me too." This got him another astonished look from Wiggins. Jury never ate crispy fish.

Jury was irritated with himself for picking on Wiggins. "I may even have dessert. Toffee bananas. Your favorite, right?" Jury smiled.

Wiggins smiled back, pasty-faced. He had, after all, already had dessert. Two helpings. But he supposed he'd have to go along or someone might become suspicious.

Though how in God's name his boss could have any idea what he'd been doing at Kenneth Strachey's (except nothing), Wiggins couldn't imagine. They ate their crispy fish.

But Jury could pick out lies like a lion sorting out the weakest in a herd of fleeing wildebeest.

"What's wrong?" said Jury, nodding toward Wiggins's all-but-untouched dessert. "This stuff is delicious." Jury crunched down through deep-fried warm caramel crust to cool banana.

Again, Wiggins blew out his cheeks.

"Dunno. I seem a bit off today."

"I bet I know why."

Wiggins looked alarmed.

"Strachey stuffed you full of tea —"

Wiggins smiled a bit, relaxed.

"— while you were asking him probing questions for over an hour."

Jury smiled, implausibly. He was the other kind, the kind you could count on.

19

A Walk through Piccadilly
Thursday, 3:30 P.M.

Ruiya was one of those near-cultish restaurants, best-kept-secret restaurants, a small unpretentious, incredibly successful, line-all-the-way-to-Charing Cross places. Located in Soho, bounded by Piccadilly, Shaftsbury Avenue, Tottenham Court Road, and Charing Cross — in other words, in the heart of the middle of London. And that explained why Jury was, at the moment, in the heart of London.

Jury had left Wiggins with the friendly threat that he himself might have a word with Kenneth Strachey, alarming his sergeant into protests that he, Wiggins, would be good to do any follow-up interviews . . . Jury knowing that he had spent the time with Strachey drinking tea and having a chin-wag and doing God-what-knows else. Jury was, of course, stereotyping the

Bloomsbury idea. Really, just how much time had Virginia Woolf spent drinking tea? She didn't write *To the Lighthouse* with a biscuit in one hand and a teacup in the other, sitting with crossed ankles round the cake- and cress-laden tea table.

He kicked off a sheet of the *Telegraph* that had blown his way down Shaftsbury Avenue. He passed by the Apollo, the Prince Edward, this theater and that theater and their offerings he would never see, as if he existed in some parallel London universe of empty Palladiums.

Along Dean Street on the other side of Shaftsbury was the Groucho Club, the cleverly named private club where the creative world went for embalming. Publishing people, writers, media people, film and TV people. Too clever by half. If the Metropolitan Police wanted their own club, would they bother to think up a name for it so profoundly (and phonily) self-deprecating as Groucho Marx's joke?

Not that police were short on ego — God, no. Think of a room full of DCIs, chief constables, a few assistant commissioners. They had their share of egos in the Met. But they were egos with guns. They had legs.

The Groucho Club had been started as an alternative to the stuffy men's clubs in

London. As far as Jury was concerned, anywhere that required a potential member to have two sponsors, two okays for membership, was stuffy enough. White's, Boodle's, and Melrose Plant's club, Boring's, struck him as supremely unstuffy. Its members were more sleepy than stuffy. All they wanted was to be left alone with their whiskies, their fireplaces, their food, papers, and smokes.

Jury made his way around Piccadilly Circus where pigeons and people shared the statue at its center in just about equal measure. He continued along the cleaner sweep of the Haymarket and its slightly more pretentiously pillared theaters. It occurred to him in London, theaters were everywhere. Here, Covent Garden, Aldwych, the Strand — nearly anywhere you set your foot.

Perhaps he should take Phyllis Nancy to a theater. Take Phyllis Nancy on a West End theater date? Ridiculous. Take Carole-anne. Even more ridiculous. She'd want a bucket of popcorn. No, it was really he himself who struck himself as ridiculous. Why? Couldn't the Met go to the theater? Couldn't they appreciate Judi Dench as much as anybody?

He stopped in front of the theater where, good lord, *Anything Goes* was playing.

Mundy Brewster was right; they were still doing it. A surge of people were coming out of the doors, matinee-goers wandering about blinking in the London light, as if they too had been inhabiting an alternate planet.

Space-Time. Wasn't that Einstein's concept? A kind of cube? He was walking toward Trafalgar Square, contemplating Space-Time. Quantum mechanics. No, that wasn't Einstein. Einstein hadn't given sod-all about quantum mechanics. According to Harry Johnson, that s.o.b. Harry, who had a sea of money and no profession except murdering women and drinking wine.

He stopped suddenly, throwing two elderly ladies off course.

They sulked past him.

Jury checked his watch. 4:00 P.M. Early for The Old Wine Shades, Harry's favorite hangout. Quantum mechanics, mathematics. He wondered if Harry knew anything about codes and the Enigma machine —

He stopped dead again, this time nearly stepping on a poodle who yapped less than his owner.

You great twit! he thought, not of the poodle, but of himself. You haven't talked to Oswald Maples about Tom Williamson's case, and here you are wandering all over

Piccadilly . . .

Jury pulled out his mobile. Dead again. Hell.

He saw a number 22 rolling up the street, ran across to the bus stop and caught it and climbed to the second level. He loved London buses almost as much as London cabs.

20

Chelsea
Thursday, 4:00 P.M.

It was a face Jury hadn't seen before, a nurse's face, who appeared at the door of the mews house off Cadogan Street, and Jury was anxious that Sir Oswald Maples had taken a turn for the worse.

But he hadn't long to worry, for the face of Sir Oswald appeared just then over her shoulder, looking both irritated and pleased, the first for the nurse, the second for Jury.

"Superintendent!" said Sir Oswald, elbowing the woman out the door as he held out his free hand, the one not gripping a cane. "Good-bye, Louise," he added.

Nurse Louise, for her part, looked even more irritated than had Sir Oswald, but not forgetting her nursy-niceness, said to him: "Now you be sure to take those tablets Doctor prescribed —"

"Thank you. Good-bye."

Louise sniffed, raised her eyebrows at Jury as if he might be going to countermand her orders, and then left.

Sir Oswald Maples shut the door. He lived here alone and had done so for many years.

Jury said, "Sorry I didn't call ahead, but my mobile died."

"The appropriate fate for it, I think. Nurse Louise has left me a mobile, with a charger, so fire yours up if the charger works on it." Oswald indicated a table near Jury.

"You've got some new ailment?" Jury asked as he plugged the charger into his mobile. Good.

"Yes. Her." He jerked his head toward the door she'd just passed through. "I was just about to pour myself a large whiskey when, lo and behold, I discover she's locked the drinks cabinet! Can you believe it? She "dropped in" to give me a new load of medicine and I couldn't get the key out of the damned woman. She thought it was so awfully cute."

Jury did have a hard time believing there was actually a lock hanging on a chain that ran between the handles of the two doors of the cabinet. "I don't believe it." Jury reached into his macintosh pocket and brought out his keys. "Got a hammer?"

"What are you going to do? Just keep in

mind that's a Louis Quinze chest."

Jury just looked at him. "Do you want a drink or do you want me to keep that in mind?"

Oswald laughed. "Go ahead and open it. If you can."

"Anyone can." Jury took a key off a ring he brought out of his pocket.

Oswald went to the kitchen at the other end of the living room and returned with a lightweight hammer.

"What's that?"

"A bump key. If you do it right, it pushes the pins up simultaneously, but only for a split second, so you're timing has to be right." Oswald handed him the hammer. Jury turned the key very slightly to the right, hit it with the hammer a couple of times. "There you go." He opened the door. "And no damage to the antique chest, *and* most important, we can lock it again and no one will ever know." He reattached the key, returned the keys to his pocket.

"Brilliant!"

"Here." Jury took out the ring of keys again, removed the bump key, and handed it to Oswald. "It might take a little practice, but you can do it."

"Well, get out the whiskey."

Jury said, peering into the cabinet, "This

197

is quite a stash, Oswald." He pulled out a bottle of Talisker and one of Johnnie Walker Black Label and set them on top of the chest. Then his hand went back in to pull out another. "What's this? Yamazaki? Never heard of it."

"Japanese. It's delicious."

"Maker's Mark, Oswald? That's Kentucky bourbon." Jury set that beside the others.

"Nurse Louise must have bought that one. There are glasses there. Do you want soda? Water?"

"Are you kidding? I'll have some of this." He lifted the bottle of Yamazaki. "You?"

"That'll do. Just don't go overboard. It costs a bloody fortune."

Jury smiled and poured two fingers into each glass, handed one to Oswald, and they sat down.

Oswald leaned his head back, stared up at the ceiling. His glass sat on the table. For all of his fussing about a drink, he'd yet to take a sip.

"I had a drink with your friend Tom Williamson."

"Did you? Good. I suggested he talk to you."

"It's a very cold case, Oswald."

"It's a very sad one. He was here the day she died in their house in Devon. In June, I think it was. A Monday in June . . . no, a Tuesday. I keep making that mistake."

"I don't see how you could even remember the month, much less the day. Seventeen years ago, my God."

"The reason I remember is that the so-called home help I had then was a woman who makes Nurse Louise look like Vanessa Redgrave. Zillah Peabody. She always came on Monday, Wednesday, Friday, and Sunday. I loathed her coming; I was glad Tom was here for moral support. I couldn't understand what was holding her up; the woman appeared with all the punctuality of a Japanese bullet train and with twice the impact. I thought I was having a holiday from her until Tom told me it wasn't Monday that day, it was Tuesday. It wasn't one of her days to come. He thought it was funny."

"Did you know her? Not the bullet train; I mean Tess Williamson."

"I'd met her, yes. Talked to her a few times. It was a bloody disaster, her dying. Well, Tom never believed it was an accidental death."

"Neither did Brian Macalvie. That was a coincidence, that he was on the case. I've just been there, to Laburnum, I mean, with Macalvie."

"That was damned decent of you."

"Not really. Tom Williamson is the sort of person you just feel you want to help . . . Know what I mean?"

Oswald nodded. "Indeed."

"Do you know anything at all about him that might shed light on this? I'm thinking about his work in codes and ciphers."

"Spy stuff?"

"Well, it was GC and CS, Oswald. It was Enigma, the German navy."

Oswald held up his hands, palm out. "That was long before Tess Williamson died. We're talking about the end of the war — forty-four, forty-five. Tom Williamson came on after that, in the late seventies, after they moved to headquarters outside of Cheltenham and became GCHQ.

"Nevertheless. It's still codes and ciphers. It's still sensitive material."

Oswald picked up his glass again and looked at it. Then he set it down, as if the expected transformation hadn't yet happened, but he was prepared to wait until it did. He looked at Jury in much the same way.

Jury said, "Was he forced to retire or was it his own idea?"

"I don't know. I only heard about his leaving GC Headquarters. Heard it on the grapevine. Remember, this was the eighties, Thatcher's government. The employees at GCHQ wanted to unionize; indeed some of them belonged to a union. The government refused to let them with the excuse that it would compromise security. A number of people were dismissed because they wouldn't give up union rights." Oswald shrugged. "Tom was one of them. That's what I heard."

"It had nothing to do with the inquest involving Tess?"

"Not that I know of."

Jury felt an inexplicable sense of relief, he guessed for Tess Williamson's sake. He turned his glass between his palms, as if there were a need to warm up whiskey. "Tell me about Tess Williamson."

"What I know of her." Oswald picked up his glass, didn't drink. "I was never really certain what I thought about her. Except she was awfully nice and, of course, beautiful. But there are some people you just can't pin down."

Jury laughed, briefly. "Most people."

"Perhaps. Well, there was the dreadful business of that child's falling into that pool and dying. Surely an accident."

"Forensic wasn't so sure. That was the problem."

Oswald massaged the bridge of his nose with his fingertips. "I can't get my mind round any of it. The way Tess died. It was very strange. Nothing I can think of explains it."

Jury looked up and around the low ceiling and blackly varnished timbers. "One thing might. Suicide."

"What? Why wasn't that proposed at the time?"

"Because it wasn't evident to anyone who knew her; they could have been in a state of what alcoholics call denial. Including Brian Macalvie. It's the first time I've ever seen him less than positive. Mentally stumbling — well, slightly stumbling." Jury smiles. "I've never seen Macalvie completely miss his footing."

Which was what he'd said, in essence, to Tom Williamson, not about Macalvie, but about Tess. They were her stairs.

Oswald frowned. "But this Commander Macalvie didn't know her."

"Yes, he did. He really liked her." Jury reflected. "I think Tess Williamson might have reminded him of someone."

"But — what would have been her motive?"

Jury shrugged. The movement was slight, certainly not registering indifference. "I would suspect because of what happened at Laburnum five years before: the death of Hilda Palmer."

Oswald's frown was deeper this time. "You're not thinking she killed her?"

"No, I'm not. To have done that seems completely out of character with what I've heard about her. Just something happened then —"

"Well, obviously something happened, man." Sir Oswald's tone was scoffing as he made to rise and pick up his glass.

He had, after all, drunk it. Jury rose while Oswald was still struggling to his feet and took the glass from him over to the sideboard.

"Thanks."

He poured a small measure into both glasses, restoppered the bottle, and returned Oswald's glass to him. Then he sat down again. "What I meant was that Tess Williamson knew."

Oswald had been about to sip, but stopped. "And didn't say?"

"And didn't say." Jury raised his own glass.

Oswald thought for a few moments, his gaze moving round the room. "And didn't tell her husband?"

"No."

"A lover?" Oswald's frown was deeper still.

Jury didn't answer right away. He too looked about the room. "I don't mean that, no."

"But if you believe she knew something about the way Hilda Palmer died — well, she must have been protecting someone."

Jury nodded. "Besides Hilda and Tess herself, there were five children and a friend of the Williamsons, Eileen Davies. She was supposed to be sitting out in front, on a bench."

"That woman. Yes, what about her?"

"I don't know. I haven't spoken with her, but she lives in Belgravia, very near, so I think I'll just drop in after I leave you. According to her, she was in the front garden the entire time."

"And there could have been somebody else that nobody saw."

"There could, yes. But it seems a little unlikely a stranger — another person — could have picked a moment he or she had no way of knowing would come, so that the person could have appeared, killed Hilda, and disappeared."

Oswald was silent. "But Tess's own death: I still think accident is more likely. A woman with vertigo standing at the top of a high flight of stone stairs —"

But they were her stairs . . .

21

Cosmetic surgery had not been the way to go for Elaine Davies; it might have made her look more youthful, but it was the look of a youth misspent. The face was all wrong, the eyes too high, the mouth too low, the nose two short for the distance between. Her blond hair, colored with highlights, was cut in a bob. She wore a perfectly cut, champagne-colored suit, silk blouse, string of pearls.

How did women find the time to maintain such a carefully wrought appearance while just puttering about the house? How did Phyllis Nancy dress around the house? He had seen her only either in her morgue scrubs, blood streaked, or in a backless black dress when they went out to dinner at Aubergine.

"Yes?" The perfectly penciled brows rose.

"Sorry. I was woolgathering." The weight-less black dress. Jury smiled.

Having nothing else to intrigue her, his warrant card did. "Ah! Scotland Yard? What have I done now?"

The simper in the question made him want to tell her something she had done.

She stood back, flinging the door wide, happy to find she'd done anything at all.

Behind him was a courtyard around which several narrow houses were arranged in a half-moon. In the center was a lavish foun-tain. Jury entered a portal, which was the only way he could put it to himself, as it seemed almost like an entry to a yacht; there was nothing actually nautical about it other than three small engravings of HMS-somethings, but the tiny room had that shipshape look about it.

The living room was one of varying shades of white, the sort of off-whites that always made him wonder why paint bothered. "Champagne" was the most daring depar-ture from stark whiteness. The side chairs and sofa pillows were the same color in silk shantung. She invited him to sit. A fire burning low in the fireplace provided the only spark of color.

When she herself took a seat on the sofa, he realized this was the color of the suit.

Elaine Davies was a hell of a color co-ordinator. The mystery of her troubling to dress as she had was thus solved: not to have done so would have messed up the tone-on-tone scheme.

But her meticulous attention to her clothes made him wonder how she could have been a close friend of Tess Williamson. Tess struck him as one who would probably favor big thick sweaters and jeans. At least when she wasn't standing at the top of the garden stairs.

Elaine was like the courtyard fountain, stilled, as if the ring of water were frozen in midfall. Tess made him think more of waves' collapsing, their uneven approaches to shore.

"It's about Tess Williamson."

Her eyes widened; her squarish mouth opened, said nothing for a moment. "Tess? But Tess has been dead for nearly twenty years."

"Seventeen. Hilda Palmer for twenty-two. You remember that."

She swallowed but remained perfectly intact, legs crossed, hands linked over a knee, silver bracelet dangling. She looked distressed or at least to the extent distress could penetrate the perfect makeup. "Tess had vertigo. Her death was an accident.

There was an inquest —"

"It was an open verdict. Tom Williamson still has doubts."

"Tom? After all these years?"

"He'll always have doubts."

"But Scotland Yard! That's rather extreme, isn't it?"

"That's an address, Mrs. Davies, not an experience. We're Metropolitan police, that's all."

"Oh, please . . ." She waved that truth away. "How is Tom? I haven't heard from him in such a long time."

"He seems fine."

"He's such a sweetheart." She sighed. "Never remarried." Absently, Elaine twisted the ring on her finger, as if she could use a refresher.

Tom Williamson would be quite a catch for any woman: still relatively young; handsome, intelligent, kind. Extremely rich. A prize, he'd be.

Jury said, "Tell me about his wife, Tess. You were a good friend, I understand."

"Tess?" Elaine fingered a pearl-studded ear. The earring flashed pink in the firelight. "There's not that much to tell. Tess was a rather transparent person. You know. One always knew where one stood."

"And where did you stand?"

She seemed a mite surprised. "As you said, I was a good friend. I knew her, I expect, as well as anyone."

Jury doubted it.

"Tess was a very positive, cheerful person. Very dependable. Very straightforward."

"So you didn't see her at all as troubled?"

"Troubled?" She would echo the end of every question.

"Was there any truth in the gossip about Tess Williamson and her photographer friend?"

She gave a little shake of her head. "I don't think so." She was vague.

He would get no more, simply because she hadn't any more to give. Again, Jury doubted the depth of the friendship

"But she wasn't an unhappy person?"

"No. Now that you mention it, yes, there was one troubling episode for her. They both desperately wanted children, but she couldn't seem to get pregnant. That really bothered her. Both of them. They went to a man in Harley Street. As it turned out, Tess couldn't have a baby. Something wrong internally. She didn't give me details." She thought for a moment. "Dr. Smiley, that was his name. I remember because of the spy stories, you know."

"George Smiley. Right. Brilliant character."

"Dr. Smiley. I wonder if he's still there . . . Well, why not? I'm still here, aren't I?"

Jury nodded. "Definitely, yes. Tell me about the day at Laburnum, when Hilda Palmer died."

That did crease her forehead. "It was awful. Awful. I doubt I'll ever get over it."

She'd gotten over it long ago. Her own role in it, Jury imagined she'd played to the hilt. Elaine would enjoy a bit of drama. "I understand you were in the front garden when this happened . . ."

"I didn't see anything, if that's what you mean."

He nodded. "What were you doing?"

"Reading. One of the other little girls, Victoria, I think her name was —"

"Veronica, I understand."

"Oh? Well, she was playing, you know, 'It,' so she was turned up against a tree counting —"

"Did you see her doing this?"

Elaine looked a little dumbfounded. "No, I didn't see anything after the game started up. Before that they were, you know, quarreling a little about who'd do this and who'd do that. Well, I turned away for my book . . .

I just know that was going on, the game, I mean."

"But you didn't actually see them? Didn't see the kids hiding."

Uncomfortably, she shifted, uncrossed, recrossed her legs. Jury heard the silk whisper. "But obviously that's what they were doing. Victor — Veronica said she'd counted nearly to a hundred; the others said where they'd hidden —"

"You're going by what the children said. They mightn't have been in the front, where you were, at all after a few moments."

"You mean you think they were lying?"

Jury looked into the firelight. The flames hadn't changed since they'd been sitting there. He supposed it must be a gas insert. He turned back to her. "That's not really my point. My point is, if you didn't know, if you didn't see where they were, then who saw where you were?"

That made the mouth, which had been ready to smile, turn down. "What are you implying? That I'm lying?"

"I'm not really implying. I'm asking. Are you?"

The well-wrought mask cracked. "That's ridiculous! Absolutely ridiculous!" She started to rise.

"Please sit down, Mrs. Davies. This is a

reasonable question for a policeman. You didn't see the children after the game started. As far as you really know, they could all have run round to the back of the house. That would leave you there alone for some moments. You yourself could have run round to the back. I'm not saying you did; I'm merely saying that the only people whose whereabouts were certain were the girl, Hilda Palmer, dead at the bottom of that pool, and Tess Williamson, down there with her."

But she did not continue to sit. "I think perhaps you should leave. I've cooperated as well as I could."

That she didn't have to cooperate at all apparently didn't occur to her. It wasn't a police interview; she wasn't a material witness. It had all happened twenty-two years ago.

Jury rose. He smiled, brilliantly. "I apologize. Perhaps I didn't put it very well. I appreciate your time, Mrs. Davies."

Thawing a bit, she murmured a few words as she walked him to the door, which she didn't slam. Her good-bye was almost cordial.

Walking down the iron steps, across the courtyard and past the stilled fountain he again wondered about Elaine and Tess's friendship.

If Tess hadn't told her anything about Andrew Cleary, why then had she told her about Dr. Smiley?

22

*Belgrave Square and Snow Hill Police Station
Thursday, 7:00 P.M.*

He wanted to sit down for a while and decided to follow the woman who had a key to the square. Only the buildings surrounding Belgrave Square — mostly embassies — were permitted to use it, but he didn't think anyone would throw him out. It was empty except for the woman who'd unlocked the gate, and she was merely crossing it to the road on the other side.

"What're you doing?" Jury was on his mobile. He wondered if that seemingly aimless question that everyone asked from time to time wasn't aimless at all, but was an appeal for connection.

What're you doing?

"Studying my library card," said Melrose, unbothered by the apparent pointlessness of Jury's opening.

"Your *library* card?"

"Yes. I like the row of stamped dates. They're like stacks of little numbers. Those rubber stamping things librarians use, packed with dates. It seems to me it'd be awfully easy to get a date wrong. This book is late. But they probably don't do that anymore in London, or anyplace except in tiny villages. It's all getting computerized, now, isn't it?"

Sitting on his bench in this green square, Jury thought he should go along with Plant's meditation on his card, given Melrose and Trueblood and the Jack and Hammer lot had saved the librarian's job, and quite possibly the library itself. He watched a couple of dusty-looking pigeons wrangle over a bit of something on the path. The washed-out blue of the sky above had faded further into pewter.

Jury half-heard Melrose's voice going on about Long Piddleton's little library, and when the voice paused, he said, "I'm resuming my interrupted visit, if you don't mind. Thought I'd come tomorrow."

"Excellent! Everyone has been vastly busy with this case of the lady in red. You can hear all the theories!"

"How wonderful." Jury shut his eyes. There was another silence, a longer one.

Melrose said, "What're you doing?"

■ ■ ■ ■

Detective Inspector Dennis Jenkins was one of the smartest cops Jury knew, capable of intuitive leaps that others considered merely random guesswork. The thing was, Jenkins lived to think.

The subject Jury wanted him to think about was vertigo.

"You wouldn't be talking about that woman who was thrown from that folly in Northamptonshire, would you. And don't you have a friend who lives around there?"

"He didn't do it." Jury smiled. "Remember, we were talking about Alfred Hitchcock?"

"*Vertigo.* I was mesmerized."

"But why?"

"Why was I mesmerized?"

"No. Why did you think it was murder?"

"Dressed like that? In that dress and those spiky heels? We're back in Christian Louboutin and Jimmy Choo–land."

Whose shoes had played a big part in Jury's last case; it had also been Jenkins's case, in part.

Dennis went on. "I'd say drugged and carried up to the top, or dead and carried up to the top. Chucked over." He made a dropping gesture with his arms. "What was the postmortem result?"

"I haven't talked to the DCI in charge of the case, so I'm only guessing a broken neck. Belle Syms was her name. It happened very late Monday night or Tuesday morning. But she was seen in a restaurant, then in the Sidbury Arms — that's a hotel there — between nine-thirty and ten. Later, back at her own hotel, the Sun and Moon. So that narrows time of death considerably."

Jenkins tossed down the pencil he'd been chewing on and said, "Why was she there in the first place? I mean, in that area? There wasn't much in the paper about background, only 'Woman Falls to Her Death in Northants Village,' et cetera."

"According to hotel staff, the boyfriend had suddenly to go to London on business. The barman, also the owner of the Sun and Moon, said the woman was 'in a right temper,' had a drink at the bar, asked about a place to eat. He said the two of them were dressed to the nines."

Dennis was looking at Jury, or not so much "looking" as fixing him in place, staring out of his light gray eyes. Jury knew the slightly out-of-focus look wasn't really meant for him but was Dennis thinking. Then he suddenly got up, unhooked his jacket from his chair, said, "Come on, let's get a coffee." He raised and lowered the paper cup containing cold tea and said, "This tea tastes like piss."

Jury followed him out of the office and out of Snow Hill station.

It was the same Café Nero they'd stopped in before when they were both working the murder of a woman near St. Bart's Hospital.

Trolling a spoon through the foam of his cappuccino, Dennis said, "This is all so much like *Vertigo,* or at least looks to be —"

Jury inhaled some foam and set down his cup. "You know that film very well. I recall you said you thought the Jimmy Stewart character was flawed."

Jenkins shook his head abruptly. "What was flawed was the vertigo angle. Killing this woman, Madeleine —"

"The chap's wife that Stewart is obsessed with?"

"Right. The success of the crime depends on Stewart's vertigo. If he could make it to the top of the chapel, that little plan would have been in ruins. If he'd made it to the top he'd have seen both Kim, who's been impersonating the wife Madeleine, and Madeleine herself. Right?" He didn't wait

218

for Jury to verify the rightness. "But instead, Jimmy, who never gets to the top, sees a woman falling past a chapel window and thinks, it's Kim. He doesn't get to the top because he suffers from vertigo. The flaw, I think, is depending on a psychological illness; it's extremely chancy for the writer, in this case Hitchcock. It's great theater, but it's hardly airtight plotting."

"But Hitchcock makes it appear inevitable. The viewer doesn't doubt for a minute that this man's vertigo is completely believable as the reason for his failure."

Dennis nodded. "Because he's Hitchcock."

They drank their coffee.

Then Dennis said, "It's all about appearances. Sometimes that's what I think life is: all appearance. No reality."

23

The Old Wine Shades, the City
Thursday, 9:00 P.M.

"You must have a new murder on your hands and you're looking for the guilty party. And here he sits."

"No, I can't tie you to this one, Harry."

"Oh, too bad. You're sure?"

"It happened too long ago. Although there's certainly a similarity of setting: large country house, gardens, woods, the victims both pretty women —"

"I'm sorry if I'm dense. But similarity to exactly what?" Harry motioned Trevor, the barman, over.

"Finished with this one, Mr. Johnson?"

"How's the '72 L'Ennui?"

Trevor frowned. "Pardon me, sir?"

Jury smiled. "He's being funny, Trevor."

"I'm being funny, Trevor. I leave the selection up to you."

Trevor moved off with a satisfied smile.

"I've just been talking with a friend, a detective with City police. I brought up Hitchcock, *Vertigo.* One of this detective's favorites. He says it's all appearances. That life is appearance, no reality."

"Smart man. I didn't know the Filth were such philosophers."

Harry Johnson loved referring to the police as "the Filth," still a popular appellation in certain quarters.

Exactly what it was that propelled Jury toward The Old Wine Shades, where they were now sitting at the bar, he had never worked out. It wasn't the superb wine; it might have been the sparring. Jury still thought it was because he would, at some point, catch Harry Johnson out. But he knew, in some part of his mind, he would never "catch out" Harry. Harry was too clever by half to be "caught out."

So when Jury got him in the end, it would not be because Harry made a mistake, but because of chance or luck or maybe a third party — whoever that could possibly be. It might (for instance) happen that the new tenants of that house in Suffolk would find something incriminating.

Harry, he thought, was smarter than he himself. But Harry, unlike Jury, was without conscience. And that made him dumber.

"You think DI Jenkins's point about appearances is an acceptable assessment of life, then?"

"No," said Harry. "There is no acceptable assessment. He's smart, this guy, because he actually thinks about appearance and reality." He held up his glass to the dim light reflecting in the mirror behind the bar and drank.

Jury drank his London Porter. Delicious.

"What was he referring to?" asked Harry.

"Vertigo."

"Ah. The ultimate imposture. Kim Novak. Hitchcock must have enjoyed the hell out of making that film; it let him indulge his own obsessions. You're interested in this because — ?"

"A case. The victim had vertigo." He was thinking of Tess Williamson.

"Did she jump or was she pushed from that tower?"

Jury frowned. "Not that case. But how did you know — ?"

"My sixth sense." With a smile just one degree short of contempt, he pulled a section of the *Sun* from his dark blue blazer and slapped it on the bar. "A sixth sense and an uncanny ability to read." This tabloid featured a story on the "folly-death," as the newspaper termed it. It was a two-page spread featuring a picture of the tower and Tower Cottage. Owen Archer probably wasn't happy.

Harry called to Trevor and crooked his finger. The knowledgeable barman came down the bar. "Mr. Johnson?"

"I hate to ruin your evening, but I think this bottle is corked."

Trevor sniffed it, shook his head. "Not corked, but certainly off." He poured a bit into a glass and tasted it. "Refermented, maybe?"

Harry said, "It does taste a bit fizzy, yes."

Jury waited until the two of them had gotten everything out of their systems about this wine debacle.

"Sorry about that, Mr. Johnson," Trevor finally said. "I'll bring you another." Trevor walked off with the offending bottle of burgundy.

Jury said, tapping the paper. "This isn't my case."

"Not officially." Harry flicked a glance over the print. "It belongs to Northampton CID. But as you've a friend who lives nearby, I'm sure you've adopted it. Obviously she was pushed or forced to take a flyer off the top of that tower."

" 'Obviously'?"

Harry sighed. "Obviously, or the CID,

including you, would not be on the case. You would not be on the case had the death been accidental, a laughable conclusion, in any event." Harry went on, "Later it seems she was seen in both the Sun and Moon Hotel, where she was staying, and in Sidbury." Harry smiled. "That's the Kim Novak part. Which is why you're here. To pick my brain."

"Don't flatter yourself, Harry."

Harry was lighting a cigarette, snapping the lighter shut and exhaling a thin stream of smoke. "You can be absolutely infantile, Superintendent. Are you then just here to have a friendly drink with me?"

Trevor came along with another bottle and turned the label to Harry. "Nice Côtes du Rhône, not awfully pricey."

Price meaning little to Harry, he merely nodded. "Go ahead and pour, Trev."

Trevor poured a small measure into a fresh glass; Harry did the usual swirl, sniff, and taste, but not making a production of it and said, "Fine."

As Trevor poured the wine, Harry nodded toward Jury. "Give him a glass."

Trevor was doubtful. "He's drinking Porter, sir."

As if Jury weren't present. "No thanks. I'll stick with this." He rolled the beer in the glass, sniffed it. "Lovely, tobacco-y scent." He sipped it. "Sweet beginning, notes of chocolate and poppy, rich, warm finish. It has Guinness on the run."

"Very good, sir," said Trevor. "Almost makes me feel like having one myself."

"I see your time in here hasn't been wasted." As Trevor walked off, Harry went on, "The point is whether this woman later seen was the same woman who checked into the hotel earlier with this chap. The woman was seen later that night at four — *four* — different times. That does seem overdoing it. And what happened to this boyfriend, anyway? As far as I can see, a better question is not who this second woman is, but why she's supplying the man with an alibi, at the same time, putting herself at risk. This man could have gone to London or anywhere and provided himself with a dozen eyewitnesses. But she was there, and all she has is the persona of the victim."

"A question I asked myself."

Harry did not appear interested in what Jury had asked himself. He went on, "So what you have are three people: one, the victim, two, the one posing as the victim, three, the killer."

"Numbers two and three could both be involved in the killing. The man and the woman who checked into the Sun and Moon."

"You're making assumptions."

"They were seen to check in," said Jury.

"Yes, but one of your assumptions is that the man was the killer. How do you know it wasn't the lady herself who killed the other woman, then pretended to be her, the murdered woman? The man might simply have left the scene as she herself said he did. Back to London."

Jury drank his beer. He said, "Somehow, that doesn't seem plausible: that a third party — the man — had nothing to do with it. And how would she have lugged the body up to the tower?"

"There are probably a dozen ways that could have happened."

"Don't be absurd."

"But I'm not being. You're the one who brought up Hitchcock. You've got it on your mind. You even brought it up with your friend in the City police. It's by way of being a minor obsession."

"Ridiculous." Jury was uncomfortably unconvinced that it was, however.

"Not really. Of course you're missing one important element in *Vertigo:* a witness. The James Stewart character was set up to be a witness. And you don't have one."

226

24

Ardry End
Friday, 6:30 A.M.

Jury woke the next morning at Ardry End in a four-poster hung with fabulously rich-looking material in heavy folds. The mattress was thick enough to keep the princess from feeling a sack of rocks; the pillows were down. He thought after the drive from London and a wine-soaked near-midnight supper, he would be completely knackered. Instead, he felt he'd been asleep for twenty-four hours.

The fire in the fireplace had been lit. It was very early; he was looking between folds of bed curtains to the window beyond which, in the dawnish-looking sky, a pale sliver of moon was still visible.

He could, he knew, get early morning tea merely by pressing a button inlaid on the side table.

My God, what a life. He thought *What a*

life every time he visited Melrose Plant's ancestral home because each time the sheer sumptuousness of it hit him with another small shock.

He would not indulge himself by pressing the inlaid button. He got out of bed (reluctantly), pulled on some clothes. When he raised the window, a little rush of morning air came in fairly glittering with clarity. He wanted to be out in it.

He left the room and padded down the tall staircase in his socks. No one was about that he could see, not even the cook Martha (who Melrose liked to say never went to bed). But he felt no need for fortification, so he didn't go into the kitchen.

In the octagon-shaped foyer, Jury looked for boots in the cupboard near the staircase. He found several pairs. The ground had looked wet and misty from the window, so boots would be better than his own shoes. He chose the suede ones, lined with some sort of shearling, and pulled them on. A perfect fit. Then he grabbed his anorak from another cupboard and went through to the living room.

On the table beside Plant's wing chair lay a battered copy of Thomas Hardy's poems. He must have sat up reading last night. Jury was impressed that Melrose was so engaged by Tess Williamson's story that he would immediately look into Hardy. There was a marker at the poem Tom had told Jury about.

Stretching eyes west
Over the sea,
Wind foul or fair,
Always stood she
Prospect-impressed.

The book was small; Jury put it in his pocket and left the house through the French door near the fireplace.

In this early light, the dew turned the grass stretching from house to hermitage to barn almost sea gray. He started toward the barn from which morning noises were coming — scuffling, a whinny, a bark. Joey out there managing things, he supposed. No, there was Mr. Blodgett, a bucket in each hand, doing something indeterminate.

His eye caught the hermitage (Melrose's name for the little stone structure), which, in this light, was showing its Cotswold origins, the stone suffused with a lemony glow. The Florida room was outlined in the pale sun. Full of wicker furniture and fake palms and a poster of Key West, the look of it made Jury smile.

He did not think Mr. Blodgett would mind, so he walked toward it, opened the screen door, and went in. He sat down on the wicker settee and outstretched his arms across the back. He raised his face to the ceiling, as if he were indeed soaking up the Florida sun. He discovered the settee was a glider. He glided and looked through the screen, taking in the scene in the distance.

Aggrieved was out of the barn, shaking his head so that his mane caught the light just prowling over the barn's roof. Then the horse lowered his head to nibble at the grass. The goat Aghast was next to stop in the doorway of the barn and look around, as if the world had just been invented. He wandered out and over to a tree to rub his head against it. Then came Joey, whose main purpose was to run circles around Aghast and the tree.

Jury shifted his gaze to the dark trees beyond the barn, thick woodland that was also part of the estate. He could almost feel the presence of Tess and Tom Williamson, as if they had sat themselves down on either side of him on the glider. *We've done all we could; now it's up to you.* They sat, the three of them, looking out over the distant line of dark trees. Prospect-impressed.

■ ■ ■ ■

Jury heard the sound of someone approaching on his right and saw Melrose Plant bearing down.

"Hey," said Plant. "I'm making my rounds." He was wearing another pair of old boots Jury had seen in the cloakroom, along with a tweed jacket over a black cable-knit sweater. He did not seem to think it odd that Jury was in Mr. Blodgett's Florida room. He stood outside, his gloved hands clapped behind his back.

"Well, are you going to see to them?"

"I am." Melrose nodded toward the barn. "There they are. Aggro isn't doing his level best."

"I can't imagine what that would be."

"Well, I'm hungry. Let's have breakfast."

"You've finished your rounds?"

"I just did. Come on." He turned toward the house, waved his hand over his shoulder, bidding Jury to follow.

Jury left the screened porch reluctantly, although he too was hungry and Martha made fabulous breakfasts. Lots of things in silver dishes.

They tramped across the now green grass. Melrose, still in the lead, threw the words back over his shoulder. "I think I'll go to Borings for a couple of days. I'm tired of here."

Jury looked at the "here" they were approaching, its gabled and crenellated roof, its high windows, its wide paths and long beech-lined drive that made its winding way down where the small traffic moved on the Northampton Road.

What a place.

"If a man is tired of here, he's tired of life."

Melrose turned. "Oh, for God's sakes, don't say it."

"I just did. What's for breakfast?"

After the scrambled eggs with smoked salmon and the featherweight biscuits and quince jam, they put on their coats again and walked the short distance from the house to Long Piddleton.

"I need to talk to DCI Brierly; I expect he's at the Northampton station. I'll go back and pick up the car."

"That old wreck?" Melrose pulled some keys from his pocket. "Here, take the Bentley."

"I'm not taking your car. I'll drive the Ford."

"Don't be dumb; take the Bentley." Melrose pushed the keys in Jury's pocket as they came to the library.

Melrose had said he needed to drop off some books and it was there they were headed. Actually, to be headed anywhere doing business in the village would take them along the same road, past the post office, the one-room police substation, seldom used. There had been no actual police presence in Long Piddleton for years.

Melrose stopped as they came to the library and checked over his books, one of which (Jury noticed) was *You and Your Goat.* "Was it helpful, that?" Jury touched the jacket before Melrose could yank it away. "Not to me. Aghast had a go at it, though."

As they had drawn closer to the library, Jury noticed the bench on the edge of the duck pond was occupied. The occupant was tossing out bread to the languid family of ducks. Jury smiled.

"Are you coming?" asked Melrose.

"No. I'll wait at the duck pond."

Still eyeing his books, Melrose walked through the library door. Jury noticed a "Coffee Morning" was announced and thought it wonderful that that little scheme had worked out so much to the librarian's advantage.

"It's been a long time," said Jury to the

back of the woman on the bench.

Vivian Rivington turned, surprised by the voice. "Hasn't it? Three days, I think."

"I mean, since we sat here. Remember?" Jury sat down.

Vivian looked at him with point-blank directness. "Don't be ridiculous. Of course I remember." Her smile was very warm. It was directed toward the ducks.

A fact that annoyed Jury. He didn't know why. He wasn't in love with Vivian. Only once he had been, and it had been love at first sight. "I remember the first time I saw you. It was back there —" He looked over his shoulder at the white lantern with the large blue *P* on it above the station door.

"I remember, I certainly do. I thought you were . . . really something. A Scotland Yard DCI. Handsome, to boot. Tall, really nice." She smiled. This time at him.

Jury took the bag from her and pulled out some bread pieces and threw them in the direction of the lazy ducks. "The ginger hair, the green eyes, and especially the blush —"

"I wasn't blushing, for heaven's sakes." Blushing, she turned away.

"Then it was the reflection of the sun. What I thought of was a Santa Fe sunset."

"No, you didn't. You hadn't been to Santa

Fe yet. That was years later." She retrieved the bag. When the duck spread his wings light glanced off the water onto them.

Suddenly, Jury missed it, Santa Fe. Hadn't thought about that evening sitting on the top of the La Fonda Hotel in a long while. But he thought of it now, the deep sunset, the light reflecting off the Sangre de Cristo mountains. "I think I'll go back."

She turned, surprised. "To New Mexico? Why?"

"If you'd been there, you'd know." Then he frowned, saying, "Tell me something: were you really serious about Franco Giopinno?" The Italian known to them more handily as Count Dracula. Vivian hadn't appreciated that sobriquet. "Would you have married him in the end?"

"Was I serious? Yes, at first. It was Venice. Dreamy, misty, romantic. Franco was the very embodiment of that part of Italy. He was like Venice distilled."

But Venice distilled was, after all, only water, thought Jury.

She went on. "I grew tired of it and him. I was looking for a way out . . ."

"The way out is: 'Sorry, good-bye.' "

Vivian's face reddened up slightly. "I didn't find it that easy. Fortunately, Melrose, Diane, and Marshall got rid of him for me."

Jury remembered they had told Count Dracula some involved story about Vivian's fortune, or lack of it. The count had taken off hastily.

"Just as well, as he was only after my money."

"No, he wasn't." Jury had taken the brown bag again and was throwing out crumbs.

She laughed. "How do you know?"

"Because no one who knows you would be after only your money."

Her smile was broader now. "Thanks."

He crumpled up the empty bag. "It would be interesting to see Plant fall in love."

"Oh, but he wouldn't. He's much too pleased with his life and himself. He's extremely pleased with himself."

"He never struck me as vain."

"I don't mean vain. No, he's more like a child who's just found he actually could rule the Wild Things." She tossed a bit of bread to the duck who'd cruised to the edge.

Jury thought that was one of the strangest estimations of Melrose Plant he could imagine. He said so. "Or under-estimation, to be more precise." He wondered then just how well Vivian knew him.

"Is it? And you a detective." She pinched

236

up his coat sleeve as she rose and bent down to whisper, "He doesn't love me."

"He's thick as two planks." Jury got up. "Well, there's always me."

"Neither do you."

And that was true now, of course, and she knew that he knew it. She had refused to marry him years before, but it was somehow hard for him to let go, if not of the feeling itself, then of the memory of the feeling. He wondered how much of love was actually nostalgia. He thought about Jenny Kennington, someone he'd been certain of, only to find that the certainty was, if not misplaced, simply for another kind of woman . . .

"Hey!"

Melrose was coming across the green, new books in hand.

Vivian looked ruefully at Jury, smiled slightly, and looked away.

DCI Ian Brierly was tilted back in his chair in the Northampton station, considering Jury's theory. "Two of them. An imposter. Interesting." He was quiet, thinking. "So the killer could have murdered Belle Syms before he took off for — allegedly — London, perhaps even at the Sun and Moon Hotel, come back, taken the body to the tower."

"Or," said Jury, "gone to the tower with her — Blanche Vesta said Belle got a kick out of heights — killed her there, then come back, had the accomplice switch clothes, and pushed her out of the tower."

"We're assuming the killer was the man she was with at the hotel?"

Jury shrugged. "What about the husband? The aunt said they were separated."

"Haven't found him either. Got some information from Blanche Vesta, went to Syms's flat in Wembley, no sign of him. My men made dozens of inquiries — the neighbors, at some shops, no one knew his whereabouts. All they found out was that Zachariah Syms was a nice guy, good with both people and animals, really loved his dog. Took him everywhere."

"Where's the dog, then?"

"Took him everywhere, as they said. So they've both gone off into the wild blue, and if it was in a car, he must've hired one, because he doesn't have a car himself." Brierly leaned forward. "Now this second woman of yours. When and where does she enter the scene?"

"Right after Belle Syms dies — unless of course she helped to kill her — when she dons the flashy red dress and later, presumably at the tower, when she strips it off and they redress the victim."

Brierly frowned. "Why? I mean why put this diabolical scheme into action? It's so damned much trouble. Why not shoot Belle Syms or put a knife in her or one of a hundred other more familiar ways of disposing of someone?"

"Well, for one thing, it's nice to avoid a weapon that might then be discovered; but for another, maybe because those ways *are* familiar. Off a tower in the middle of the night — that has us sitting here talking about it. The method rather than the motive."

"True."

"I'll say this, though," said Jury, who was rising to leave, "if we discovered there was an imposture, it would certainly make mincemeat of an alibi dependent on that eight-to-early-A.M. time frame for the murder."

"It would. Problem is —" Brierly paused.

Jury stood, waiting. "What?"

"I haven't got an alibi to make mincemeat of."

Brierly got up and walked with Jury to the front door of the station. "That's some car you've got there." He nodded toward the Bentley parked by the curb. "That's police issue, is it?"

"My other car's a Jaguar XKB." Jury took out the keys and twirled them round his finger. "See you."

25

"Chief Inspector Brierly hasn't got an alibi because he hasn't found a suspect," said Melrose Plant.

"Right. They haven't located the man she was with. He doesn't have form; any fresh prints found in the room didn't turn up anyone with a record; the hotel people didn't get a registration plate number, and nor could anyone identify the car itself."

"What about her husband?"

"The husband might be a suspect, although I got the impression from Blanche Vesta he really loved Belle."

"And she left him. Rage is always a good motive."

"Yes, but why would he choose that peculiar way of killing her?"

"Why would *anybody*?"

Jury had returned to Ardry End after leaving the Northampton station. They had wandered around the grounds, visited the barn and its occupants, argued yet again about Aggro/Joey, and were now sitting in the living room, having a drink before dinner.

In answer to Plant's question, he could only repeat what he had said to Brierly.

"A *distraction* you're suggesting?"

"Yes. It's possible. Or maybe the killer is playing games, or has a flair for the dramatic . . . who knows?"

"If Belle Syms was being impersonated, police are looking for not one but two people. This other woman might have furnished an alibi, but she adds a danger."

"What?"

"When you include someone in your plan, you'd better be able to trust that person. And if it's murder, well . . ."

"Anyway, it's not my case."

"You keep saying that, but you keep doing things about it."

"I'm thinking more about Tess Williamson."

"I wondered if it could have been suicide."

"Possibly," said Jury. "It certainly wasn't an accident."

"You don't think she killed that child, do you?"

"No. She didn't do it. But I'm betting she knew who did."

"And she told no one, not even her husband?"

Jury frowned. "That was what finally got to her, I think: that she'd let Tom Williamson suffer. That she'd let him down."

Melrose gave him a look of disbelief. "You don't kill yourself because you've let somebody down."

"Maybe you've never been let down."

Melrose reached into his pocket for his cigarettes. "Mind if I smoke?"

"Mind if I mind?"

"Not at all." He removed a cigarette, lit up.

Jury's eyes followed the smoke scrim as Melrose exhaled.

"You know," Melrose, unbothered by Jury's longtime smoke-yearnings, worse than any alcoholic's need of a drink, said, "there's another side to her wanting to make her death appear accidental. I'm assuming, of course, she did this so that her husband wouldn't have to go through the shock of his wife's suicide. If that's what it was. Now, she's tried to save him from one thing only to drop him into another; and that is, he would never ever know what happened to Hilda Palmer. And now look what's hap-

243

pened: Tom Williamson wants her case reopened. He's never put any of it to rest. And sounds like he never will, unless you do something."

"It's down to me, is it?" Jury felt a little resentful.

"Well, it certainly doesn't seem to be down to Brian Macalvie. Macalvie, who's the only one with the kind of imagination to get beneath all of this, appears to be hung up on the woman."

Jury looked at Melrose, disturbed by what he said. He rose, went to the fireplace, kicked back a bit of sparking wood that had gotten free. He stood there. "I guess you're right. She should have told Tom what she knew."

Melrose leaned forward, elbows on knees. "So here she is, Tess Williamson, in a dilemma: not to tell her husband is to leave him forever wondering. At the same time, she's too ashamed to tell him because she's kept quiet about it for years. We look at this dilemma from our vantage point and it seems easily solved. Just tell him —"

"So we're back again to the question of who Tess Williamson was protecting. Assuming you're right. There were eight people at Laburnum on that occasion, two adults and six children."

"Devon police didn't think the presence of some other unidentified person was possible?"

"It seemed logistically impossible."

"Who was the other adult?"

"Elaine Davies. Tess's friend. She's divorced and looking for number two."

"Tom Williamson?"

"I'm sure of it. He isn't interested. He isn't interested in any woman but Tess. I doubt he ever will be."

26

Jack and Hammer
Saturday, 11:30 A.M.

Stanley was missing.

Jury and Plant walked into the Jack and Hammer just before noon to find a woebegone Diane being uncomforted by a chipper Theo Wrenn Brown, who was spinning his theory of the double-recent visit of a stranger to the Blue Parrot. "Man walks into a pub. Then again. Calling attention to himself —"

"Put a sock in it, Theo," said Melrose. "What happened, Diane?"

"I went to Sidbury early this morning to that new pet store that just opened along the main street. I wanted to pick up something for Stanley to wear when he gets cold at night. Of course, I took him with me. We were in the shop, looking at the sweaters, and Stanley was sitting right at my feet. All of a sudden, the shop assistant calls out,

'Madam, your dog!' I looked at her, then looked down, and saw Stanley was gone. Then she said, 'He nipped right out onto the pavement.' I ran out of the shop and looked in the direction she'd pointed and didn't see a sign of him. I hurried along the street; there were a lot of people; it seemed everyone in Sidbury had decided to shop that day. When I got to the corner I looked and looked and *still* didn't see him. So I ran back and got my car and drove up and down and around for half an hour. No sign of him." Diane stopped as if she'd suddenly hit a wall.

No one seemed to know what to say. A silence fell.

Irritated that he'd been cut off simply to hear this story all over again, Theo picked up his theory-spinning where he'd left off. "As I was saying, this man walked into the pub, did it twice to call attention to himself in order to set up his alibi."

"Alibi for what?" asked Vivian, who was sensibly drinking coffee.

"We don't know yet, do we? That's to come."

Vivian insisted, "It's been four days. If anything were to come, it would be here by now."

Jury, who had sat down next to Vivian,

247

said, "I'm really sorry, Diane. But why didn't you call us so we could help you search?"

"I did call Melrose. He wasn't home, or at least Ruthven couldn't find him. You were in Northampton. I got hold of Marshall, though, and the two of us drove over what seemed like half of Northamptonshire and saw nothing, no sign of Stanley at all."

Another sad silence ensued with another attempt by Theo to pick up the story of the stranger in the Blue Parrot.

Jury cut him off this time. "Theo, the man must have anterograde amnesia." He and Melrose had discussed this possibility.

"What's that?" asked Vivian.

"An inability to make new memories."

How Melrose wished he had it when the door of the saloon bar suddenly opened to admit Agatha and Lambert Strether. Leaving Strether to fend as he might (which he did by sidling up to the bar), Agatha wedged her way onto the window seat by Jury. "Your deliberations won't get very far, as you're not aware of what's happened." She smirked and removed a strange beaded cap, which she placed on the table. Then she fluffed her hair, which was all a big dust ball anyway, and paused dramatically. "You know where those smart little shops have opened just outside of Sidbury?"

Strether had shambled over to the table and placed a glass of sherry before Agatha. "Police all over, cars all anyhow. Quite a mess. Something's afoot! Aha!" Strether stood and drank his beer.

Jury waited. Nothing. "Exactly what's 'afoot'?"

Agatha sipped and set down her sherry. "It looks quite serious, people spilling out of doorways, all along Reacher's Road . . ."

"Wretch's Row!" Melrose sat up straight as a die, staring. "Who? Where?"

"There's been a shooting of some sort in the alley behind the shops, apparently. That antiques shop. Or, no, I think it might be that dusty little bookshop on the end."

Melrose and Trueblood exchanged a startled look. They said the name together: "Enderby?"

"Where's your car?" said Melrose to Trueblood as he scraped back his chair.

"Same place as always," said Trueblood, pushing out of his own chair. His antiques shop was right next to the pub.

"You won't see anything!" Agatha exclaimed, afraid they would where she hadn't. "You won't get past the police."

"He will." Melrose jerked his head toward Jury.

Jury was about to say something when his mobile started chirping. He rose and walked a few feet away from them. It was Wiggins.

"John McAllister, guv. I've found him."

"Good, where?" Jury took a seat at the bar. Scroggs was drying glasses.

"Lives in Hackney. He's an M.D., as you already know. Also a post-doctoral in Natural Sciences. Both degrees from Cambridge."

"What in hell is a doctor with two Cambridge degrees doing in Hackney? The whole borough's a veritable crime scene."

Wiggins chortled. "I wouldn't say that. It's just got a high population of immigrants, mostly Bangladeshi."

"It's also got Newham as a neighbor. I'm not talking about immigrants. Newham's and Hackney's jobless rates are worse than Alabama's."

"You mean the U.S.?"

Jury assumed that was a rhetorical question and didn't comment. He heard papers being shuffled against a background of traffic noise.

"Sorry," Wiggins said. "I'm in the street."

"Okay. See if Dr. McAllister's available anytime today. I can leave here right now."

"Right."

Jury shut the mobile and went back to the

table. Responding to Plant's "He will," he said, "Actually, he won't. I'm going." He pushed into his coat.

Melrose and Trueblood were astonished. Melrose said, "It could be a murder, for God's sake!"

"But it's not my murder."

"Then where are you going?"

"London. Can you drop me at the end of your driveway on the way to your murder?"

Half an hour later, Jury was in his car, heading for London on the Northampton Road when his mobile jittered again.

It was Melrose Plant. "I wish you'd get over here, Richard."

"Why? What's going on?"

"That chap's been murdered."

"Who? You say it as if we know him."

"Well, we do, in a sense. I mean it's Trevor Sly's chap."

Jury put his foot on the brake. Fortunately, this particular stretch of road was not heavily traveled. No one was going either way. He pulled over to the edge; the engine idled. "Are you saying they've got Trevor over there I.D.ing the victim?"

"No. It's more like Stanley is."

Jury's mind went blank, as if it had suddenly collided with anterograde amnesia.

Stanley. "You mean the *dog*?"

"Right. The dog. Diane's in a swivet."

The engine still idled. So did Jury's mind, for a moment. "What in bloody hell's the dog doing there?"

"He's in the alley with the victim. We're standing about here in a clump. We tried to talk to them — police, I mean — but can't get them to listen. Look, stop asking questions and just get over here. Where are you now?"

Jury told him.

"Well, you're only two miles away from the Old Post Road. Just drive on a bit, you'll see the sign at the next crossroad. We're in the alley behind Reacher's Road. It's right off Old Post."

"Why isn't Trevor Sly there, then? If you think it's the same man, Trevor's the one who saw him, not us."

"Trueblood and I tried to tell this inspector in charge but we can't get anybody to listen. The only one who's gotten up close is Stanley. Diane's having a fit. They'll listen to you."

"Why are you so sure — ?"

"We're not *sure,* except it's certainly possible. This victim more or less fits the description — but it's mostly Stanley."

Jury said all right, snapped the mobile

shut, threw it on the seat, and headed for the next intersection and the Old Post Road.

■ ■ ■ ■

WRETCH'S ROW

■ ■ ■ ■

27

The body lay in a narrow alley that ran behind the shops in Reacher's Road. A tall brick wall ran along the other side of the alley, separating it from an old garage and a row of lock-ups. The body had not been removed by the time Jury arrived. The delay had been caused by the wait for the doctor, who had been out with the Fanshawe hunt, meeting at some swank estate a dozen miles from Sidbury.

It was Detective Chief Inspector Brierly who had come again. He looked to Jury as if he'd aged between finding a woman gone off a tower and this body in an alley. He had deep dents between his brows, as if his worries had been multiplying for decades. He was accompanied by a sanguine and sandy-haired, gum-chewing detective sergeant named Crumley. Crumley did not look a bit worried, as if he always expected to find dead bodies in the alleyways of Northamptonshire villages.

Jury had gotten through the police cordon at the end of the alley by explaining who he was and that he wanted a word with the CID man in charge.

DCI Brierly was more than happy to listen to Jury, since he was getting little enlightenment from anyone else. Not a clue. "No ID," said Brierly. "No wallet, no keys, no cards." He looked down. "Just a dog."

It was Stanley. He lay as still as stone and looking ten times heavier, his head on the dead man's arm. Stanley looked as if he had decided to lie down and die himself.

Diane Demorney, at the end of the alley with Melrose and Trueblood and a clump of curious onlookers, looked as mournful as Stanley.

The dead man, who lay half in the alley, half on the back doorstep of Mr. Enderby's bookshop, looked poignantly young, thought Jury. He was dark and good-looking, or had been before life had drained from his face.

Although the doctor, whose name was Keener, had lately been with the Fanshawe hunt, he did not seem to Jury to belong to that particular social class. Dr. Keener seemed quite small-townish, careful, and smart. He chewed on the corner of his mouth, thoughtfully, as he hunkered down beside the body. He was wearing a suit and tie and a fedora. Jury found that almost quaint. Dr. Keener pushed the hat back and said to DCI Brierly, "I'd say he's been dead anywhere from three to six hours. Rigor is firmly established, but that only helps to a certain extent. Say fairly early this morning." The doctor looked at the back of the shops. "Since these shops don't open until noon on Saturday, no one saw him until shortly after. So that doesn't help much, either. You found bullet casings, you said."

Crumley nodded. "Three of them. A .38, looks like. Revolver. One bullet went into his back. Two others hit the road. Lousy shooter."

"Strange," said Dr. Keener, thoughtfully. Then he rose, giving Stanley a pat on his way up. "What about the dog?"

Crumley stopped chewing his gum. "Could be anybody's."

Dr. Keener chewed his lip and gave Crumley a chilly look. "Do you really think so, Detective?"

Trevor Sly was stepping out of a police car as Dr. Keener was stepping into his old

Morris Minor. Trevor, the center of attention for once, and not wanting to be (for once), was brought up the alley, his head down, as if the shooter might still be around and waiting.

Chief Inspector Brierly spoke to him, and Trevor nodded and looked down at the dead man. He shuffled his feet and mumbled something that sounded to Jury like "that's 'im." So Trevor Sly was the only person DCI Brierly knew of at the moment who had the slightest knowledge of the dead man before he appeared in this alley face-down.

Poor Trevor, thought Jury. They would have him going over every detail of the victim's appearance in the Blue Parrot; police would have Trevor at the station all the rest of the day trying to sort it.

That left Stanley. Jury gazed down sadly at the dog, whose eyes were following every movement of the crime scene officers. The whimpering sound he made lasted as long as had the zipping of the zipper that closed the victim in its dark blue body bag.

One of the men had tried to move Stanley out.

"Let him be," DCI Brierly had said.

"He's a dog, guv; he doesn't care this is a bloody crime scene. He'll muck it up."

Brierly said it again: "Let him be."

And they had.

Stanley sat, raising one paw, then the other, again and again, helpless to keep the body from being stowed in the mortuary van, and the van from driving off. He sat and watched it until the red blink of its turning signal disappeared into the Old Post Road.

Then Jury picked up the leash, gave Stanley's back a good rub, and said, "Come on." Stanley followed him obediently.

The huddled onlookers at the end of the alley were still held at bay by a police constable.

Diane Demorney's eyes were ordinarily as smooth and black as onyx. Now they were clouded. She had set down the bowl she carried around and was pouring water into it from her thermos.

Questions were coming at Jury from all directions: "Who —?" "What — ?" "Who was he?"

Jury said nothing, and nor did Melrose or Trueblood. They stood watching Stanley lap up water.

"I'm sorry, Stanley," said Diane, giving his head a rub.

Jury thought that for all of Stanley's misfortunes, it had at least got them to call

261

Stanley, Stanley.

A few months before, Trueblood had dragged Melrose to (as they called it) Wretch's Row because he'd heard one of the shops, St. Germaine, carried some fabulous French Empire antiques. This had turned out to be an inexact description, as the place was crammed with cheap reproductions. The tall, spindly armed proprietor, a Cuthbert Egg, could have been Trevor Sly's brother, with his long-faced, cunning look. He'd only to say "Ah, gentlemen, pleased, so pleased . . ." The slight lisp, the hands sanding each other, the trace of a limp, and the thin smile, made Melrose think he was back in the Blue Parrot.

There was a Mrs. Gooding, a grandmotherly type who dealt in antique quilts of satiny, velvety little squares and diamond shapes that hung all over her walls. The quilts had become quite fashionable in Sidbury, where they hung on any number of residents' walls, sweating out stuffing, unsuitable for anything but wall hangings.

There were the Feasters, husband and wife who both wore large dark glasses for some reason, hers outlined in bits of shimmer that could have been either marcasite or shreds of foil. They called their shop All

262

Requests Considered and sold "luxury," in the form of their services as event planners — births, weddings, funerals, and holidays. Melrose especially liked the funeral-consultancy.

Then there was a little cookery shop that sold overpriced tableware, pots and pans, table linens, and every sort of kitchen gadget. Did people really need battery-operated cheese graters?

The only shop they both liked was at the end of the row, a tiny bookstore called BookEnds, owned by Mr. Enderby, a mouse of a man who could have sat comfortably on a thimble, but who was usually sitting on a ladder-back chair behind his counter doing his "accounts." He wore round frameless glasses and a green eyeshade, although the shop was full of shadows and lit only by a few metal-shrouded incandescent bulbs. Mr. Enderby was unfailingly polite and soft-spoken and very honest in his pricing.

"Much too modest," Trueblood would say as he plunked down one thing after another from the floor above, where Mr. Enderby displayed a wonderful collection of Minton blue china, Wedgewood, and pressed glass; and unusual objects such as a marble egg with a strange, suffused inner glow for which Trueblood had offered a hundred pounds. Mr. Enderby objected. "Oh, my, no, that's much too much."

"Mr. Enderby, I deal in antiques. I know what things are worth."

"Well, sir, I don't want to cheat my customers."

A laugh from Trueblood. "Then you're running with the wrong crowd, Enderby." Here a nod toward the shops up the street.

As Trueblood loved the first floor, Melrose loved the downstairs, where he would sit on a stool and leaf through featherweight pages of an old Robert Louis Stevenson volume, or a fifty-pence paperback of Raymond Chandler. But he especially liked the long table back by leaded glass windows on which sat boxes of photographs and a stereopticon.

While Melrose slid brown and cream photos into this museum piece (wondering whose little dog this was and by what sea these arm-linked young women stood in bathing costumes), Trueblood floated about upstairs like a bat looking for God knew what but always finding something rather remarkable which he would bring down and argue up the price. A miniature dollhouse (if dollhouses could be said to be miniaturized) complete with tiny bits of furniture and family, including a black dog not much bigger than a cinder; or a child's delicate tea service of very thin china that Trueblood thought was Belleek, ancient. When he paid 500 for the dollhouse and 150 for the tea set, Mr. Enderby pointed out once again that the provenance was uncertain. The china was unstamped and undated.

"You put too low a price on things, Enderby," argued Trueblood, who would never agree that he was overpaying, not even to Melrose.

The shop was never crowded, never more than one or two other customers, and often he and Trueblood were the only ones. Melrose was so concerned that the shop might close for lack of business, that he had suggested he would like to invest in it or even become a silent partner. "You see, books have always been a hobby of mine." Books had never been a hobby; they were a necessity.

Mr. Enderby had been quite pleased by this offer and had told Melrose that he would keep it in mind. Melrose knew he wouldn't.

Melrose loved the shadowed aisles, the atmosphere of dust and desuetude, the little fireplace in which lumps of coal burned intermittently, reddening up, turning to cinders, going out. Mr. Enderby, behind his counter in the shadows, head bent over his "accounts," seemed to Melrose always in danger of going out himself.

He and Trueblood had been to Enderby's bookshop only the past week. As Trueblood stood negotiating, Melrose had looked up from his stereopticon to see misty waves of rain coming out of nowhere, as if from an uncertain and questionable sky. Like Mr. Enderby's china, unstamped, undated.

Mr. Enderby had not been taken away for more questioning, DCI Brierly having been apparently satisfied for the moment with Enderby's statement, a statement amounting to very little. He had not even been the one to find the body on his back step.

"Mr. Enderby," said Jury, when he had gone into BookEnds with Melrose, "customers use the back way in, do they?"

"Yes. Not often, as there's no reason to be going through the alley. But my shop, being the end one, well, a person might find it easy just to park his car near the alley's end and come in. I've got book displays all along the side of the shop in the windows, and someone looking at the windows might come to the end and just decide to pop round to the back door instead of walking back to the front." He shrugged and fell silent, as if words failed him or were meaningless.

They were gathered round Mr. Enderby's counter-table, Melrose and Jury sitting on tall stools as Enderby sat in his chair, his books closed in front of him. He drummed his fingers on them.

Jury said, "He'd been in the area for a few days, apparently, and he was looking for the Old Post Road, so there was something or someone in this neighborhood he wanted to see."

Mr. Enderby removed his glasses and wiped the lenses with a square of silky material. He looked thoughtful. He said, "That inspector asked me if I knew anyone round here might be expecting a visitor, anyone saying, 'my cousin, my nephew, Gloria's husband,' you know, somebody turned up or expected. Just trying to jog my mem'ry, he said." Mr. Enderby put his glasses back on, adjusted the earpieces. He folded his hands over his small belly and shook his head. "No. Nothing like that I remember."

"What about Stanley?" said Melrose.

They both turned to look at Melrose, settled on his stool. He said, "Was anyone expecting Stanley?"

■ ■ ■ ■

Someone was, as it turned out.

Her name was Hildegard Tallboys, and Melrose was perfectly happy that Stanley had not reached his destination.

They had found Miss Tallboys because they had, on the off chance of finding out how Stanley fit in, gone to each of the shopkeepers and asked about pet owners in the neighborhood of Reacher's Row and Crutches Close on the other side of the Old Post Road.

Here there were small, boxy, many-hued houses, poorly placed, as if a child had walked away after tossing down his building blocks.

Number 13 was a dingy gray with dark green trim outside. Inside, the lighting was dim, which was just as well, since it helped to hide the unattractive, bulky furniture and the old, rather sinister wallpaper with its dark ivy rolling upward like tentacles. There was a great deal of tile — in the entryway, around the windows, and outlining the fireplace in which sat a single-bar electric stove, unlit. The room was cold and clammy and reminded Melrose of one of London's underground public toilets.

He eyed the mantelpiece with its display of stone cherubs on either end, each holding a fold of stone cloth. He bet they wanted mittens.

Miss Tallboys had followed the direction of Melrose's gaze. "Got that pair across the way at Germaine. Quite pricey, but I expect they're worth it."

Melrose expected they weren't but just sipped the tea that had been served them from a pot covered by a rose-colored crocheted tea cozy. She could have served it boiling from Hell's Kitchen and it would still have gone cold by the second sip. But then Hell had long frozen over in number 13, Crutches Close. Miss Tallboys simply had a knack for a chill.

Anyway, the tea had been served only to keep the talk of the murder going. Hildegarde Tallboys was disappointed by the flimsy findings of Scotland Yard: Jury was not exactly a font of information. She had, after all, gone to all of this trouble with tea. Nor had she apparently given any thought to the fate of the dog that the victim had, as nearly as they could work out, been there to deliver to her.

"Miss Tallboys, how did you contact the dog's owner?"

"Well, I didn't, did I? I'd no idea who the

owner was. Are you saying it was this man that got murdered?"

"I don't know. If you didn't contact the owner, what was the procedure? How did you come to pick this dog?"

"I haven't seen the dog, have I? So I don't know if it's the same one."

Blood out of stones, Jury thought, his tight smile wanting to snap. "Right. But you contacted *someone.*"

"Yes, of course. It's this Web site, PetLoco. My friend Louise Phenn told me when I said I thought I should have a watchdog."

"PetLoco?" Loco, he gathered, being some misdirected form of "locator." "How did this organization work?"

"You go on their Web site and have a look at pictures and read the bit about the dog. They're all up for adoption, and not on the cheap, I might say. Seventy pounds mine cost. Looked to be a nice Staffy."

"Staffordshire terrier for seventy quid? Sounds like a bargain."

"Well, you have to pay extra for delivery. Another fifty."

"Wouldn't it have been much cheaper just to go to a shelter in Northampton?"

"Need a car, wouldn't I? Anyway, I don't like those places. Noisy, all the barking and everything. Depressing."

"So you paid and arranged for the dog to be brought to you here."

She nodded, lifted the rose cozy from the teapot, lifted the lid, replaced both, satisfied. "Don't think I don't know about scams. Louise checked this PetLoco out quite thoroughly before I sent any money. No, they're on the up-and-up. The dog was to be brought here this week. That is, the one just past. They said they could only assure the exact day forty-eight hours ahead of time because of schedules of the people who bring them. I expect they get volunteers from nearby. I mean, no one's going to bring a dog all the way from London, are they?"

"Given today's Saturday, you should have heard from them at the latest on Thursday, shouldn't you?"

Curtly, she nodded. "Heard nothing, looked at the Web site, rang them. Well, they were just as surprised as I was. Woman I spoke to looked up the records, said the dog should have been delivered Tuesday or Wednesday. I asked who was supposed to bring it; well, they wouldn't give out any names, would they? Very cloak and dagger. Like that writer, John le Carré."

Melrose liked it that she pronounced it La Car.

271

She sniffed. "Silly waste of time."

Melrose frowned. "What is? Waiting for the dog?"

"No. Those spy books. People chasing all over Europe. Life's not like that."

Melrose cleared his throat of mild laughter. "Actually, I imagine Mr. le Carré thinks life is." He was careful to pronounce it La Car.

"Oh, he just goes and makes it all up. Pack of lies."

"No, he actually worked for MI6 before —" When Melrose saw Jury giving him a smile that definitely didn't reach the superintendent's eyes, Melrose shut up. He'd only wanted a bit of entertainment to take his mind off his toes, which were frozen to stubs.

"Do you think we could have a look at that Web site, Miss Tallboys?"

"On my computer? It's not working properly. Anyway, I didn't use mine, I used Louise Phenn's. Mine, it takes hours to get anything on it with pictures. You know what they're like. Slow as Moses."

"Then I think we'll be going. Thanks very much."

It was then she raised the teapot. "There's a bit more, if you'd like another cup."

Melrose couldn't believe she'd still be

pouring from that pot. Tea, like revenge, was best served cold.

They both got up. At the door, Jury said, "What about the dog, though? I mean, assuming the dog who came with this man is the one. He's certainly a Staffordshire terrier."

"Oh, my goodness, no. A dog that's been involved in a murder. I think not." They stood in the open doorway as she added, "That place'll have to return my payment, of course."

"But the dog will have to be returned too, to them."

"I expect police'll have to take care of that, won't you? It's not my dog, is it?" The door closed with a cold little thud.

28

Jack and Hammer
Saturday, 3:00 P.M.

They had, after the events in Wretch's Row, retired to the Jack and Hammer, where Melrose and Jury had told them the story about the chilly interview with Miss Tallboys.

Mrs. Withersby, with a fag caged from Trueblood in the corner of her mouth (another stuck behind her ear), leaned on her mop and listened and smoked.

Stanley was lying under the table on a comfortable old quilt Diane had bought for him.

Agatha, enjoying another Shooting Sherry, was scandalized by the quilt's being a "genuine Goodings" and Stanley on it. "That quilt probably cost twice what the dog did! It's an antique!" That Diane was not defending this profligate purchase annoyed Agatha far more than Strether getting buzzed at the bar and probably trying to sell Dick Scroggs a useless investment.

Vivian, puzzled, said, "If this man had merely been enlisted to deliver him, why would Stanley have been so upset? He was ready to jump into that van with the dead man."

Trueblood fiddled with his Montblanc, rolling it over his fingers like a small baton. "How do we know Stanley is the dog this Tallboys woman was to get?"

"We don't," said Melrose.

Jury drank his Adnam's, set the glass down, and said, "You can debate this, but I've got to go to London."

"But wait," said Vivian to Jury. "What do you think?"

"That you're all a bunch of nutters." The voice was not Richard Jury's but Mrs. Withersby's, she of pail and rag. "Every one of you lot's got a mobile phone. 'E told ya" — here she nodded toward Jury — "that there dog might of come from this PetLoco place and not one of you tried to ring it. All you lot do is sit around and talk."

They all turned to look at Jury again.

He slid a couple of pound coins from the table and handed them to her. "Have a drink, Mrs. Withersby. Me, I'm off to London. They can sit here and talk."

■ ■ ■ ■

He was in the car and heading for London on the M1 when his mobile stuttered in his pocket.

"John McAllister, guv. Says he'd be free to see you whenever you get back."

"Good. I'm on the M1, just passed the Dunstable turn off."

"Okay. I'm looking at this file. The shot of the kiddies who were at Laburnum. This one where they're standing together. Strachey's pretty tall. John's the shrimp of the lot. Funny little kid. Why did his parents have him wear those black-framed glasses, poor kid?"

"He didn't have parents, Wiggins. He had minders."

"I was reading her testimony. Tess Williamson didn't call him 'John.' She called him 'Mackey.' "

Jury felt a sudden sense of desolation, the way you do sometimes on a Sunday when your street is empty of the usual foot traffic.

"Tell him seven. And try not to get bogged down in afternoon tea and the D'Sousas."

"Ta, guv."

Jury floored the accelerator, thinking of

the empty street, thinking he could outrun
it.

29

Clapham Common
Saturday, 4:00 P.M.

But there was to be no serving of tea and cheesecake on this Saturday afternoon in the D'Sousas' spartan little house on Clapham Common. Both of them, mother and daughter, looked thin as rails, as if they might have stopped eating altogether.

The only interesting thing Wiggins had seen was a coal-black cat, who had been, understandably, playing dead, curled up by the cold grate, until Sergeant Wiggins walked in. The cat followed him to the sofa and sat pushed up beside him, paws nudged under chest, blinking.

"Nice cat," said Wiggins, who wasn't much of a cat, or for that matter a dog, person. But he gave the cat a few strokes. The cat was clearly happy to have something living and breathing in the room.

"Sookie seems to like you," said Colleen

278

D'Sousa. "What was it you wished to see us about, Sergeant?" Then, "Oh, would you like a glass of water?"

Wiggins had never understood "water" as a social refreshment. "No, thanks." Then he went for it. "But a cup of tea wouldn't go amiss." His smile included Sookie, who purred. Jury would have killed him. But he was frankly already bored with these two, and had it not been for the cat, he'd be snoring inside of five minutes.

Colleen and Veronica, her daughter, looked at each other in an almost startled way. "Tea? Why I don't believe we have any, do we, Veronica? You could have a look."

Wiggins thought he was hearing things; his eyes widened to moons. This was England, wasn't it?

"That's all right, Miss D'Sousa," he said as she began uncertainly to rise to search the kitchen. "Just have a seat, please." No tea was to have serious consequences. He slapped his notebook onto his knee and clicked his ballpoint into action. "Twenty-two years ago —"

"Surely, you're not going to question Veronica about that Hilda Palmer girl?"

"Dead girl, Madame. Hilda was only nine."

Colleen raised her hand to her rolled-back

dark hair, as if to press the upsweep into place.

Wiggins hadn't seen a do like that since *Mildred Pierce*. It had looked terrific on Joan Crawford.

"I can't think why —"

Wiggins held up his hand to stop her. "It's Veronica here I'd like to do the thinking. Now, miss, you were the one in the game who was 'It,' right? Meaning you had to be the finder."

Nodding, she said, in her surprisingly little-girl voice, "Leaning against the big oak. I was to count to a hundred. You've got to do more than just ten or twenty, don't you, to give everyone a chance to find a proper place. And the grounds of Laburnum were very large. It was boring to have to do all that counting."

"You peeked, then, didn't you?" Wiggins had flipped to a page in his notebook, as if he were confirming this bit of information that he'd just invented.

Insulted for her daughter, Colleen said, "She did no such thing!"

Wiggins looked from one to the other. Veronica D'Sousa was by now thirty-one or -two years old. Still living with Mum, poor lass. Being controlled with a heavy hand, if the missus had to react to his comment as if

Veronica were still nine.

"Pardon me, but you weren't there." He turned again to the daughter, smiling conspiratorially. "Everybody peeks, don't they? God knows I always did."

Seeing it was a bit of a game, just as hide-and-seek had been, she said, "Only a tiny bit. Just the once. I was looking to see if Kenneth had gone behind one of the big stones there in front of the house. It was just a quick look-see. I didn't see him, or anybody else, but that's where he was in the end."

Wiggins absently stroked the cat, who was snoozing now. He said, "But there was somebody, miss."

She frowned. "No. They'd all hidden."

"Not Mrs. Williamson's friend."

"What do you mean?"

"Mrs. Davies. Elaine. She was sitting on the stone bench, reading."

"I guess she was, yes."

"Were you often at these outings Tess Williamson organized? What I mean is, was it always the same group of kiddies?"

"Always. Except, of course, if one or the other of us had a cold or for some reason couldn't be there, but that almost never happened. Mrs. Williamson organized such treats. Like taking us to the winter fun fair in Hyde Park at Christmas. Or to Fortnum's for tea. Mostly, it was to Laburnum; we loved going there. Sometimes we'd all meet at their house in Knightsbridge."

"Hilda was always one of the group, was she? Yet she wasn't much liked by the other —"

Colleen, of course, interrupted. "Do you think this is appropriate, Sergeant Wiggins?"

Wiggins smiled what Jury liked to call his Death's Head grin. "I wouldn't be asking if I didn't."

"Really, Mum. You'd think I was still nine years old!"

Wiggins was glad to see Mrs. D'Sousa sink back into her chair. Perhaps Veronica wasn't as much under the thumb of her mother as he'd thought.

Veronica went on. "Hilda was a hard little girl. Even cruel. But often it's better to keep such people around than to get rid of them."

Wiggins appreciated the thought that went into that. "Keep your enemies closer, right? You mean because she could be vengeful? I heard she was."

"That, but also because she could be a scapegoat for us."

That surprised Wiggins. It surprised Mum too, obviously.

"Veronica! What a thing to say!"

Veronica smiled round at her mother. "Mum, don't you think we should give Sergeant Wiggins some coffee? As we don't have tea? Can't you organize that?"

Without a question, Colleen rose and said she'd see to coffee, yes.

Again, Wiggins half-smiled at his note-book. He said, "What do you mean by that, miss, exactly? The 'scapegoat' business?"

She thought rather seriously as she looked round the room, as if trying to fix on something. "Well, sometimes you can tell, say, if you're amongst friends, if one of them is a little put-out by another, or angry — I mean on a deeper level, something not showing, like anger or envy on some level she doesn't show. Johnny, say, mightn't like something about Kenneth, but wouldn't come out and say it. Or Mundy being ir-ritated with Mrs. Williamson. We could turn the resentment onto Hilda." She paused. "I'm not explaining this well, for it sounds mean. It was really very subtle. And Hilda more or less wanted it —"

"The misdirected anger?"

"Yes. Some people are like that. It makes them feel important. That's not to say, though, that Hilda wasn't awful. She was. She was a troublemaker, an insinuator, if you know what I mean. The person she

283

hated most was Mundy Brewster. But Mundy's looks kind of protected her — she was so beautiful. Arabella Hastings didn't fare as well; she had a terrific crush on Kenneth Strachey, and Hilda was always embarrassing her in front of him. But the one she picked on the most was Johnny. John McAllister, because he was so defenseless. He had such an awful home life. Both his parents dead, living with guardians. He needed protection. Mrs. Williamson was his protector —"

"Here we are," said Colleen, surging back into the room with a silver-handled tray.

Wiggins was sorry to see her; the last few minutes had been interesting.

She set about pouring coffee. There were no biscuits. So he wouldn't linger over coffee. Wiggins drank up, patted the cat, said he had to be going. With her mother present, Veronica probably wouldn't be as forthcoming.

But she insisted on seeing him to the door, and outside of it, to the top step.

Wiggins said, "My notes tell me you're an actress."

"Not much of a one. I've had just tiny parts in a couple of West End productions. I'm afraid I don't have what it takes."

She set that out there, of course, to be

told that she did. Wiggins said, "I wouldn't agree to that at all. The way you hold yourself, the way you move — no, you're an actress, all right. You're a first-rate" — Wiggins almost said manipulator, but it sounded offensive — "organizer."

At first she seemed not to understand; then she said, "Oh, you mean . . . of Mum?"

"And me." He smiled. "Thanks for the coffee." Down the steps, he turned. "Next time, have tea." He winked and waved and was gone.

30

Hackney, Plaistow Street
Saturday, 7:00 P.M.

Jury hadn't been in Hackney in some time. It appeared to be going through the process of gentrification that had overtaken other boroughs, only here Jury wondered at its chance for success. Bulldozers were plowing under eyesore council flats; one sat idle in an enormous vacant lot that would soon make way for a high-rise and probably smart little terraced houses to be sold or let to workers from the City.

Hackney was always getting ripped off. There had been many instances of council corruption over the years. It would sell a street of little businesses to a developer or a private party with the assurance that everything would be rebuilt and restored to the owners. That, of course, never happened.

Hackney was skirted by Newham and Tower Hamlets, a triple play in unemployment. To Jury, a London enigma. He lived in Islington, which had its own poor pockets. But he felt surprised by Plaistow Street, and naive in his surprise. He'd lived in London all of his life; he'd been with the Met for thirty years. He was used to the city's differences. But he'd never felt as if he'd passed out of one century into another as he did turning the corner into Plaistow Street. It was like crossing over an unsealable crack in the city's surface.

The coming of darkness didn't help, as it was a street of lamps that didn't work. No leafy trees, no front gardens. It was a street of small, profitless shops; lock-up garages; gray, Soviet-style council flats; and red brick low-rise ones, narrow houses in a street already almost claustrophobic in its narrowness.

On the corner was a pub whose name he couldn't make out because the sign had been virtually rubbed out by wind and weather, and the light above it broken. "Three"-something was what he made out. Three globes or three bells, possibly. It must be fairly popular, given the buried laughter that dug its way to the surface whenever a customer went in or out the door. The few people he saw were mostly going in and mostly by themselves. Not a pub for the owners of the condos and flashy flats in Canary Wharf or the other refurbished haunts of Docklands.

On an impulse, Jury walked in, and silence dropped like a blanket of fog. The pub was not overflowing with custom, but it was a comfortable and wieldy crowd of under two dozen. Some looked at him with faces as bland as a custard; others glanced around and looked away. He sensed something other going on than the usual Saturday-night revel; they were here for something that made him, for some reason, uncomfortable.

A lightweight conversation resumed after Jury had made his way to the bar, but he knew from the few words floating past him that it was meaningless. The barman raised his eyebrows in question rather than asking Jury aloud what he'd have. Jury ordered a whiskey, as it would be quicker to drink than a pint, and stopping here longer would make him that much later in seeing Dr. McAllister.

But he did find out the name of the pub: THE THREE TUNS was carved into a long piece of wood that hung above the bar mirror.

As he paid for the drink, he wondered what a man with John McAllister's qualifications was doing living in Plaistow Street. Perhaps he lived at the other end of it, and the other end would bring Jury to a pleasanter world of trees and gardens.

But 31 Plaistow Street was not far from The Three Tuns. It was not one of the council flats, but still a red brick block of flats, probably on the Social's list of low-rent living space.

The big glass door in front looked thick enough to be bulletproof, but wasn't. The rows of metal letterboxes were well worn, largely from fingers working hard to pry them open. MCALLISTER was 31B, the number the same as the building number. Not a terraced house with a garden flat, then. Far from it.

Inside was a lift on the right. Jury was surprised to see one, and this one was presently serving as a lounge area for a group of five kids dressed largely in baggy pants, ink, and bits of metal randomly stuck into eyebrows, earlobes, noses, and lips. Even the one girl in the group hewed to that dress code, except for the baggy pants. Hers were tight jeans. She wore a great deal of makeup, purple lipstick being the most pronounced.

When Jury paused for a second, looking at the lift, one said, "Broken, mate" and pointed to the OUT OF ORDER sign taped to the door. Jury was looking at the old-fashioned floor indicator, the metal arrow on the slate that jerked from one number to another. It was now on the top floor, number six. Jury nodded toward the arrow.

"Stuck, in't?" said the girl.

"Then why are you waiting?"

"Us? No. Just talking."

Jury nodded and proceeded up the stairs. He was surprised the dun-colored paint wasn't graffitied over and that the iron railing was secure in its sockets. Someone was taking decent care, he thought, although there was still that stairwell smell of beer, chips, and the dole.

He reached the third floor and found 31B. A howling fight was going on between the occupants of the flat directly across from McAllister. He was tempted to break it up when McAllister's door opened.

"Superintendent Jury? Hello." McAllister put out his hand.

If John McAllister had been a funny little kid back in the days of Laburnum, he was no longer. He was well over six feet, nearly as tall as Jury, and handsomer. He still wore black-framed glasses, but instead of hiding his eyes they served to enhance them. Eyes and hair were a brown the color of cognac, the hair, lit from behind, especially beautiful, as it had been in the snapshot Jury had right now in his pocket, the one taken at Laburnum.

The flat's door led onto a narrow hallway, which in its turn led on to what would have served as a living room if the flat were used in the ordinary manner. But any comfort that might have been in the living room had been dispatched. In its place stood a long counter where microscopes were positioned among other instruments Jury was unable to identify. There were also piles of plain folders and stacks of books. Most of the books, though, were shelved, and there were two walls full of shelves. The only concession to comfort was one overstuffed chair in a corner, a lamp, a side table, and more books. Otherwise, seating took place on one of the tall metal stools lined up at the counter.

It was on these that they sat, elbow to elbow, leaning on the counter.

"My sergeant tells me you've a boatload of degrees."

John McAllister laughed. "He exaggerates. I have a couple."

"An M.D.?"

"Not much of one."

"Where did you get it?"

He smiled. "Oh, the where was all right.

Cambridge. I meant that I don't practice in the U.K."

"Why did you get an M.D. then?"

McAllister looked at his hands, as if they'd failed him.

Surgeon's hands, Jury thought, practicing his stereotyping. But they were, either a surgeon's or a pianist's.

"I expect I wanted to do some good."

"Did you?"

"Some."

"You're modest, Dr. McAllister. According to someone who thinks a great deal of you, you've done much more than a little."

"Who could that be?"

The look was genuine puzzlement, as if he couldn't imagine anyone thinking a great deal of him.

"Madeline Brewster."

"Mundy? My God, how is she?"

"Fine. Wondering how you are."

Again, he looked down at his hands. "I should keep more in touch with her."

"Yes, you should." Jury pulled the snapshot from an inside pocket, placed it on the counter, turned to face McAllister. The children were lined up, the large sarsen stone and one end of the front of Laburnum as backdrop.

John McAllister picked it up, adjusted his

glasses, and started to say something, but didn't. He shook his head. "Twenty-two years ago this was. And yet it was yesterday."

"Is it that clearly printed on your mind?"

He nodded. "I'll never forget it."

"Describe it, then. What happened."

His thumb and index finger went to his glasses again. Jury wondered if this gesture was what a gambler would call a "tell."

"I'm going to disappoint you, I fear, because I can't describe much. When the game got going, we took off on our separate ways. I ran around the side of the house to the woods. I do recall Mrs. Davies peering at us or me from the bench where she was sitting when I passed. Then I climbed one of the laburnum trees."

"If you were up a tree, you'd have had an excellent perch for viewing what happened."

"Sorry. You see the branches hanging over that section of the garden veiled part of the terrace steps and the pool where Hilda went in. I didn't see it happen; I didn't see her."

"You didn't like her, did you?"

McAllister's smile was thin. "I couldn't stand her. I probably hated her more than the others did. I expect I was a target for her because I was the smallest. I just looked like a little kid." His voice was very sad.

"You *were* a little kid, John."

He nodded. "I was, yes."

"You chewed some of the laburnum seeds and got sick, right?"

"Yes. It was a pretty stupid thing to do. Cytosine is an alkaloid."

Jury smiled. "A little too stupid."

McAllister looked at him.

"What I hear about you is that you were extremely sharp and very knowledgeable in science and maths. Anything that had to do with flora and fauna, you knew. So you obviously knew about the toxic properties of the laburnum — seeds, bark, all of it toxic."

"Everybody knows that. I wanted to see how toxic."

"Why would you decide during a game of hide-and-seek you needed to know the toxicity?"

McAllister shrugged. "I don't know, other than curiosity."

Jury didn't believe him. "Were you trying to make yourself sick so you'd be noticed?"

The look was unwavering. "To get attention?"

Jury nodded. "Until something far more attention-getting happened."

John McAllister looked away. "If I hadn't been thinking only of myself I might have prevented it." He turned back. "Charging Tess Williamson with Hilda's death was unthinkable." He was fiddling with the microscope, as if he wanted to escape into its complex properties. Then he shoved it aside. Silence.

"Why are you living in Hackney, Dr. McAllister? Why in Plaistow Street?"

That took him by surprise. "Why?"

"A man like you, a distinguished career, superintelligent, degrees in two disciplines, why would you choose one of the most impoverished and violent boroughs in London?"

McAllister thought for a moment. "I'm a research scientist. My surroundings don't mean much to me, so here is as good as there. And I spend a lot of time in Kenya. I'm not here that much."

"That you're here at all surprises me."

McAllister laughed. "Does ambiance matter all that much to a policeman?"

"We're not talking about ambiance. All of that shouting across the hall. Doors slamming. The neo-Nazi group downstairs, the general racket?"

John McAllister's tone was slightly exasperated, but he didn't want to show it. "I'm not sure what this has to do with Hilda Palmer's death — would you care for a coffee?"

"Thanks, yes. I'm not sure either. That's

why I'm asking."

McAllister had walked back to the small kitchen area and was taking out a large tin of Kona coffee and a Jura coffeemaker. Obviously, Dr. McAllister was not living in Hackney out of need. He measured some beans into the machine's grinder. It was quite loud, but it then went about its work without further help.

"You're talking in circles, Superintendent Jury; my point is why would you be asking me questions about my flat, and your point is pretty much the same. Why would you?"

Jury smiled and watched the expensive machine quietly dispense two cups of coffee.

McAllister said, "Let me tell you something about myself."

"I wish you would."

John poured coffee into two cups, took one to Jury, asked if he wanted cream and sugar.

"No, thanks."

After John reseated himself, he said, "The people I lived with when I was a kid: they were, or she was a distant relation of my mother. Of course you know my parents both died in a motor accident. One moment, they were there; the next moment they were gone. In an eye blink. I was six.

Both of them just gone. It's hard to understand what that feels like to a six-year-old."

Jury said. "I do. I lost both of my parents
during the war. Not at the same moment,
but not far apart." He did not add that he'd
been a baby, remembering nothing of his
father and with false memories of his
mother. He'd fantasized years of his life
with her.

"Then you can understand that I was not
at all fond of my guardians or grateful to
them or anything. Our house was cleared
out and sold. I was taken with my suitcase
to the house of these people in St. John's
Wood. I don't know who delivered me
there, like a package, and then went off.

"These people, my guardians the Lewises,
were polite. They showed me my room,
which was much bigger than my old room.
The house itself was much bigger, grander,
I suppose. We had dinner. I think mine was
minced beef and chips. I sat and looked at
it without eating. Would that upset them so
they'd offer something else? 'Come on love,
there's tart and custard for pudding.' They
didn't say that; I just made it up. They
didn't say anything about me not eating."
He looked up at Jury. "Do you think they
were being diplomatic, then? Not insisting?"

"No. It sounds more like they were uninvolved."

Jury had apparently said exactly what John had believed, and he seemed to relax a little. "It would have made no difference if they'd offered me a dish of Smartees or a chocolate soda or anything at all. I don't think there was a taste in the world I could have tolerated sitting there where my mum and dad weren't.

"The grounds behind the house were large. There was a stream; there was a pond. The pond was quite deep, or looked so to me. Dark and deep. I must have visited it a hundred times, each time thinking I'd just throw myself in. I expect it would have been a nice place for swimming, but I couldn't swim. I drowned in it a hundred times.

"One day I was standing, looking down at that pond, at its dark depths, into which I had jumped so many times in my mind's eye, when she came up behind me and I heard her say,

'Hello, Mackey.'

I turned, and there she was, Tess Williamson, with that smile. It was so welcoming that it literally made up for all of the lack of welcome over the past months. What a smile."

He smiled himself, and every trace of disappointment vanished. "And that 'Hello,

Mackey.' I said, 'My name's John' and would have felt utterly stupid and awkward except Tess Williamson took all the awkwardness away. She could do that; she could neutralize bad feelings. She took every trace of failure I'd ever felt and blew it off the way you blow filaments from puffballs.

"She said, 'I know. Your name is John McAllister. Mine's Tess Williamson. Do you mind if I call you Mackey?'

"I shook my head so hard I must have looked like a dog shaking off water. I nearly cried I was so happy that someone wanted to call me Mackey. She told me she was having a party at her house and would I like to come? I had no idea how she knew my guardians, nor did I care. I just said yes.

"So she took me by the hand and said, 'Then come on, Mackey.' "

He went on to tell Jury of his introduction to the Williamsons' house in Knightsbridge and how he met the others — Mundy and Kenneth, Arabella and Veronica and Hilda Palmer. How, in the next two years, Tess supported him, championed him, encouraged him to do great things. She realized his potential, even at his young age, and was determined he would become, well, what he had become. Although Dr. McAllister didn't put it that way at all.

He told Jury that when Tess was accused of the murder of Hilda Palmer all of them knew it was a lie. No matter what police said, no matter what evidence was turned up, they knew it was impossible. The hand of God would more likely have come down and pushed Hilda Palmer into that dry pool than the hand of Tess Williamson.

The evidence had turned out to be completely circumstantial and spurious. And she wasn't indicted and all five of the children went crazy with joy.

And except for Mundy Brewster's mother, who had some sense, the others — the Stracheys, the Lewises, the Hastingses, Mrs. D'Sousa — none of them would allow their children to see Tess.

" 'Tainted' or other things equally stupid was what they said. 'You just can't be sure about her' was what they said. And of course the Palmers, or at least Mrs. Palmer, would never give up thinking Tess had shoved Hilda into that pool.

"The day she died — that was the darkest day of my life. It was like my parents dying all over again. The funeral. Mundy had a Morris Minor. She was sixteen or seventeen by then; she could drive. We all arranged to meet, even Veronica got away from her mum. Mundy picked us all up and we went.

Nothing would have kept me from going. I had to say good-bye, you know, properly."

Silence fell. Jury finished his coffee. He could think of nothing to say and finally rose to leave.

"Thanks, John. I'll see myself out."

He did. With his hand on the doorknob, he turned at McAllister's voice.

"Without her," he said, "I'd be nothing."

Across the hall, the fight appeared to have been stalled or stopped.

But there was a new noise that Jury couldn't place. He couldn't determine the source, the direction from which it was coming. It sounded like growling and then whining. He thought at first the sounds were coming through the broken window at the end of the hall.

As he walked toward the stairs, he reached the lift with its OUT OF ORDER sign. The growls and whines were coming from the lift shaft. The floor indicator stood now on number four. He was on three. He pressed the down button and waited. The sounds were not loud, but chilling — the scuffle and whine — as the lift passed his floor without stopping.

Jury made for the stairs at a run.

The kids were still in place on the ground

floor. They didn't see him coming, not at first, because their attention was totally fixed on the floor indicator. They were watching the lift descend. They were clearly excited. And then one heard Jury approaching and said something quickly to the others.

Jury had his ID out and yelled, "Police, hold it right there!"

They broke like a covey of quail, banged through the door, flew out into the street. By the time he reached the street, they were gone off in different directions.

He went back to the lift whose doors had opened on carnage: two dogs, one dead — or nearly. It moved its rear legs as it lay on the lift floor as if it were running or trying desperately to. It was torn and bloody, one ear bitten off. Jury thought the other, bigger dog, the victor, he supposed, would charge at him as he took off his coat, but the dog merely sat, staring glassy-eyed past the lift door.

Jury put his coat over the downed dog and called emergency and told the operator he wanted the Met's Animal Control Unit and then the RSPCA. Then he got out McAllister's number, called him upstairs. "Do you keep any medical supplies around your flat?"

"Yes. What's wrong?"

Jury told him there'd been a dogfight in the lift. "I'm on the ground floor."

"Bloody hell. Not again? I'll be right there."

Again?

Jury had thrown his coat over the downed dog because he thought he saw him shiver. The other dog growled deep in his throat but did nothing. They were both pit bulls, unfairly matched, to say nothing about being illegally kept. The one whose breath was so shallow it didn't even raise the surface of the coat was much smaller. He wondered who would bet on the smaller of the two to win this fight.

The big pit bull still stared out at nothing and seemed transfixed. He too was streaked with blood.

"Jesus," said John McAllister, setting down a bag like any G.P.'s except it was ox-blood tan, not black. It opened like a drawbridge. McAllister very carefully put his fingers on the dog's neck. "Still alive, but just barely." He got out bandages, ointment. With a hypodermic he drew something from a small tube, flicked the needle, and inserted it under the dog's skin. "Anesthetic. This guy must be in some pain."

"There were five kids standing here when I came in —"

"I know. I've seen them."

"You said 'not again.' You mean this has happened before?"

"Lift dogfights." He was swabbing one of the cuts across the dog's side. "I keep reporting them. But the RSPCA can't seem to do anything without seeing it actually happening." He shook his head. "What a bloody awful racket."

"That one doesn't look too hot, either." Jury nodded toward the other, bigger dog, who was lying down now, next to the one McAllister was treating. He held the dog's neck with his hand. It was covered with blood.

Jury rose, leaned against the wall, turned, and stood there, as if facing the wall were somehow a child's penitential pose, as if he were himself one of the kids responsible for this.

"Sorry, Superintendent," said John McAllister. As if he were echoing the thought.

Headlights were hurled across the big glass door. Car doors slammed. People, four of them, rushed in: two from the Met, two others presumably from the RSPCA. A stocky man and his equally stocky female partner.

Jury produced his ID, told them about the fight in the lift. They nodded, apparently used to it. The first man spoke to McAllister, said "Good," gathered up the badly wounded dog, handed Jury the coat. The woman managed to get a harness round the other, this dog not really protesting, and led him out. The man followed with the smaller dog.

They watched the van pull out from the curb and drive away. They stood in silence for a minute. Then Jury said, "There's a pub down there that interests me. I'm not sure why. But it smacks of lawlessness."

McAllister laughed. "Three Tuns? I know what you mean."

"Care to go along for a drink? I feel the need of one." He checked his watch. "It's only eight."

"Good idea. I'll get my coat." He picked up the pigskin bag.

"Someone's going to have to clean that up." Jury nodded toward the lift. "Who's the building super?"

"Man named Moggs."

"If you have a number, I'll call him."

"I'll get it." McAllister went toward the stairs.

Jury looked into the lift again. It had its complement of graffiti; there'd been some attempt to wash it off, unsuccessful. He was about to take out the wedge so that the door could close, thought better of it, and left it there. He retaped the OUT OF ORDER sign to the door, wondering if there were signs on each floor. Looking at the streaks of blood, the bit of flesh that he decided was the torn ear of the losing dog, he guessed that the people in this building were no strangers to violence. Still, someone who passed this scene might be appalled.

John McAllister was back, wearing a dark Burberry and carrying a piece of rug or carpet. "It's left over from the living room I had recarpeted awhile back." He placed it over the floor of the lift. It no longer looked like the site of a massacre.

As they walked the two blocks to the pub, Jury said, "What do you do in Kenya?"

McAllister turned up the collar of the pricy raincoat. "Medicine and research."

"Madeline Brewster told me you were with Médecins sans Frontières."

"I wasn't with them, but something like it called DOCS, meaning 'doctors on call.' Mostly though I just work by myself with several small villages. Most of the diseases are common and preventable. All they need is vaccination, for the most part. The grinding poverty is pitiful."

"You travel and work at your own expense?"

"I have money; Tess Williamson left me quite a lot, so I can afford it. But sometimes I wonder if what I see in Africa has desensitized me to stuff like that." He turned his head to nod back at his building.

"No," said Jury. "It hasn't."

McAllister opened the door of the pub onto a raucous scene that was more of a brawl than a group of people gathered in a public house for drinks and chat. There were twice as many customers now as there had been at Jury's first visit, a few couples with kids small enough to have bypassed their bedtimes; the men at the bar seemed to be clinging to it rather than merely standing.

When the two of them walked in, that fog of silence that Jury had experienced before descended again. Talk simply stopped; movement was stayed. They were all glancing and glancing away, as if they'd seen and hadn't seen Jury and McAllister walk in.

"I've wondered," said John McAllister, amusement in his voice, "if a certain kind of person always knows when a cop turns up."

Talk resumed, but not in the brassy way it had been going forward; the customers were moving around, but warily. The two men's presence had damped things down and only their absence would bring back the original noise level.

McAllister found a small table in the window. Jury said, "What'll you have?"

John said, "Bitter," and pulled some notes from a pocket of his raincoat.

"No way, Doctor. Drinks are on Queen and Country."

As Jury passed up to the bar, eyes followed him; the low-key conversation stopped. It was like being in the middle of some pantomime. He ordered two pints of the pub's best bitter, put down the money, and when the drinks were drawn, carried them back to the table.

He set down the pints, pulled up his chair, and said, "Can you tell me anything else about the other kids who were at Laburnum? You must've known them rather well."

"Except for Mundy, not really." He shrugged. "I only knew Hilda as someone who liked to pick on me. That's the only side of her I ever saw."

"Maybe that's the only side she had. I have yet to hear anyone speak well of her."

"Hilda liked to hold people hostage. Her forte was gathering information and threatening to use it."

"What did she know about you?"

"Nothing. There was nothing to know. With me it was just continuous needling. I was a small kid, the runt of them; I wasn't clever, like Kenneth. I wasn't good-looking like Mundy or talented like Veronica, or wonderfully devious like Arabella." He smiled. "If you can call deviousness a virtue."

"Devious? That sounds like Hilda Palmer."

McAllister shook his head. "Arabella was very different. She wasn't out to hurt anyone. Hurt was Hilda's work ethic." He took a small drink of beer.

"Veronica D'Sousa I haven't talked to; my sergeant was doing that this afternoon. We haven't yet found Arabella Hastings. What were the feelings between the five of you — I'm leaving out Hilda, since everyone seemed to dislike her. I take it the rest of you weren't fast friends."

"No. Nothing so simple as that. I liked Ken, at the same time I envied him his social ease. I had a crush on Mundy. I think she had a crush on Kenneth. But then so did Veronica."

"Mundy didn't have a crush on Kenneth Strachey. She had one on you."

"Never." He laughed.

"She did, trust me. You said Veronica was clever."

John nodded. "She was quite a gifted mimic. She'd do screamingly funny impressions of some of the teachers. I remember her mother. Very domineering. That may be why Veronica never married."

"It occurs to me that all of you are in your thirties, but none of you ever married, except for Arabella Hastings."

"You're right about the rest of us, as far as I know. It's odd, especially when it comes to Mundy. You'd think she'd have been snapped up long ago."

"Perhaps she didn't want to be." Thick as two plants, thought Jury, smiling to himself. Bad as Melrose Plant.

"What? Oh. I'm guilty of typical male stereotyping. All women want to marry." He thought for a moment.

"My sergeant spoke to Kenneth Strachey, found him very personable. He lives with another chap, in the theater or wishing he were. So here's more stereotyping: Did you think Strachey's gay?"

McAllister made wet circles with his glass. He'd drunk very little of its contents. "You probably think I'm comatose, but I never thought about it one way or another."

Jury smiled. "Not comatose. Just uninterested." Jury watched as a man, short and paunchy, got out of his chair and started toward the toilets, then stopped and went to the bar.

"We've been sitting here for over a half-hour and no one has gone back there to that alcove where the phone and the toilets are located. This place is crowded. And the crowd has been putting away a lot of beer."

John turned his head, looked toward the "Gents" and "Ladies." Then looked back at Jury. "What do you mean?"

Jury got up. "Be back in a minute." He started away, then turned back to the table. "Have your mobile with you?"

"Sure. You want to use it?"

Jury shook his head. "I want the number." John gave it to him, and Jury tapped it into his own mobile. "Sit tight." He walked back to the alcove and went through the wooden beaded curtain. The men's room was on the left. He knew it was empty but knocked for show, in case anyone out in the pub was watching him. And he was fairly sure a lot of them were. He walked a few feet toward the telephone on the back wall. There he found a staircase. He went down six steps, where the stairs turned and continued on to the bottom. Here, a man with big biceps wearing a black T-shirt that said ARSENAL was tilted back in a chair. There was a door beside him.

He looked up at Jury, chewed his gum more thoughtfully, and said, "You lookin' for somethin,' mate?"

"Just curious. What's through there?" Jury nodded toward the door.

"Private party." As if he had something to grin about, Arsenal grinned. He had a mouthful of bad teeth.

"Private party? Not anymore." Jury reached for his ID and his mobile. "It just turned public."

The supercilious grin turned humorless. Arsenal took a step back, probably thinking that Jury was reaching for a gun.

Jury nodded toward the door. "Open it." He spoke into his mobile. "John, come down here. There's a staircase next to the Gents." He snapped the phone shut.

One minute later John McAllister was down the steps.

Jury nodded at him. "This is DS McAllister —"

John flashed an ID at Arsenal, who barely looked at it.

"Now, open up, Aladdin."

His back still to the wall, no doubt so he could keep an eye on them, the big man reached toward the knob and pushed the door open.

There was so much smoke the room could have been on fire. But the smoke was only a canopy from endless cigarettes, cigars, and, no doubt, weed.

Jury didn't know what he'd been expecting to find, but not this; and then he wondered why not this? For it was the natural progression from the lift dogfight.

A dogfight as one ordinarily saw or imagined it: a lot of booze, blood, money, and drugs. Some looked up when the two of them came into the room, but as the fight was in progress, the shouts of encouragement to the two dogs in the pit went on unabated. The pit was perhaps fourteen or fifteen feet wide, with wooden walls. The dogs looked to be some version of American pit bull terriers or Staffies; given their entanglement at the moment, it was hard to tell.

What astonished Jury was that all of the noise was coming from the persons in attendance and practically none from the dogs themselves. Both of them looked to be losing, given the bloody cuts on them. Neither looked as if he wanted to be here, although they both had probably been starved, or worked on a treadmill until they were exhausted, or otherwise "trained" for the fight. Jury had a hard time wrapping his mind around this scene. He yelled into the crowd "Call it off!" He got onto his mobile to call the Met.

John McAllister shouted "This is over!" as if he'd been enforcing the Animal Welfare Act every day of his life. There were two teenagers near him, both wearing black cords and T-shirts, arms swamped with tats. The bulb in a metal shade hanging over the pit swayed and picked up the glint of knives. There was a blurry movement of an arm coming up and just as suddenly dropping at the sound of McAllister's voice.

"Drop it!" He had a .22 cradled in his hands. The knives were dropped.

When neither of the handlers made a move toward the dogs, John grabbed up one of the breaking sticks about a foot long and an inch in diameter. He jumped into the pit and was about to force it into the jaws of the dog when one of the handlers came up behind him. John turned fast with the stick and landed it on the man's neck. Then he wedged it into the mouth of the dog that had his teeth clamped on the other dog and drove him back.

The crowd around him was seething and yelling. Jury held his ID up in the air and called out "Special Ops Unit. We're holding all of you on felony charges. Who's the organizer of this event?" He wasn't expecting an answer. But that announcement sent some of the crowd surging toward the door where Arsenal was, presumably, on the other side and used to this noise.

Both of the dogs were being held now by their owners or handlers, and it would have been very hard to pick out the winner. They were in awful shape, bleeding and with broken bones. Neither looked as if he were eager to carry on.

"You got no rights here, mahn," said the referee, a Nigerian Jury thought by the look of him.

Jury didn't bother answering that aimless charge. He had Animal Control on his mobile. He told the person at the other end what was going on and where and asked them please to send their officers as soon as possible.

Then he called the police.

"Too bloody bad we can't take the lot in right here and now," said Karl Mindt, the man in charge of this unit from the SPCA as he watched the dogs being carried on small stretchers out to vans. "There are kids here; that's obviously illegal. Not the best way to get them to relate to the animal world. We'll collect all contact information for all this crowd; we can deal with most of them later. You know this goes on all over London. That kid's parents should be put away." He nodded toward a bewildered-looking boy of seven or eight.

"I never would have guessed at fights in lifts."

"Fights just about anywhere these idiots can find an enclosure. Trunk fights are popular. Throw two dogs in the trunk of a car and drive around for a while. Teens don't bother as much with guns now. Instead, they lead these dogs around. They're status dogs. And if one gang meets up with another, they can always let the dogs go at it. Superintendent, I've been at this job for thirty years and will never fail to be amazed at what people think to do to animals. If such ingenuity were put to work in support of the public good, the crime rate in this city would be halved."

Jury watched the officers at the door letting the onlookers file through only after they'd collected their contact information. He said, "You know these online adoption services?"

"I do. Some of them serve this business." He looked toward the pit.

"Ever hear of one called PetLoco?"

"PetLoco?" Mindt looked disgusted. "No, but the name alone gives me the creeps. Marsha!" He called over to one of the officers at the door. Marsha was taking down names. She was a burly-looking woman who Jury would want on his side, not on his opponent's. She moved toward them.

"Marsha here knows a lot about those Web sites."

But not about PetLoco, she said. "In general there's a lot of trafficking in APBTs. You know, American pit bull terriers."

"PetLoco's site doesn't give an address," said Jury. "I'd like it."

Marsha honked out a laugh. "No surprise there. They don't want us turning up to go through their computer files. Brixton's a good bet, since a lot of this shit goes down there."

"Can't go into files without a warrant, too bad," said Karl Mindt.

"I don't give a rat's ass about a warrant anymore."

Mindt laughed. "Better be careful with that talk, Marsha. This guy's a superintendent, Scotland Yard."

Marsha looked at Jury with eyes the color of steel balls. "Not a rat's ass. Sir. Nice to meet you." She walked away, then threw back over her shoulder, "I'll get you an address, Superintendent."

Jury called out his thanks, checked his watch. He was astonished that only an hour and forty-five minutes had transpired since he had set foot in John McAllister's flat. "Mr. Mindt, thank you very much for getting here so fast and taking care of this. I've got to be somewhere." He put out his hand. Mindt shook it.

Jury said to McAllister, "John. If this had been an audition, you'd have been hired by the police several times over. Are you used to facing down crowds like this? People like this?"

John McAllister was wiping blood from his hands. "The dogs', not mine. I've come on the odd fracas in Kenya." He didn't elaborate. "Ready to go?"

"Bloody right, I am."

31

Dr. Phyllis Nancy was still in the white-walled rooms of the mortuary, gazing down at one of London's latest victims. In this case, a middle-aged woman. Dr. Nancy was speaking into a recording device that hung by a wire hooked to a pole.

Phyllis Nancy was the most dependable person Jury had ever known. She was a legend. She was always where she said she'd be and when she said she'd be there. If she promised an autopsy report by 3:00 P.M., it was in the hands of the person who wanted it by 3:00 P.M. Given the uncertain and chaotic lives of those who did the policing of London, Dr. Nancy was really that old cliché: the lighthouse, the beacon in the dark. One wag, a detective known for his drinking habits, called her "the cocktail hour."

"As dependable as five o'clock."

There were many reasons to love Phyllis Nancy, and Jury knew all of them.

She stopped speaking into the recorder, replaced it, and saw him. "Richard." Her smile was bright. Then she added, after looking him over, "Where in the name of God have you been?"

"A dogfight." He told her how that had happened.

She was taking off her green cotton top. Beneath it she wore another shade of green in a cashmere sweater. "You look in need of a very stiff drink."

"How'd you guess? If you're finished." He held up the folder Macalvie had given him. "I want your opinion on something."

She tapped the device she'd just been speaking into. "After I write this up. I promised DS Stevens by ten." She looked apologetic.

Jury checked his watch. "It's almost nine-thirty. Can you do it in a half-hour?"

She looked at him as if he'd missed something. "I've got to."

Jury laughed. "Meet you at The Feathers when you're done, okay?"

The bright smile returned. "Fine."

The Feathers sat across the road from New

Scotland Yard, near the St. James Tube station, an old two-story pub that served good beer and passable food.

Phyllis came in spot on 10:10. He didn't need to ask if she'd gotten the autopsy report to DS Stevens. She crawled up onto one of the high stools. "Half-pint of Guinness, thanks." She pulled over the file folder by his arm. "I'll have a look at this while you're gone."

He went to the bar, looked back to see her reading, head down, chin propped between hands.

When he was back, setting down their mugs, she said, "This was twenty-two years ago, Richard. Why — ?"

"Why am I into it now?" He told her about meeting Tom Williamson, about his visit to Laburnum with Macalvie.

She looked down at the last page of the report. "The main theory was accidental death. It says she suffered from vertigo." Phyllis frowned.

"I think it was murder. So does her husband."

She nodded. "So should the coroner, it seems to me. First, a fall down a flight of long steps wouldn't have enough momentum to take you all the way to the bottom; you probably wouldn't get more than halfway down. It would take, really, a headlong dive in order to carry yourself to the bottom of these stairs. A running leap, something like that. If you just lost your balance, or if you, say, swooned, as one might from vertigo, the fall would have you landing much farther up the stairs. And given the evidence here" — she turned the pages and pointed — "the blood, the shoes, the flowers scattered down the steps didn't reach the bottom. If she'd wanted to kill herself and make it look like an accident there are far better ways to do it. Why choose one that in all likelihood is not going to work?"

"That's what Brian Macalvie said."

"Your cop friend in Exeter?" When Jury nodded, she added, "I agree with him. So accident isn't likely, not with the way she went down. Why was that put forward as a theory?"

"Because there wasn't evidence of anything else, and because of her vertigo. Her history of that automatically made it appear to be accidental. She'd taken falls before, fainted, swooned, whatever." His mobile twitted. He fished it out. "Jury."

Melrose Plant told him they were all at the Blue Parrot: Trueblood, Vivian, and he.

"You're really trying to find this other dog?" He was looking at Phyllis, whose eyebrows went up, fractionally. Jury smiled. Phyllis had never been one for the grand gesture, not even in the matter of a raised eyebrow. Then she rose, gestured toward the bar, and walked off. Phyllis would do that: absent herself from others' space.

Jury listened as Plant told him about the various views in the matter, then said, "Aren't you going rather far afield, gathering at the Blue Parrot —" Melrose interrupted, telling him the Blue Parrot *was* the field, after all. "You think there was another dog . . . oh, yes, the Tallboys's dog . . . Now it's a dead dog?"

Phyllis was back with two packets of salt and vinegar crisps. She sat down, opened one as Jury said to Melrose, "You're ignoring the obvious." When Melrose asked why he'd do that, Jury answered, "Because it's more fun."

Squawk from Melrose. "Look, if you don't mind," said Jury, "I've got company. We're having a right rave here, so let's continue this discussion after you've found a dead dog. 'Night." Jury snapped the mobile shut, stuck it back in his pocket.

Phyllis had been trying not to overhear, turned away from him, looking out over the room, but now she turned back. "Dead dog? Is that code for something?"

"No. It's really a dead dog. I mean, it would be if they found it. Which they won't. Melrose Plant." As if that explained the call to the world. "My friend in Northants. It has to do with the man who was shot in the alley." Jury explained the whole Stanley-Staffordshire terrier thing.

"Great heavens." Phyllis ate a crisp and turned this over in her mind. Then she said, "This woman went off the tower on the Monday night and the man was shot on Saturday? Do you think their deaths are related?"

"I can't imagine how." Jury took a few crisps, ate one, drank his beer.

"Well, try. I mean, this is a little town in Northamptonshire. I'd guess the homicide rate in — what's the name?"

"Sidbury."

"The homicide rate in Sidbury is minus zero. Now here are two murders in five days. And you don't think there's some connection?"

Jury took another drink, ate another crisp. "Well, when you put it that way . . ."

"You're supposed to be on a week's holiday. Lord, but you have the most interesting holidays. Who needs Greece? Who needs Rome?"

"Not when they have you." He munched on another crisp.

32

Putney
Sunday, Noon

The address that Karl Mindt had passed along to Jury from his coworker Marsha was a terraced house conversion-to-flats in Putney.

Jury and Wiggins were standing in front of the panel with mailboxes located on the ground floor just inside a set of glass doors. The logo printed on a card and taped to the mailbox of number forty-one showed a dog whirling about, mouth agape, tongue out, eyes crossed, as if the dog had gone crazy.

"It thinks itself pretty cute," said Wiggins. "But are they sending out the right message with that logo?" Wiggins rarely employed an ironic tone.

"I don't think they're sending any message at all. I've an idea they don't have one."

"Number forty-one. Sounds like four

326

flights up. No lift."

"We'll steel ourselves."

The same "crazy dog" card was taped to the door of number forty-one. The expression on the face of the young fellow who came to the door was not unlike the dog's: mouth slightly open, one eye wandering off. His uninviting greeting was "Yes?"

"We're here about your pet-locating service."

"Sorry, the office isn't open to the public. We're an online service. If you want, the Web address is on our card." He produced one from his shirt pocket, handed it to Jury, started to close the door.

"If you want," said Jury, sticking his foot between sill and molding, "our address is on our card too." Jury shoved his card toward the kid.

"I don't —" Then both Jury and Wiggins had their IDs out.

"Bebe!" the kid gave a yell, turning toward wherever Bebe was. The door opened wider because his hand, which was on the knob, turned with him.

Jury could then see a frizzed ginger-haired head poking out of a door on the left.

"What?"

"Police."

The rest of Bebe followed. Jury thought

her a bit old for the tight jeans, the cherry red, off-the-shoulder top, and the spike heels.

Bebe in turn looked at the card and IDs.

Wiggins said, "And you are — ?"

"Brenda Bluestone." From her jeans pocket she pulled what resembled a Nicorette and popped it into her mouth. Jury was familiar with Nicorette from the hard days of stopping smoking. He felt a moment's sympathy for Brenda Bluestone. "They call me Bebe." She continued. "I can't think what you'd want. Has somebody complained? We're a sorting business; we can't help it if a person is unhappy —"

"We can exchange information inside, Miss Bluestone." Jury smiled.

Once in the PetLoco official office, she said it again, "I can't think why police would come round."

There was a big metal desk with a computer facing away from Jury and Wiggins where Bebe-Brenda sat. Along the wall behind her was a long shelf that held three more computer screens. The screens were filled with small pictures of dogs, cats, and the odd rabbit. Their locations were given below their pictures. Jury could make out a few: Bermondsy, Shoreditch, Fulham. On the wall above them was a big poster featuring some two dozen dogs.

"What's this about?" asked Brenda while Jury and Wiggins were settling in folding chairs that Wiggins had pulled over from the mismatched ones around the room.

"Just a few minutes of your time, Brenda."

"Call me Bebe," she said with a twinkly smile they were unlikely to get again.

Call me Ishmael. Jury said, "Thanks. This is just a routine inquiry that has to do with a woman in Northamptonshire — Sidbury's the name of the village — who'd contacted you for a dog and had paid for a Staffordshire terrier. Her name is Tallboys. Hildegard Tallboys. Could you look up that account?"

"You understand we have a strict confidentiality policy —"

"Oh? Did that Maltese on the screen behind you have you sign a document?"

She was not amused. "Our clients don't want their details given out. It's like adopting children. See —"

"It's nothing of the sort."

A flush spread up from Bebe's throat over her face, lending her even more color. With great reluctance she typed in the client's name, at least Jury presumed so.

"Yes. That's her. Crutches Close, Sidbury, Northants."

Jury nodded. "According to Miss Tallboys the dog was to be delivered on Tuesday, but wasn't. Your records must show that."

Bebe kept looking at the screen, as if something would appear that would help her situation. "Well, not exactly. The delivery of the dog was never confirmed."

"But it's been six days. Don't you follow up? Miss Tallboys claims she called that evening to tell you and also the next morning. And that she got a runaround." This was Jury's invention.

Now Bebe's frown deepened as she brought her face closer to the monitor. "I don't understand why there's no record of such calls."

"What about your coworker, the one who answered the door?"

"Nigel? Oh, he wouldn't know anything. He doesn't handle listings or deliveries. He's a kind of night watchman, isn't he? He sleeps here."

Jury wondered about this but didn't pursue it. "Who was the person in charge of taking this dog to its destination?"

"We don't give out —"

Wiggins got in on this one. "Miss, we're from Homicide, not the RSPCA. This is a murder investigation. There's a dog was to be delivered to this Miss Tallboys by Thursday. That didn't happen."

"But two other things did," said Jury. "A man was murdered near Crutches Close, and a dog, a Staffordshire terrier, was found wandering around by a resident. The dog was wearing a leather collar with a metal name plate: STANLEY. Jury was aware that for the length of this recitation, Brenda Bluestone was sinking like the Wicked Witch of the West, after Dorothy tossed a bucket of water on her. "So who was the handler of Miss Tallboys's Staffordshire terrier?"

Bebe was recovering quickly. At least enough to post a denial. "I've no idea what you mean."

Jury rose. So did Wiggins. "Then we'll have to come back with a warrant."

"And then," added Wiggins, "you'll likely know what we mean."

Bebe waved them back down, temporarily furious. "Listen, it'd be my job if I gave out information like that. Instead, why'n't you ask Digby? That's Digby Horne, he's the owner of PetLoco. Tell him about the warrant, I'd like to see his face." She gave them the details, address in South Kensington, and phone number. Wiggins took it down in his notebook.

"You can tell us how this operation works, can't you?"

"Oh, sure." She sighed, back on safe ground. "People look at our Web site, see a dog or cat they like and contact us —"

"Where do you get these animals?"

"Well, people get in touch with us if, like, their dog's had a litter and they can't find someone to take the puppies; or people bring in strays or homeless dogs. Then there's hoarding. You know about that?" She looked from Jury to Wiggins, hoping to educate them and regain some of the popularity she thought she'd lost. "Some of them are in awful shape, poor things."

"Then you must have a vet on call."

Pause. "We do have someone who takes care of that sort of thing."

"Not a licensed veterinarian, right?"

She just shrugged. "Digby covers that, seeing the dogs have places to live."

"Where are the dogs housed?"

"Different places around London. Then there's this farm in Kent where they go, some of them. See?" She turned the framed photograph around so that they could see it. There was a farmhouse off to one side and farm animals dotting the far, green fields. Closer in, there were dogs who appeared to be playing.

Wiggins had been taking notes. He said, "Where exactly is this farm in Kent?"

Bebe's eyebrows stitched together. "I'm not sure. Digby has that information."

"You mean it's not in your database?" When she shrugged again, he asked, "What about the London addresses?"

Again, the head shake. Jury left it at that, went back to the operation. "After a person contacts you, then what?"

"Usually, they say they'll think about it. Then perhaps the next day or day after, I hear from them again saying they'd like the particular dog or cat. Not cats so much, they're not as popular. I have them either give their credit card details or, if they want, post me a check. Then it's turned over to Digby."

"Mr. Horne? And he takes care of getting the dog to a handler and having it delivered. It's pricey though, that, isn't it?"

"A little. All of our fees are posted on the Web site."

"So your customers don't see the dogs before they actually buy one?"

"Well, you can see, we're not set up for meets and greets, so to speak." Her little laugh went nowhere as she looked about the room.

Jury looked with her. The drab walls, the cracks in the ceiling. Not exactly what you'd call a shelter.

"You don't do a background check?"

"Of the dogs?"

"The people."

"Not exactly. But we tell whoever's making the delivery that if anything looks, you know, iffy, they're to stay right away from it and bring the dog back."

"Do you have a number of people who make these deliveries?"

She seemed to be weighing the price of giving out this information. "Yes. The people who do the deliveries seem to like it; the pay is good. Depending on the location, they could get anywhere between thirty and a hundred quid. Plus expenses, of course."

"This is added to the customer's tab."

"Of course."

"So it would cost at the very least eighty or ninety pounds. Depending on how much the adoption costs in the first place."

"That's right. But it's almost always more. The more desirable dogs are in the hundred-pound range. Then plus delivery . . ."

"How much is your overhead?"

"Oh, now, I can't give out that information. I can say, though, that it's not much. There's rent and our salaries. And the equipment. Electric, phone, all of that. But Digby's had this place for years as a private residence. It's only the last five or six he decided to run PetLoco out of it. So the rent, it comes under regulated tenancy."

Dirt cheap, then. Jury got up. "Thanks very much for your time, Bebe. You've been a big help."

As she rose with them, her expression said she wasn't sure whether that was good news or not.

Jury nodded toward the blowup picture behind her of the dogs. "Are those the dogs you have now for adoption?"

"That's right. Well it might be a wee bit out-of-date, as we get twenty to thirty clients per week."

"You get that many adoptions?" Jury was still looking at the picture; there were probably thirty dogs listed.

"Oh, yes. Digby works very hard at this."

"We'll try and reach him."

"You won't be back tomorrow with a warrant?" She sounded hopeful.

Jury shook his head. "I don't think so."

"Sounds a bit dodgy to me, sir," said Wiggins as they walked the few feet to the car. "You think she was being truthful?"

"Truth as Bebe knows it, Wiggins. The person to talk to is this Digby Horne. Speaking of dodgy." They got in the car,

Wiggins driving, and pulled out into the road. Traffic was heavy. "When we get back I want to ring DI Brierly about this. He's in charge."

Wiggins guffawed. "But you don't yet know what 'this' is."

"Some of it I do. Careful!"

Trying to enter a circle, Wiggins nearly closed daylight between their Ford and the fender of a vintage Rolls.

"That was close."

"That? Missed him by a mile, sir. Never fear."

Jury always feared.

It was Wiggins's mobile that rang this time. "Wiggins. Yeah. Good, I'll tell him." He put the mobile beside him on the seat. "That was Fiona, sir. Andrew Cleary returned a call, said he was in London and could meet you this afternoon. He's staying at Number Eleven Cadogan Gardens."

"Good. She has his number?" When Wiggins nodded, Jury said, "Call her back and tell her I'll be at his hotel at four o'clock."

Wiggins made the call, then tossed the mobile into the well between the seats.

Jury said, "Did you notice her reaction when I mentioned Stanley? Bebe, I mean."

"I did. She went pale."

"No wonder. To know Stanley gets her a

little too close to murder."

"How'd'you figure that?"

"Because Stanley was one of their dogs. They should update their poster, Wiggins."

33

New Scotland Yard
Sunday, 1:30 P.M.

"His name was Roy Randall," said DCI Ian Brierly. Jury had called him from the office. "Lived in Wembley-Knotts. There was a torn envelope with that information on it in — you'll never guess — his shoe. Folded and refolded and stuffed into the toe. That's why we missed it at the scene. What's written on the back of it looks like instructions or directions, more — 'M1 . . . X Nth . . . SB' . . . might as well be in code, right? 'TL . . . TR . . . OPR . . .' et cetera."

"Possibly Motorway? Exit Northampton? And *SB* could stand for Sidbury, couldn't it?"

"Yeah. But why would any driver who had any acquaintance with the U.K.'s motorways have to remind himself of motorway one? Or Northampton, for that matter? I mean, if I said to you, 'Take the M1 to

Northampton,' would you have to write it down?"

"No, but I'm a detective. Scotland Yard." After Brierly laughed, Jury went on. "Mr. Randall might have suffered from anterograde amnesia."

"You're kidding?" Brierly paused. "Oh, you mean that turning up again at the pub — the Blue Parrot? Forgetting he was there before? I'll be damned. So he was writing notes to himself?"

"Probably."

"But why stick the thing in his shoe? It makes no sense."

"It makes perfect sense if you might forget you wrote the note. Maybe he put it in his shoe so he wouldn't have to depend on his faulty memory. Every step he took would let him know there was something there."

"Good lord." Brierly sighed. "Anyway, when we put his name in the system, what turns up is he lost his job and went on the dole six months ago; he got laid off from his job at a BP station. Also, he had form: petty thieving, exposing himself in public lavatories Half-dozen citations. Looked a lot scruffier too. Long hair, facial hair —"

Jury was surprised. The dead man hadn't looked the part.

Brierly went on. "Not married, lived

alone. House was empty. The neighbors said Roy had gone off on a short holiday. According to them, he did have dogs. Sometimes, more than one."

"I can help you out there: the dog appears to be one of PetLoco's animals."

"That Internet service that the Tallboys woman was using?"

"Yes. A service of questionable provenance. The owner is a guy named Digby Horne." Jury gave Brierly the details of his address and number. "You'll want to talk to him, I think." Jury told him what had gone on in the PetLoco offices.

"Thanks. I've got somebody in London right now. I'll tell him to look up Horne. Where does he get these dogs, then?"

"According to the girl who handles the adoptions, they come from various sources. People who want to get rid of their animals, maybe a litter of puppies; strays. My guess is the dogs are discards, maybe from gangs who use them as weapons, maybe dogfights. Some may be genuine rescues, and by that I mean nothing altruistic, just opportunistic. Lost dog, Digby collars it, stows it, sells it. The man's charging as much as a hundred quid; he's got a hundred percent profit, since he doesn't have to buy the dogs in the first place. They get twenty or thirty a week adopted on average. At up to two hundred per dog, that could be four or five thousand per week. The overhead is minimal."

"I'm looking at the site now. Most of these dogs appear to be Staffies or some form of pit bull, APBTs. In all likelihood. Where's this farm they're touting as a place for a wonderful romp in the sun?"

"I doubt very much the dogs you see running around there belong to PetLoco. I doubt he'd go to the expense and the trouble. He'd have to drive to Kent — or have one of his handlers do it," said Jury. "But going back to Roy Randall. Was there anything at all to connect him to the Tallboys woman?"

"Not a scrap. Not the name, not the address, nothing."

"He was looking for the Old Post Road, Ian, so he had some destination in mind. No connection with Belle Syms either, I take it? Two apparently unconnected killings five days apart in a little place like Sidbury." Jury paused. "What about the Blue Parrot? Trevor Sly said he heard a shot. Did you find evidence of that?"

"Bullet casing? No. But that publican, Sly, was adamant that he'd heard one."

"Why the alley? Could this Randall have been in one of those shops?"

"Not according to the owners. They were all in a muck sweat about that, I'll tell you, afraid that it would link them to the shooting. Only Mr. Enderby didn't seem disturbed by that, I mean, that his doorstep was the one the poor fellow went down on. He was of course very disturbed this fellow had been shot. He's a nice old guy."

"Couldn't Blanche Vesta give you any more information about her niece?"

"No more than she told you. It's been a year, she said, since she'd seen Belle."

"Why did the niece see her now? I can't understand that."

"And nor can Blanche Vesta. There seemed to be no bloody reason for it."

"It might have been simply to show off that dress and those shoes. To make her aunt think she was successful."

"I guess that didn't turn out very well for her, did it?"

34

Bloomsbury
Sunday, 2:00 P.M.

"Mr. Strachey," said Jury to the young man who was holding a bundle of clothes to his chest. "My name is Richard Jury, New Scotland Yard." He had his warrant card out. "You spoke to my sergeant, DS Wiggins?"

"Sergeant Wiggins! Good detective. Make a good cook too."

Jury didn't want to visit that point for any length of time, so he merely smiled. "I'm sorry to disturb you on a Sunday. May I come in?"

"Absolutely. Don't apologize. That's what Sundays are for. People popping in. Otherwise, they're boring. I was just on my way to the dry cleaners with this lot, but it can wait." He deposited the clothes on a nearby chair. Among the browns and grays of jackets and trousers Jury saw a strip of black

343

jacquard with what appeared to be a deep pink lining. A smoking jacket? Yes, Strachey seemed to be the type.

"You know a dry cleaner who's open on Sunday?" asked Jury.

"Just until three P.M.," said Kenneth, ushering Jury into a large living room and depositing the bundle of clothes on a footstool.

From a cream-slipcovered sofa with its back to them, a strand of smoke was spiraling upward in magazine-advert fashion. The smoke was followed by a head wearing an enormous hat that reminded Jury of a bird of prey with its feathers and beads; shoulders dressed in lace and satin followed the hat, both rising over the sofa's back. "Police! Marve!" exclaimed the young man who wore this Edwardian ensemble with seemingly great enthusiasm.

"This is Austin," said Kenneth, last names apparently unnecessary. "We were just doing a scene from *Earnest*. Austin's into costume design and makes a wonderful Lady Bracknell."

Austin half-rose in a mass of pinkish brown ruffles, a high collar, and puffed sleeves in an elaborate tapestrylike material of pinks and browns. "Not quite as good as Kenneth's," he said.

"Austin," said Kenneth, "was hugely disappointed that he missed out on the police experience the other day. He was so looking forward to being grilled on where he was and what he was doing at such-and-such a time on such-and-such a day."

Austin smiled. So did Jury, who said to him, "I'm awfully afraid you're going to be hugely disappointed again, unless you happened to have been at a house in Cornwall called Laburnum twenty-two years ago."

"Bugger all," said Austin. "How completely unfair." He levered the rest of himself off the sofa, sighed, and removed his bird-of-prey hat, into which he stuck a couple of hat pins. He was of medium height, thin, almost starved-looking in a Romantic way. Wiggins had been right; both of these young men were delicately handsome.

"I'll just go out in the garden, then. But if you're serving the crème fraîche tarts for tea, expect me back." Austin took himself off through a French door in what Jury thought was an overabundance of swishness, part of which was caused by the many petticoats.

Kenneth called after him: "Take off Lady Bracknell and I'll take it to the cleaners with the rest of the stuff."

"Oh, all right," said the put-upon Austin, returning and crossing over to another room.

Jury said, "It looks like it weighs a ton."

Kenneth laughed. "I'm used to it. Let me have your coat and do sit down, Superintendent." Strachey directed Jury to a furniture grouping near the French door, a love seat and two dark wicker chairs covered in a pale, zigzag pattern of linen. The walls were white, the floors very dark.

"Thanks." Jury took one of the chairs as Strachey stowed his coat in a small cupboard near the front door. "You're a descendent of Lytton Strachey, I understand."

"Not I, Superintendent. Pop seems to forget that Strachey had no children. Any relationship with Lytton is very watered down. I mean, with his ten siblings, you're going to wind up with countless cousins, cousins who had countless children, of whom Pop claims to be one. But frankly, I don't think he's got the family tree down to its last leaf. He must read *Eminent Victorians* once a year."

Kenneth went on. "My father says Lytton's father was viceroy of India, which appeals to Pop no end; he's still living in the British Empire. Well, I shouldn't admit it, but I rather like the whole idea of the British Raj."

Looking around the room, Jury thought, it would seem so. There was the colonial style of dark wood and light walls. But besides the wood and walls, a large palm sat next to the fireplace; in a sunny corner sat an even larger fern. Yet, with all of this colonialism, there were Mies van der Rohe cantilevered cane chairs with chrome frames.

On a coffee table sat a glass vase with an inch or two of sand, a large shell, and several gold coins, one snapped in two, as if the halves were to be handed out to a couple of secret agents. It made Jury smile. It was the most studied arrangement he'd ever seen in a home, but not overbearing, as the table on which it sat was itself an eye-catcher of carved mahogany.

The French door through which Austin had made his theatrical exit and reentry opened on the promise of a rose garden of which Jury could see only a fraction: part of a stone wall with climbing roses and a willow tree. Stationed by the door was the figure of a black servant boy in a white jacket and fez. Between the two wicker chairs was a table whose base was in the form of an elephant topped with a smooth marble surface, and above the fireplace was a dramatic painting of a parrot. One wall was papered with a pattern of palm fronds and bamboo, and there were stalks of bamboo in a tall vase on the other side of the French door.

Jury thought of E. M. Forster. The elephant table, the fez-hatted servant holding a tray; the wicker and mahogany and bamboo. All he could think of was British colonialism.

"Superintendent, you look bemused." Strachey smiled broadly.

"To tell the truth, Mr. Strachey," and Jury knew he wouldn't, "I haven't any authority here; I mean, the events at Laburnum have nothing to do with any investigation of mine." That, of course, had nothing to do with Jury's "bemusement." He was bemused by Kenneth Strachey and all of this British Raj stuff; he was bemused by E. M. Forster and *A Passage to India* and the young female teacher's betrayal of the Indian doctor. He did not know why this had grabbed his imagination.

"Perfectly all right with me, Superintendent, though I don't think I can add anything to what I told Sergeant Wiggins. Tea?"

"That would be nice, as long as you're serving the crème fraîche tarts."

Kenneth was much amused. "You pick up

on everything you hear?"

"No. I just find your friend Austin memorable."

Kenneth laughed. "Come through to the kitchen." With a wide and wind-milling motion of his arm, he motioned for Jury to follow him.

Jury did. When he saw the kitchen he said, "God, but this looks right out of a Smallbone's advert."

Kenneth filled an electric kettle, spooned tea leaves into a china pot. "No. There are different pieces here. The Aga is the best of the lot. I love it. I always wanted to be a chef. That drives my father crazy." He moved to the big butcher-block island, where Jury sat on a tall stool, and clattered two cups into saucers. He placed these on a tray, together with a sugar bowl.

Everything was fine china and everything matched. No mugs from the Burnhams here, Jury thought, wistfully. "I hope you don't mind covering some of the same ground as you did with Sergeant Wiggins."

"Not at all."

"It's about that day at Laburnum —"

"That's always been a mystery."

"You think so?"

Kenneth smiled. "Well, so do you, I take it, or you wouldn't be here."

Why was everyone doing his job for him?

The kettle screamed and Kenneth switched it off. He poured water into the waiting teapot and sat down across from Jury. They both looked at the teapot, as if it would steep the faster for being watched.

"Let's take this through to the other room. Wait, milk." Kenneth went to the stainless steel fridge, got out a pint of milk, filled a small jug, and brought it back. "Carry the pot, will you?" He picked up the tray, and they went back to the living room.

Kenneth poured out the tea and shoved cup and saucer and milk and sugar across to Jury.

Jury added milk and a lump of sugar from the irregular little lumps that looked sandblasted or excavated from some sugar mine. Probably cost ten times what his regular sugar did. He said, "There's also the death of Tess Williamson."

Kenneth frowned. "Now, that I never considered a mystery. She fell down those stone steps —"

"That's one theory."

"Oh? There are others?"

"Yes, or I wouldn't be here." Jury tried to keep his tone from being too snarky.

"I don't understand. If not an accident, what?"

"Then the only choices are suicide and murder."

Kenneth stared at him, putting his cup back in its saucer, contents undrunk. "Tess a suicide? I find that hard to believe."

"Why is that?"

Kenneth picked up the smallest of three small elephants and held it. "Because I don't want to."

Jury liked that answer. He drank his tea. "Did she ever strike you as being unhappy?"

Kenneth shook his head and ran his thumb over the elephant, back and forth. "No, but then she wouldn't show that around us, would she? She tried very hard to make us happy."

"Did Hilda Palmer ever indicate that she knew something about Tess Williamson?"

Kenneth's brief laugh was derisive. "Hilda into one of her little blackmailing schemes? No, she didn't. But Tess wouldn't have paid any attention to Hilda Palmer." He picked up his cup, tasted the tea, set it down again, put his hand on the teapot. "I can't stand lukewarm tea." He picked up the pot and went back to the kitchen.

Jury looked at the little parade of elephants: the more bejeweled small one that Kenneth had put back in its place; the middle one, with its bright green eyes; the plainer large one. It was as if the elephant, as it grew, was shedding topaz skin and emerald eyes. Coming to terms with reality, perhaps. Jury studied the room. It was an expensive room, and he imagined "Pop" had sprung for this lot, fond as he was of the British Raj.

He felt the room's charm, but more by way of being held captive than beguiled. The brilliant-winged bird in the painting made him think of the Blue Parrot and Trevor Sly's poorer, but more painstaking attempt, to make a strange and out-of-reach landscape familiar and close by, with his movie posters and creaking fans and little boxes of camel matches. Jury thought of faces behind fans, figures behind screens, and the skittery sound of beaded curtains. "It's all appearances," he heard Dennis Jenkins saying. "No bloody reality."

But that, he thought, was a Romantic notion. There was a reality; you just had to scrape for it, like scratching away the imitation jewels on the littlest elephant. He had moved over to the fireplace, where there was only the black grate. He thought of Forster and the Marabar Caves, which the doctor had shown the teacher who later betrayed him.

All of this reflection took only the five

minutes or so that Kenneth Strachey was in the kitchen boiling up water and pouring it over fresh tea leaves.

Now he was back, offering tea. He had also brought a plate of pistachio biscuits. "Homemade." Kenneth smiled and poured the tea.

"I think it's pretty obvious, myself, that Tess Williamson's death was no accident, given the forensic details. And if it wasn't suicide — although I'm not convinced it wasn't — she must have been murdered. Can you think of any reason for that?"

"My God, of course not. Except for the Palmers, the mother, who was furious that Tess was acquitted, I can't think of any reason."

"Did she betray someone?" Jury could not have said why he asked this; the linkage was not wholly conscious. The rightness of the question was certainly questionable.

Except for its effect on Kenneth Strachey. His expression should have been caught in paint or bronze or at least a photograph. It was there and gone in two seconds. Jury could not penetrate it. Only he had an impression of something caving in, which led his mind back to the Marabar Caves and Dr. Aziz. (He wondered how he could suddenly remember the name, the details of this story, much less what Forster's story had to do with the here and now.)

But Strachey, if he indeed had been thrown completely off balance, regained it very quickly. He gave a kind of choked laugh. "Good God, Superintendent. You mean her husband? Did she betray him?"

"No." Jury had to admire Strachey's recovery. Most people would have said, "What do you mean?" And Jury didn't know exactly what he did mean. But he knew it wasn't Tom Williamson. "No. Not her husband."

Strachey frowned. "Hilda Palmer. Hilda was the person set on betrayal." Strachey had the air of one no longer standing on shifting sands. "As I told Sergeant Wiggins. No one liked Hilda Palmer, including myself."

"Me. People are always making that error." Jury smiled.

That little foray into grammar threw Strachey completely off guard again, and Jury took advantage of it. "Tell me, which one of you did it?"

From Strachey's expression, this time anger, not the other thing, Jury knew Strachey was aware that he might lose control of an interview he had clearly thought he would control. He now looked as if he'd jump up and exit as theatrically as had Austin.

But he didn't. Instead, he made light of it. "You're trying to catch me out, Superintendent. Now, why do you think that one of us shoved Hilda?"

"Because Tess Williamson didn't do it."

"Well . . . there was that friend, that woman who was more or less keeping an eye on us —"

Jury shook his head. "Elaine Davies didn't even know Hilda Palmer."

"Again, Hilda's death was ruled an accident —"

"No. It was an open verdict. But some of the evidence said Hilda was pushed. I think it was one of you kids who pushed her. Or perhaps more than one of you."

It was almost as if a sirocco had swept across the room and they'd now have to deal with this unexplained drift of sand at their feet.

There was no more to be gotten out of Kenneth Strachey, and Jury blamed himself for his own missteps at the end of that interview. He left a few minutes later, when Austin returned, dressed in jeans and a black T-shirt imprinted with a rococo design of red and black. Jury realized after a second look, the design was a skull. Austin went out to the patio.

Outside, Jury stood and looked around, rather aimlessly, for he was thinking not of Bloomsbury but of India and the Marabar Caves.

He could not get that image out of his mind.

35

Hyde Park and Cadogan Gardens
Sunday, 3:00 P.M.

Why had he asked that question about betrayal?

Why had Kenneth Strachey's reaction been so anxious? Panic-stricken, really?

And why did he keep thinking about Forster's novel and the Marabar Caves?

It disturbed Jury that the question about betrayal had no source. But of course it had to have a source; he just didn't know what it was.

Jury was sitting on a Hyde Park bench, trying to empty his mind and then see what floated to the surface. What came up was the Blue Parrot. Of course, the posters of *A Passage to India*. But there was more, surely, to the connection than a film poster.

The Marabar Caves. The woman claiming the good doctor who had befriended her had raped her when they'd visited the caves. He hadn't, but he was an Indian and she was a white Englishwoman. Who was more likely to be believed? It was a rather wonderful metaphor for colonialism. All of those well-heeled and self-righteous Brits demanding service and servitude.

His mind returned to Trevor Sly and the Blue Parrot. Stanley. Tess Williamson. The lady in red. Stanley. How could there be any connection among those three things? A shot rang out and killed Stanley's handler.

Jury's mobile jumped around in his pocket. It was Wiggins.

"I'm still looking for Belle Syms, guv. Syms was her married name. We want her maiden name."

"Of course. Get hold of Chief Inspector Brierly and see if he's got that information. Or, no, better yet, I'll call the aunt, Blanche Vesta."

Wiggins rang off and Jury still sat, thinking. *"We all seem to hate our given names, especially girls."* That had been Mundy speaking. Madeline, Mundy; Veronica, Nicki; Arabella . . . *Belle?*

Jury pulled out his mobile again, tapped in a number (glad he'd had the presence of mind to put it on his contact list), and when Blanche Vesta answered reintroduced himself and engaged in a few moments of mutual sadness about her niece's death. And asked if he could see her that evening.

He thought for a bit and then called Dr. Keener with the same question.

Then he left the park, walked to Piccadilly, and took a cab to Cadogan Square.

Number 11 Cadogan Gardens was quite an opulent little hotel, a lot of velvet, a lot of embossed wallpaper, dark wood, crystal chandeliers. He asked for Andrew Cleary and was shown by a porter into the drawing room.

Andrew Cleary was seated on one of the many comfortable-looking sofas, reading a paper and drinking tea. Jury walked up to him. "Mr. Cleary?"

Cleary turned. "Yes? Oh, it's Superintendent Jury, right?" He rose and shook Jury's hand. "Let me get some more tea. Or would you like something else, Superintendent?"

"Tea would be fine." Jury removed his coat and sat in one of the down-pillowed chairs opposite the sofa.

Andrew Cleary was a slightly bald, thin man who one could tell had been handsome in his youth. He still had the aquiline nose, the thin, but well-shaped mouth. The light brown eyes, though, had been aged by the puffy skin beneath them, and the skin begun to loosen about the throat. Cleary was probably Tom Williamson's age, but he looked ten years older.

"You wanted to talk about Tess Williamson."

"I do, yes. Primarily about Laburnum and the children she so often had around her. And the T. S. Eliot poems you gave her."

The porter was there and Cleary asked for another pot of tea. He then looked at Jury, puzzled.

" 'La Figlia che Piange,' in particular."

"You speak Italian?" said Cleary.

"Lord, no. I just speak that."

Cleary picked up his cup, took a sip. "Ah, yes. Tess was fascinated by that poem. 'The double-dealing,' as she put it."

"The poem is all about appearances. The reality was quite something else, wasn't it? The speaker is interested in the appearance of anguish, not the anguish itself. Yes, I guess you could call that 'double-dealing.' "

"Interesting. Most people would just take it at face value."

"But that *is* the face value. It's clearly not a poem about two distraught people parting. He's giving her directions: stand there; do this; do that. The speaker is telling her how best to project the trauma of a love affair ending. It was he who ended it, but there's a callous disregard for that ending. The speaker is interested in the woman as some sort of model. He could be a painter. Or a photographer. It's an artistic experience for him, not an emotional one."

Cleary looked impressed. "My word, you've really studied that poem. Now, do you think it reflects our relationship? Do you think Tess and I were having an affair?"

Jury cut him off. "Nothing of the kind, nor do I think your attitude toward her was that of the person speaking in the poem, but —" He stopped talking as the waiter returned with the tea tray, set it down, poured cups for both of them, and left.

"Tess wasn't interested in me or any man other than Tom. She told me that she loved him from the moment she saw him."

"I believe that," said Jury as he added some milk and a cube of sugar to his cup. "But I was going to ask, why did this poem interest her so much, since it didn't really describe anything that related to her?"

"Betrayal. Tess was fascinated by the idea of betrayal."

It came to Jury again, the image of the Marabar Caves. "Was she, then, betrayed?"

Cleary went on. "Remember *Tess of the D'Urbervilles*? Tess — the fictional one —

was betrayed by Alec d'Urberville and then sought out Angel Clare, who was a young man of very high expectations regarding people and who believed in ultimate goodness. He was, I guess, a secularist. Yet his love for her seemed abstract. It was Tess's favorite book. Hardy was her favorite author; his novels, his poetry too. There was one she especially liked that pictured a woman looking out to sea. I think it was called 'The Riddle.' She was a riddle, Tess; I always felt she was looking over my shoulder, over everyone's shoulder really, for something that lay just beyond her reach."

"What was she looking for?"

Andrew Cleary shook his head.

"Do you think it had anything to do with her idea of betrayal?"

Cleary frowned. "I'm not sure I follow you."

"I mean, something like, oh, one's giving a child up for adoption. How would she take that?"

"Well, the circumstances would count —"

"Why? Can you think of a context for that which wouldn't be betrayal? Abandoning a cat would be less than abandoning a baby? A cat might *mean* less than a baby to a person, but aren't they equal acts of abandonment?"

"Perhaps so. But by whom was Tess abandoned? Someone like the speaker in the poem?"

"Or whom did *she* abandon? Is that who she was looking for?"

"She wasn't about to tell *me*!" rang out Cleary's answer.

36

Sidbury
Sunday, 7:00 P.M.

Blanche Vesta clapped her hand to her cheek. "Good lord, I should have said!"

"Don't blame yourself. There was so much going on — and she was being referred to as 'Belle,' which, as you said, was her nickname."

Blanche was determinedly apologetic. "Certainly, I do blame myself, withholding such an important bit of information. Arabella never did like her name. Everyone was told to call her 'Belle' and if you forgot, she could be quite cheeky."

"Is Hastings the family name?"

"Dad's name, yes. Oh, I forgot my manners, Mr. Jury. You sit right down by the fire and I'll fetch you a cup of tea. Water's nearly on the boil right now."

"Please don't put yourself out, Blanche."

"Since when's a cuppa putting a body

out?" She walked away and Jury heard the comforting sounds of a tea ritual: kettle shrieking, cup or mug retrieved from a cupboard, frig opening and closing for milk.

Jury looked around the room: nothing stylish, nothing pricy. Old photos in round maple frames of cheerless-looking adults and children.

On another wall, a large poorly wrought painting of a woodland scene, with a not-to-scale deer standing in front of it.

"Here we are!" called Blanche, so cheerily Jury would have thought she was trying to make up for the grim-looking people in the photographs. She set down an aluminum tray and poured from a teapot covered in tiny pink geraniums into a cup similarly flowered.

"Sugar?"

"Just one, thanks."

No question arose about milk. Jury accepted the cup, sipped the tea. "You said before that you seldom saw Arabella. So I expect you don't know much about her friends."

Blanche shook her head. But then she stopped. "Wait a tic. Remember, I mentioned a call on her mobile. It was someone calling her — aren't they dreadful, the way people just stop whatever they're doing? —

and she went to the little foyer there to talk. As if it made any difference to me if it was the bloody queen inviting her to dinner."

Jury laughed. "You don't know who the caller was?"

"Had to be a man, didn't it?"

"Oh? Why?"

"A woman doesn't get all cagey and mysterious over a call from another woman, does she? I'm guessing the man she came here to meet. Too bad I couldn't hear more of the conversation." Blanche leaned over the tea tray and selected a biscuit with ivy-like white icing. She held the plate out to Jury.

He took a plain shortbread biscuit. "Good point." He liked her deductive ability. "But she didn't mention any man?"

"Didn't have to, did she? She certainly wasn't wearing that getup to please *me*. Wait. She had me take her picture with one of those new kind of cameras, and then she forgot to take the camera." Blanche got up, went to a small table in the corner, pulled out a drawer. "Here it is. Maybe you can get the picture. I'm no good at this." She sighed at her own lack and handed the camera to Jury, who fooled with the buttons and brought up the picture. "This is a great help, Blanche." Stunning dress, even more stunning on the live woman. Sequined top, very low V-neck, draped skirt. Almost black bobbed hair, silky and worn with a fringe that obscured her eyes in the picture. The strappy sandals with a vinelike embellishment — how could women manage in such heels?

Jury chewed the shortbread and reflected. "Do you know anything about Arabella's childhood? I'm thinking specifically of her being one of six children who went to a house party —"

Blanche threw up her hands. "You're talking about that terrible business in Cornwall — or was it Devon? — where that little girl died. The woman who owned the house got arrested? I didn't believe it myself. But my sister Nancy couldn't talk of anything else."

"Nancy?"

"Belle's mum. She wanted to bring a civil suit against the woman after she got off on that murder charge. I said, 'Nance, you're balmy. What would you charge her with? And Nancy says 'endangering the lives of children.' Well, as she's already got off the murder charge, it's not likely you could make that stick."

"Where's her mother now?"

"Dead. So's her dad. Died within six months of each other — heart attack and cancer. Sad, that. Arabella went to live with an aunt on the father's side. I was just as glad it wasn't me who got asked. I couldn't take to the girl."

"Why not?"

"She was just too — needy. That sort of thing scares men off, I once told her. You make too much of a fuss or want too much attention, it puts people right off."

"Did she ever talk about that day at the house in Devon?"

Blanche shook her head and crimped her lips together, as if in imitation of Arabella's tight silence. Then she spoke again. "Not to me, and from what Nancy said, not to her either. Nothing beyond saying they — the kids — were playing hide-and-seek."

"Did she ever mention those children in any other context?"

Blanche shook her head.

Jury picked up his cup and swallowed the lukewarm tea. He said, "Thanks so much for your time, Blanche. I've got to be going." He rose, picked up the camera, and said, "Mind if I keep this? I'd like to get some prints made. All we have are crime scene photographs and you don't always want to show one of those for identification."

"Oh, go right ahead and take it."

As they walked to the door, he said, "One other thing. You said that Belle had never worn the kind of clothes she was wearing in that picture."

"You're right there." She snorted. "Never saw her in anything but jumpers and skirts or trousers."

"But you never saw her much, anyway. So how can you be sure?"

Blanche gave him a long-suffering look. "Some people you wouldn't have to see often to tell if they'd wear that red dress and those crazy shoes. If you'd known her, you'd see what I mean. Belle just wasn't the sequined-red-dress and four-inch-heel type. That's all."

37

Dr. Keener had his surgery on the ground floor of his home in the outskirts of Northampton. The house was a modest brick and stone structure with two front doors, one for the house and one down a little walk for the doctor's office.

Jury walked through that door into an empty waiting room. A bell tinkled when he opened the door, no doubt to alert one of the doctor's staff. But it was Dr. Keener himself who opened the inside door to his office and said, "Superintendent Jury, do come in." He was wearing the waistcoat and trousers of a three-piece suit, the jacket temporarily draped over a headless plaster torso that stood by a window. The torso was clearly a teaching device, as all of the organs and arteries were marked in brilliant colors, and all named.

370

"Please have a seat."

Jury sat in the chair usually filled by a patient.

Taking the swivel chair on the other side of the desk, Dr. Keener said, "What can I do for you, Superintendent? I've an idea it's about the young man who was shot in Reacher's Road."

"You're right, doctor. Do you recall you hesitated over your diagnosis — or not your diagnosis, exactly, but the circumstances. You seemed perplexed by something in the scene."

"Quite right. I still am. I'm waiting for a forensic report."

"May I ask what you found so puzzling?"

"There were three bullet casings, right? Meaning three shots were fired. The shooter wasn't very good, was he? One shot hit the ground; another grazed the victim's ankle; the third was the one that killed him, struck him low in the back. The shots were fired from behind the victim, perhaps fifteen or twenty feet. That's truly remarkably bad shooting, wouldn't you say?"

Jury smiled. "I would."

"I noticed it particularly because a couple of days before that I'd been one among a half-dozen others at a shooting party on the Windmill estate, not far from here. Grouse, pheasant, that sort of thing. I thought I could have done better than this person, and I'm not a very good shot. Of course, the shooter might not have been trying to kill him, but to warn him. That seems a rather extravagant warning, though, don't you think? Three shots?"

"To scare him off, possibly? But then he would have killed him by mistake, which is even a grosser error than merely bad shooting."

"Hm. The trajectory of the bullet suggests he was aiming low. That dog belonged to him, didn't it?"

"The dog was certainly sticking to him at the site."

"Strange . . ." The doctor sighed. "Well, put that incident together with the woman falling from the tower and it strikes me Sidbury is not the place to buy your holiday cottage."

"What did you make of that fall?"

"That she didn't fall is what I made of it. It wasn't an accident. Have you been up that tower?"

Jury shook his head. "It's really Northampton police's case."

"You're a tall man. The window ledge would hit you about here —" Dr. Keener placed the edge of his hand against his chest. "Now, this woman was tall for a woman — a little over five-nine — but certainly not six feet. The window ledge would hit her about here." He moved his hand halfway up his chest. "It would have been extremely difficult for her to hoist herself up and position herself for an accidental fall. Putting herself in that position — she would have had to have suicidal intentions. The alternatives to accident are suicide and homicide. And for either of those, that tower would be an awkward venue."

Jury liked the "awkward venue." He smiled.

Dr. Keener went on. "But that's our problem, isn't it, the awkwardness, as it had to be one of three."

"Afraid you're right there, doctor."

"So I'd go for homicide, simply because it means there was a second person choosing the site for reasons we can't fathom. At least I can't."

"Perhaps that in itself is the reason: that we can't fathom it. And the site will distract us from other things, such as motive. But I agree with you, it's impossible for that fall to have been accidental, and I can't imagine a person bent on suicide putting herself through a lot of difficulty in order to com-

mit it. Homicide is the most likely explanation. She has a date; she's dressed up for it;
they go looking for fun. The tower's a lark."

"I don't think it was for him, though."

"And ultimately not for her, either."

38

"The dog?" said Melrose "Stanley?"

Jury had driven to Ardry End after leaving the doctor's house. "But how would a dog be a threat?"

Jury raised his eyebrows. "Have you forgotten Mungo?"

"By no means. Mungo is unforgettable. Still —"

"That must be what Dr. Keener is suggesting. The terrible marksmanship, the shots aimed so close to the ground."

"Good lord, trying to shoot the *dog*?" Melrose drank his wine. They were having dinner.

"DCI Brierly hasn't been able to find the person the dog was meant for."

"Perhaps he wasn't meant for anyone. Perhaps he was in town for some other reason. Both of them, Stanley and his

375

handler. Or owner, possibly.

"Is there a connection between the two killings? Or is it a coincidence?" Melrose's tone was doubtful.

Jury just gave him a look. "If I knew that I wouldn't be sitting here eating your cook's coq au vin." Fresh peas and tiny new potatoes completed the meal. "I'd be out doing something."

"You're in a bit of a mood."

"Yes, I am in a bit of a mood. That this Belle Syms is really Arabella Hastings isn't getting me closer to an ending."

"Don't be daft. Of course it is if Arabella was one of the kids at Laburnum. So now you know that this present murder has something to do with Tess Williamson's —"

"I've considered that possibility, yes."

"Why in God's name kill somebody by tossing her out of a tower? What if the fall doesn't actually kill her? That's a damned awkward murder site. Why not just toss her off a cliff?"

Jury set down his fork, spread his arms. "Do you see any cliffs around here? The tower makes sense: you want something high enough to account for the broken neck."

" 'Account for' a broken neck? That sounds as if the neck were already broken."

"It was."

"Aren't you begging the question?"

Jury sighed. "Two murders and you're making up a syllogism?"

Melrose shrugged. "I still think the method is crazy."

"Maybe the killer is, or maybe he's bored; this is a game to him."

"But why choose here? Sidbury and Long Piddleton?"

Jury shrugged. "Because her aunt lives here? Perhaps Arabella was coming here anyway, and her killer saw an opportunity to get her outside of London."

Melrose worked up a frown that had Ruthven (who was removing the plates) worried. "Are you quite all right, m'lord?"

"Yes, of course. How about some cognac with the pud?"

Ruthven smiled. "There's cognac *in* the pudding, sir." Ruthven seldom allowed himself to make little jokes. "It's Martha's bread pudding. The hard sauce."

"Better and better."

Ruthven swanned out with the dinner plates.

Jury thought about his conversation with Harry Johnson. "What if there were two of them? Two women who looked enough alike that no one would suspect it?"

Melrose groaned. "That old gimmick? I don't like it."

"Oh, well, I'm sorry if this strikes you as unoriginal. Maybe after a vat of that Courvoisier, I'll come up with something a little more outré. For whatever reason, there's definitely a question of identity here. Remember Harry Johnson?"

"Good lord, your favorite sociopath. You still talk to him?"

"He pointed out that she went to four different public places that evening. One wouldn't do that unless one wanted to establish a presence."

Melrose wasn't listening but thinking his own thoughts. "Two women? Remember *Vertigo*?"

"If I didn't, I'd be the only person on the planet."

"Her husband kills her, finds a woman who looks like her, finds some sucker to follow her around — in the film James Stewart — who attests later to seeing her fall out of a church tower."

"In the film the sucker is Stewart; in real life, I take it, it's me."

"Who else?"

"Thanks. Well, I'm going to Laburnum tomorrow morning."

"Again? What do you hope to find?"

"A letter. A note. Do you want to come?"

Melrose poured out some more cognac. "No, thanks. I'm too busy."

"You? Busy?"

"I do have this house to run —"

"No you don't. Ruthven runs it."

"There's the livestock to see to."

"Yes, I can see that's a full-time occupation."

"Anyway, you don't really want me to come. You're on a mission, best carried out by you yourself."

"I don't know what you're talking about. I'm merely trying to find answers to Tess Williamson's death."

"A mission."

39

Jury got out of the car and slammed the door, which sent a flock of pigeons beating upward. This left behind an even more deathly quiet that stayed with him as he mounted the stairs and felt under the thriving holly in one of the planters for the keys the housekeeper was to have left for him. He had called Macalvie; Macalvie had made arrangements for the keys.

He unlocked the thick oak door, closed it, and stood in the Great Hall and listened for some little overture of sound. Any house as old and big as this one would have its portion of creaks, groans, and sighs. But there was nothing. This was one of the things that had slipped through the net when he'd been here with Macalvie: total silence. Tess Williamson had spent long periods of time here alone.

Jury walked into the sitting room and dropped into a down-cushioned chair that sent forth a cloud of dust that reminded him of the pigeons' flight.

Had Tess needed to come here to exorcise some kind of guilt? But hadn't she had her share of punishment and for what she hadn't done? If she hadn't killed Hilda Palmer, what had she done? She must have felt she'd betrayed someone, and the only one who would have been that important to her would be her husband.

Tess must have been covering up for somebody else.

He thought about the children and their uniform dislike of Hilda Palmer. Mundy Brewster had said that adults didn't understand what Hilda was like — how could they unless Hilda had one or the other in her crosshairs. On the surface she was sweet. She'd pretend to save things, some little creature she'd hurt in the first place. "She was the most vicious person I've ever known . . . Imagine the ruination that lay in her wake if she'd ever gotten to our age now."

Jury smiled again at the "our age."

He took out the diagram that forensic had made, showing the positions of the people who'd been at the house that afternoon, both adults and children. None of them had clear alibis, with the possible exception of John McAllister, who was lying at the bottom of a laburnum tree. And possibly Elaine Davies, who'd been on a bench and not paying attention.

Jury was by now through the dining room and standing on the patio, looking down to the drained pools. He looked at the urn at the top of the marble steps and at the angle of the steps themselves. He looked beyond the steps to the grove of laburnum trees, at the one Johnny McAllister had supposedly climbed and wondered, why?

"He loved formulas . . . Can you imagine a ten-year-old fascinated by molecules and maps of numbers?" Mundy again. She wasn't surprised when McAllister turned out to be a brilliant doctor. "He was wizard in science and biology."

Even though the coroner's verdict had been an open one; even though there'd been a lack of convincing evidence, the suspicion that Tess Williamson had been guilty never lifted. He sat down on the top step of the patio, by the urn. Had there been contact between Tess and John McAllister during those five years before she died?

Possible, but not likely. She would have discouraged it, and he? He might truly have wanted to step forth and admit to killing Hilda. Had the case been presented with John McAllister as the killer, any solicitor with half a brain could have gotten him off . . .

Only, Tess Williamson knew how fragile this boy was, how little support he was getting at home, how little it really was "home" for him. What would have happened to him? Was she afraid he'd be put in an institution?

And Tess's own death?

Tom Williamson was convinced it was murder. "I expect I'd better get a solicitor," he'd said, jokingly. But as for Tess's fortune, Tom already had it. She would probably have allowed him any part of it for anything he wanted. Tom, from what Jury could tell, didn't want anything but Tess.

Money and revenge. Those were the two motives that might apply in this case. Revenge? The only people who could logically have wanted revenge would be Hilda Palmer's parents. Hilda's mother was the only person who professed any desire to kill Tess Williamson. The rather awful truth (Jury suspected) was that more than one adult, and any number of children were relieved the girl was gone. Yes, any one of those children could have pushed her.

Jury sat with his head in his hands. If Tess

Williamson had indeed committed suicide and tried to make it appear an accident, there had to be a note. Or a journal. Something so that Tom would know not only about her own death but also about what had happened to Hilda. She would have left a note and left it someplace where Tom would be sure to find it, but not someone else.

He rose, brushed the dead leaves from his coat, turned and stirred the detritus of leaves and twigs up in the urn. "Stand on the highest pavement of the stair / Lean on a garden urn . . ." As if. The forensic net would certainly have swept up small journals buried in garden urns.

Where would Tom be likely to find a note, but not someone else?

Suddenly he remembered the ships-in-bottles. Jury left the patio, took the stairs two at a time, and got to the door of the study, which he opened with the second key the housekeeper had left. Inside, he looked at each of the bottles. The tightly rolled pieces of paper were contained in five of them. He took down the schooner from a top shelf, but couldn't get at the paper with his finger. On Tom's desk he found a letter opener that he was able to shove into the neck of the bottle, pin down the paper, and coax it through the neck until he could just wedge his little finger in and pull out the paper, which he unrolled. It contained nothing but the short history of the boat. He re-rolled it tightly and reinserted it. He performed this on two others, but could not catch onto the paper in the last two and gave up. No note from Tess.

And then he realized that Tom would have found it long ago, perhaps straightaway, since Tom wouldn't have put it in the bottle himself.

Jury left the study and went back down the stairs to the library, where he sat down for five minutes, feeling deflated. He got up and went to the bookshelves, looking for Thomas Hardy. *Tess of the D'Urbervilles,* her favorite. Jury pulled it out, quickly riffled the pages, shook it. Nothing fell out. Stupid idea, anyway. He shoved the book back in line. Poor fictional Tess, doomed and damned and all because the confession she had written out to Angel Clare had gone under —

Jury took the stairs again.

The floor in Tom's study was covered not with carpet but with a big rug, consequently, it was not tacked down. He ran his fingers carefully beneath that section of the rug that met the sill of the door. He found nothing.

He went into the room. He was able to roll that part nearest the door back a couple of feet. He found it: an envelope addressed TOM. It wasn't sealed. He opened it to find three pages of ordinary white stationery covered with a neat handwriting with a fountain pen.

My dear Tom,

You'll wonder why after five years I've decided to tell you what happened that awful day Hilda Palmer died. I was in the kitchen by the window when I saw Hilda standing by the edge of the pool. I assumed she'd come round from the front. Then Mackey came running around and saw her and stopped. They were talking, or, rather, Hilda was talking, no doubt heaping abuse on him the way she liked to do. Mackey looked as if he were trapped between rage and tears. I went outside and was starting down the steps when I saw him pick up a rake Sturgis had left behind and swing it at Hilda with all of his very small might. He knocked her over and she fell into the empty pool. I ran down to where he stood, staring at her body and I thought she was dead. Straightaway I grabbed Mackey and told him to run into the grove and climb a tree. "This didn't happen. You had nothing to do with it, Mackey. You weren't here. Now, run." He ran.

Mackey, the love of my life, with that patched-up backpack, those inappropriate black-framed glasses, the light in his hair —

The dash ended it. That was the last sheet and nothing was written on the back of the page.

Jury got up and pulled the rug farther back, moving from one side of the room to the other. He yanked it back as far as he could before it was trapped by Tom's desk and the heavy cabinet that held the boats in bottles. There was nothing else underneath. He knew it was unlikely there would be another page, since the pages he'd just read had been folded into an envelope.

And yet there had to be, he thought. How could she have just left it there?

He put the letter in an inside pocket, pulled the rug to its original position, locked the door, and went downstairs.

40

M5 and Northampton
Monday, 3:00 P.M.

"I'll be bloody damned," said Brian Macalvie.

Jury had called Macalvie on his mobile to let him know he'd left the keys in the planter where he'd found them. He told him about the fictional Tess and the letter to Angel Clare. "I think Tess Williamson was ambivalent about telling her husband the real story. And the letter-under-the-door was a mark of that ambivalence. It wasn't deliberately shoved under the rug, but she might have hoped he'd never find it."

"You're thinking it's a suicide note?"

"No, I'm not thinking that. It doesn't read that way; she certainly thinks she'll see him again."

"Yeah, well, I think that's a kind of overinvolved explanation." Macalvie was silent for a moment, then said, "And now you've got

388

this bizarre murder of Arabella Hastings, who was at Laburnum when the girl Hilda was killed. Connection? Someone who knew something? But what?"

"Enough to get her killed."

From Exeter, Jury was on the M5 to London when he decided to get off and take the A417 to Northampton. It would take him three hours, but he was betting DCI Brierly would still be in his office.

He was considering stopping for a coffee at the next Little Chef when his mobile bleated. It was Wiggins.

"I took the photo to four different places, the Givenchy salon on Sloane Street, Harvey Nicks, Selfridge's, and Harrods. None of them carried that particular dress. I can't find any other shop that sells Givenchy."

"Fortnum's? Liberty's?"

"No, sir."

"I'm going to try to see Brierly. I'll ask him if he had any luck."

Three hours later he was sitting in the Northampton station.

"No joy, there," said Brierly when Jury asked him about the red dress.

"My sergeant has tried all of the usual department stores and the Givenchy place."

"I'll just keep looking."

When Jury told him about his talk with Dr. Keener, Brierly said, "The dog? You're kidding."

"No. Dr. Keener made a good point. How could the shooter have missed the target twice, if the target was Randall himself. Why were the shots aimed so low to the ground? You've got a forensic report. It tells you the trajectory of the bullets."

Brierly nodded. "It does, of course. We were puzzled by that. Nobody thought of the dog. After all . . ." His voice trailed off and then returned with "Why?"

"I don't know. This PetLoco outfit. That's an online pet clearing house, you could say. It's a site that should be shut down. I expect the owner is into dogfighting."

"And it's your opinion the shooter was afraid Stanley would be traced back to this PetLoco outfit?"

"I don't think it was that. No, there'd be other ways of finding out the dog's history." Jury paused. "How about Randall, the victim? Any more on him?"

"Only what I told you. I still don't understand, if the shooter was trying to kill the dog, what in hell was his motive?"

Jury shook his head. "I don't know."

"Then this poor guy Randall was just collateral damage. Wrong place, wrong time."

"Wrong dog," said Jury.

41

Islington, London
Monday, 10:00 P.M.

If it had to do with clothes psychology, Jury knew where to look. And he was looking at her right now in his flat in Islington.

"Only a man would make that mistake," said Carole-anne Palutski, sitting on Jury's old and rather tattered sofa purchased some years before at Heal's. Carole-anne was applying a nail varnish called Hotsie-Totsie, a shade in the deep pink family of colors.

Jury had been on his way to the kitchen for more tea when she said that, and it stopped him. "What do you mean?"

"I mean that color red with that skin — it just runs riot. That red completely blots the poor girl out." Carole-anne had been looking over a photo spread supplied partly by the Sunday *Telegraph;* partly by the sexiest of the tabloids; and partly Jury himself: the picture taken by Blanche Vesta when her niece had visited her.

Jury returned to the sofa, tea-less, and said, "I didn't think the red swamped her own coloring."

"Of course not, you being a man." She ran a tiny trail of Hotsie-Totsie over her little finger.

"Well, if it's so wrong, the color, I mean, then why is she wearing it? Why did she buy it?"

Carole-anne gave him a long, pitying look. The look you'd give a simpleton. "Don't be daft. She didn't buy it. Some gentleman-friend probably bought it. And that's why she's wearing it. And with those shoes." She blew on her nails.

"What's wrong with the shoes? I think they're quite smart."

"You being a man." She had her head bent over her nails, applying another little smear of polish.

"Me being a man, I ask you: What's wrong with them? They're Jimmy Choo." Jury was quite proud of his shoe knowledge. He'd gotten the name of the designer from the insole, of course; still, he enjoyed tossing the names about.

"Yeah, and I can tell you this: Jimmy didn't design that shoe to go with that dress. They're beautiful shoes, red patent leather and what — four-inch heels? — but not with that dress."

"Why not? They match."

" 'Match'?" She clapped her hand to her forehead in utter disbelief. "That's the point! They shouldn't match. One or the other, one at a time, but not both. The shoes, the dress, are each one screaming for attention. Then add that little gold bag with the skull clasp? That's Alexander McQueen. Somebody paid a fistful for that getup, but it wasn't her."

Jury thought this generalization about men's lack of taste very annoying. He said, "You think I'd be incapable of walking into Harrods and walking out with a dress and shoes and bag for you that you wouldn't wear?"

"I'd wear them all right, but that's because you went to the trouble and expense — notice I'm not holding my breath — of getting them for me. Which is what she did." Carole-anne pointed a hot-pink nail at the array of pictures, then held out her hands, fingers spread to look at the total Hotsie-Totsie effect. "And nor would she be wearing that pink nail polish either."

"Don't tell me he bought the nail polish too? That's a bit much!"

"No. She had her nails done before she

knew what dress she'd be wearing. There was probably another dress. That artwork on the nails is something. But the color's more like this." She held up her fingers so he could have a good look. "Hotsie-Totsie."

"Should be red, you mean."

"Of course."

Jury thought about this. He got up, went to the phone, and called Wiggins.

"What's up?" Wiggins's voice sounded drowsy.

"Were you asleep? It's only ten. You're going to see Kenneth Strachey tomorrow, right? Ask him more questions about Arabella Hastings. We're going to want a warrant."

42

Dr. Robert Smiley, OB-GYN specialist was still practicing from his office in Harley Street.

When Jury walked into the ground floor of the building in which his surgery was located, the receptionist pointed out that he didn't have an appointment and that the doctor was booked straight through until four, when the office closed.

Jury produced his ID. "I have a few questions, that's all. It won't take more than ten minutes."

"Oh, my. Police. If you would just care to have a seat in the waiting room. That's on the first floor." She pointed to the staircase on her right leading upward. "I'll see what I can do."

This minor commitment was weighted with importance. Jury took the stairs.

There was no one in the waiting room, which rather undermined evidence of the doctor's fully booked day. In about five minutes, a nurse appeared at the door to the office and ushered out a patient, an unhappy-looking middle-aged woman. The nurse beckoned to Jury; he rose and followed her into the office, almost as well appointed as a library in a stately home.

Dr. Smiley entered through another door, one that connected this consulting room to the surgery. "Superintendent Jury, what can I do for you?"

"I'd like to ask you a few questions about a former patient."

Dr. Smiley sat down behind his desk, signing for Jury to sit in the chair opposite. "As long as it doesn't breech confidentiality —"

"I'm sure it does, but I don't think the answers will compromise you. The patient is a Tess Williamson, and she died seventeen years ago —"

"Ah, yes! That was tragic. I don't remember her medical history — Had she some sort of condition?"

"Vertigo. But I don't think that accounted for the fall. Her death isn't what I wanted to see you about, though. You ran some tests on her and her husband, Tom Williamson, trying to work out why they'd been unsuccessful in having a child. I'm interested in the test results."

Dr. Smiley raised his eyebrows, saying, "This is where you get into the confidentiality problem, Superintendent. I can't answer that question."

"Even though she's been dead for seventeen years?"

"Yes, but there's still her husband."

Jury had forgotten that part of the "confidentiality" issue. "True, sorry. The thing is, I'm investigating three suspicious deaths, and this information would help." Jury sat back, then forward again. "May I make a guess?"

Dr. Smiley said nothing.

Jury said, "Tess Williamson wanted to save her husband's feelings, so she asked you to tell him that the trouble was hers, not his."

Dr. Smiley still said nothing.

The two men just looked at one another for moments, then Dr. Smiley broke the silence and said, "She was an exceptional woman. I got the impression she always put her husband first. Her death must have been devastating for him." The doctor looked away.

"It was, Dr. Smiley. Thank you for your time." Jury rose, and so did the doctor. They shook hands, as if sealing a pact.

■ ■ ■ ■

In the cab taking him to Clerkenwell, Jury thought he could answer the question now as to why Tess had told the gossipy Elaine Davies of this visit to Dr. Smiley. She wanted someone else to know, because that would reinforce her story that the problem lay with her, not with her husband.

The taxi stopped along the Clerkenwell Road and Jury got out and paid the driver, who sped off.

Clerkenwell was another London borough that had fast become a hot spot for young professionals and artistic types. It was going the way of many London neighborhoods. The old places like Docklands that had been spiffed up enough that the owners of these rentable properties could ask for high rents and higher sales figures. Converted warehouses were prominent in these overhauls. What once had been big drawbacks, like exposed pipes, were being turned into assets. Painted in hot colors, the pipes were now part of the warehouse conversion aesthetic. Anybody not making close to six figures was being squeezed out of Central London these days. Jury might have taken a couple of hikes in rent for his one-bedroom in Islington, but he'd also taken a couple of hikes in rank and pay.

Arabella Hastings had lived by herself, her marriage to Zack Syms having lasted less than a year. He left the ex-husband to DCI Brierly, also the people at her workplace, concluding he himself would get nothing new. He would be told she was quiet and shy and probably a good worker.

The building, one of the block of new flats in which she had lived, stood at the confluence of Clerkenwell Road and a street so narrow one would have taken it for a walkway. The place was so spanking new it looked as if it would have no attraction for any life form — mouse, roach, spider, or human.

Wiggins had arranged with the building super to open the door to Arabella's flat. The flat was on the first floor, so he took the stairs.

Hardly larger than a bedsit, Belle Syms's rooms gave away almost nothing about their owner. Sherlock Holmes would have taken one sweeping look round and nailed her, the essential Belle. But Jury was a long way from Sherlock.

The little flat consisted of a very small sitting room, a larger bedroom, a galley kitchen, and a bath. Jury bet the first room had been part of the bedroom and then been sectioned off, raising it a step above the bedsit category and, consequently, raising the rent by half.

The furniture was mostly that blond, streamlined stuff often called Scandinavian. The only color was supplied by the rug, and that faded. The only thing Jury was interested in was the cupboard in the bedroom that held Arabella's clothes. He found shirts, skirts, and slacks in a spectrum of shades that ranged from fawn to beige to dark brown. No spectrum at all. The most riotous shade in the closet was a sort of copper, a suit that would have served her for job interviews. There were no dresses at all except for the inevitable black, sleeveless linen. That was pretty much Belle's venture into femininity. There was certainly no other dress that matched in quality and color to the Givenchy. In this cupboard it was Marks and Sparks, Army-Navy. The most expensive item was a cashmere sweater from Selfridges.

The shoes were no more adventurous than the clothes. A couple of low-heeled taupe ones; a brown pair of one-inch heels; a pair of black pumps with a bow; and one pair of oatmeal-colored fuzzy slippers. No other designer dress, no designer shoes. All that

Belle had seen of color and designer fashion were the clothes she stood up in. This taste of glamour and the high life she'd barely had a chance to sport around Sidbury.

Somebody else had done it for her.

43

"She's having her elevenses," said the woman who oversaw the Armani collection.

Jury had always liked "elevenses" — the break one had to honor, much like a special dispensation from the Church. Jury checked his watch to find indeed it was 11:20 to be exact.

"Could you tell me where she's having it?"

"She likes the pastry shop just opposite Harrods." The woman pointed as if through the many-walled, huge store.

"Thanks. And if she returns before I find her, would you kindly tell her I need to speak with her?" Jury handed the woman a card.

"Yes, of course."

Jury thanked her again and made his way through the Harrods throng, like an exodus

403

into another world.

It was the same pastry shop where Jury had enjoyed a cup of coffee and a doughnut the week before. Mundy Brewster was sitting at a little table against the wall with a cup of tea and a small plate holding half of a custard doughnut.

"Hello, Mundy," said Jury, pulling out the one other chair. He put the file he was carrying on the table.

"Mr. Jury! You found me!"

As if she'd been lost. Jury suddenly thought of Stanley.

"Right. I've talked to Kenneth Strachey and John McAllister since I saw you."

"You found Johnny!"

As if he too had been lost and Jury had accomplished some incredible feat in finding him

"I did. In Hackney."

Mundy shook her head. "I can't think why he lives there."

"He gives me the impression of one who doesn't care where he lives."

Mundy reflected for a moment. "He seems to have a need almost for deprivation."

"I wonder why."

She shrugged. "He's got a lot of empathy. Even when he was little, he had all of this empathy for living things. Hilda used it to torture him. Once she took a bird and killed it. She really did wring the bird's neck, standing in front of Johnny."

"What a delightful child. I'm not surprised somebody killed her."

Mundy's eyes widened. "You don't believe it was an accident?"

"No. Have you read the papers recently?"

She shook her head. "Haven't had the time, really."

Jury took the two newspaper articles from the folder and placed them before her. "This."

She bent over them, first retrieving her glasses from her bag. Wire-rimmed, round. For some reason Jury found this endearing — glasses instead of contact lenses. "Recognize her?"

She looked up. "Should I? I don't."

"Arabella Hastings."

She stared at the pictures, then at Jury. "My God! But it says here, 'Belle Syms.' "

"She changed it. Remember what you said: none of us liked our names?"

"I can hardly believe this."

Jury produced the other photo. "Her aunt took this when Arabella went to see her."

Mundy tucked a strand of hair behind her ear. "Arabella. All got up like a dog's dinner." She bit her lip. "Sorry, that wasn't nice; I simply meant she's dressed to the nines."

"Apparently she had a hot date."

"Can't imagine that, either. I mean, Arabella was always so withdrawn and shy, she had a hard time even engaging with us."

"I wonder what you think of her clothes."

"They're good. That's certainly a designer dress, and I'd guess the shoes are too. But —"

"Givenchy and Jimmy Choo. We've canvassed London — Harrods, Liberty's, Harvey Nichols, and the Givenchy salon, of course; none of the people in any of those places have sold it. Can you think of any other place that sells Givenchy?"

She frowned. "No, but I can research it for you. Fortnum's doesn't, I know . . ."

"Well, if you find anyplace let me know. I've a friend who's fashion conscious and claims the dress, shoes, and nail polish weren't meant to go together. What do you think?"

"I agree." She picked it up and brought it closer to her eyes. "The nails are gorgeous — though I don't care for that kind of thing — but the color isn't right with all of that red. And she shouldn't be wearing red shoes, either."

"My friend thinks she must have been going to wear another dress, not that one."

"Very possibly. So why didn't she?"

Jury shrugged. "That I don't know. But
there certainly might have been two
dresses." Jury frowned.

Mundy said, "I think that dress and shoes
would have made it hard to recognize
Arabella, even if I'd seen her last week. I
haven't seen her since Tess Williamson's
funeral. Seventeen years ago." She stopped
and looked at him, puzzled. "This happened
in Northamptonshire, yet it's your case?"

"Technically, no. But I think it means
something in the larger view: the Laburnum
business and Tess Williamson's death."

"If it wasn't an accident . . ."

"It was something else. Suicide or homicide. Or rather homicide made to look like
an accident, I believe."

"You think Tess's death is related to Arabella's?"

"I do."

"No, it must be a coincidence that one of
us — you don't really think it was one of us
kids that killed her?"

"It's certainly a possibility. Given Arabella
was murdered."

Mundy thought for a moment. "Do you
think it was something Arabella did? I mean

do you think it's revenge?"

"No, I have the feeling that Arabella knew something about the man who killed her and had threatened to tell what she knew. She might have been using the knowledge for leverage."

"You think it was the man she was with here?" She turned the newspaper round so that he could see the small picture of the Sun and Moon Hotel in case he'd forgotten where "here" was.

"Yes, I do. There's also the strong possibility he had help from another woman."

Mundy sat back in silence. Then she said, "Was Tom Williamson ever a suspect?"

"In his wife's death? Of course he was. It's always the spouse who's under suspicion, especially when there's money involved. Tess was rich; Tom wasn't. He inherited everything. But he was in London at the time of her death. But homicide wasn't a popular theory. Especially since Tess had vertigo and those steps were rather a challenge. At least that's the way it appeared."

"So why has that changed?"

"Because it would be difficult to kill oneself by accidentally falling down a flight of steps."

"In crime fiction it happens all the time.

Someone pulls a wire across a top step, the victim stumbles over it and goes down."

"True, but there'd be more momentum in that situation. It would be more like a straight dive down the steps. It would still be hard, though. In any event, there'd be bodily injuries from a person's trying to break the fall and stop herself in an accident."

"Why would anyone want to kill Tess Williamson?"

Once again, Jury had a sudden image of the Marabar Caves. "Betrayal?"

44

Plaistow Street was not improved by the light of day. Boarded-up buildings, cafés with steamy windows, newsagents, aimless knots of boys and men passing around something drinkable or smokeable who had nothing else to do.

Jury walked into the building where security was always on the mend. He walked from the anteroom through the glass door and passed the lift. No kids were grouped there this time, but the OUT OF ORDER sign was in place. He wondered if it simply meant what it said. He guessed the lifts were often not working in earnest.

He took the stairs.

"Dr. McAllister, sorry for the short notice. But it's important."

John McAllister stood aside and gestured

410

Jury in. "I imagine a lot of your job is short notice. Come on in. What's this about?"

"I have something I want you to read." Jury had drawn the letter from an inside pocket of his jacket. "It's a letter Tess Williamson wrote to her husband before she died Tuesday, June 17."

John looked shocked as he took the letter but didn't open it immediately. His look at Jury was speculative. "I don't understand. If it's to Tom, why should I — ?"

Seeing the look on Jury's face, he didn't finish; he opened the folded pages and read the first of them. Then he sat down and read the rest. It was a long time before he spoke. He folded the pages and put them back in the envelope, saying, "Where, after all these years, did you find this?"

"She'd slipped it under the door of his office, you know, where he kept his ships-in-bottles, thinking he'd find it within a few days. It went under the rug."

John McAllister looked rather wildly around the room, stopped, bent his head. Shook it. "I can hardly believe it."

"I know. But her story about you, that's all true?"

He nodded. "It's what happened, yes."

Jury was somewhat taken aback. "So you hadn't forgotten?"

John took off the black-framed glasses, misted over. "Forgotten? Hardly." He wiped the glasses, put them back on. " 'Those inappropriate, black-framed glasses . . .' "

Jury had never heard her voice, but in his head he heard it now. "I was only thinking of buried memory. You know, something brought on by great trauma. She ordered you to forget."

"She did, yes. Then you think she did throw herself down those stairs. Deliberately."

Jury didn't answer this. Instead, he said, "You knew this all of these years, and yet you remained silent. Why?"

"Because she wanted me to."

"Yes, when you were just a little boy —"

John shook his head. "After that. She knew it would ruin my life. Which it would have."

He said this so matter-of-factly, Jury was astonished. "But when it happened, she made a decision on the spot, suddenly, rashly —"

"You mean she wasn't aware of the implications of her taking the blame?" said John.

"Exactly. She couldn't at the time have known —"

"But she could. She thought at lightning

speed. She would have made a brilliant surgeon."

"She could hardly have known Tom might have to resign."

"Yes, she could. But even if we say she made a rash decision, it was hardly irrevocable. Ten minutes, ten hours, ten days later, she could have told the police what really happened —"

"As could you."

McAllister looked disappointed in Jury. He walked over to the table where he kept the whiskey, put an inch in two glasses, walked back and handed one to Jury. "Look, Superintendent. Right now, at this point in time we could go round the stations of the cross of selfishness and find me at every one. But as to Tess: Tess was making an adult's decision. I was only capable of a kid's decision, which wasn't even deciding. Tess told me what to do, no, it was more that she ordered me to do it: to blot it out, to run. 'This didn't happen, Mackey.' She clutched my shoulders and looked at me with those hypnotic eyes. You've no idea the effect she could have on others. Or maybe that was my ten-year-old self's wishful thinking."

McAllister held Jury's gaze with his own hypnotic brown eyes. "She said, 'You weren't here, Mackey, you had nothing to do with this. No matter who asks you, you don't know anything about it. Promise me . . . promise' — she shook me — '. . . that you'll forget it, that you believe you had nothing to do with it.' And I promised. I was terrified of what I'd done; I didn't realize I'd hit Hilda so hard it would push her into that pool and she'd die. And here was Tess, just taking the fear away. Do you know what it's like to feel completely weightless? To be borne up as if by water? 'Let the deep, deep sea hold you up.' Joseph Conrad said something like that: that if you fall into the sea, don't flail, just submit. 'Let the deep, deep sea hold you up.'

"Tess was the deep blue sea. She held me up. Without her, I'd have drowned. I said it before: without her, I'd be nothing."

Jury looked at the drink in his hand, feeling himself at sea and helpless. He swallowed the whiskey, felt it burn his throat, and he thought he knew why alcoholics drank: a moment of clarity. It was so obvious, so crystal clear: "She wanted Tom to know."

John looked at him doubtfully and more than a little worried. "But that's exactly what Tess didn't want; she wanted to take the blame —"

"She's been dead for seventeen years. Tom Williamson has had to suffer not only that, but the unknown —"

"If you mean by 'unknown' that Tom wasn't sure she was innocent —"

Jury shook his head. "No. He knows she didn't do it."

John tapped the letter. "Then what purpose would be served by letting him read this? Would this be the truth of the affair? That Tess was willing to place him, Tom, in jeopardy in order to save me? It would surely make him miserable."

"By your own reasoning, I'd have to show him this letter. You did nothing, you said, kept silent, you said, 'because she wanted you to.' That was true, no matter the consequences; she was willing to bear them. By the same token, she wanted Tom Williamson to know what happened. Just as she wanted to save you from what would have been an appalling outcome right then, some years after that, she wanted her husband to know. Our conjectures have nothing to do with it. She wanted him to know."

"You're going to give him the letter."

"Actually, I thought you would."

"*Me?* Why?"

"Because you should. You should first tell

him what happened. Then he could read this."

"Superintendent, I realize you think I should do penance —"

"No, I don't, Dr. McAllister. You've been doing penance for years, in Africa. You're doing penance by living in Hackney. You want to serve time among the disadvantaged, the downtrodden, the misbegotten. To me, that's crystal clear. I just think it would be more — I don't know — humane, that's all. A letter written seventeen years ago from his dead wife is going to be very hard for Tom Williamson. It was hard for you; imagine how hard for him. I think it would make it easier if you were to tell him beforehand what happened. Then he could read the letter."

Jury went on. "I'll tell you something else. You said before you supposed Tess did throw herself down the stairs. No, she didn't. I think she was murdered."

John sat down again, suddenly. "My God. Please don't tell me you think I —"

"You? No I don't think that at all."

He had his head in his hands.

"I don't know if you've seen this in the papers, but do you remember Arabella Hastings?"

"Arabella? Yes, of course. She was one of

us at Laburnum that day. What about the papers?"

"She called herself 'Belle,' and her married name was 'Syms.' She was divorced. She was murdered in a little place near Northampton."

"What? What are you telling me. First, Tess; then, Arabella? Murdered?"

"Arabella Hastings was thrown from the top of a tower. You haven't read about that? The tabloids of course were all over it. Very dramatic." Jury wondered at that for a moment, at the drama. "Let me change the subject a little. Tell me anything you can about the children present that day at Laburnum."

"I thought I'd told you all I know."

"You answered my questions. But now I'm asking about your interaction with one another. Arabella Hastings was murdered, after all."

"You think that involves the rest of us?"

"Absolutely. Were any of you ever at Laburnum on other occasions? By yourselves?"

"Yes, I was. So was Mundy. So was Kenneth. I don't know about Arabella and Veronica."

"Was Tess's attachment to you something the others resented?" Jury settled back for a no.

He got a yes. "Kenneth was jealous as hell. It pleased me, that, since he was so adored by the girls."

"Not by Mundy," said Jury.

"No, perhaps not. But Kenneth adored Tess. He seemed — consumed by her."

Jury sat forward, hands laced between knees. "That's a powerful word. How did he treat you, then, seeing she preferred you?"

"Oh, Ken was cool. He wouldn't have let it show by being nasty to me. No, he treated me very well."

"And Tess was how toward Kenneth?"

"Perfectly nice, as she was with all of us."

"I understand Arabella doted on Kenneth. Did he have any interest in her?"

"None. Arabella wasn't cute or pretty and nor did she have much personality. But I think the main thing that put one off was her neediness. I hate that word, *needy,* but I can't think of another. She clung to him. She was like a limpet. The more he tried to brush her off, the harder she clung."

Jury set down his glass. "There's another thing. Going back to those laburnum seeds, you knew how many it was safe to eat. The fact that you were sick pretty much saved you from suspicion. Right?"

"Yes, I expect so."

"And you knew traces of the poison had to be in your stomach when it was pumped out. For someone in such danger, you were thinking pretty clearly. It wasn't foolproof, of course, but it was a pretty good alibi, that toxic illness. It got you off the hook for Hilda's death." Jury rose. The letter was lying on the table beside John, who was not looking at it and nor at Jury.

Jury picked it up, folded it, returned it to the envelope and waited for some sign of encouragement from John McAllister, some sign he should leave it. But he got none. He left it anyway.

"Good-bye, John." He had never seen a sadder look on any man than the one on John McAllister's face.

45

Brown's Hotel, Mayfair
Wednesday, 2:30 P.M.

An hour after leaving Plaistow Street, Jury was sitting in Brown's Hotel in Mayfair with Phyllis Nancy. He'd phoned her and asked her if she could get away for an hour or two. He told her he needed help. He chose Brown's because it was so comfortable, so beautiful, and so old-fashioned.

Phyllis agreed. "I'd never have thought of Brown's for tea. I'm glad you did. I love real teas." She sighed and settled back comfortably in her armchair. Between them on the table was a tiered plate from which she took a little scone.

They sat in wide, soft, cretonne-covered armchairs in a section of the hotel's lobby that was given over to afternoon tea. There were perhaps a dozen other guests sitting about on sofas and in armchairs.

"What is it you need help with?" She

poured each of them more tea.

"This." Jury pulled the letter from his pocket and handed it to Phyllis. "When I went to Laburnum, I found this. It had been shoved under the door of Tom Williamson's study and had also gone under the rug. It's been lying there for seventeen years."

"Why haven't you turned it over to Tom Williamson?"

"Because I couldn't. I think it would break his heart all over again."

"That's not for you to decide," she said, a little testily. She pulled the sheets from the envelope. As she read, her face bore an increasing expression of alarm. When she came to the end, she turned the page over. "Where's the rest of it?"

"There isn't any 'rest.' That's it."

Phyllis shook her head. "No. There's at least one more page."

"There wasn't." He told her how he'd continued searching for a missing page.

" 'Mackey, the love of my life' "? She shook her head. Is it this you don't want Tom Williamson to see?"

"No. 'Mackey' refers to Doctor John McAllister; that is, he's a doctor now; then he was only ten years old, and Tom told me Tess had a way of making exuberant declarations of love and affection. She was very sentimental. That appears to be what that is."

"It's too unlikely she'd end there. No, there's another page somewhere . . . unless . . ."

"Unless what?"

"Could she have been interrupted?"

"It's possible. But the letter still went under the door in that form. I mean, being interrupted wouldn't explain the missing page."

"It would if somebody else shoved it under the door, not Tess." Phyllis pushed part of her scone to the side of her plate, drank her tea. "If the person with her thought it could be read as a suicide note. Which it could."

"You think someone could have turned up while she was writing this —"

"The someone might have read it and become crazy-jealous or angry."

"Her husband, you mean? No, not him."

"If not jealous, then very angry over her protecting 'Mackey,' the one who'd killed Hilda Palmer. Or could it have been he himself who was there and didn't want to be found out?"

"Doctor McAllister?" Jury shook his head. "I no more think he could have hurt her than could her husband."

"Isn't this dated the same day that she died?" She showed Jury.

"It is. Of course anyone could have added a date."

"Yes, I expect so, which suggests murder." Phyllis leaned across the table, shoving aside a basket of sweet rolls. "How do you see what happened? The sequence of events? I mean, assuming I'm right about her being taken by surprise?"

"Okay. Say that someone she knew turned up, uninvited, and she asked him or her in. This person might have asked what Tess was doing. She says, 'Writing a letter.' She offers the visitor a drink — 'tea, coffee, whiskey'? — then leaves the room to get it. Visitor reads the letter, is angered by it, so much so that he threatens to kill her. And does. Then tries to make it appear as if she fell down those steps. On the other hand, the person could have come in the first place with that intention, and the letter had nothing to do with it."

"I still say it could have been this Doctor McAllister discovering in the letter that what happened was about to be revealed and he had to silence her."

"But surely he'd have got rid of the incriminating letter, were that the case, or rather that page of it, since he might have wanted to leave the letter as a suicide note," said Jury.

"The page that's missing, Richard. What if she discovered that she hadn't put it with the rest? What would she have done? Probably shoved it under the door too."

"It wasn't there."

"You mean not under the rug. What if the loose page had gone on top of the rug? Then someone would have found it. Her husband might have done."

Jury shook his head. "He'd have told me; it would have been too important a detail to omit."

"Before you show him this, though, go back and find the missing page."

"Phyllis, there is no other page."

"Yes, there is." Phyllis cut a Bakewell tart in two. "Find it."

46

Bloomsbury
Wednesday, 3:00 P.M.

Kenneth Strachey opened the door, looking
more billowy than on Wiggins's previous
visit. The white shirt had long balloonish
sleeves and gave Strachey a poetical or
piratical look. Wiggins couldn't decide
which.

"Sergeant Wiggins! Good to see you.
Come in, come in?"

"Thank you, sir. I'd just like to ask you a
couple of questions, if you don't mind."

"Absolutely ask away, but let's do it over
tea. I've just wet the tea leaves."

"Be glad to join you." Wiggins followed
him into the kitchen where steam was coming out of the spout of the blue-glazed pot.
Again, Wiggins pulled up a stool, put his
mobile on the counter at the end of which
sat a beautifully decorated cake. "Did you
do this, sir?"

425

"I did. Care for a slice?"

"Oh, no, sir. I'd better not start in eating again. It looks delicious. Is that caramel icing?"

"It is. Chocolate cake."

"And did you do all of the fancy decorations?"

"Yep. Sure you won't have some?"

"Not today, I'm afraid. I'll forget why I've come again."

Strachey laughed. "No harm done." He went to one of the cupboards to pull down cups and saucers. While his back was to the counter, Wiggins pulled a small camera out of his pocket, and took a quick picture of the cake. He dropped the camera back in his pocket, and as the mobile was close to hand, he picked that up as Strachey turned back. "Been trying to call Superintendent Jury. He's in Devon. Exeter."

Strachey poured Wiggins a cup of tea, shoved the jug of milk and sugar to him. "So what do police want to know?"

"Just me, sir. I was thinking of that unfortunate day at Laburnum for all of you kids and got to wondering, have you kept in touch with any of the others into adulthood?"

"Yes. Madeline Brewster, somewhat."

"What about John McAllister?"

426

"John? Not really. He seems to do rather a lot of traveling, and he's not in this country much of the time."

"How about Arabella Hastings, sir? The one who's dead."

Kenneth sighed. " 'The one who's dead.' Right. Poor girl. Threw herself off a tower, the paper said."

"From what we've gathered, Arabella, or Belle, as she called herself, had quite a case on you when you were kids. That so?"

"That's so, yes. It was rather tiresome."

"And did this tiresome crush linger into adulthood?"

"I don't know what you mean."

"No? I thought it quite a clear question. Was Arabella still devoted to you?"

"I've no idea," replied Kenneth, a little irritably. He drank his tea.

"You don't? What we were told was that her feelings for you were very intense. That she was one of those needy people who stick on you like a limpet. That was the description."

Kenneth didn't respond.

"Did you take her out at all in the last year, say? Go clubbing? Go for a meal? That sort of thing?"

Kenneth's irritation increased. He also looked a little wary. "No. I wouldn't have

427

given Arabella any encouragement."

"And why's that?"

"Because it was bad enough as it was, her suddenly turning up at places where I was. Coffeehouses like Nero's; Dillon's books; other public places. If I'd invited her for a meal, I'd never have been able to get rid of her."

"Is that what you mainly wanted, sir? To get rid of her?"

Kenneth had raised his cup, but now he set it down. "Sergeant Wiggins, are you implying that I did it?"

Wiggins raised his eyebrows. "Did what?"

"Got rid of her. In other words, murdered Belle — Arabella?"

"Did you?"

"Of course not. Furthermore, at the time of her death in Sidbury, Northants, I was here in Bloomsbury, London. I've already told you this, Sergeant. I came in sometime between eight and nine and had an early night."

"And your housemate can confirm that? Austin?"

Impatiently, Kenneth nodded. "Of course."

Wiggins had taken out his small notebook and ballpoint pen. "Does Austin have a last name?"

"Smythe, with a *y*. What motive would I have for killing her?"

"That of course I couldn't say." Wiggins's cup was empty. He was sorry his questions were offensive; that undoubtedly accounted for the lack of scones. He picked up the pot of tea. "May I?"

"Sorry. Of course, have more." As Wiggins refilled his cup, Kenneth said, "Her death must have been accidental."

"Oh? Why do you say that?"

"The shoes, Sergeant. The four-inch heels. According to the papers, she was wearing the shoes when she fell. She'd surely have removed them if she'd meant to fall."

"Why's that, sir?"

"Because of where the window was. She'd have had to climb up on a chair or a bench in order to get herself in place to jump. Automatically, she'd toss off her shoes."

"If it were an accident, wouldn't there have been the same problem? Getting herself in place?"

"Perhaps so." Kenneth poured himself some more tea.

"But one wonders why she'd have worn those high heels in the first place, seeing as how she'd have to climb that long circular staircase." Wiggins paused. "At least, you'd think she'd have worn her other shoes."

Kenneth looked a bit surprised, then said, "What shoes?"

"Oh, sorry. We got some prints left by a low-heeled shoe, though we didn't find any low-heeled shoes, which was very odd in itself. It's especially odd that she didn't keep them on for climbing that staircase. Given she wore them to tramp across the mud." A fact that Wiggins was not sure of, but he put it out there anyway. "She climbed those stairs in high heels, when she'd got this other pair. It strikes me as being significantly overprepared for suicide."

"So you're quite sure she was murdered?"

"Yes. Why and by whom we don't know. Yet. We also have an idea that it's tied to the death of Tess Williamson."

Kenneth looked completely taken aback. "Why in God's name would you think that?"

"Because Arabella Hastings was one of the six children Mrs. Williamson took along to Laburnum."

Kenneth forced a laugh. "That's really a stretch, Sergeant. Just because Arabella was at Laburnum that day twenty-two years ago."

In a mild tone, Wiggins said, "Why didn't you report her stalking you to police?"

"Stalking?"

"What you described certainly sounds like

it. It must have been dreadfully annoying, her turning up that way."

"Well, perhaps I exaggerated."

"But you were very clear about this incident, like the description of the window in that tower." Wiggins added, with a spring in his tone, "I must say, sir, you're really up on the details —"

"All from the papers, Sergeant. Journalists were making a meal of that event."

"I expect you're right there." Wiggins collected his notebook and clipped his pen into his shirt pocket. "Thanks for your help. Sorry I can't stay and share that cake with you."

"You're very welcome, Sergeant Wiggins." Kenneth got up too.

At the door, Kenneth said, "I'll be sure to put a piece of the cake by for you for your next visit."

"Two pieces. Superintendent Jury will come along too. Ta, sir."

I REMEMBER YOU

"When my life is through,
And the angels ask me to recall
The thrill of them all
Then I shall tell them
I remember you."
        Johnny Mercer and Victor Schertzinger

47

Jury remembered Tom Williamson's speaking of the housekeeper at Laburnum: "She comes in from time to time." He called Tom for her number.

"The Sturgises, they're not on the phone, Superintendent. But they're located nearby." Tom gave him directions. "When would you be going?"

"Tomorrow."

"I'd always put bits and bobs of papers on his desk," said Mrs. Sturgis, who had been extremely surprised to have police on her doorsill and still inquiring into the death of her former employer at Laburnum.

"Chuck it in the dustbin?" she had earlier responded to Jury's question as to how she handled papers left lying about. In her tone was a kind of housekeeping horror. "I

435

should say not! Who am I to tell if a piece of paper is worth keeping or disposing of?"

"I realize it's been seventeen years, Mrs. Sturgis, but can you cast your mind back and try to visualize the room and the things in it. Do you recall whether you found a page of stationery — plain, white paper, about five inches by seven inches — lying on the rug close to the door to Tom Williamson's workroom?"

Mrs. Sturgis sat quite still, apparently trying to visualize, as Jury had asked her to. Laburnum following Tess's death. She had earlier weighed in with conventional comments regarding the awfulness of that death.

"All right, I remember how brown the flowers in that crystal vase looked, so I took it upon myself to throw them out. I didn't think dead flowers would be much solace to her husband, would you?" She didn't expect an answer and went on. "Now I was lugging in the Hoover through the study door . . . my foot came down on something — yes, a small sheet of paper. I picked it up but didn't, mind you, read what was written on it, as that was none of my business. It wasn't full of writing, I could tell that. So I pushed it onto one of those metal spearlike things Mr. Williamson used to hold papers. He had more than one. It kept 'em from flying about, I expect. Since I didn't know what the paper said, I thought no more about it."

"Good for you, Mrs. Sturgis. You've a remarkable memory. Few people would recall a thing after so many years, something that must have struck you as trivial at the time."

Now she seemed a little distressed. "Actually, Mr. — What did you say your name was?"

"Richard Jury."

"Oh, yes. Well, actually, Mr. Jury, I'm not sure I thought it trivial, not after police were looking all over for a suicide note. But I knew it wasn't."

"You said nothing to police about that paper you'd found?"

"No. The notion of Mrs. Williamson committing suicide was preposterous. It would never have happened."

"You're quite positive."

"Of course I am. Not in a million years. Never would she have done that to her husband, for one thing. She was not an unhappy woman, either. Kill herself? Suicide and Tess Williamson? Different as chalk and cheese, Mr. Jury. Chalk and cheese."

Jury wished only that he could find more witnesses as sure of their testimony as was

Mrs. Sturgis. "Let me ask you something else, Mrs. Sturgis. I'm sure you remember that awful day at Laburnum when Hilda Palmer was found dead in the empty pool."

"Do I remember? Well, of course I do. Police thought the girl was hit with something hard. I asked Sturgis could it've been one of his rakes or hoes. His tools were always lying about."

As if on cue, a tall, rangy, elderly man came into the parlor, looking displeased. "Where's my lunch, Edna? It's gone noon already."

"Well, pardon me for living, Gabriel. I was interrupted making your sandwiches by police at our door. Scotland Yard, in case you're interested." She turned back to Jury. "This here's my husband, Gabriel. He was gardener at Laburnum for over thirty years. Still is, in a manner of speaking."

Gabriel Sturgis had stopped dead when he heard "Scotland Yard" and stood blinking away his astonishment.

Jury rose and extended his hand, but Gabriel seemed to take the outstretched hand as a threat and took a step back.

"Nice to meet you, Mr. Sturgis. I've been speaking to your wife, who's been extremely helpful. You weren't there, either of you, the day Hilda Palmer had her fatal accident?"

Mrs. Sturgis sniffed. "Indeed not. I wish I had been. I'd've sorted it."

And probably she would have, thought Jury, taking his leave.

Tom, of course, would have been in his study a few times over the years since Tess's death, but if he had found this page of her writing, Jury was sure he'd have mentioned it. Jury expected no revelation other than the one about "Mackey."

He parked, got out of the car, and hastened up the outer steps, unlocked the door and ran up the broad staircase to Tom's study.

The large desk that Mrs. Sturgis still polished to a glitter was covered with small stacks of papers. There were two of the "spears" she had mentioned, pinioning small and large pieces of papers. A lot were receipts, a few were bills. Tom would not have had the electricity, gas, or central heating cut off, despite his rare appearances here.

Jury flipped through the papers on one of the needlelike metal spears, found nothing, started through the papers fixed on the other. Halfway down, he found it — the page of stationery that had sat here between a bill from a roofer and an electric bill.

There were only two lines of writing at the top of the page:

But you, Tom, you were the thrill of them all.

Love always,
Tess

Jury looked at the thin spear that had punctured this page and felt it like a penknife in the heart.

It was just as well Tom hadn't found it, for how could he have read it and not thought of suicide, even though such a fall was too uncertain a method for suicide?

Jury called Brian Macalvie.

Macalvie wanted to see the end of Tess's letter and drove from Exeter.

They were standing by his car when he read it.

"I knew it wasn't suicide. Someone bent on suicide isn't going to hit on such an uncertain method. At the very least you'd come out of it with all manner of cuts, bruises, and possibly broken bones. So you'd just mess yourself up and you'd still be alive, only messed up. There was a gun in the house; there were pills; there was poison. And don't forget the car, which has always been popular because of its accident potential. No, you don't choose a fall down stairs."

"Yet many people settled for 'accident.' "

"Yeah. If it had been an accident, we certainly would have seen more signs of defensive wounds. One of the most common in that scenario is a broken wrist, because you automatically put out a hand to break your fall. And she wouldn't have gone far before the momentum slowed. She'd have landed maybe halfway down those stairs."

"Tom Williamson assumed you thought it was an accident."

"I know. I let him think that. If he knew I agreed with him that she was murdered, it would have driven him crazy because the investigation wasn't turning up evidence to prove murder."

"But he still thinks it was."

"But there's no real evidence. So he knows it's a guess."

"If you thought it was murder, who did you think did it?"

"One of them."

"The kids?"

Macalvie nodded.

"Why?"

"I told you I'd never worked out a motive.

But I'm sure it had something to do with that day at Laburnum twenty-two years ago."

"Macalvie, all she was doing was protecting one of them: John McAllister."

"Maybe one of the others worked out what had really happened and didn't like it. Someone might have been fanatically jealous. I think it's interesting that she died in much the same way as Hilda Palmer."

"But how did the killer do it?"

"Maybe with a gun to her head or maybe just by getting behind her and pushing her. That would have created a force she couldn't have managed by herself. And finished off the job with a blow to the head that mimicked hitting her head on that marble pediment."

"Forensic would have been able to tell the difference between those two events, though."

"Well, forensic didn't, in this case. There were arguments on both sides about the kind of skull fracture, the force of the blow, and so on." Macalvie opened the car door, started to climb in.

He stopped when Jury said, "Tess Williamson told her husband that their not having children was because she couldn't. I spoke to the doctor they'd consulted."

"And he said she could."

"He wouldn't tell me, of course. Patient confidentiality. But he did hint at the truth: he said she always put her husband first." Jury paused. "The thing is, three of those children at Laburnum were adopted."

"Four."

"No, three: John McAllister, Arabella Hastings, Madeline Brewster."

"Four. Kenneth Strachey."

48

Little Chef, M5
Wednesday, 3:00 P.M.

As Jury sat in a Little Chef on the M5, he called Wiggins. "Ring the D'Sousas and tell Veronica I have a few questions. This afternoon, if possible. I'll be there in two or three hours."

"Right. Me, I've been back to Strachey, sir. You're right about him. For one thing, he knows just a bit too much about that tower. He claims he got it from newspapers, but I've been through every major one and I can't find the details Strachey mentioned about the room at the top, the window she fell from, et cetera. I can take this to a magistrate and get a warrant, I'm pretty sure. But I've got to specify exactly what it is we're looking for."

"Clothes. A dress. I think he bought the Givenchy for her and I've an idea he bought more than one dress. As backup. He wanted

444

her to look sensational, and since he could hardly take her on a buying spree, he'd have wanted more than one dress."

"You think there's a relationship between this vertigo girl and Tess Williamson?"

"Yes. I think Belle Syms knew something about Tess's death." Jury picked up a piece of toast, inspected the burned places. They never did that at the Happy Eater. "In the meantime, I want you to check hospitals, private clinics in particular, where a woman might go to have a baby. Someplace near London in the early seventies. See if there's any record of a Tess Hardwick being admitted. Hardwick was her maiden name."

"Wouldn't it be easier to ask her husband?"

"Not if he doesn't know she had a child before they were married. I don't know that she did; little Hilda Palmer was rumoring it about, though."

Wiggins said, "You're thinking she was the mother of one of them?"

"It's possible. McAllister is probably the best bet, given her intense feelings for him. He was ten at the time, so we're talking twenty-two years later. He's thirty-two now. You can walk that back and get the year. Same for the other three: Mundy Brewster, Arabella Hastings, and Kenneth Strachey."

445

"Strachey? But he's got parents."

"Not the original ones. Apparently he's adopted."

"Well, but he doesn't know it, does he?"

"Oh, he knows it, Wiggins. When I commented on his relation to Lytton Strachey, he said, 'Not I. Pop seems to forget that.' His tone is sardonic whenever he talks about his father."

"Yeah, now I recall, he said something to me about his relationship to this Lytton Strachey that didn't follow."

When Wiggins started to ask another question, Jury said, "Ah! Here comes my breakfast. I'm in a Little Chef on the M5. We'll talk when I get back."

"Wish I was there, guv." Wiggins loved motorway restaurants, especially the Happy Eater, but that chain had been taken over by Little Chef. "Incidentally, you got a funny message from Madeline Brewster: 'Check out Paris.' What's she mean?"

Jury pondered this. He said, "The dress, Wiggins. Givenchy. So check it out."

"Must be a thousand places there." Wiggins grumbled this out.

"Quite possibly. Listen. If you can set it up, I'll go to the D'Sousas."

"Right. I'll tell them five-ish? That gives you a couple of hours. Is that enough time?"

"Five sounds good. Teatime."

"Lots of luck with that, sir." Wiggins gave a huffy laugh and hung up.

49

Clapham
Thursday, 5:00 P.M.

"Mrs. D'Sousa," said Jury, standing at the front door. "I'm Superintendent Richard Jury. I believe my sergeant rang you."

Colleen was not happy with either of them — sergeant or superintendent. "I don't understand what you could possibly want. We've told police everything we know."

"To the extent that you think you know it, Mrs. D'Sousa."

This rather runic reply seemed to convince her that he wasn't going away until he'd asked what he wanted to ask. He'd been standing outside while Colleen filled the doorway. Her shoulders drooped, her mouth along with them, as if she'd lost a battle, if not a war. "Oh, very well. Come in."

"Thank you." Jury stepped into a foyer that had once been largely a coat cupboard (he bet), and she preceded him into the living room, where sat Veronica D'Sousa with a black cat, or rather beside a black cat, as the cat didn't seem to be interested in Veronica.

Jury was left on his own to guess who this young woman was, as Colleen didn't introduce him.

"Miss D'Sousa? I'm Superintendent Jury, New Scotland Yard. I'd just like to ask you a few follow-up questions to those Sergeant Wiggins put to you when he was here last Saturday."

Veronica repeated a version of her mother's "I don't understand" by saying "Well, I can't imagine what questions would be left to ask. That Sergeant Wiggins covered everything that happened that day at Laburnum." She stroked the cat, who moved out from under her hand to the other end of the sofa.

Colleen had ensconced herself in an armchair, covered in a cold blue that matched the sofa. Left to sort out his own seating arrangement, Jury sat down beside the cat. The cat promptly rubbed against his coat sleeve, purring.

"Not necessarily everything. You had a particular fondness for Kenneth Strachey, is that right?"

Veronica looked at him dumbly. "Why

449

ever would you say that?"

"Because somebody said it to me. Both you and Arabella Hastings were fond of him."

"Oh, her," said Veronica dismissively until she suddenly remembered that Arabella was dead and took another line. "Poor Arabella. What rotten luck!"

"You think it was just bad luck that landed her at the bottom of that tower? That it wasn't intended?"

"Intended? You mean she threw herself off? She did it on purpose?"

"Or somebody else did."

Veronica, in a stage gesture, put her hand to her face.

Colleen gasped. "Are you saying the girl was murdered? But that's impossible!"

"Unfortunately, it isn't. Arabella Hastings presented a problem to someone. I was hoping you might assist me in understanding what sort of problem." Jury smiled. The cat was stretched out along its whole length, lying against him. The fire was out. The room was cold. He wondered how often the fire was lit and the cat got to lie in front of it.

"Me? But I haven't seen Arabella in absolutely years."

"As a child, what was she like? You were friends."

450

"She was just — a regular girl, I suppose."
Veronica shrugged.

"Was she happy?"

"Happy? I expect so."

"Why would you expect so? She was an orphan; her only family, aside from the uncle who took her in, was an aunt in Northamptonshire. Did she get on with the rest of you all right?"

Veronica frowned slightly. "Well, yes, or more or less."

"The 'less' might have been because she resented you, you being so much prettier." Which she wasn't; indeed they had much the same coloring.

This left Veronica at sea as to how to respond to a compliment from a Scotland Yard detective. "Well, in a way —"

"And jealous too, since she was attracted to Kenneth Strachey."

"Good heavens, Superintendent! Nicki and Arabella were only eight and nine years old," put in Colleen.

"And Kenneth was thirteen. All the more understandable he'd look good. When you were playing hide-and-seek, Kenneth was the first one you discovered, right? Did you keep your eyes open until you saw where he went?"

Veronica first looked surprised then guilty,

casting her eyes down. She didn't answer.

Jury said, "When you found him behind that huge rock, did you stay for a minute or two?"

She looked quickly at Jury, then away.

"Were you kissing?"

"Superintendent!"

"Pardon me, Mrs. D'Sousa, but if you continue to interrupt, I'll have to insist that I speak to your daughter alone. Veronica?"

"Nicki. Why do you think that? That we'd be kissing? I was just a little girl."

Her mother looked smug.

"Little children are fascinated by sex, Nicki. Because he was handsome and you were pretty. And you haven't said no."

She was silent. Her mother opened her mouth but shut it again when Jury shot her a look.

"Anyway," said Veronica, "why would you be interested in all that?"

"Good question. I'm interested because I'm trying to sort out the relationships among you all. For example, all of you disliked Hilda Palmer."

"That's no secret. She was trouble."

"She knew things — or thought she did — that she'd use to blackmail people."

"She drove a teacher to resign, is what she did."

452

"I heard about that."

Veronica suddenly turned to her mother and said, "Mum, you haven't offered Mr. Jury anything. I bet he'd like a coffee." She gave Jury a questioning glance.

"I really would, if it's not too much trouble." He didn't want coffee, but he did want to get her out of the room without appearing to threaten her. Wiggins had been right about his interview.

Colleen stood. "Cream and sugar?" she asked, as if it were a dare.

"Both."

She mumbled something and left the living room.

When she was out of earshot, Veronica said, "I didn't want to say this in front of my mother because she'd demand to hear every last detail."

"Good. You can say it to me and *I'll* demand to hear every last detail." Jury smiled, winningly enough that he could see her beginning to melt a little.

"Well, Hilda Palmer claimed she knew something about Mrs. Williamson."

"What?"

"That before she got married she had a baby."

Jury feigned astonishment and said, "What was Hilda going to do with this knowledge?"

"If Mrs. Williamson tried to do anything to her, Hilda would tell her husband."

"But how did Hilda find this out?"

"Listening to people talking. She was always listening outside of doors and things. I don't know. Hilda was just good at finding things out. Really, she was dangerous. She knew something else too about Mrs. Williamson. That she went to a 'baby doctor.' Well, that's what she called it. I expect she meant a gynecologist."

"Many women do. Nothing shocking in that."

"She overheard Mrs. Davies talking to her mother. What she said she heard was that Mrs. Williamson couldn't have children. And she didn't think that was true because of what she said she knew."

"Couldn't Hilda simply have been lying? Showing off?"

"Yes, she could have been. I'd guess she lied a lot." Veronica looked puzzled. "The thing is, how do you know something's a lie until you know the truth of it?"

"A good point."

"And enough of what she said did turn out to be true."

"It certainly sounds as if people hadn't much privacy with Hilda around. What about Arabella?"

"Why are you so interested in her?"

"Because she's dead," said Jury.

"Oh. Sorry. Arabella was all right. She didn't run and tell on you if you did something wrong. But the trouble with her was she was kind of cling-y. You know?"

Jury nodded. "Meaning she'd stick to you and you couldn't scrape her off?"

"Exactly."

"Anyone she'd especially cling to? You?"

"No. Kenneth. You could tell he hated it."

Approaching footsteps told them Colleen was coming back. She entered, carrying a small tray that Jury rose to help her with, but she merely set it on the coffee table and told him to help himself to milk and sugar, which he did. He said to Colleen, "I was told the parents of the children at Laburnum were quite friendly with one another. Is that true?"

"No. If you mean by that sharing a social life, no."

"You didn't get together for coffee or drinks or meals?"

"Oh, the occasional coffee, I suppose."

"Did any of the others?"

"Not so far as I knew, and one can generally tell if people have struck up a friendship that goes beyond seeing one another when the children are together. We were

455

perfectly pleasant, though; we did talk. Especially Gilbert Strachey. He had a way of going on about his forebears. 'Descended from Lytton Strachey' he was fond of reminding us. I said to him that would be rather difficult, as Lytton Strachey had no children. He was —" Quickly she flicked a look at her daughter and then returned her gaze to Jury. "— You know."

"I don't know, Mum. I don't even know who Lytton Strachey was."

Jury put in, "He was a famous nineteenth-century writer and critic."

Colleen went on. "So it's absurd talking about Kenneth's carrying on the writing tradition. Poor Gilbert lives in a fantasy world, but then if you have Gilbert's money, I suppose you can live anywhere you want."

Jury liked the way she put that. "Mr. Strachey is rich, is he?"

"Very. Kenneth doesn't know how lucky he is. It would be nice if Nicki could keep on seeing Kenneth —"

"Mum! That's nothing to do with this. Don't parade my personal life in front of strangers."

It apparently didn't occur to Veronica that she was doing the parading with that last comment. " 'Keep on seeing'? Then you've recently been together?"

456

"Only once or twice —"

Colleen said, "Oh, more than that, dear."

Jury welcomed the interruption this time. It confirmed what he'd already suspected: Kenneth and Veronica were, as Wiggins liked to say, "going at it." Veronica was caught between not wanting it known she was seeing Strachey and wanting it known Kenneth found her desirable.

She made another weak protest. "Hardly more than that, Mum."

"All right, dear, if that's what you say."

"You and Kenneth, Nicki," said Jury quite deliberately, "sound like an item."

50

Jury left in the aftermath of Veronica D'Sousa's displeasure with both his comments and her mother's about Kenneth Strachey. He assumed the intensity of that displeasure mirrored the intensity of her feelings for Strachey.

A half an hour later, he was sitting in his office at New Scotland Yard with Wiggins, talking about Tess Williamson and that his search had turned up the final page of the letter she'd written to Tom.

Wiggins said, "Kenneth Strachey was obviously devoted to her."

"Why do you say that?"

"I think he's still making the cake, guv."

"What are you talking about?"

"Just that. Literally." Wiggins pulled the picture he'd taken out of his pocket and walked it over to Jury's desk. "This cake was on the counter when I went there; chocolate cake with caramel icing and chocolate swirls all around it. Don't you think they're quite similar?"

Jury looked at the two pictures and nodded. "In her testimony she said she'd been making a cake."

"Strachey is a first-rate cook, you know. Especially cakes and pastries, from what I can gather."

"I saw the kitchen. Both cakes appear to be similarly decorated, but it's a little hard to tell from this old photo —"

"It was enough to make me wonder, so I rang Elaine Davies. I thought she might remember. And she did remember, in part because she'd helped make the caramel icing."

"Well done, Wiggins. You're right, that strikes me as pretty obsessive behavior. But what did he say about Arabella Hastings and Veronica D'Sousa?"

Wiggins told him about the "casual" "occasional" coffees and lunches. "Obviously, he couldn't just deny it, not with her probably telling us they were having a flaming love affair."

"But she did try to deny it; it was Mum who brought it out. Veronica was furious. So now they've both — Kenneth and Veronica — denied something, which makes it look all that much more suspicious." Jury reflected, holding his teacup. "Would you say, Wiggins, that Veronica and Arabella are about the same size and shape?"

"I'd say so, yes, sir, from the photos I've seen. I never actually saw Arabella Hastings."

"Same coloring too, except for the hair. Arabella's was dark, almost black."

"Easy to do that with a wig. You're thinking —"

Jury nodded. "I can think of only one reason Kenneth Strachey would be seeing his old friend Nicki: he needed someone to stand in for Arabella, and somebody devoted enough she wouldn't give all that much thought to the fix she'd be in if police ever settled on Kenneth as a suspect."

"And she's a good actress too, I remember."

"I think that red dress would fit both women; anyway, Strachey could have sussed out their dress sizes, and shoes, for that matter —"

"Speaking of shoes, Strachey went pale when I mentioned the 'other pair' of shoes, the low-heeled ones that Brierly's SOCO team found prints of. Those prints couldn't have been made at some other time, could they?"

Jury shook his head. "They were fresh. I'd guess Belle brought more sensible shoes in case the sandals turned out to be too, well, strappy." He smiled.

"That'd be my guess too, only it doesn't make sense, does it? Thing is, why didn't she walk to the top of the tower in them?"

"I can think of no reason at all. You're right; it doesn't make sense. On the other hand, if Belle was already dead and carried up to the top, it would explain the red sandals, but then, what about the other shoes?" Jury paused; then he said, "The stand-in, the woman who posed as Belle would have to be insanely in love with the perp because she's giving *him* an alibi and leaving herself exposed. Dangerous for her."

"What was the motive, though?"

"It must have been something Arabella knew that presented a danger to the killer. Something that went back to Laburnum."

"Possibly, except we know who shoved Hilda, so what's left is Tess Williamson."

"Her death, you mean?"

Wiggins nodded as he poured boiling water over tea bags in two cups. "Was Doctor McAllister any help?"

"Not about that. He's too taken up in his

461

job to think about much of anything else."

"If he killed Hilda Palmer and was afraid Tess Williamson might tell the police —"

"I don't think so, Wiggins. Why would she? She was the one who protected him at great personal cost to herself. Why would she give him up five years later?"

"You really think one of those kids killed Tess Williamson?"

"Yes."

"But after five years? Why wait that long?"

"Perhaps because the killer found out something he hadn't known before." Jury rose. "I've a dinner engagement; I'm late for it already. You should go home, Wiggins."

"Soon as I finish writing up my notes, sir."

This was said in a tone of such gravitas, Jury felt a mite ashamed he wasn't writing up his own.

"There's an obvious candidate you're ignoring: Madeline Brewster —"

"No. Not Mundy." Jury picked up one of the teacups and added milk from a pint bottle.

"If you don't mind my saying, sir —"

"Any statement that begins that way always ends with the person minding."

Wiggins didn't care; he went on. "Your emotions are getting in the way here. It's the first time I've ever known you to discount witnesses because you didn't want to believe they were guilty. In this case there are three of them: Tom Williamson, John McAllister, Madeline Brewster."

"Tom Williamson has an alibi. Just look at Macalvie's notes. Tom was in London at Oswald Maples's house. Doctor McAllister was in Kenya. Or Botswana."

"So he said. It wouldn't be the first time someone managed to get in and out of a country with, say, a fake passport."

Jury nearly laughed. "I can't picture that; sorry."

Wiggins frowned. "Anyway, I'm talking about the murder of Arabella Hastings. Where was everyone when that happened?"

"But the same person did both, I'm almost certain. As to Mundy Brewster" — Jury shrugged — "she's not involved."

Wiggins grunted. "We didn't really investigate them. Especially Madeline Brewster. You think the killer had a female accomplice. Besides D'Sousa, she's the only female left amongst the kids at Laburnum. You don't even know if she has an alibi."

"You're right, Wiggins."

"Then do you want me to talk to her? I can call her right now —"

"Check the alibi."

51

Boring's, Melrose Plant's club, was located in Mayfair, not far from Brown's, with which it had something in common: exclusivity. But here the testament to money and changelessness was mirrored not in chintz and tea, but in leather and whiskey.

As they sat in the light and warmth of one of the Members' Room's several large fireplaces, Jury said, "Have you got the two dead dogs sorted yet?"

"One dead dog. There was never more than one. That one is Stanley as you very well know and Stanley is quite alive."

"Glad to hear it. And did you find *any* dead dog, never mind the number?"

"No. You might remember, though you're pretending you don't, I was never in favor of the dead-dog theory." Melrose sat up a bit and looked over his shoulder. "Where's

464

Young Higgins?"

"He appears to be the only porter in sight; he has to wait on everybody, as far as I can see."

Melrose slouched down again. "What's he doing out of the dining room?"

Jury shrugged. "I wouldn't know, would I? I'm not a member."

"Don't be so literal."

"All right. Now, where does the failure to find a dead dog point you in your search?"

"Nowhere. Are you doing any better with your case?"

"Probably. But I'm not looking for a dead dog."

"Funny," said Melrose, glumly.

"We know Belle Syms was really Arabella Hastings, one of the kids at Laburnum."

"Aha! That's certainly progress. Hold on a tic. There's Young Higgins." Melrose raised an arm and swept the elderly porter to their chairs.

"Yes, my lord." Young Higgins bent toward them.

"Another whiskey, Higgins."

Jury nodded. "The same. Thanks."

Higgins moved off with exceedingly great care so as not to break something — an arm, a leg, or a glass.

"Does any of the staff ever retire here?"

"No. They just die. Young Higgins has been here since I came here with my father. He must be into his nineties now."

Jury turned the talk back to the dead man in Wretch's Row. "You're no closer to solving that mystery, then?"

Melrose frowned. "I wouldn't say that."

"What would you say?"

"That Stanley's affinity for the murdered man bespoke a relationship of long-standing, not merely one between dog and handler, no matter how good the handler."

"Interesting. Continue."

"His alleged name, Roy Randall, wasn't taken from any official document, such as a driver's license."

"True."

"So how can Brierly be sure that was his name? He can't. The victim had only an envelope addressed to a Roy Randall. The assumption is that's who he is. But he isn't. Or wasn't."

"You say that as if you really knew."

"I do. It's interesting."

Jury stared at Melrose. "Well, come on. Give."

It was at that moment when Young Higgins returned with their drinks and the announcement that their table was ready in the dining room whenever they were ready.

"Thanks," said Melrose, and to Jury, "come on. We'll take our drinks through. I'm hungry and it's roast beef and Yorkshire pudding night."

Jury rose, saying, "Who the bloody hell is Roy Randall?"

"Over dinner, Richard, over dinner."

Boring's dining room was, as always, an expanse of white linen and dark wood and voices kept so low that it was more an island of silence in a sea of hush.

Their waiter was a brash young ginger-haired fellow who addressed them as "gents."

"Evenin' gents. We've a nice Stilton and leek soup, as well as a London particular tonight."

"Those soups are rather heavy with roast beef and Yorkshire pudding, wouldn't you say?"

The young waiter had no fear of saying, "I like a good thick soup meself?"

"Do you, now? What about the rest of the cast from *Oliver*?"

The waiter's eyebrows rose over eyes of denim-colored blue. "Sorry?"

"Never mind. I'll have the London particular."

Jury said, "The Stilton, since I don't know

467

what that mystery-soup is."

"Pea soup, ain't it?" said the waiter. "You must've been round in the time o' the 'thick as pea soup fogs' London useta 'ave. 'Particular' to London, they was. I take it you'll both be 'avin' the roast beef?"

"As that's the entrée of the evening, I expect so."

The waiter thanked them and took off for the kitchen.

"Young Higgins would have a hernia," said Melrose. "That one won't last long."

"As long as he lasts through your story, that's okay. Continue with Roy Randall."

Melrose said, "Right, as soon as I've settled the wine."

"Oh, come on, just get the house plonk."

"Boring's does not serve a 'plonk.' Let's see, let's see . . ." He consulted the list. "What do you say to a Saint-Émilion?"

"I'd say stop stalling."

"All right." Melrose raised his hand and motioned the waiter over and ordered the wine.

Jury said, "You're just going to milk this information for all it's worth, aren't you?"

"That is correct." Melrose moved his wineglass nearer to his water goblet. "Now, I heard there were a half-dozen receipts from a turf accountant in Mr. So-called

Randall's pocket, the envelope addressed to him in Snide Street, E6, and the label of a Savile Row tailor in his coat. A rather unusual combination, don't you think?"

"I'm sure DCI Brierly had his men on that."

"He did and he didn't."

"Would you mind not sounding so damned inscrutable."

"Inspector Brierly was working under the assumption the man's name was Roy Randall, which would rather skew the result."

Jury waited. There wasn't much use prompting.

"They found Roy Randall, who took off like a bat out of hell when he spotted a cop on his doorstep."

"But how did you find —" Jury stopped when Melrose held up a hand like a crossing guard. Then they waited while soup was served and wine uncorked. Poured. Tasted.

Jury put his hand to his head. "I take it Roy has form."

"All kinds, but largely petty thieving, including making off with garments from coatracks in cafés; and several citations for indecent exposure in public lavatories." Melrose stopped and spooned up his soup. He buttered a roll and drank some wine.

Jury was about to cuff him. But he restrained himself, saying, "And DCI Brierly gave up all this information to you, a mere citizen?"

"Well, he didn't, did he?" Silence, another swig of wine. "I did manage to get in to see him by telling him I had some information for him about Belle Syms."

"What information?"

"What you told me."

"I also told him."

"Not before I did, though."

"Ta very much."

"That's okay. Naturally, he got out the file on the case. And as people sometimes tend to do, even policemen, he read off the address as if he were speaking to himself."

"He was."

"As I told you — Snide Street, London E6. Ring a bell?"

"Of course it doesn't."

"Perhaps not. It did with me. I got out my *London A to Zed.* You know where Snide Street is?"

Jury was silent.

"Right around the corner from Catchcoach."

"Catchcoach Street? Isn't that's where the Crippses live?"

"The same. That address, combined with petty thieving and public toilets, was enough

to bring me to London. I spent a pleasant
afternoon with Ash the Flash and White Ellie. Let me tell you about it."

52

Catchcoach Street
Thursday, 4:00 P.M.

Melrose told him about it.

He always preferred coming on number 24 Catchcoach Street stealthily in order to apprise himself of the dangers — it was not too strong a term — that lay in wait, or that would do if the Cripps kids spotted him first. He had fortified himself with a half-dozen screws of candy to give out when it became necessary to save himself.

He stopped by one of the few healthy trees in Catchcoach Street, hiding himself behind its trunk. He watched the loose ring of kiddies in the front garden — or rather the dirt — of number 24. As he hadn't been here in a couple of years, there were one or two new ones among the gang of old and he wondered if the tot in the middle of the circle was actually the former baby, Robespierre, who had managed to survive for two and a half years and who could prove useful now, instead of just an object to be pushed around in his carriage and crib. The former baby was still a victim but now one with legs and hence more versatile. Each one of the Cripps kiddies had played that role in his or her turn.

The same baby carriage stood outside the door, housing, Melrose supposed, a fresh baby. He counted six children in the ring, the one the others were dancing around making seven. He recognized two or three of them. Piddlin' Pete was the one who had formerly occupied the center of the circle, but he now appeared to be the ringleader, which apparently offered him more opportunities to urinate on whatever struck his fancy, which at the moment was a stray cat wandering in from the road. The cat did not stay long.

The front door slammed back and the matriarch of the household yelled, "Petey, ya stop that this minute or I get yer dad!"

This was not much of a threat, considering Ash the Flash's own quixotic behavior in the public toilets hereabout. It was this particular penchant of Ashley Cripps that had put Melrose onto him as a possible source of information about Roy Randall. Melrose had discovered the terraced house in Snide Street, only one street over from Catchcoach. Wembley-Knotts, that part of London in which all of this activity took place, was now almost wholly occupied by Pakistanis and Bangladeshis, with a sprinkling of Taiwanese, Japanese, and an even thinner sprinkling of the original British settlers. On every street there was probably a token Brit whose pale face tended to get lost in the crowd of many-hued others.

From behind the tree, Melrose watched the action as White Ellie (short for Elephant, a tribute to her girth) kept up her threats and bawled at them to "stop pickin' on Robespierre." So Melrose had been right; the crying child in the center of the circle was the former baby in the pram.

But Robespierre, weeping like all get out, was getting precious little help from the adults on either side of the street. The kiddies were singing one of their original songs, as they danced about, jumping higher and higher in the air:

"Robespierre, Robespierre
Always keeps 'is bottom bare.
Robespierre, Robespierre,
Always got 'is prick in the air."

The idea was, of course, to get the child

in the center crying (which he had been and still was), and the more he cried, the higher they all jumped.

Melrose crossed the street.

When they saw him, they yelled and broke the circle and spewed around him like vomit. He heard among their whoops and hollers, "Candyman!, Candyman!" He was not sure he cared for that appellation in these times, but he still pulled from his pockets the white screws of lemon drops, sherbets, milk gums, fruit bonbons, and jelly beans. He also had one small box with a breathtaking assortment of colors and textures; this he gave to the tearful little Robespierre.

He also gave a rap on the fingers to the child who tried to grab it away and was surprised when this eight- or nine-year-old started bawling. Melrose told him to shut it. The boy was so surprised by this stranger's command that he shut it.

The doorway now was filled — rather, stuffed — with the figures of White Ellie and Ash, who were hurling greetings at Melrose and waving him in. The kiddies, now mildly quiet as they shoved candy in their mouths, were told to come in for their tea.

When Melrose stepped into the living room, Ashley said, " 'Ave a drink, 'ave a drink, Lord Ardry."

The Crippses liked having a friend with a title so much that Melrose didn't see the point of telling them he was now a commoner. "Thank you, Ash, I will."

Ash, in a generous gesture, swept his arm over a card table holding bottles containing various substances that could as well have been crankcase oil as gin.

"A cup of tea would go down a treat," said Melrose.

Ellie waved her own arm toward the kitchen. "Come on in whilst I fork up the kiddies' tea!"

Melrose had avoided the kitchen after Sergeant Wiggins's description of a frying pan with hardened lard in which were lines of tiny footprints. But here it was, the Crippses' kitchen, with wallpaper on which gladioli had been transformed into phalluses; where grease-smeared dishes were piled in and out of the rust-stained sink; where open cupboards did little to protect dishes from those same creatures with tiny feet; and where the corners of the ceiling were festooned with cobwebs. A real lived-in look, all-round. The room was so crowded with stools and chairs and baby paraphernalia it would be easier for a roach to ride in a Nascar race than to cross this kitchen.

"I've wet the leaves already, so it should be good and strong. There you are." Ellie handed him a chunky mug, and shoved a carton of milk and a box of sugar toward him.

"Thanks," he said, shoveling in a couple of spoons of sugar and looking rather closely at the milk before he poured it.

What he liked about the Crippses was the assumption that Melrose was here simply because he wanted to be, and they didn't waste time asking the reason for his visit. Ash and Ellie assumed they were as much a destination couple as were the queen and Prince Philip. There could be no purpose in his visit beyond his delight in seeing them.

"Ash," he said, "do you happen to know a fellow over in Snide Street named Randall?"

"Roy Randall?" bellowed Ash. "Yeah, o' course." He leaned closer to Melrose. " 'eard there was a bit of bother with the cops."

Ellie put in, "Randy Roy, we call 'im. Been done a few times for flashin'."

"Have you read the paper lately?"

Ellie barked, "Makes ya' think Ashley can read?" She turned then and yelled to the urchins in the yard, "Yer mash's up!" On six plates Ellie was spooning up globs of mashed potatoes. Alongside of that she put a forkful of boiled cabbage, and the kiddies came barging in.

Ash curled a hand round his ear. "What you sayin', Lord A?"

Melrose loved the *A*. "There was a man found in Northamptonshire. Sidbury, near where I live. He was with his dog, walking behind some shops."

The kids grabbed plates and bottles of ketchup and crowded onto chairs around the table where Ash and Melrose were sitting. Ash got up, saying, "Come on into the parlor. Can't hear bugger all in this racket."

Melrose followed him, saying, "I wondered if you knew any of Randall's mates."

"Mebbe. Yeah, I do."

Melrose slipped one of the snapshots Theo Wrenn Brown had taken at the scene across the card table. "Could this be one of them?"

Ash took some time adjusting the wire earpieces of his glasses, picked up the picture, and said, with surprise, "Bugger if that don't look like Zeke. What's wrong with 'im?"

"He's dead. Walking his dog down an alley. Shot dead."

The cigarette Ash had lit and stuck between his lips stayed glued to the corner of his mouth when it dropped open. "Dead? Zeke's *dead*? But I just saw 'im — when was it? Last week? Roy never tol' me about this."

"Maybe Roy doesn't know. Who's Zeke?"

"Friend of Roy's lives over near the Park, Wembley Park. Elephant! Ellie, get in 'ere!"

White Ellie managed to loosen herself from the grip of the table and entered the living room.

"Looka 'ere, El—" Ash held out the picture.

She stared at it, squinted at it, brought it up to her eyes. "That's Zeke!"

"He was shot," said Melrose. "So his name is Zeke — what?"

"We just call him Zeke. Name's Zachariah. Zachariah Syms. Oh, my God!" White Ellie had her plump hands on both sides of her face. "Poor fella."

Ash looked at Melrose. "You said 'e was walkin' a dog? What 'appened t' the dog? Where's Stanley?"

53

Boring's
Thursday, 9:00 P.M.

They were into their dessert by the time Melrose reached that point in his narrative.

"Bloody hell," said Jury, dropping his fork into his pie. "Zachariah Syms? Belle's husband."

"The same." Melrose's tone was a little smug. "Thought that would interest you."

"Why was Zack Syms in Sidbury?"

"Looking for his wife. Looking for Belle. According to Ash, by way of Roy Randall, 'Zeke,' as he calls him, had been trying to get back together with Belle ever since they separated. They were still on friendly terms, even met up at the pub for a beer."

Jury nodded. "Yes, Blanche Vesta said Zack was still crazy about Arabella. Blanche liked him."

"But Belle wasn't interested. When she told him she was going to Sidbury, he as-

480

sumed it was to visit Blanche, who he knew from Blanche Vesta's visits to Wembley Park to see them. So he took off for Sidbury. He didn't know where the aunt lived, though."

"That's why he was looking for the Old Post Road."

"I expect so. He'd never been there before."

"But he never got there, poor fellow." Jury frowned. "What about Stanley?"

"Ah. Now, that's very interesting. Stanley's a bit of a personality in his own right, though Lord knows, we haven't seen much evidence of it. Stanley's not a Staffie; he's a pit bull. One of your APBT dogs. Roy Randall breeds them —"

"That's illegal," said Jury.

"So? Since when have the Ashes and the Roys of this world worried over that detail?"

"But he'd have been reported by someone, surely. Breeding dogs in your back garden must create a bit of a ruckus. How many dogs are we talking about?"

"A dozen, maybe. And he doesn't do this on his property. He has a small parcel of land in the Norfolk Broads, near Hinckley Broad, I think. He does keep a couple of dogs at a time at home —"

"Again, the neighbors would report the presence of a couple of pit bulls."

"Let me quote Ash's response when I made that point: 'You think people round 'ere give a toss? You think we ain't got better things t'do than finger some poor sod that's got a dog the Filth don't like?' " Melrose chortled. "White Ellie put in, 'No love lost for your RSPCA, neither.' "

Melrose wanted to congratulate Ellie for citing this organization's initials correctly.

"So how did Stanley end up at PetLoco?" asked Jury.

"I'm getting to that. Roy has sold these dogs of his to online pet adoption services, many to PetLoco, which I take to be the most questionable of the lot. They turn around and sell the dogs to dog men, who, in turn, fight them. When they're either no good or used up, the dogmen turn right around and unload them to places like PetLoco. Or they just shoot them. Now, the thing about Stanley is that Zack Syms had developed a real fondness for him. There was a hell of a row on Snide Street when he found out Roy had sold the dog. He went on PetLoco's Web site, found Stanley and paid the price, which for Zack was hard, as he had barely enough for rent and booze. And the thing is, Stanley really liked Zack. In a short time they were inseparable. Indeed, anyone who as much as looked at

Zack cross-eyed had to deal with Stanley, who was happy to sink his teeth in them; and if Stanley didn't get him first time, he remembered who the ignorant git was. One mugger will not be mugging anytime soon; one bloke outside of a pub tried to hustle Zack for money. Stanley soon routed him.

"Which might have been," Melrose went on, "what happened outside of the Blue Parrot. We'll never know, I guess; we can only infer."

"Infer, perhaps, that the killer met up with them somehow in that vicinity and tried to shoot Zack?"

"By 'killer' I take it you're talking about Belle Syms's?"

Jury nodded. "But I don't think just because he killed the wife, he was gunning for the husband."

"But wouldn't that make some kind of sense? Or are you still thinking the shooter was —"

"— after Stanley. Or both of them They both presented a danger, or he thought so."

"Yes, the dog was certainly protective of Zack."

Jury was shaking his head. "I think it was his memory. The killer had run into Stanley before and Stanley would remember him."

Melrose knocked back some brandy. "Oh,

come on! Not that old hoary device — furious animal recognizes killer?"

"I'm just nothing but clichés and hoary devices, aren't I?"

"Syms didn't have a gun, did he?"

"Not when his body was found."

"How is it Stanley got separated from him?"

Jury shook his head. "Must have had something to do with the possible fracas."

"And then there's the matter of the Highboys woman and *her* dog."

Jury thought for a moment. "It's possible Stanley had already been delegated to Highboys and Zack Syms came along and offered more."

"And PetLoco kept Highboys's fee and told her the dog would be delivered?"

"That's easy enough to check. That place will be out of business in two days when I tell Karl Mindt."

"Who's Karl Mindt?"

"RSPCA."

"Does this get you any closer to Belle Syms's killer? It certainly wasn't her husband. He was sitting in Roy Randall's parlor on Monday night. Do you have a prime suspect?"

"Oh, yes. Trouble is he has an alibi."

"How inconvenient."

"It's not a perfect alibi, however. The thing is, he had an accomplice, I'm pretty certain. That explains Belle Syms's appearance around Sidbury after ten P.M. Eight to ten P.M. is the time period when Kenneth Strachey was seen in London. So he could hardly have pitched the body off that tower then. And since he allegedly turned in — or so his housemate thought — he would also have been at home at midnight. That's the squishy part of the alibi. His housemate didn't actually see him at midnight."

"This supposed accomplice: she doesn't have an alibi. Would a woman be that stupid?"

"Yes. We're talking about a grand passion, remember? Woman or man, anyone might supply a lover with an alibi even though it left him or her exposed."

"This is the *Vertigo* girl."

" '*Vertigo* girl' — I like that. That's what Wiggins calls her."

"There's something I just can't understand. Why in God's name would a killer go to all of the trouble of luring a woman to the top of that tower to kill her? Or, if she's already dead, haul a body up there?"

"So we'd ask the question."

"What?"

"So police would spend a lot of time trying to sort out the scene. As if it really were relevant."

Melrose frowned. "Sorry, that's too subtle for me."

"It's not subtle at all. This elaborate charade makes one think it must have been necessary for some reason. No. It was simply a distraction. Like the red dress, the spike-heeled shoes."

Melrose waited. "I must be in my default mode: stupid."

"The *Vertigo* girl. In the film, Kim Novak looked exactly like the wife. Exactly. In this case, the accomplice's face only approximated the face of Belle Syms. Coloring was the same; hair was different, but a wig took care of that. Makeup, cleverly applied, could create the illusion of a likeness, but certainly not enough that if a person such as the Sun and Moon's owner looked closely, he couldn't tell the difference. So the point was to make people look not at the face but at what was beneath it, and that dress was sensationally good at that. Everybody mentioned it."

Again, Melrose frowned. "How did she have the money to buy the outfit in the first place?"

"Well, she didn't, did she? And he'd never have left the clothes up to her anyway. He bought it, I'm sure. He had to have something that was a standout and that would fit both women."

"If there *were* two women."

"There were. Another brandy?"

"Hell, yes. Where's the unspeakable — ah, there." Melrose raised his hand. "Let's get out of the dining room, though." When the "unspeakable" waiter arrived at the table, Melrose instructed him to bring more coffee and more brandy into the Members' Room.

"So you're saying this Strachey bloke killed Belle Syms before he took off for London and possibly got the body up to the tower at that time —"

"Yes. The accomplice who'd arrived at some point, perhaps met him there, I don't know, would already have been made up and wigged and then donned the red dress. Strachey takes off for London; she returns to the Sun and Moon, then appears a little later in the bar, and then makes her circuit of the town. Since Belle Syms hadn't gone to those places herself — the club, the Sidbury Arms — this second woman wouldn't have had to contend with recognition. When I said Strachey's alibi wasn't perfect, I meant that he would just barely have had time to leave London at ten, get to Sidbury at, say, half-eleven. That's if he's got a very fast car. There is no way he'd still have the time to murder Belle Syms and get her body up to that tower. No way. So if there was no accomplice, Strachey couldn't have done it, not given the time-of-death window. But I'm sure it was him; so there must have been another woman."

"Who was —"

"My guess is one of the other kids at the Williamson house that day: Veronica D'Sousa. She and Kenneth Strachey were seeing one another. She was clearly nuts about him, had been when they were kids, still is."

"Well, but do you think this all has anything to do with the death of Tess Williamson?"

"I think it has everything to do with the death of Tess Williamson. Look: two of the kids at that party were killed. Although Hilda Palmer's death was more of an accident, and certainly unpremeditated. Three of these kids were currently involved with one another: Kenneth, Arabella, and Veronica. The two women were in love with Strachey."

"But you still haven't mentioned a motive."

"I think Belle knew something. Incidentally, Belle — Arabella was apparently a stalker. There was every sign she was stalking Strachey."

"Is that relevant?"

"Yes."

"What do you think she knew?"

"Who killed Tess Williamson."

54

Jury sat at the bar of The Old Wine Shades, drinking a pint of Fuller's on tap and incurring Trevor's disdain. He had offered Jury a very fine Pinot Noir that he had just opened, and Jury turned it down in favor of beer.

He had also eaten a surprisingly good sandwich, and all the while he ate, he had thought about Mundy and his idea that she might have modeled that dress in the course of her afternoon's work. Kenneth might have picked it out and asked her to model it. Customers could, he supposed, do that.

No, he couldn't believe the accomplice had been Mundy Brewster. She was not that stupid, and nor venal. And certainly she was not besotted with Kenneth Strachey. Dr. John McAllister was another story, but Jury doubted she would go along with murder, even for him. When his mobile twitched in

490

his pocket, he pulled it out.

"Sorry, boss," said Wiggins. "It's a non-starter."

"What is?"

"Veronica D'Sousa. The night Belle Syms was killed, the D'Sousas — both of them, daughter and mum — were at a charity bash at the Connaught. I've already tracked down a half-dozen guests who could verify different times in the evening that Veronica was present. Their statements covered the time from eight to midnight."

Jury was stunned. "You mean she has an alibi?"

"Up to her earlobes."

Jury sighed. "Damn. Did you come across any other women he was seeing?"

"No joy there, either. I put two DCs on his trail after I interviewed him. That's the bad news; but there's also *good* news: Madeline Brewster has an alibi that sounds solid, as soon as I can check on the people who saw her in this pub —"

Jury was surprised at the relief he felt. While Wiggins talked, Jury signaled to Trevor by raising his empty glass.

"Oh, and I had much better luck with the clinic inquiry. Private clinic that sounds pretty posh, even over the phone. Called the Oldham Clinic in Surrey, near Dorking.

They had a Tess Hardwick there in the relevant window of time."

"I'm surprised they'd give you the information. Didn't they balk?"

"Of course. But you can really make headway if you threaten them. I just told them I could have a warrant and a black ops team at her door within twenty-four hours."

Jury laughed. " 'Black ops'? We have a black ops team?"

"No, but it sounds really sinister. I just tossed it out."

"I'll keep that in mind. Where is this place?"

"Box Hill, just north of Dorking, A24. It's only around twenty miles from London. I expect you can do it in an hour, hour and a half."

"Okay. Thanks, Wiggins."

Jury put his mobile back in his pocket as he thanked Trevor for the drink the barman was setting before him.

"You look as if you'd lost your last case, Superintendent," said Harry Johnson, pulling out the bar chair beside Jury.

"Hello, Harry." Jury looked down toward the floor. "You forgot Mungo again."

"Sorry, I don't know your schedule. Trev!" Trevor turned and Harry nodded.

"Nice to see you, Mr. J, as always. What'll it be?"

"Um. How about a good Sancerre, Trev? I'm in a flinty mood."

Trevor laughed and went down the bar.

Harry turned back to Jury. "You're here early. As am I. What's the matter? Not making progress? No Hitchcockian solution? I assume you're still working on the vertigo murder?"

Jury nodded. "Actually, Harry, I followed up your suggestion of an imposter. Now I'm stuck with it."

"What do you mean?"

"I'm cornered. I'm fairly certain I've identified the killer, but the accomplice, the woman I was sure was his accomplice — she has an alibi. Ironclad. A dozen or more people saw her in London at the time this murder happened. The next woman we thought might be a contender for the role also has an alibi. She couldn't have got to Northants and given her performance in the time frame set by the pathologist. The killer is probably gay, and that limits considerably the possible women who could have played the role. The list of women has struck out."

In the midst of this, Trevor had returned with the Sancerre, a glass of which Harry now held in his hand. He sipped it and said, "Who said it had to be a woman?"

55

London and Box Hill, Surrey
Friday, 1:00 P.M.

Jury was too stunned to speak.

Which made no difference, as Harry was still talking. "Your suspect certainly must have men-friends."

Jury thought of Austin — the languid, effeminate, "girl-y" Austin — and frowned. Was that possible?

Harry still went on. "Of course, anyone you choose as an accomplice to a murder you'll be bound to for life. You want to dump him? You can't. You're stuck with him. How hideous." Harry shuddered.

Jury sat, staring at his beer. Austin as Lady Bracknell. He tossed a ten-pound note on the bar and rose. "Thanks, Harry; for once. Or twice. Right now I've got to go to Surrey."

The Oldham Clinic sat on a few wooded

acres near Box Hill overlooking the River Mole. This part of Surrey was only about twenty miles from London, and Jury made it easily in an hour.

This clinic was a posh place to be sick in. A semicircular drive, both ends gated and pillared in stone, ran to and from an ivy-clad red brick building planted in the middle of grass so green it looked fake enough to be a film set. This was a private hospital catering for people who could afford to be upscale sick. Jury put his finger on the buzzer, and a bell toned inside, sounding gloomy.

The door was opened by a well-groomed, expensively suited middle-aged woman. Her "May I help you?" could have been mistaken for a friendly inquiry, but it wasn't.

"You may." Jury pulled out his warrant card and brought it up to her face.

"Police?"

"It would seem so. And you are?"

"The charge nurse here. Mrs. Stewart-Stevens."

It could have been her husband's first name, but Jury guessed it was simply one half of a double-barreled one. "Mrs. Stewart-Stevens, may I come in, please?"

"As I told the other policeman, I don't

understand why you'd be interested in the clinic."

"It's about a former patient, as he told you."

She stepped back from the door and nodded him in with great reluctance.

The room was dull with old wood and old Oriental carpeting, but bright with fresh flowers. "I need to speak to the person in charge of records."

That astonished her even further. "*Our* records?"

"Unless you're holding somebody else's records."

Now her look was smug, a "gotcha" sort of look. "For that, you would need a warrant."

"I will certainly return with one if the clinic refuses to let me see the records I need to see. Right now, I'm making a request, that's all." Jury smiled. "If you're the charge nurse, I expect you yourself have the authority to do that." He wasn't, but she took him up on it. So far he had seen no sign of life here except for this woman, either inside or out.

She was saying, "— but I don't see any reason to do that. What records are you speaking of?"

"Tess Hardwick's. Thirty-five years ago

she was a patient here."

Although the woman didn't move, mentally she had taken a step back. "Yes, I was here then."

As if that solved all problems. "What was she here for? Was she pregnant?"

"No. It was a nervous condition. She was treated by our psychiatrist then, a Dr. Samuels."

It was Jury who took a step back mentally at this: "You mean she did not deliver a baby here?"

"As she wasn't pregnant, that would follow, wouldn't it?" was Mrs. Stewart-Stevens's rakish response.

"This Dr. Samuels, is he — ?"

"No, Superintendent, he isn't here anymore. He passed away two years ago." More helpfully, she added, "There was another patient named Thessaly, called Tess; perhaps you're confusing the two? Thessaly Durban was the woman who had the baby. She put it up for adoption. You might inquire at the adoption agency in Camden Town. That's where the child was sent."

Jury was surprised. "You remember this right off the top of your head? Even though it was over thirty years ago? I'm impressed, Madam."

"It was my first nursing post. Here, I

mean. I made a lot of mistakes. The reason I recall Tess Hardwick is that she was the soul of kindness and was always trying to buck me up. Tessa Durban I remember only because I connected the two women in my mind, probably because they both called themselves Tess."

"If you'll give me the name of the agency —"

"I'll just get it. Wait here."

There was no problem in getting Eleanora Crick at the Camden Gardens Adoption Agency to divulge the name of the baby's mother. Perhaps it had been a relief to people in Miss Crick's line of work when the Adoption and Children Act was implemented because they wouldn't have to stonewall anymore.

"Thessaly Durban," said Miss Crick in answer to Jury's question. She had pulled an old ledger down from a stack on a shelf behind her.

"The baby was a boy, correct?" That was Jury's best guess.

She nodded.

"Tell me, have you had any inquiries about this adoption? I mean other than from police? And I don't mean recently. I'm talking about seventeen years ago."

"Seventeen years — ?" Eleanora Crick consulted a large ledger, with entries in various hands. Jury watched the pages turned. "I don't see any note made to that effect."

"It would have been written in that ledger, I assume?"

"Yes . . . only —" Her face clouded over.

"Only what?"

"You see, over the years we've sometimes been short of experienced staff and have had to engage people who weren't. Experienced, I mean."

How much experience did it take to write down a name? But Jury didn't bother asking her. Instead, he thanked her and left.

56

A24 to M25
Friday, 7:00 P.M.

"You were right, Wiggins, about the Camden Gardens adoption place. Only the baby wasn't Tess Williamson's. The mother was a woman named Thessaly Durban, also calling herself 'Tess.' "

Jury was on his mobile, calling as he drove the A24 to meet the motorway to London.

"Then Tess Williamson wasn't pregnant; she didn't have a baby."

"She didn't, no. I should have paid more attention to Macalvie's post-mortem report. Had she ever delivered a child, it would have shown up there. I guess I wasn't looking for what *wasn't* there."

"But the Oldham Clinic is for obstetrics, isn't it?"

"Yes. But they take people with other conditions. Especially if the patient has the Hardwick money behind her."

"Then she couldn't have been the mother of one of those adopted kids at Laburnum. Specifically, Kenneth Strachey."

"That's right. Only, he didn't know that. Imagine if you suspected a woman named Tess Hardwick was your birth mother and went looking for her and found a Tess Durban. Bingo!"

There was a frown in Wiggins's voice. "But that's a different name, guv —"

"Consider the difference, though. 'Durban' could so easily be taken as a short form of 'D'Urberville.' That Tess loved Hardy's book was common knowledge. So 'Durban' would simply be the name Tess might have used in order to keep her identity secret."

The frowning tone was still there. "I dunno about that. Seems a bit of a reach."

"Of *course* it's a reach, Wiggins. Kenneth Strachey is given to reaching. He can convince himself of anything he wants to. He's an extremely disturbed man, as you've probably noticed. And an extremely plausible one. I think it's time we charged Mr. Strachey."

"Tonight, sir?"

"No, we'll leave it till tomorrow morning."

"What's the charge, guv?"

502

"Three counts of murder."
"Three? Who's the third?"
"Tess Williamson."

57

Saturday, 10:00 A.M.

When Kenneth Strachey saw the two of them on his front step, he did not look as if he planned to cut them a slice of cake.

Jury smiled pleasantly. "Good morning, Mr. Strachey. I hope we're not disturbing you too much. May we come in?"

"Yes, of course." Strachey seemed trying to project the same goodwill he had managed when Jury and Wiggins had stood there separately. But he couldn't muster the energy. He simply nodded, said "of course," and waved them in. "I was just about to have tea. Care for a cup?"

Fully expecting Jury to say no, Wiggins was in a hurry to say yes. Then they both said "Yes, thanks." Wiggins looked at Jury in surprise as they followed Kenneth into the kitchen.

"Why are you here?" The tone was hostile,

but the expression tried to hide the hostility.

Jury ignored the question anyway, saying instead, "You know what I'd really like with my tea?"

Kenneth was moving the classy designer kettle off the hob and looked puzzled. "No, what." He got some cups and saucers from a cupboard and lined them up.

"A piece of that wonderful cake Sergeant Wiggins hadn't time for."

This was not on the menu. Strachey just looked at him, saying nothing.

"You don't remember? This cake." Jury drew a photo from his coat pocket and placed it on the butcher-block table.

Wiggins was on the verge of making some comment when Jury stepped on his foot. Wiggins grunted.

Strachey frowned. "When did you take this —"

"That cake was baked by Tess Williamson twenty-two years ago. And that, of course, is Tess," he added, pointing to a figure standing near the cake. Jury did not know that he'd ever seen, literally, blood drain from a face. But Kenneth Strachey's did and left his skin waxy white.

Wiggins picked up the picture as if he really did intend to see if it matched Ken-

505

neth's cake.

Jury snatched it out of his hand, and Wiggins moved his foot back.

Strachey said, "Is this a joke? If it is, it's quite tasteless."

Strachey, remarkably (thought Jury), continued with his tea preparation. He put two tablespoons of loose tea into the pot and poured freshly boiled water over it.

"Not a joke at all," said Jury. "Murder rarely is."

The drama at this point was quite accomplished: too much hot water in the pot, and tea overflowing onto the table, cups unsettled in their saucers. Wiggins looked as if he might say, "What a waste."

"Murder? What in hell are you talking about?" Kenneth grabbed a roll of paper towels and started mopping up. He shoved the roll toward Wiggins.

"A better question might be *who,* not *what,* in this case."

"What do you mean?"

"Well, as we're dealing with three murders and three victims — Arabella Hastings, aka Belle Syms, Zachariah Syms, and Tess Williamson, I'd think you'd be interested in which one I'm talking about."

The mention of Tess Williamson had frozen Kenneth Strachey in place for three seconds, but then he was back to pouring more water over tea leaves with just that brief hiatus of spilled tea; Jury marveled at the man's composure.

"All right, who are you talking about?" said Kenneth.

"All three."

"*What?* You're saying that Tess Williamson was murdered?"

"Yes. I thought I just did."

"The court didn't think so. It was an open verdict."

Kenneth was pouring tea into the cups, sliding the milk jug and sugar bowl toward them. Only Wiggins seemed less fazed by the real world encroaching on his teatime than did Kenneth. Wiggins added three lumps of sugar, a good dose of milk, and drank.

"I know one of the detectives who was on the Williamson case. As far as he was concerned, the alleged accident wasn't a compelling theory. I myself played around with the idea of suicide, but he found that even less likely."

As if Jury hadn't spoken, Kenneth went on: "As for Arabella Hastings, she was one of us kids who Tess took to Laburnum, but what could she have to do with all of this? It's absurd. Why would anyone go to the trouble of getting the woman to the top of that tower — ?"

"Oh, I expect the tower jaunt was already settled before you left. She apparently liked heights: Ferris wheels, the Swiss Alps, fire ladders, the lot. And the tower served as an excellent distraction."

"Hold it, please. 'Before you left' you said."

"You and Arabella."

"You're serious? You think I killed Arabella? *I* did?" Kenneth half-laughed.

"Yes. Didn't we tell you that's why we came? Sorry."

"Superintendent, have you forgotten I have an alibi? Austin has told you —"

"No, I haven't forgotten. Interesting to speculate, though, on why you thought you'd need one. I mean, why would police even think of you in terms of Arabella Hastings, given you'd had nothing to do with her since Laburnum; that is, beyond her unwelcome attentions? That, of course, turned out to be a blessing in disguise, as it made her putty in your hands, poor girl."

"I was in London that night."

"If you were, and I'm not at all sure you were, it would have been for only part of that night, although Austin believed you were here for all of it. Either you killed

Arabella before you left the Sun and Moon, or you got her up to the tower and then did it. In any event you waited until you got back to toss her body out of the tower window. You needed an accomplice, someone to take her place so as to fix the time of death much later and give you a chance to get back to London. But we found no woman you knew who couldn't account for her whereabouts that Monday night.

"Lacking a woman, how about a man of slight build and pretty looks? My first thought was Austin, a good Lady Bracknell, and then I realized you were an even better one. So why put yourself in the hands of anyone else when you could do the imposture yourself? You donned that sensational red dress and heels — killer shoes, I might add — made yourself up, pulled on a wig and went down to the bar of the Sun and Moon, making a point of talking to the bartender, who was also the owner. After that you made several stops around Sidbury, establishing the fact you were very much alive until after ten P.M. Then you recostumed the body, took Belle Syms up to the tower, and shoved her out of the window.

"But at one point a problem came up that no one could have foreseen: a dog."

"A *dog*? Well, I'm sure you can weave a

dog into this fanciful fabric."

"Thanks. I'm sure I can too. So can Sergeant Wiggins. When he finishes his tea." Jury gestured from Wiggins to Strachey. "Go ahead."

"Yes, sir," said Wiggins. "Exactly where you came in contact with this dog enough to make an enemy of him, we don't know. However, the dog got away from his owner sometime Monday evening. He was seen by several people and seen on the grounds of Tower Cottage." Wiggins did not even blink over this lie. "That was around midnight. The dog could have seen you with the body. Thing is, this dog once belonged in part to Arabella Hastings when she was married to Zack Syms. If the dog was close enough to see you carrying or dragging her, he'd have gone for you. Not only that, he'd remember you. His name is Stanley."

"Stanley." Strachey tried on a condescending smile, but it didn't work.

"Stanley," said Wiggins, "is a very protective dog. As you found out."

"Jesus Christ." Strachey shook his head.

"He won't be of much help," said Wiggins, quite seriously.

"Is that all? Are you finished?"

"By no means," said Jury, holding his teacup out for a refill; Kenneth lifted the pot and poured the tea. Jury continued the story:

"We're still with Stanley, only now he's back with his owner, and one or two things happened. We know the second did because we've got the body. That is, in Sidbury. The first, though, I'm speculating about. You were looking for Stanley because you thought Stanley's owner might have been watching you at the tower. You didn't know where he lived but assumed it was in Sidbury. Or Stanley might even have belonged to the owner of the cottage. So the dog and his master could be around if and when you had to return, either of your own volition, or were forced back by police. You couldn't stay in Sidbury, of course, so you drove back and forth and on the last occasion, Saturday, you spotted Stanley somewhere around the village in the company of his owner. You followed them to that alley behind the shops and tried to shoot both Stanley and his owner and did manage to shoot Zack Syms. Killed him."

Kenneth Strachey seemed fascinated with this accounting despite himself. He said, "My God, Superintendent, that's one of the most incredible reconstructions of a crime I've ever heard." He got up and started collecting the teacups. "Sorry gentlemen, but

I'm a little peckish, and I'm getting a few things to eat. Do you like caviar?" He looked from one to the other.

Wiggins supplied an answer. "Tell the truth, I don't think I've ever tasted caviar."

"Well, then you're in for a treat, Sergeant."

"Oh, don't get up, Mr. Strachey, the worst is yet to come."

Kenneth raised his well-groomed eyebrows. "Then I need sustenance to get through it, don't I?" He paid no attention to Jury's request; instead he went to the giant fridge, opened the door, and started whisking small plates out of it and lining the dishes up his arm.

Fascinated by such self-possession, Jury watched him prepare all sorts of things: crushed ice filling a glass bowl and a smaller bowl set within the ice; bread sliced thinly; an arrangement of crackers circling a large platter, smoked salmon on a green glass plate set beside that; wineglasses brought down from a cupboard, three of them upended on the counter at which they were sitting, and a bottle of Chablis that he uncorked as smoothly as a sommelier and poured. "Sorry there's no champagne."

Jury found Strachey's capacity for suppressing emotion unnerving. But he waited until the plates had been brought to the table and Strachey reseated. "Now, the worst?"

Jury nodded. "Much the worst: the murder of Tess Williamson."

Strachey this time did register alarm. "Again, the court's ruling was an open verdict. Probably, it was an accident. Everybody knew she had vertigo."

"Vertigo isn't what killed her. And an accidental fall down those steps wouldn't have done it, either."

"Why not, if her head struck that pedestal at the bottom?"

"She never reached the bottom. Her head was struck, all right, but a hand was holding the piece of marble."

"You make it sound as if you were there."

"I wasn't. You were."

"What?" For the first time, the sangfroid slipped a little. "What about Tom Williamson? I passed him —" He stopped, realizing his error.

"You passed him? And where was that?"

"All right, I was there. I passed Williamson on the road, the old one that led to the house."

Jury was taken aback. "No you didn't. Tom Williamson was in London that afternoon, visiting a friend."

Strachey's smile was tight. "Well, there's

an alibi worth checking."

"That's a very weak defense, Mr. Strachey." When Kenneth didn't answer that charge, Jury said, "Now, Arabella Hastings . . . Somehow threatened to use the knowledge unless you saw her, went out with her, or who knows what? Remember, you told Sergeant Wiggins she was 'always turning up' in unlikely places. I'm saying Arabella followed you all the way to Laburnum that day. But it was years before she played that card. Perhaps because she married Zack Syms. It must have come as a very nasty shock that she knew about Tess's death. So you dated her a few times, and when she said she was going to Northamptonshire to visit her aunt, you saw an opportunity.

"The impostor-thing was quite a clever idea, Mr. Strachey. Chancy, but not as chancy as it would have been to have someone else put on that dress. This way, there's only you, no one else to witness it —"

"Except a dog," said Wiggins, interrupting as he popped a biscuit laden with caviar into his mouth.

"Except a dog," said Jury, smiling.

58

Knightsbridge
Saturday, 11:00 A.M.

Tom Williamson heard the brief rap of his front door knocker, which stopped as suddenly as it started, as if the visitor wanted to take it back.

Rarely did Tom get surprise visitors; he thought it must be the postman wanting something signed or one of the delivery services — UPS, FedEx. These thoughts occurred as he walked to the door, opened it, and saw a complete stranger with nothing in his hands.

"Mr. Williamson," he said.

"Yes? May I help you?"

"I expect you wouldn't remember me; it's been so long. John McAllister." John smiled.

Tom was utterly taken aback. He stood for some time looking at him. "McAllister. Wait, you were one of the children at Laburnum . . . You're *Mackey*?

515

"Mackey, yes."

Tom found the man's smile absolutely heart-melting. No wonder Tess had adored him. "But . . . come on in, please."

John McAllister entered rooms he had seen once or twice as a little boy but remembered nothing of.

Tom said, "Look, would you like something? Tea? Coffee? I could use something stronger, myself." He didn't doubt that McAllister could too. "Whiskey? Vodka?"

"A whiskey would do well, thanks."

"Just have a seat anywhere; I'll be right back."

After he walked out of the room, John looked around it, avoiding the mantelpiece, since he'd noticed pictures lining it and didn't think he could take looking at them too closely.

Tom was back with the Macallans and two cut glass tumblers. "Water? Soda?"

John shook his head. "Just plain, thanks. I'm sorry to barge in like this, but it's important. It's about Tess."

Tom handed him a tumbler holding two fingers of whiskey. "Tess? But she's been dead for seventeen years, John."

John nodded. "This is something I just found out and that you probably don't know yet. There's a letter —"

"What letter?"

"From Tess."

Tom frowned. "I don't understand."

"Of course you don't. You've never seen it."

59

Bloomsbury
Saturday, Noon

Jury and Wiggins had run through two possible scenarios as to the way Kenneth Strachey had managed to get Tess Williamson from the top of that set of stone stairs to the bottom.

"Maybe with a gun pointed at her, she was trying to get away and took a running leap, which is about the only way she could have propelled herself down those steps by herself," said Wiggins.

"But perhaps you actually picked her up and threw her down. Forensic had a set of figures to determine the varying distances: the depth of the patio would show how much of a run she could manage in order to throw herself down; the distance of the time the person would be in the air; the landing distance. What we're thinking is that you must have read the letter she wrote to

Tom and were infuriated by her words about John McAllister: 'Mackey, the love of my life.' "

Kenneth smiled sourly as he poured another glass of the Chablis — two glasses. Wiggins cupped the top of his glass with his hand. "Yes, I was furious. She had written this note and left it under a glass heart paperweight. I thought that glass heart a nice touch. It says so much about the human heart, doesn't it? Heavy, brittle, breakable, weighted, transparent, cold — one could go on for a long time reflecting on that symbolism.

"And you're right. I did go looking for my biological mother when I turned eighteen. I never forgot what that beastly little Hilda Palmer told me. That Tess had a baby several years before she'd married Tom Williamson and had put it up for adoption.

" 'And how do you know this, brat?' I asked her.

" 'My mother heard it.'

" 'Why do you think this is such exciting news? It wouldn't hurt Tess if it were known.'

" 'Maybe not hurt *her.* But what about one of *you*?' "

Jury said, "How did she know that? It wasn't common knowledge at all; I imagine your father went to some pains to hide the fact that you were adopted."

"He did. Hilda? How did she know anything? But she did; she found out things that astonished people."

"The search for your mother led you to the Camden Gardens Adoption Agency."

"And I did discover there was a woman named Tessa Durban who'd put a child up for adoption. Tess just made that name up. She was my mother."

Jury and Wiggins exchanged a look. "Didn't it occur to you that Hilda Palmer was lying to you, Kenneth?"

"Of course it did. But it turned out she wasn't. It was the brightest moment of my life, finding that out. And Tess didn't know; at least I don't think she did. How could she have? I found out she was going to Laburnum that week; I went too. I drove up out front and went in. I called her name, but nobody answered. I went into the library, her favorite room in the house, but she wasn't there. That's where I found the letter. Of course, I shouldn't have read it, but I felt I had earned the right now. When I found that she'd been protecting John and that he'd been the one to push Hilda, I didn't know what to think. 'The love of my life'? For the first time I wondered if I'd made a mistake, or the agency had —

"I went looking for her. You think I killed her? Don't be ridiculous; I could never have done that. She was dead when I got there."

60

Jury snapped out of his self-satisfied summing-up, stunned. "What are you talking about?"

"I went out to the patio and saw Tess lying at the bottom of those stone stairs. I ran down to help her, thinking she must be unconscious and she . . . was dead."

He looked genuinely grief stricken.

Wiggins said, "Were you absolutely sure? Didn't you call police? Or a hospital for an ambulance?"

"Yes, I did."

"But you didn't wait?"

"No. Caught in those circumstances? Alone with a dead body? I don't think so." He shook his head. Then he added, "So that probably was Tom Williamson I passed on the road."

Jury shook his head. "He was in London

522

with a friend, a mutual friend. He couldn't have been there."

"But he was. At least he was on the road, and where else would he have been going?"

Jury made a few swift calculations in his mind. "London is two hours —" Then he stopped. No sense telling Kenneth Strachey what he thought. He said, "Why haven't you said anything in all of this time, for God's sakes?"

"Same reason. Police would have been all over me and they'd manage to supply a motive, wouldn't they, in my discovery she was my mother? She abandoned me and I was furious . . . something like that."

"You didn't know how long she'd been dead?"

"I could take a guess that it wasn't long. Her body was still warm. I don't know much, but doesn't it take at least a couple of hours for rigor mortis to set in?"

Strachey was a little too nimble with words for Jury's taste. He looked at Wiggins, who appeared to be thinking something of the same thing. "About that. I can't get over the fact you just left her there," said Jury.

"Self-preservation, Superintendent."

Jury narrowed his eyes. "Let's go back to Belle Syms's death."

"Now, that's really a facer, isn't it? What

possible reason would I have for doing away with Arabella Hastings-Syms if she wasn't a danger to me? And if I hadn't killed Tess, Arabella wouldn't be a danger, right? And of course if I didn't dump Belle from that tower, neither the dog and nor the husband would have seen me. Which means I'd have no reason to kill *them,* correct? It's like dominoes, isn't it, Superintendent? The first one falls, then they all do." Kenneth smiled brightly. "So I've done absolutely nothing wrong" — he bit into one of the biscuits — "except to put too much salt in these clotted cream biscuits." He frowned.

"Very neat, Mr. Strachey, but I don't believe it for a moment."

"No? Then why don't you check Williamson's alibi?" He took a drink of wine. "Because the thing is, you don't have any evidence that I'm guilty of any of these murders, do you?"

"Get a warrant, Wiggins. Bloody hell."

"We've still no concrete evidence, sir. Just theories," Wiggins said, uncertainly. "Is it possible Tom Williamson was there?"

"How can it be? He was with Sir Oswald that afternoon. And if Tom killed Tess what about the others? Arabella Hastings and Zack Syms. You don't think he did those murders too?" Jury wiped his hands over his face. "No, it couldn't have been Tom. He loved her too much."

Wiggins gave Jury a look.

"Well, what?"

"It's just that you're so emotionally involved in this case."

"Okay. Then *you* check his alibi. Go to Knightsbridge, talk to him."

"Wouldn't it be better to talk to her?"

"Her? Who?"

"The nurse, or housekeeper back then? Zillah Peabody. I saw her name in the file. Sir Oswald was waiting for her, couldn't understand why she didn't show up because it was Monday, and she regularly came on Sunday, Monday, Wednesday, and Friday. But Williamson told him, no, today was Tuesday."

Jury, whose hand was reaching for the phone, stopped in midair. "Surely, all of that was checked out seventeen years ago? Tom would have been the prime suspect. Police surely would have picked over that alibi like searching for fleas on a dog."

"That's *Williamson's* alibi. It isn't Sir Oswald Maples's. I mean, Maples established Tom Williamson's alibi. Did anyone think to wonder if Sir Oswald was lying to protect him?"

"Oswald Maples wouldn't have done that."

"But think about this: Tom Williamson could have been establishing an alibi. He had to be with someone on Tuesday at least late enough into the afternoon that it would have made it impossible to get to Devon by the time Tess died. But, of course, he wouldn't know that, would he, unless he'd killed her?"

"Then go to Chelsea instead of Knightsbridge and see Oswald Maples."

"Right."

61

Chelsea
Saturday, 2:00 P.M.

"Sir Oswald Maples? I'm Detective Sergeant Wiggins. May I come in?" Wiggins had his warrant card out and Sir Oswald was adjusting his glasses the better to see it.

"Wiggins? I know that name from somewhere."

"Superintendent Jury's my boss. Maybe he mentioned me."

Sir Oswald broke out a big smile. "Of course! Yes, come on in. I was just having a hot drink. Care to join me? Toss your coat over a chair, why don't you?"

"Thank you, sir. Are you having tea, then?" Wiggins got out of his coat and, as Sir Oswald had suggested, tossed it over the arm of a chair.

"No. It's some concoction called — what is it? — Chee?"

"Chai," said Wiggins, correcting the pronunciation. "Real spicy, isn't it? Lots of cardamom and things?"

"Ah. You're a cook, Sergeant? Splendid."

"Not me, no. I just like to drink things."

Sir Oswald laughed. "Well, then, allow me to get you a cup."

But seeing that it was difficult for Sir Oswald to walk, even with a cane, Wiggins said, "Oh, please don't. I've just had a pot of tea and I'm pretty well tea-d out."

"All right. Then what can I do for you? Superintendent's sending round the rozzers?"

"No, sir. He just wanted a couple of questions answered."

"Why didn't he send himself round?" Oswald reclaimed his chair and balanced the tea on its arm.

"He couldn't. This is to do with Tom Williamson, sir. As you know, Superintendent Jury has been looking into Mrs. Williamson's death. We just wanted to get one thing straight. You confirmed Mr. Williamson was with you the day she died. He was here at your house."

"He was, yes. I recall we were arguing about the day. This is seventeen years ago, you know; I think I should be congratulated for remembering."

"I do too. But in this case could you have

been wrong? Or right, I should say?"

"Well that just about covers the bases, Sergeant Wiggins. I was either wrong or right. About what?"

"The day. You were expecting your housekeeper, Zillah Peabody. That's what you said in your statement. She came four days a week: Sunday, Monday, Wednesday, and Friday."

Oswald put on a long face. "Didn't she just. Like clockwork. That's why I couldn't understand why she hadn't come, it being a Monday. Tom said because today's Tuesday."

"But when she showed up, sir, it was *two* days later, Wednesday. Not the next day. If it had been a Tuesday when Mr. Williamson was here, your housekeeper would have appeared the next day, Wednesday?"

"Now *that* is one of the most confused statements I've ever heard."

Wiggins nodded. "As it would have been seventeen years ago."

Oswald sipped his Chai and made a face. "You've got the days all turned round, Sergeant."

"No, sir. Tom Williamson had them turned round. You were right. It *was* Monday when he was here. Not Tuesday. Mrs. Peabody was supposed to have come on the Monday, but her hubby was taken ill."

"How do you know this?"

"I've been to see Zillah Peabody, sir. She told me about her husband being ill. And told me she couldn't understand, when she apologized for not being here, you said, 'My mistake.' "

Oswald stared at Wiggins. "But Tess Williamson was killed the day Tom was here. Wasn't she?"

"No. She was killed the next day. That was Tuesday. He was here on Monday."

"But how could Tom think he was here the day Tess died if he wasn't? My God, wouldn't the death of your spouse pretty much pin down the day?"

Sir Oswald looked utterly distressed. Wiggins said, "Not to worry, sir. We just wanted to straighten out that one detail."

Oswald Maples sat quietly, apparently turning over this news. He said, "Are police all idiots?"

"Very probably, sir. Do you have any particular idiot in mind?"

"I do, indeed. If Tom was actually here on Monday, and he needed an alibi, well, man, he didn't have one! But how could those two mixed-up days not have been pointed out at the time? It takes you seventeen years to work out that puzzle?"

"I think the reason is that it was Mr. Williamson's alibi that was checked. Not yours. Your substantiating his alibi wasn't questioned. That, and the fact police are idiots."

Oswald Maples was struggling to get out of his chair. "That remains to be seen. The big question is, can you pick a lock, Sergeant? I think she hid that damned bump key."

62

Boring's, Mayfair
Saturday, 5:00 P.M.

Jury was sitting in the Members' Room with Melrose Plant when the call came from Wiggins. Since mobile calls were not permitted in that room, Jury walked out into the lobby to take it.

"Sorry, boss, but it looks like Tom Williamson wasn't with Sir Oswald Maples the day his wife died." Wiggins told him about the conversation.

"Tom *wasn't* with Oswald Maples?"

"He was with him, all right. It was just the wrong day — Monday — when he was. We don't know where he was on the Tuesday."

Jury couldn't believe what he was hearing.

"Sir Oswald was expecting Zillah Peabody. She always came four days a week: Sunday, Monday, Wednesday, and Friday. When Sir Oswald wondered where she was and said she always came on Mondays, Williamson said, 'But today's Tuesday.' "

"That can't be," said Jury.

"Fraid so, guv, if we can believe Zillah Peabody. It's true she hadn't gone to the Maples house on the Monday before Tess Williamson was killed, but that was because her hubby was sick and she was taking him to the doctor. She'd told Sir Oswald on Sunday that she'd be missing Monday, as they'd be going to the surgery. He'd forgotten, that's all."

"This Peabody woman; are you sure *she* didn't make a mistake about the day?"

"I think we can believe her. See, her husband was sick for nearly a week after they saw the doctor the first time. She'd made an appointment four days before, on the Friday, to take him in on Monday. She was certain of this and gave me the name of the doctor so I could check it if I wanted. I haven't yet because this is Saturday, but I can go round and see him, if you like. The thing is, sir, that amongst these three people — Tom Williamson, Sir Oswald, and Zillah Peabody — if you look at it this way, only one of them had anything to gain by getting the day wrong."

"No, don't see the doctor yet. I'll have to talk to Tom Williamson. Thanks, Wiggins."

"Sorry, guv."

Jury slapped his mobile shut. "Bloody hell," he said under his breath and walked back to the Members' Room.

Melrose Plant was looking at the dinner menu as Jury bolted his whiskey.

"Uh-oh. Looks like bad news."

Sitting down, Jury said, "I've just had my whole case blown to bits." He recounted what Wiggins had told him, adding, "I don't believe it."

"Then don't," said Melrose, equably.

"I can't ignore the lack of an alibi."

"Of course you can. This all happened seventeen years ago. Do you really feel the need to turn everything upside down because one additional detail has come to light? And a detail hardly beyond dispute."

"Why 'beyond dispute'?"

"What about Ms. Peabody's memory? Could she be wrong?"

"Possibly, but unlikely. Wiggins pointed out to me that of the three of them, the only one who stood to gain by that faulty date was Tom Williamson."

Melrose shook his head and slid down in his chair. After a few moments of thought he said, "Have you been to Greenwich?"

"Greenwich? Of course I have. If you're referring to Greenwich mean time, what has that to do with it?"

"No, that was just a point of reference. What I'm talking about is the prime meridian."

"That's to do with longitude, isn't it?"

"It's a line of longitude. The prime meridian is zero longitude. It goes through the Royal Observatory and divides the Eastern and Western hemispheres. The thing is, of course, there are many other meridians in many other locations. Why the one that runs through Greenwich is 'prime' is simply because everyone agreed to its being that. It's completely arbitrary."

"This is in aid of exactly what?"

"Your case, of course. You had it beautifully tailored. And now, it appears to be lying in tatters at your feet. Or, at least, to have shifted, so that now you've got a new suspect and a completely different playbook. Your longitudinal line, which was running straight through a doorway in Greenwich, has now shifted to a spice stall in Marrakech. Or Crete or wherever the hell any dingbat who comes along chooses to draw it."

"By 'dingbat' I take it you're referring to —"

"Your original suspect."

"Yet it's true that the alibi of the second

suspect is leaking all over the place."

"My God! You cops and your alibis!"

"It usually works. It usually holds that a man can't be in two places at the same time."

Melrose thought for a minute. "I think I'd challenge that, if it were meaningful. What kills me is this: here are these people — say, these three people, two of whom you've been absolutely convinced were above suspicion. Then, suddenly, your prime suspect says, I didn't do it, he did it, and instead of standing firmly on the prime meridian, you're all over the map. You've completely shelved insight and intuition for 'the alibi.' " Melrose made air quotes.

Jury felt a combination of irritation and elation. "Thank you." He looked over his shoulder. "Is there any tea in this place?"

"You're welcome. I'm sure there is." Just then the young porter who had waited on them the week before was passing with a tray. Melrose beckoned him. "Could we have a pot of tea, please?"

The porter grinned. "No problem."

Melrose winced.

While they had tea and a few uninspired biscuits (about all Boring's could manage, since few members ever asked for tea at this hour), Plant continued to say a cheering word or two about the misplaced alibi, such as: "That Williamson wasn't where he said he was doesn't mean he wasn't somewhere."

"Great," said Jury as he bit into a round of stale shortbread. "MI6 is always in the market for agents fluent in arcane languages."

"You know what I mean. Tom Williamson could well have been with someone else who could supply him with another alibi."

"That's true. But, you know, thinking about all this I see a problem: Why is Tom still saying it?"

"Saying what?"

"That he was with Oswald Maples the day Tess died. It was one of the things he told me when I met him in Vertigo 42, which is, incidentally, where I have to be in about an hour. I'm meeting Phyllis Nancy. It would have been abundantly clear to Tom the next day that he hadn't been with Sir Oswald. Assuming his innocence, of course."

"Of *course,* assuming he's innocent! Richard, I'm telling you, trust your instincts and remember the library card."

"What?"

"You recall I was telling you about my library card, that stack of dates and how the librarian could get a date wrong if she doesn't push the rubber stamp forward.

How easy it is to get a day or a date wrong."

"I'm a cop. I can't go by instinct. Wiggins has told me half a dozen times I'm too emotionally wrapped up in this case."

"That's different."

"How?"

"It just is. Okay, look: say you walked into the foyer of Ardry End. There you discovered Agatha lying dead on the floor, a bullet hole in her head. I'm standing over her with a gun in my hand. I say, 'I know how this looks, but I didn't do it.' Would you believe I shot her?"

"Of course."

"No, you *wouldn't.* Certainly not after I said I *didn't!* You know I'm incapable of killing someone."

Jury nodded. "Except her."

They both started laughing. Which was better, Jury supposed, than not laughing.

He suddenly thought of Carole-anne and stopped on the pavement to call Harrods.

"Mundy," he said, after he got her cell phone. "Would you do me a huge favor?" He told her what it was.

"Be glad to."

He had his Visa card out, started to give her the number.

Mundy said, "Pay me later. This way, I'll

buy it and get a huge discount." She laughed.

"Is Harrods still making deliveries?"

"Don't worry. Consider it done."

How nice. Someone else taking a task on, without comment, without an endless round of questions. He felt such a sense of relief he wondered which three little words were the greater balm for the soul: *I love you* or *Consider it done*?

63

Jury was sitting in one of Vertigo 42's marine blue chairs, watching the night deepen as the sun set over St. Paul's, when Phyllis Nancy walked out of the elevator and toward him in a black dress and a silk coat in the colors of the setting sun, the hem of it swirling in different shades of orange and pink, as if the silk were on fire.

He was reminded of the ensemble he had seen in Harrods, the orange shirt and hot-pink skirt. "Juicy Couture," he said, rising and kissing Phyllis on the cheek.

"What?" Phyllis laughed and sat down in the chair he held out. "I had no idea you were so fashion conscious. This dress isn't Juicy; it's Lanvin." She turned her head. "My lord what a stunning view! How did you find this place?"

"Tom Williamson," he said and changed

the subject. "It's amazing what color combinations look really great. Orange and pink, for instance, that was the Juicy Couture outfit I saw in Harrods."

"This is like having lunch with the girls," she said.

"You don't know any girls." He helped her off with the silk coat to reveal the black dress beneath. "My favorite dress. The backless black. Champagne?"

"Definitely." Phyllis took a seat beside Jury.

The waiter was there ahead of him to lift the bottle from the cooler and pour Phyllis a glass. He then refilled Jury's. The champagne was a nonvintage Krug, certainly not one of their most expensive, but perfectly good, a "reliable" choice, as the server had said, and not patronizing Jury either. He had picked up, in spite of himself, from his visits to The Old Wine Shades, the ability to ask for help in the wine department, something Harry Johnson had no problem doing despite his uncommon knowledge of wine. Jury asked the waiter for smoked salmon, remembering that Phyllis loved it.

As the server took himself off, Jury's mobile twitted. He took it out of his pocket.

"Good heavens, haven't you changed the Tweetie-bird ringtone?"

"I don't know how."

"Well, you could have asked."

"Ask you? You're the one who put the bloody thing on in the first place." Jury looked at the screen and saw Tom Williamson's number. "Would you excuse me for just a moment. This doesn't look like a place receptive to mobile calls."

"Go ahead," said Phyllis, smiling.

Jury walked past the desk out to the entryway near the one-stop elevator.

Tom said, "I had a visitor earlier today. I've been trying to get hold of you ever since. Where are you?"

"Vertigo 42. Who came to see you?"

"John McAllister. Twenty years since I've seen him."

Jury felt one weight lift off his shoulders, as another, heavier weight settled. It was the thought of having to ask Tom about that day seventeen years ago when he'd visited Oswald Maples. "Sorry, Tom, I'm terrible with mobile phones. I'm glad he went to see you."

A bit testily, Tom replied, "Of course, it might have helped had I seen Tess's letter myself."

"Again, I'm sorry. I should have given it to you straightaway."

There was a silence. Tom said, "I know

why you didn't. You thought it would be easier if John appeared in person and told me what had happened."

"Well . . . yes, I did. I was afraid you might look at the letter as a suicide note."

Another pause. "I probably would have done. It isn't, though, is it?"

"Absolutely not. You were right. Tess was murdered."

Tom gasped. "You know that?"

"I do. Look, can I bring this letter round tomorrow?"

"You'd better. Incidentally, it would be pretty small-minded of me to take you to task considering everything you've done."

He could have waited, Jury scolded himself, until tomorrow to ask Tom the next question: "Tom, there's something I have to ask: Why do you say you were at Oswald Maples's place on the day Tess was killed when you weren't? Why did you concoct that elaborate alibi and involve Sir Oswald?"

There was a silence; Jury expected one. Tom finally said, "Oh, that. But you're wrong about the alibi. I'm terrible about days and dates. It was a genuine mistake, if you can believe that."

"I'd like to, but it's hard. You'd have known at least by the next day that you weren't at Oswald's on Tuesday."

"I did, yes. But when police turned up, I kept to the alibi, thinking Oswald would confirm it. He did. What purpose would it have served to tell the truth? Which is that I was here, at home, with no witnesses."

"That's the thing about truth: it doesn't have to qualify; it doesn't have to have a purpose. The truth is its own purpose." Jury paused, but Tom said nothing. "I've never worked on a case before where so many people kept so many secrets. Good night, Tom."

"Wait!" said Tom quickly. "Let me have a word with the maître d'."

"Just a moment." Jury walked over to where the two men were standing, and said, "Mr. Williamson would like to speak to the maître d'."

The taller of the two took the phone, spoke to Tom, and returned the phone to Jury.

Jury returned to Phyllis.

Phyllis picked up her glass. Her other hand lay against the shoulder of the black dress. Her nails were a deep pink, that unusual pink Carole-anne had been applying to her own nails. This surprised Jury into saying, "Hotsie-Tot—." Almost saying. His mind swerved. It was like dropping his hands from the wheel of a car or a boat and having the thing jerk away out of control and then grabbing it back. "My God, Phyllis —" He rose suddenly.

"Richard, what's the matter?"

"It just came to me." He yanked out his mobile. Dead, all the power eaten up with the last call. "Hell."

She opened her small purse and pulled out hers and handed it to him.

"Thanks. Pardon me again for just a minute." He hurried over to the small reception area and put in a call to Wiggins.

When Wiggins answered, Jury told him what he wanted and where to get it. "First thing in the morning, Wiggins. Thanks."

Heading back to the table, he saw one of the waiters with another cooler and another bottle of champagne. Closer, he saw it was a Krug. The other kind, vintage.

"Compliments of Mr. Williamson, sir. Should I pour?"

There were also two fresh glasses.

"Pour, by all means."

The waiter did so, saying, "I'll have your smoked salmon in just a few minutes." He moved away.

"Do you think you'll remain stationary for at least ten minutes. I *am* your date. Remember me?"

"I remember you, all right." Jury raised

his glass. "Thank God for the girls."

One of the girls was waiting for him when he got back, very late, to his flat in Islington. For once, he was glad he hadn't talked Phyllis into coming with him when Carole-anne turned up in the doorway he had come through only two minutes before.

"Wow!" he said, seeing the orange-and-hot-pink outfit so winningly displayed. "Hotsie-Totsie!"

"It is, isn't it?" She gave a twirl so that he could take in all of the angles. "I love it. How do I look?"

"Juicy. As if you didn't know."

"I couldn't believe you actually went and got this for me." Her look was a little chagrined.

"Not bad. For a man."

She sat down on his sofa and smoothed out the skirt. It was exactly the color of her nail polish. "Delivered this evening right to my door. What service! But I don't think she was a regular delivery person."

"She?"

"Tawny-haired, really pretty. I mean, a raving beauty."

Consider it done. She'd done it herself. He smiled. "Glad you like it."

Carole-anne crossed her legs, swung her

strappy sandal, and said, "So who was she?"

64

Kenneth Strachey looked even more displeased today than he had the day before at the sight of Jury and Wiggins on his doorstep. "Gentlemen, this is beginning to amount to harassment."

"Really?" said Jury. "But we haven't said anything yet."

"The case against me is closed, Superintend — what are you doing?"

"Coming in." Jury and Wiggins crowded past Strachey. It was the load each carried that made the crossing difficult.

Strachey stared at the plastic-bagged clothing. "You picked up your cleaning on the way here?"

"No, sir," said Wiggins. "We picked up yours." He deposited his load of garments on the sofa and relieved Jury of his, which he tossed on a chair. He separated the

548

plastic covering from the garments and then the garments themselves. The black jacquard dress with the deep pink lining was nestled between a fawn corduroy jacket and a suit of windowpane plaid.

Kenneth stiffened. "Where did this come from?"

"As I said, we picked it up for you," said Wiggins, smiling insincerely. "Your cleaner is open on Sunday."

"I mean, the dress. It doesn't belong here." He shrugged. "That cleaner's always mixing things up. Obviously, he got someone else's cleaning in with ours." Kenneth poured himself more tea from the pot on the coffee table and sat down on the sofa.

"Nice try, Mr. Strachey. But you may remember I was here when you were holding this bundle of clothes and told me your dry cleaner was only open until three on Sunday. I saw this garment, or a bit of it, and assumed it was some fancy jacket, dinner or smoking. As to where the dress originally came from? It came from Alexander McQueen in Bond Street, same place the little purse came from. Since the dress is now here, one might assume you bought it —"

Strachey's smug expression lasted only until Jury added, "Or had Austin buy it."

"Someone calling my name?" fluted Austin, entering from the rose-bedecked patio, brushing at his shirt. "It's started to rain. Police again? How devastatingly wonder — Oh, my God!" He had by now taken in the dress. "Kenneth — ?" He was looking from Jury to Wiggins to Kenneth a little wildly.

"Never mind, Austin," said Kenneth.

Jury said, "You yourself got the red Givenchy in Paris because you knew it would be simple for police to trace it in London, if it ever came to that. You didn't think it would come to it, though, since you didn't think we'd connect you with Belle Syms."

"Don't be ridiculous; if I'd wanted Arabella to wear a certain dress, I'd've had her go round and try it on, surely."

"Surely not. Not in this case. You'd have needed to try it on *yourself* first, to see if you could get away with it. That's the reason you wanted two very memorable dresses. If one didn't work, the other would. "So on one of Austin's visits to Alexander McQueen, you had him pick out a dress —"

Kenneth shook his head. "Absolutely not! Austin had nothing to do with this dress —"

"Oh, but I think he did, Mr. Strachey. You certainly wouldn't have chosen it."

"Why not?" said Kenneth, walking straight into an admission of guilt.

Jury smiled. "All you have to do is look at it. It's gorgeous; the material is exquisite. But it's what's called a pencil dress. It would fit like the paper on your wall. It might have fit Belle Syms —"

"It would have."

"But not you, Kenneth, and you were the one the dress had to fit. It was clever, sending the dress to the cleaners instead of trying to dispose of it in some other way. It could have stayed there for a long time. As for the shoes, you must have practiced a good deal to be able to manage those heels. At the tower, you put on Belle's other low-heeled ones in order to carry the body. You've got slender hands; probably slender feet. And I recall Austin commenting on how well you played the part of Lady Bracknell in *Earnest*." Jury paused. "Come on, Kenneth, make it easy on yourself and just tell us the rest of the story."

"Make it easy for *you,* I think you mean."

"It's already easy for me; we have a genius of an artist at the Yard. All I have to do is get him to put makeup and a black wig on your picture and show it around to the places you visited in Sidbury. Believe me, we'll have an ID within an hour. And if not easy for yourself, how about Austin? You don't want to incriminate him, do you? Right now he's an accessory and he's looking at serious prison time." Hearing a gasp from the direction of the fireplace where Austin was huddled in the chair by the plaster figure wearing the fez, Jury looked at Wiggins, nodded his head toward Austin. "Have a word, Wiggins."

Wiggins led Austin out on the patio to have that word.

Jury looked at Kenneth, who was no longer drinking tea, and who was staring at the floor. "Here's what I think: I think Zack Syms, who was looking for Belle's aunt, got in your way, or his dog did. Syms lost Stanley on Monday night. We know this because the dog turned up at the house of a friend of mine. Syms was very attached to Stanley and wouldn't give up looking for him. Possibly, the man or the dog saw you at the tower —"

Wiggins and Austin came back to the living room, Austin looking bloodless, drained of strength. When Kenneth saw him, he sat back and with a seeming sense of relief, began talking:

"That damnable *dog* came racing out of the shadows toward the tower and I just escaped getting its teeth clamped round my leg. I kicked at it, but it went on barking. It was wearing a collar, and the collar had a lead attached. This really worried me because there must have been a person on the other end of that lead. But where? I saw, heard nobody. It struck me that someone should have been calling for the dog. Not a sound. Not a glimmer of the dog's owner. The cottage was still dark, no one there, apparently, so I thought it unlikely the dog belonged to whoever lived there.

"I managed to get to my car, and the dog gave up. I drove back to the Sun and Moon, gathered up Arabella's stuff from the room, shoved a hundred pounds under the brass bell, and left. I was back in Bloomsbury by four A.M. Austin sleeps like the dead. I couldn't, so at six A.M., I tossed on my robe and was making coffee when he appeared and obviously had no idea I'd been gone half the night." Kenneth's smile was almost fond.

"But then you went back, and more than once."

"Every day — until I found him."

Jury interrupted. "What happened at the Blue Parrot?"

Kenneth frowned. "The which?"

"A pub just off the Northampton Road where Mr. Syms was seen that Tuesday afternoon."

"Oh, that place: I picked up his car on the Old Post Road and followed him. He kept stopping and getting out and looking round. He went back to that pub twice. Made following pretty hard. The second time I took a shot at him when he was getting into his car. I'm a bad shot, not at all like Pop. It's his gun."

"Too bad for you," said Wiggins, which earned him a look from Jury.

"Early Saturday morning I got back to the village, drove around it for over an hour before I saw his car pulled up and parked on a side street near the alley behind those shops. The guy started running and disappeared into the alley. I pulled over, got out of the car. There was no one else about; the shops were still closed. He was in the middle of the alley, down with the dog, hugging him for dear life . . ."

The expression on his face said that he had no idea how a bond could exist between man and animal. "Didn't you ever have a dog, then?" Jury said.

"Me? No." Kenneth gave him a black look, gave all of them black looks, including Austin, who'd been trying to shrink small between the black plaster boy in the fez and the fireplace.

"I shot at them, didn't I? Both of them. Two shots that did nothing but nick the alley wall, but that got this guy up on his feet and the dog running toward me. I shot at the dog and missed, but turned him back; my last shot was at the guy, whose back was to me for that moment. The shot took him down. Naturally, I wanted to get closer to make sure he was dead, but with the dog there, I could see that was impossible. The gun was a .38 with only five shots and I'd used them. I ran."

"For one who'd so carefully thought things through at the beginning, this was extremely reckless behavior — tracking Zack Syms down and shooting him."

"Perhaps. But I could control the beginning; I couldn't control the end."

Austin was sitting with his head in his hands. He might have been silently weeping.

"As for Tess, you have no evidence for my killing Tess Williamson."

"As you yourself said, it's like dominoes, Kenneth," said Jury. "Knock over one and the others follow in its wake. We've pretty much covered your murder of Tess; whether you admit to it or not, I know you did it. What reason would there have been for killing Belle Syms other than that she knew something extremely incriminating? You admitted you'd been to Laburnum the day Tess died; you knew about the letter. That's established. Only, you didn't put that letter under the door, she did, in the little time left before you killed her. Of course you killed her. You didn't see Tom Williamson."

For some odd reason Kenneth took this as a question rather than a statement and answered it with a shake of his head.

"So we're arresting you, Mr. Strachey, for the murders of Arabella Hastings, Zachariah Syms, and Tess Williamson. Wiggins —" Jury nodded toward Kenneth Strachey.

"Right, guv." Wiggins took the handcuffs he'd had under his belt and walked behind Strachey, handcuffing him as he read him his rights. He looked toward Austin, raised a silent question with Jury.

Jury nodded. "Mr. Smythe, you'll come along with us, okay? You'd probably be very helpful."

Kenneth Strachey offered no resistance. Austin rose from his chair and went to join them.

Seeing Austin's distress, Jury said, "We know you had nothing to do with any of this, Mr. Smythe . . ." Closer now, Jury could see that parading down along the three buttons of Austin's T-shirt was a placket covered with a design of tiny skulls. Jury smiled. ". . . Except perhaps for your fondness for Alexander McQueen."

Then, as if ushering Kenneth and Austin into a formal dining room rather than the rainy day, Jury swept out his arm.

"Shall we?"

They left in the wake of the air stirred by that sweeping gesture.

ACKNOWLEDGMENTS

My deepest thanks go to:

RSPCA Chief Inspectorate Officer Kevin
  Degenhard
Dr. Elizabeth Martin
Debra LaPrevotte, Supervisory Special
  Agent, FBI